CRISTINA ODONE was born in Nairobi, Kenya. She is the author of *The Dilemmas of Harriet Carew*, based on her 'Posh but Poor' columns, which appeared weekly in the *Daily Telegraph* from August 2006 to January 2008. A frequent broadcaster (*Question Time*, the *Today Programme*, *Woman's Hour* and the *Jeremy Vine Show*), she is a former editor of the *Catholic Herald* and deputy editor of the *New Statesman*. She lives in London with her husband, step-sons and daughter.

CRISTINA ODONE

The Good Divorce Guide

Harper
Press

Harper*Press*
An imprint of HarperCollins*Publishers*
77–85 Fulham Palace Road
Hammersmith, London W6 8JB
www.harpercollins.co.uk

Visit our authors' blog: www.fifthestate.co.uk
Love this book? www.bookarmy.com

First published by Harper*Press* in 2009

A catalogue record for this book
is available from the British Library

This novel is entirely a work of fiction. The names, characters and incidents portrayed in
it are the work of the author's imagination. Any resemblance to actual persons, living or
dead, events or localities is entirely coincidental.

ISBN 978-0-00-728974-5

Typeset in Minion by Palimpsest Book Production Limited,
Grangemouth, Stirlingshire

Printed and bound in Great Britain by
Clays Ltd, St Ives plc

Mixed Sources

Product group from well-managed
forests and other controlled sources
www.fsc.org Cert no. SW-COC-1806
© 1996 Forest Stewardship Council

FSC

FSC is a non-profit international organisation established to promote the responsible
management of the world's forests. Products carrying the FSC label are independently
certified to assure consumers that they come from forests that are managed to meet the
social, economic and ecological needs of present or future generations.

Find out more about HarperCollins and the environment at
www.harpercollins.co.uk/green

*To my parents, and to Edward and
Claudia, for trying to make theirs
a civilised divorce.*

1

Five steps to take if you suspect your husband is having an affair.

1. Check the paper trail. If he told you that he was going to Woking for a conference on hair-regeneration therapy from the 9th to the 12th, but you found a Stansted–Venice boarding pass stub for the 11th–12th in his suit pocket, beware.
2. Study his reactions. 'You'll never believe this.' I stood in the bathroom, brushing my hair and watching my husband in the mirror as I spoke. 'Remember the Pearsons?' 'Doug and Ginnie?' Jonathan continued methodically polishing his shoes. 'Yup. She's found out he's been sleeping with their children's French tutor!' Jonathan looked up, surprised – but I could see no sign of a guilty conscience. 'Poor Ginnie,'

I went on, eyes on my husband. Jonathan shrugged: 'Yeah, she's a sweetheart. Never liked HIM much.'

3. Provoke him. Saturday morning over breakfast: 'Oh no, not another marriage quiz!' I rolled my eyes, *The Times* in my hand. 'OK, let's see how we measure up. "On a scale of one to ten, how annoying is your spouse's worst habit?"' I studied my husband over the paper. Jonathan roared with laughter: 'You're not the one with annoying habits. I am.'

4. Make unexpected changes to your routine. Arrive home in the middle of the day. Pretend the film you were supposed to see was sold out and you came home early. Announce you're off for a haircut but come back after a drive around the neighbourhood. If he gives any sign of irritation or alarm, you're on to something.

5. Finally, taking a step I had promised never to take, a last resort I regarded as the stereotypical first resort of the paranoid wife, I check his BlackBerry for compromising messages. Even the most cunning man leaves some clues – like the 'I wnt U2. Lst nght = hotvolcanicsex XXX' that I found in the message inbox on Jonathan's BlackBerry when it slipped out of his jacket pocket. I look at the sender: 'L'. Who is 'L'? Or is L for lover? lust? LOVE?

There he is, asleep on the sofa, *The Lancet* trembling on his chest, *Newsnight* on the telly. Here I am, standing beside him, wondering how to survive this revelation.

Jonathan, my husband of twelve years, is having an affair. After months of suspicion and covert investigation, I've found him out. I stand quite still as the answers to a hundred questions whirl around me: so this is why he's had so many business trips recently. This is why he jumped when I walked in on him whispering to his BlackBerry last week. This explains his personal trainer, his new interest in what he wears, his locking his desk drawers. I want to cry, I want to scream, I want to smash his framed photo of the 1989 University Challenge team, from which he smiles, bright-eyed and long-haired.

Yet even now I cannot quite believe it. An affair. Sneaking, cheating, lying, faking . . . Can this be true of my solid, steady, scientist husband? I feel as if I've stepped out of the house on an errand, and come back to find it burgled and vandalised. Nothing is how it should be any more. How can Jonathan be having sex with someone else when only two days ago we had a fabulous marital moment that had him whistling 'Love is in the Air' afterwards in the shower? How can he betray me when he told me only last Saturday that we should go out for supper, a film, anything, to have some 'us' time? How can he cheat on me, the woman with whom he'd once said he was sleep-lessly in love? I'm not saying our marriage is perfect. We can be boring, tense, uncommunicative; but we've never, in a dozen years, lied to each other. 'You're the only person I can be one hundred per cent honest with,' Jonathan used to repeat to me. Until now.

I don't know where we go from here. Do I play dumb and

let the affair take its course? Do I confront him? Do I fight for my husband?

Worst of all is the thought of the children. Kat, twelve, and Freddy, nine, were never to have a worry in the world. Jonathan and I were as one on that score, always: we wanted the best for them, no matter what the sacrifice involved. Even when, over the past four years, I've had a vague feeling that I've been short-changed; that instead of the best I might be stuck with an ill-fitting companion; even then, I never once voiced a complaint. How could I moan about Jonathan, or trade him in, or simply dump him and move on? To do so would have upset our family. And no amount of freedom was worth that.

I study my husband asleep on the sofa. A nice face, broad forehead under brown hair (no longer long, but still plentiful), strong jaw without a hint of a double chin. But the parted lips and low rumbling of his snoring give him a slightly comical air: a sex god, he ain't. Which is why it never occurred to me that he would find someone else. Or that someone else would choose him or chase him. Wrong.

'Ahhhhh . . . I fell asleep in the wrong position.' Jonathan blinks and winces as he starts massaging his neck. 'Will you have a go with your healing touch?'

'Let me see . . .' Reluctantly, I knead the flesh, wondering with a kind of horrified curiosity if I might find a bite mark or a scratch there. I'm surprised at the jealousy that fills me. *This man's MINE,* I want to tell the woman who texted him her lusty message. *Keep your hands off him, L.*

4

'Hmmm . . . you are a genius . . .' My husband beams with gratitude.

'You are tense.' Worn out by his double life, I reckon.

'Work's been non-stop.' Jonathan gets up, stretches. 'Tomorrow's Tuesday, isn't it?' He follows me into the kitchen in his socks. 'I'd better go through the rubbish, just so there's no bottle caps in with the glass.'

'Good-oh.' I turn my back on the fussy sorting that will now take at least half an hour. Jonathan's big on recycling, and can spend hours discussing landfill, the merits of compost, and the logic of climate change.

'Damn, I missed *Newsnight*.' Jonathan places four bottles of wine neatly in a carton that he will bring outside tomorrow morning. 'Tea?'

'Yes.' I boil the kettle, set out two mugs on the counter. We stand there, sipping from our Charles and Diana Royal Wedding mugs, surrounded by children's school books, white cabinets half-hidden by Blu-Tacked schedules, a half-opened bottle of wine and a bowl of fruit. You'd never know one of us was getting hot, volcanic, adulterous sex.

'Ta.' Jonathan takes the tea from me. 'New dress?' He gives my new Whistles wrap-around an appreciative look. 'Nice.'

'Thanks.' I feel flustered: Jonathan can look at me like *that* while seeing someone else?! 'I'm off to bed.' I climb the stairs.

'I'm off to Paris.' Jonathan's voice sounds flat and expressionless as he follows me upstairs. 'On Wednesday. A conference on folliculitis.'

'Not hair transplants? Or hair restorers?' I ask innocently,

5

and turn to see Jonathan start nervously: he can't decide if he's been caught out or I'm simply teasing him.

'No. Definitely folliculitis.' My husband switches off the lights downstairs and climbs up after me. 'Definitely.'

Until recently, being married to Jonathan was easy. When friends would mock marriage as outdated or unrealistic, I'd stick up for it as the best of all possible unions. 'Married people are healthier, and happier, than singles,' I'd quote the latest research. 'Married people are less likely to end up in jail, commit suicide, or go bankrupt.' I was the marriage merchant in a world of marriage break-ups.

But am I facing a marriage break-up of my own?

Lying beside my husband on the bed, his feet hot against my cold ones, I test my reaction to this evening's revelation as if I were a doctor trying to find the source of pain in a patient's body. My ego is shattered, my nerves shaken, my heart in upheaval. Worse, my conscience is uneasy: have I been taking Jonathan for granted? The children, changing and growing, present a constant challenge; did I see Jonathan as something settled, someone I'd figured out? In fact, I realise with a jolt, I haven't *thought* about Jonathan for years. I've listened to him, I've distracted him when things were difficult at work, I've co-opted him in sorting out the children's rows. But I haven't really engaged with Jonathan in a long time now. I didn't feel the need to – nor did he. We talk about Kat's homework, Freddy's football, my mum's pension, his mum's prescriptions, the rise in our heating bills, the fall in house prices. Not ever about *us*. Somehow, I thought it a subject best left untouched. Yes, I've been vaguely conscious of leading life against a backdrop of mild disappointment; but I put it down to working in Dr Casey's practice, not to marrying Jonathan Martin.

Jonathan is snoring again: a low grumble, reassuring, utterly familiar in a terrifying new landscape. I venture alone into this alien world. I can see me, on my own, at a friend's party. Me, on my own with the children on holiday in Devon. Me, without Jonathan, cooking in the kitchen, or listening to the *Today* programme, or swearing at the sat nav. Me, without my husband. I blink, stare at the dark shapes in our room. I won't sleep tonight, I know. My failures keep thumping inside my head. It's because I'm thirty-seven. It's because I take off my makeup in front of him. It's because I don't know the periodic table, or why $e = mc^2$ or who edits the *BMJ*. What is Jonathan's affair about? Improving his sex life, or . . . or satisfying his yearning for the best mate? If this is not just about sweaty grunting sex, it could mean divorce. My children robbed of their father, me robbed of my companion, all of us robbed of our peace of mind.

No, I'm not going to stand by and watch my life being kicked around. I'm going to fight to keep my husband. I must act quickly.

Within twenty-four hours, I am sitting in L'Avventura, staring at Mimi, his personal trainer, over a basket of focaccia and a bottle of mineral water. I've asked her to lunch on the pretext of sounding her out about taking me on as a client.

I would no more hire Mimi to teach me kickboxing than go back to being mousey-brown, but Mimi is my chief suspect. Mimi has been on the scene for months now. My husband has never been thin, but he's also never shown the slightest interest in losing weight, building his pecs, or achieving his target working heart rate. As of last winter, though, we have been getting a constant stream of 'Mimi says my body weight:muscle ratio needs improving . . .' and 'Mimi says I need to get my heart rate up three times a week minimum.' I noticed that Jonathan had started weighing himself with an absurd regularity, and stealing glances at our bedroom mirror. More suspicious still, his sessions with Mimi never seemed to take place around our home, but rather, near the office in Harrow. It took me three months to arrange an accidentally-on-purpose meeting with the Australian fitness freak, and I didn't like what I saw: slim, blonde, and extremely young.

Just his type. In fact I can't think of many men who would deploy great physical exertion to get her out of their bed – even though she moves her lips when she reads the menu, and pronounces prosciutto 'prose-cutter'.

I have a plan.

'Sometimes,' I begin, 'I think it's such a miracle that Jonathan manages anything at all. I mean' – I look full of loving concern – 'I'm so worried he'll end up getting like his father . . . it was a blessing he passed away when he did.'

'His father?' Mimi looks bewildered.

'Jonathan puts on such a brave front. Especially considering he's doped up to the eyeballs half the time.'

'Doped up?' The waiter brings Mimi five teeny ravioli on a rocket leaf. She doesn't look at them.

'Yes . . . he is so good about covering it up. The doctors are worried, though.' I look mournful. 'They're scared it might be taking a turn for the worse.'

'What?!' Mimi looks gratifyingly frightened.

'It's been hard at times, especially because of the worry about the children. It's genetic. The doctors say *any* child' – here I look intensely at Mimi – 'any child of Jonathan's will be affected.' I taste a forkful of risotto. 'I think we've got it in time. I mean, Kat did try to throttle her guinea pig and there was the incident with Freddy biting his school friend, but . . .' I lower my voice, 'with the injections they're getting, it should all stay under control.'

Mimi, food uneaten, shakes her head in disbelief. 'He seems so normal . . .' she mutters uncertainly. 'He wouldn't hurt a fly. It makes him hopeless at kickboxing.' She crosses her arms on the tabletop and I notice a heavy gold charm bracelet. On a personal trainer's salary? I shake my head sceptically. 'It must be so difficult for you.'

'It's been hell.' I shut my eyes as if the memory were too painful to bear.

How long has this affair been going on? I've been suspicious for about five months now – but it could have started even earlier. When I took the children to my mum's for half-term? When Jonathan went to Glasgow for that conference on hair regeneration?

'Poor you,' Mimi whispers. 'It must be hard to cope.'

'It can all get a bit much.' I nod, voice cracking with grief.

Mimi's eyes are wide with sympathy. She leans across the table, puts her (beautifully manicured) hand on mine: 'If there's anything I can do to help, let me know.'

'Yes . . .' I whisper.

'You've been very brave.'

'I have to be.' I shrug.

'I won't forget what you told me, Rosie.' Mimi looks sincere – and shaken.

I breathe a sigh of relief: I've pulled it off. As I turn to ask the waiter for the bill, I spot Jonathan through the restaurant window. He's across the street, sheltering beneath an umbrella with Linda, his American colleague. They're looking at one another and suddenly he reaches to touch her face. It's only a second – but I know immediately that I've been lunching the wrong woman.

I look away, and hold the tabletop to steady myself. I wasn't expecting this. Mimi, yes: sweet, obvious, none too bright. Jonathan would have fun with her, and nothing more. But Linda? When Linda first arrived at the lab, Jonathan had said she was 'impressive'. 'She knows her stuff': he'd sounded admiring. She knows her stuff and is tall, dark and handsome (if you like a red pout, double-D breasts and legs that go on for ever). American, and half my age (or just looks that way).

I pay the bill and stay behind while Mimi, looking thoughtful and slightly worried, goes on her way.

I step out of the restaurant and begin walking towards the tube station.

It's Tuesday, one of my two days off, so I'm not rushing back to work. Yet still I walk quickly, trying to put some distance between me and the sighting of my husband and his lover. Passers-by brush against me, cars whizz past, bicycle brakes screech. It's muggy and grey – a bad beginning to the summer. I'm walking uphill, and my cotton dress sticks to my back. I breathe in slowly, with difficulty. I'm feeling uncomfortably sweaty, and keep tugging at my dress where it sticks to me. This is serious. But what do I do? Confront him? Ignore it? Talk it through in a friendly tête-à-tête?

Jonathan wakes up in his five-star hotel room in Venice. Linda stands, gloriously naked, by the balcony, looking down at his open case. 'My love!' Jonathan pulls off the sheet, inviting his lover back into the bed. 'What *is* this filth?' Linda throws a handful of seamy fetishist mags on to the bed. 'You know what? You are sick!' She snatches her clothes and runs from the room.

Scenario number two: Jonathan is in the kitchen of the little love nest he and Linda are renting from a friend of hers. He is opening a bottle of wine (Châteauneuf-du-Pape – nothing but the best for his beloved) and looking forward to the cinq-à-sept he has so brilliantly organised. Suddenly he hears what sounds like sobs from the bedroom. He rushes next door to find Linda weeping, holding a letter in her hand. 'How could you? You're two-timing me!' She throws the sheet of paper at him. Jonathan slowly unfolds the letter and reads, in a handwriting that looks vaguely familiar, a breathless declaration of love from someone who signs herself as T. 'It fell from your jacket pocket . . .'

Or scenario number three: Linda sits, massaging rose oil into her naked body, in anticipation of an afternoon's love-making. She and Jonathan are attending a conference on folliculitis in Florence. He's in the shower. The phone rings.

'Hello?' she purrs.

'Hello, this is Gould Jewellery in Hatton Gardens. Is it possible to speak with Mr Martin?'

'Afraid not. Can I help?'

'Oh, I don't know . . .' the woman's voice sounds reluctant.

'I'm his partner.'

'Well . . . just to let him know the emerald ring he wanted tightened is ready for collection.'

'B-b-b-b-b-but what ring?'

'The one with the engraving in the band – "For Lola with Love".'

'What?!!' Linda splutters as the line goes dead.

This is how I deal with my jealousy in my imagination: I wreak revenge. I spend hours at my desk at Dr Casey's surgery planning the different vendettas, and imagining the shock on the lovers' faces.

'Rosie, did you hear what I said?' Mrs Stevens startles me. It's always the way: Mrs S ignores me all day, pretending I'm but a speck of dust in her beloved Dr Casey's wood-panelled offices. Then, just as I am deep in texting Jill or in a phone conversation with the children after school, she pounces, beady eyes gleaming with dislike, and exposes me for what I am: a medical receptionist and administrative assistant desperate to swap this part-time job for a full-time one as counsellor. Kat and Freddy are old enough now, and I've sent in my application for a four-year course. By the fourth, I'll be allowed to have my own 'clients', with a qualified counsellor monitoring our sessions.

'Did you put Mrs Morrow's file back?'

I start rummaging through the metal filing cabinet.

'Should be here,' I mutter, as I search among the alphabetically arranged manila envelopes. In fact, I suddenly remember to my horror, I have left the Botox patient's substantial file beside my coffee in the kitchenette.

'I don't think you'll find it there.' Mrs S smiles smugly. 'My question was purely rhetorical. I found the file by the coffee machine – you managed to get a stain on it, as well.' An eyebrow shoots up: 'I do wish you would concentrate on the task at hand.'

With a triumphant air, she watches me turn red. Then she slaps down the file, turns on her sensible heel, and sails away. She leaves me wondering, for the umpteenth time, if I shouldn't hand in my resignation now, rather than wait to see whether I've been accepted on the counselling course. I've been working for Dr Hugh Casey, well-known dermatologist, since Freddy was four and I decided the children would not be traumatised if I were to step back into the work place a few days a week.

When Jonathan and I met, I was twenty-two and working at HOME, a charity for the homeless. Jonathan was a pharmacologist bent on finding new drugs to revolutionise existing treatments. He yearned for the glory of being published in the *BMJ* – and the profits that would come in the wake of his discovery. By the time we had been going out for about a year, Jonathan had started talking about our future family; then the family was no longer just talk but a loud and needy wail from the little pink room I grandly called the nursery. I left HOME for home and soon found my daughter so engrossing, and Freddy's arrival so overwhelming, that work languished. Jonathan encouraged me to stay with the children, taking pride in the fact that he could provide for his family.

Five years ago, though, I decided to ease my way back into work. I wanted something not too taxing, part-time, that would allow me to do what I enjoy doing most: listening to people. 'You certainly have a knack for getting people to open up,' my dad's patients would tell me when, as a teenager, I earned pocket money by helping out in his GP's practice. I soon realised that often the men and women who filed in were distressed not so much because they were ill but because they were lonely, worried, unhappy, or just a little down. I only needed to give them an opening, and they would lean on the counter and unburden themselves about the daughter who hadn't shown up at Christmas, or the husband who had died last spring.

When I joined Dr Casey's practice as a part-time receptionist, I looked forward to working with his patients – or clients, as Mrs Stevens likes to remind me: they might not work the land as my father's Somerset patients did, or have priceless stories about their barnyard animals; but they would surely be eager to share similar small triumphs and secret sorrows. Dr Casey had recently cottoned on to the way he could more than double his profits by offering cosmetic treatments such as facial peel, Botox and collagen injections to his existing clients. He soon had back-to-back appointments to freeze foreheads, plump out lines and remove age spots for long queues of elderly dowagers and their daughters and daughters-in-law. Our waiting room filled with glossy women in sunglasses deep into copies of *Vogue* and *Tatler*. Most were forty- or fifty-something, but there was also a clutch of unbelievably young girls who thought they had to act now to stop time from having its wicked way with them.

Unfortunately, Dr Casey was already sixty-plus when he discovered the riches he could make from cosmetic treatments. His plump white hands might not tremble, quite, but they are not as sure as they once were; and in the trade, and among some of the less than satisfied clients, he has been dubbed the Butcher of Belgravia.

Dr Casey's patients believe that their money entitles them not only to a timeless face but also to unending sympathy. This is where I step in: I book their appointments, greet them when they come, and above all listen, as temporary confidante, when they tell how their husbands tease them that they're no longer spring chickens, their careers depend on their youthful looks and friends have recommended a make-over to inject a bit of wow! into their lives.

Comforting wealthy women whose faces have turned to stone, or lips to balloons, is a far cry from the cutting-edge work among drug addicts I once dreamt of. But Dr Casey is an amiable man: 'Top o' the morning!' he cries cheerily in a cod Irish accent as he steps into his elegant offices. The women who flock to him stir my protective instincts. I manage to remember their names and most of their family members', and for this they are grateful and praise me to Dr Casey, who winks at me, pleased; and to Mrs Stevens, who sniffs, unimpressed. Despite Mrs S's best efforts, the hours are flexible and my tasks not too onerous. Getting to Hans Crescent after the school run takes twenty-five minutes max by tube.

Only Jill, now a GP, expressed disapproval of my decision to work for Dr Casey's practice: 'Why be with that old fraud? What about all the good work you were going to do? All those kids you were going to help?'

'Working here suits me right now. It's easy.'

'Since when is easy best?' Jill scoffed.

'If I have to commit full time to a demanding job, I can't look after the children, the house and Jonathan.'

'Jonathan shouldn't need looking after!' Jill shook her head crossly. 'You've got a gift for listening – you shouldn't limit yourself to hearing about botched lip jobs.'

'Oh, Jill!' I cried, stung. 'It's not like I'm a paid-up member of the ladies-who-lunch club.'

'Don't you think it's a bit dangerous to dumb down? I mean, I know I shouldn't say this, but what if you and Jonathan ever split up?'

From across the room, Mrs Stevens is watching me, so I pretend to look through Mrs Morrow's file – she's overdue for her Botox appointment, it's more than four months since the last one – while steeling myself for the difficult campaign to keep my marriage from collapsing.

After work, I go to Tesco's. I come home lugging three carrier bags that would break a donkey's back. I'm slightly out of breath as I make my way to our large kitchen. The appliances are ancient and the wooden table scarred, but I love this room with its Aga, bay window and white tiles. Jonathan prides himself on his gourmet cooking – 'the fastest way to relax outside the bedroom' he always tells me – and sets great store by the Magimix, the collection of Le Creuset casserole dishes and Sabatier knives, plus a whole alphabet of glass jars of exotic herbs. I enjoy watching him frown as he takes up a pinch of this, a dash of that, mixing ingredients as if they were solutions in his lab. On weekends he takes over the kitchen to produce succulent cassoulet, or Thai coconut soup, or spicy salmon tartare. Weeknights are mine, though, and I cook my hearty if less sophisticated favourites. Jonathan is usually kind about my efforts – though he can't resist sharing a tip or two: 'That cauliflower cheese hits the spot, Rosie. But have you tried sprinkling it with breadcrumbs before you take it out of the oven?'

'Mu-um!' Freddy calls out from upstairs. 'I need you to help me glue my Viking ship!'

'Where's the please?' I shoot back. Even while contemplating your husband's adultery, manners matter. 'Let me get supper going and then I'll help you.'

'Mu-um,' Kat looks over the banister, 'Molly's here. She needs advice.' Molly's head pops up beside her. Molly Vincent lives next door but can be found here most afternoons, munching biscuits and telling us about her difficulties with her boyfriend, her teachers and her mum. 'What should I *do*, Rosie?' she always moans, picking at the chipped black polish on her nails. At twelve, she's the same age as Kat – but mercifully my daughter seems about five years younger. Carolyn Vincent is always apologetic about her daughter 'bending your ear,' but I don't mind – or rather, I didn't. Now I wonder if I should confess that I'm in no position to advise anyone about how to lead their lives.

'I'd love to, girls, but Molly's mum just texted me that she wants Molly over for supper now.'

'Oooooooooh noooooooo!' Molly's dramatic disappointment is followed by her sloping down the stairs, with Kat disappearing back into her room before I can ask her to give me a hand in putting away the groceries.

'Bye bye, Kat. Bye, Rosie. Goodbye, Mr Martin!' Molly waves over her shoulder. 'See you tomorrow.'

'Goodbye.' Jonathan, sunk into his favourite armchair, doesn't look up from his paper. Then, to me, 'Hullo!' The sight of my treacherous husband infuriates me: he sits there, waiting for me to cook, pour him our 6.30 glass of wine, chit-chat as if nothing was going on. I start unpacking, slamming doors, banging drawers shut.

'A hell of a day . . .' Jonathan comes into the kitchen.

When did we stop greeting each other with a kiss? He takes a bottle of Rioja from the wine rack he and Freddy built for my birthday present last year. 'I think old Bill really is getting past it. He was practically snoring during the

18

CostDrug presentation.' My husband shakes his head over such a lapse. 'What's for supper?'

'I'll tell you what's NOT for supper,' I burst out, as I slap the haddock fillets on to a baking tin. 'Hot volcanic sex!'

2

Jonathan blinks at me, mouth open. 'Wh-wh-wh-what . . .?'

'You heard.' I stare at him across the table where we have shared meals, card games and late-night discussions about us, the children, our friends, the world.

'You've been spying on me!'

'You've been cheating on me!'

I wonder if the children can hear us upstairs. But Kat is bound to be glued to her mobile, and I can hear the rhythmic thud of Freddy's computer game. So I let rip: 'You thought you had it all worked out, didn't you? Me here, her there – you would have kept the whole thing going for years if I hadn't caught you out!' My voice breaks, but I go on: 'How could you? Sex with someone in the office – it's so . . . squalid!'

Jonathan looks as if he's about to shout back, but then he breathes in deeply and issues a slow sigh. 'It's not squalid. She's not squalid. She's beautiful, she's kind, she's . . . clever.'

The word hits me and I jump back, as if it had been a splatter of grease from a frying pan.

Jonathan sees my reaction and looks pained. He draws nearer, and starts to put his hand out towards mine, before letting it fall. 'I'm sorry. I know this hurts. You deserve better.' He shakes his head. 'We've been working side by side for a year. She's been involved in the hair follicle regeneration project. It was bound to happen.'

'Bound to happen? You're shameless!'

'Stop it, Rosie.' Jonathan speaks quietly, patiently, the embarrassed husband of a fishwife from the backstreets of Naples.

'How long has it been going on for?'

'I . . .' Jonathan looks sheepish. 'I realised she was interested in everything I was interested in back in January. But' – here he looks proud of himself – 'it didn't start until three months ago.'

'You've lied to me!'

'I was going to tell you,' Jonathan replies quietly as he sits on the bar stool at the counter.

'What? That you've been cheating on me?' I'm standing, hands on hips. 'That you don't love me any more?'

'Don't pretend *you* love me any more,' he snaps back.

I gasp. 'How can you say that?!'

My husband looks at me unblinking: 'It's true.'

I swallow hard. I look away from the man in front of me. Do I love him? Of course I do. Don't I? What else has kept me by his side for twelve years? I've given him two children and given up a job. I've put up with his parents' dislike and his colleagues' condescension. I've put up with his constant sharing of such riveting facts as an elephant defecates twenty kilos a day and the longest river in China is the Yangtze. I've reassured him when he thought his colleagues were being promoted above him, supported him when he had to work 24/7, cheered him on when he was ready to give up on his great invention, or buying this house, or building Freddy's Lego castle. For twelve years I've worn pastel blue because it's his favourite colour and Diorella because it's his favourite scent. If that's not love, what is?

'Look,' Jonathan brings his hands up to cover his face, 'I don't want a row.' His voice is quiet, convinced. 'We were both growing bored and giving less.'

Growing bored? Well, yes, it can be a bore to be shush!-ed when we're driving back from a party, while my husband yells 'The Congo!' and 'Elizabeth I!' and 'Tin!' in answer to *Brain of Britain*. And yes, Jonathan gets on my nerves when he turns our friends' incipient baldness into an opportunity to plug his invention – 'I think Ted's coming along nicely. He'll soon be asking me about Zelkin'; or 'Sam's grown incredibly thin on top, have you noticed? I wonder if I might not tell him about Zelkin . . .' And I remember how boring he gets when he insists on updating his files with newspaper clippings on everything from 'Chinese restaurants' to 'children's museums'. But it doesn't amount to grounds for divorce. At least, not in my book.

'We both deserve better,' Jonathan continues.

Do we? It's true that when I spot our lovey-dovey neighbours, the Vincents, patting one another on the bottom or

23

cooing at one another over a barbecue in the garden, I feel that I too deserve someone with whom I can be in tune, rather than in denial.

Our marriage, then, could be better. Yes, I do sometimes think that the elastic has given way, and what was once a support that made us the best we could be, now hangs loose, feels uncomfortable and risks dropping altogether, making us look ridiculous and shoddy.

I look down, to see whether my marriage is round my ankles.

'You're only cross,' my husband is telling me, 'because I beat you to finding the Right One.'

I know when I'm beaten. I draw up the second bar stool and perch on it, across from my husband. 'I trusted you.'

'You still can.' Jonathan looks earnest. 'I'll look after you and the children, no matter what.'

'What does "no matter what" mean?' My voice trembles: I'm scared now, as well as angry. 'You can't seriously be saying that you're going to risk upsetting our family for a bit of nookie with some . . . some . . . slut!'

Jonathan draws himself up, and a familiar expression, but not one I have seen him wear for years now, comes over him: 'Take it out on me, Rosie. I understand. You're angry and hurt. But don't call Linda a slut.' I breathe in sharply: Linda! The 'L'! But Jonathan ignores my reaction and goes on: 'She tried to fight this for months. She was ready to get out of hair and get into skin. She almost took a job in California to get away.' He shakes his head. 'She has been worried about you and the children from the start.

She wants to meet you, you know, she wants to explain herself . . . Will you?'

'Oh please, Jonathan!' I cry. 'You can't expect me to be ready for a tête-à-tête with your lover.'

'No, no, of course not.' Jonathan looks sheepish. 'Not *yet*.' He shoots me a look. 'But you will, won't you, at some point? It will make everything so much easier.'

I've suddenly recognised the expression that has altered Jonathan's features: love.

'What happens now?' I ask, defeated.

Jonathan doesn't answer.

I bite my lip. The only way I can see him putting this behind him is if the children and I are not on tap. Once he starts missing us, I doubt Linda stands a chance. I study my husband's dazed, faraway expression. I remember it from sunny afternoons when we lay, exhausted after lovemaking, on our bed. Jonathan doesn't stir. I'm damned if I'm going to sit here waiting passively for him to dictate the terms of my life.

'I think a period of separation would be sensible, don't you?' I don't want a divorce. My husband may be a habit, not a soul mate; and my marriage may be tired, not thrilling: but I won't be pushed out of either.

'Yes, if that's what you want.' Jonathan doesn't meet my eyes.

'It's what I need.' I cross my arms resolutely. 'At least this way I'll have time to sort things out in my own mind.'

Jonathan looks up and finally meets my gaze. 'You've got a lot to offer, Rosie. You're a good-looking woman, kind, and a great mum and . . . and you're still the easiest person to talk to.'

A lot to offer – but not enough for him.

The thing to remember about a separation: there is your separation, his separation, and everyone else's view of your separation.

Jill rushes over the next day: 'That rat! God, I want to kill him! . . . look, don't worry, I've been there. I'll help you.' She stands in the doorway, a bottle of wine in hand. Beneath her glossy black fringe, green eyes shine wide with sympathy.

'I'm actually fine,' I try to say, but she hugs me so tight the words are crushed against her yellow shirt dress.

'Don't breathe in, whatever you do. I've sweated my own body weight. I've just come from my Bikram yoga session.' Since marrying a man five years younger, Jill has been trying out anything that promises to restore her youth. She smiles: 'Brought some vino. God knows, we both need it. Though I shouldn't be drinking.' Jill shakes her head disconsolately, sending the short glossy black hair swinging, left to right. 'The latest research says three units of alcohol a day are more ageing than a week in the sun without SPF.'

Looking slim and tanned in her short dress, Jill strides past, pulling me in her wake, as if I were the visitor rather than the hostess. 'Let's stick two fingers up at that pig. He was chippy, an intellectual snob, and had no sense of humour.'

'Jill, do you mind!' I stop my ears, looking cross. But I always listen to Jill: she's been my protector since the first day we met at University College, when a trendy third year in a black patent leather miniskirt was teasing me about my old-fashioned Laura Ashley dress. 'At least Rosie doesn't look like one of Nature's little jokes,' Jill had snarled, giving my critic a withering look.

'You need a drink.' Jill beckons me to follow her into the kitchen where she slides off her Prada rucksack and places it on the back of a chair. 'Glasses,' she murmurs and rummages through the cupboard to find two. 'When Ross left me, wine became like a saline drip to a comatose patient.'

I watch her, a little dazed, as she twists the wine open and pours it. Jonathan used to call her terrifying: my best friend effortlessly takes over most gatherings, and most situations. 'She makes a man feel redundant,' my husband had complained when they'd first met. *Only men like* your *friends*, I'd felt like answering. There was Tim, capable of amazing work in the lab but only of locker-room banter outside it; and Perry, who'd left pharmacology for the City and only thought of money. Jonathan kept assuring me they were clever and kind, and when Jill and I shared a flat in Islington after uni, he'd encouraged them to chat her up. But Tim's idea of breaking the ice had been to let out a wolf-whistle as Jill swivelled her legs out of her Mini; while Perry had spent most of their dinner at an Italian restaurant calculating on the back of his napkin what he reckoned the takings were. 'I really appreciate your looking out for me,' Jill had told us, 'but Tim's only interested in getting it on and Perry's only interested in raking it in. There might just be more to life, don't you agree?'

'Now' – Jill sits at the table and motions me to sit in front of her – 'tell me all about it.' She crosses her arms on the tabletop and looks me straight in the eyes: 'Who is she?'

'A colleague. But actually it's my decision . . .'

'Bastard.' Jill kicks off her high-heeled mules, stretches her legs out. With her long, lean frame and sharp haircut my best friend always makes me feel small and floppy in comparison. 'It's an open-and-shut case. He's dumped his loyal, loving wife of twelve years.' She beams a big grin: 'He's cheated on you and he's gotta pay for your heartbreak.'

'Actually, I'm not heartbroken.'

'That's the spirit!' Jill's red-nailed hand pats mine. 'Don't let the bastards get you down.'

'I mean' – I shake my head – 'it's not how you see it. Jonathan has found another woman, but I'm not devastated. The separation is my idea.'

'Hmmm.' Jill shoots me a look that shows she's not convinced. 'A bad marriage is like two drunks fighting: it doesn't get any better, and someone's got to break it up.' She pours more wine. 'Let me give you a few tips. First: you can see a shrink, a marriage counsellor, a clairvoyant – anyone – but you MUST get yourself the best divorce lawyer in town. Mine was known as the husband beater.' Jill winks. 'She left Ross battered and bruised.'

I have a fleeting image of Ross Warren, the dopey and dope-smoking younger son of a wealthy Gloucestershire farmer. He was a potter, charmingly hopeless and totally unsuited to Jill. They were married for three years, until he left her for a Latvian waitress. Or was she a dog-walker?

'This is a separation, not a divorce.'

'Second tip' – Jill ignores my protest – 'only ring your ex during office hours.' Here she gives a sharp mirthless laugh. 'I can't tell you how many nights I spent snivelling on the phone to Ross. I told him I loved him, I'd forgive him, I'd take him back and never complain about a thing again . . . all kinds of stuff that at three p.m. would never have crossed my lips but by midnight sounded fine. Sooooooo embarrassing. Third tip: don't, whatever you do, find out the other woman's address, email, telephone numbers . . .' Jill pauses and for a nano-second looks embarrassed. 'Unfortunately, I had gone through Ross's computer and had every possible contact detail for Inga.'

'You didn't . . .'

'I did.' Jill nods her head and can't hide a smile. 'She got quite a few calls from Immigration requesting she show up at their offices. Then her name and mobile number somehow ended up in the *Time Out* personal ads – in a box that said something along the lines of "Busty Inga is just the thinga when you're hot to trot".'

'Jill, how could you?!' For the first time in days, I'm laughing.

'I know, I know – wicked, isn't it?' Jill laughs too, then grows serious. 'What do the children know?'

'That their father and I need a break from each other. Just for a while.' I swallow hard. 'I can't bear the thought of anything hurting them.'

'No. Of course not.' Jill's eyes grow dark with longing: my best friend is thirty-eight and on her third cycle of IVF. Then she shakes her head. 'You've got to move quickly, and club him before he can collect his wits.'

'I don't want to club him. I don't wish him ill.'

Jill's eyes widen into round Os. 'That's the shock talking. When you come to, you'll want to milk him dry.'

'He's my children's father . . .'

'She's your husband's lover.' Jill takes a long sip, then twirls her flute pensively: 'You should get your revenge. Leave them penniless.'

'Jill, I don't want a nasty, messy break-up. Neither does Jonathan.' I finish my glass. 'I believe we can separate in a really civilised, non-traumatic way.'

'And I bet' – Jill leans over, up close – 'that you believe in Father Christmas too.'

Mealtimes, I discover over the next few days, are tricky. Even though I've moved his chair into the garden shed, and leap in to fill every conversational gap with some innocuous comment about their school or my work, nothing can disguise the Jonathan-shaped hole at our table. I've taught myself to check the table setting before calling the children: if I'm not careful, I'm on automatic pilot to set for four, which then means I hurriedly whisk plate, fork, and knife away while Kat and Freddy look on, sad but silent.

But mealtimes could be tricky with Jonathan around, too. There was hair: 'I'd be very interested to see if Louis Vincent keeps that head of hair,' Jonathan would say, raking a hand through his own thick dark curls. 'He's what – forty? Forty-one? It really is phenomenally full. Unusual in a fair, Nordic type. Far more common in a dark-haired Latin. Which why Zelkin sales are not very good in France or Italy.'

30

There was food: 'Hmmmm . . .' Jonathan would savour the mouthful of risotto, then cast me a suspicious look. 'Did you make it with proper stock or is this a stock cube? I'm getting a slight aftertaste of monosodium glutamate . . .' And I'd own up, feeling criminal for having failed to spend two hours boiling a chicken carcass with onion (four cloves stuck into it), bay leaf, carrot and two stalks of celery, as my gourmand husband insisted gave the best flavour.

Then there was the 'Quiz': 'Let's see, children, who can tell me how many wives Henry VIII sent to the block?' Or, 'Can anyone remember what a coniferous tree is?' While I'd roll my eyes at supper being turned into quiz night at the local church hall, the children enjoyed their father's inquisition, giggling openly about their ignorance and looking admiringly as Jonathan answered his own questions.

Without Jonathan, suppers were quieter but less testing.

'Freddy, elbows off the table,' I warn, ladling gravy over each plate. 'Kat, put that phone away.'

I watch the children eat. Freddy's round cheeks fill as he slowly chews the chicken. His expression is serious, brows gathered in thought. Freddy hasn't shed a tear over our separation, but he's coming to my room every morning at five, a toddler's habit he'd shaken off six years ago. *Your son needs you, Jonathan,* I mentally address my husband, *it's no good pretending a part-time dad will do.* I turn to Kat as she pours herself a glass of water. She has my mum's colouring, darker than mine, but the shape of her mouth, her profile, even some of her mannerisms are reminiscent of a younger, fresher version of me. As she sits now, head to one side, a faraway look in her eyes, I am reminded of my twelve-year-old self, sitting between Dad and Tom at supper, eager to join in the grown-up conversation. I took our family's wholeness for granted; it was a given that Mum and Dad were together, and would stay that way for ever. No such givens in Kat's life. And without them, can she grow up confident and happy and independent?

A bleep brings me back to the supper table; under the table, I see Kat's fingers busily tap-tapping away on her mobile.

'Kat! The phone! It's rude.'

'OK, OK, it's off!' Kat sulkily switches off her mobile. 'What's the big deal?'

'It makes us think we don't mean anything to you.'

'Mum . . .' Freddy sets down his fork and turns to me, suddenly serious; 'do you think that's why Dad left?'

'Apparently one in two marriages end in divorce.' My mother sets down her weekend bag. 'We're getting worse than the Scandinavians.'

'It's not divorce, Mum,' I explain patiently. 'It's a trial separation. We need some time to think.'

'I don't think he'll be using the time to *think*.' My mum extracts her flowery toiletries bag.

We're in the guest bedroom, once taken up by a succession of Latvian, Polish, and Hungarian au pairs. Now Otilya, our cleaner for the past ten years, has stemmed the flow of au pairs by offering to watch the children until I get home from work.

'I never thought' – my mother shakes her head mournfully – 'it would happen in our family.' She sighs. 'It's horrible. What am I going to tell your Aunt Lillian? And Cousin Margaret? Oh, it's so . . . so embarrassing.'

Embarrassing? I give my mother a look: ever since I was this high, my mother has managed to embarrass me. Other mums accompanied the class responsibly on school trips; mine got caught smoking with the sixth formers and led the back of the bus in rousing renditions of 'The Good Ship Venus'. Other mums might gently query their child's mark with the relevant teacher; mine would write them five-page letters warning them not to be so provincial in their thinking. Other mums would put off any talk of the birds and the bees; mine was drawing diagrams and labelling them with rude words and inviting my friends to have a look 'and see what's what'.

Embarrassing, indeed.

With a huge effort I swallow my reproaches. She's here and the summer holidays have not got off to a great start, as Jonathan has just announced that he thinks our usual fortnight in Devon would be 'inappropriate' this year.

'Cup of tea?' I volunteer.

'I'll come down with you, let me just organise my things,' my mum says as she starts unpacking. Quickly and methodically, she hangs up her summer dresses and places her shirts and underwear in neat rows in the chest of drawers (I must have been looking for my mum when I married a neatness freak). She is always organising things: her house in the little village in Somerset she and Dad retired to; the members of her local Ladies' Lawn Tennis Club; my dad's life as a GP; mine and Tom's as their none-too-ambitious children. She didn't organise Dad's untimely death, though, or my brother's marriage to an Australian, who insists on Tom staying in Oz. And these failures spur her on to be even more in control of what is left.

'I'll come right over,' Mum had said when I rang to tell her about Jonathan leaving home. 'You need your mother at a time like this.' She would brook no argument, and rang me within half an hour with station, platform and arrival time. Exhausted from days of poor sleep, I was too tired to argue – or remember that my mum's assistance is not quite the balm to human suffering she believes.

'I always did worry about your different backgrounds.' Mum shakes her head as she hangs up her dress.

I haven't forgotten the scene she made when she found out I was marrying a working-class boy from Leeds: 'You are mad, barking mad! He won't know how to hold his knife and fork!'

'Mum, he's lovely and so clever. His boss says he's got a brilliant future ahead of him.'

'I bet they have illuminated reindeers on the porch at Christmas.'

But Mum calmed down when Jonathan impressed my dad by confessing that he read the *BMJ* for pleasure. My parents' grudging acceptance turned into positive praise when Jonathan made money with the patenting of Zelkin and invited them to stay with us the summer we rented a villa in the Dordogne.

34

'Honestly,' Mum now says, mouth set, 'I don't know how he could do it.'

'He's in love,' I say, and I don't think I sound too bitter.

'Thank goodness your father's not here to see it.' My mother is rustling through her weekend bag. 'Here, I brought you this –' She pulls out a brochure and hands it over. 'I know it's not really your age group, but an older man might be just the ticket. And I thought it might take your mind off things.'

I look down at the glossy photos of a SAGA cruise around the Med.

'Mu-um, I'm getting separated, not Alzheimer's!' I hand her back the brochure. I think ruefully of Jill's comment about 'the three stages of womanhood: "Aga, Saga, Gaga."'

'Well,' my mother sniffs, 'I found it very helpful when your father passed away.'

'It's not the same.'

'No. Your father never chose to leave me.'

In her eyes, clearly, I'm a reject, she's a survivor.

'You've got to protect those poor children.' My mother follows me down to the kitchen. 'I know you're still . . . raw, but I hope you're not going to take this lying down, Rosie.'

I fill the kettle. 'Mum, you're just thinking in stereotypes . . .'

But Mum interrupts, cocking her head to one side to look at me appraisingly: 'You look as if you've put on weight. Do you think that's why –'

'Mu-um!' I cry, exasperated.

'Sorry, darling, didn't mean to upset you.'

Mum has never been one for diplomacy. When I was ten, miserable because my classmates were teasing me about my braces, Mum looked at the silver twin track that ran across my face and told me, 'You *do* look dreadful, darling, but only for another two years.' I catch sight of my reflection, distorted into a swollen shape on the shiny metallic microwave, and feel the tears sting: I *do* look dreadful.

'You gave him the best years of your life.' My mother shakes her head woefully.

'I've still got a few left, Mum.'

'They're all the same' – Mum ignores me as she sips from her mug – 'these modern men. Not a thought about duties and responsibilities. It's all about fun fun fun.'

'That's not fair on Jonathan.'

'Fair? I don't want to be fair. Is it fair for him to dump you when you're nearly forty?'

'He hasn't dumped me,' I protest. 'Remember? The separation is my idea.'

'What makes me spit is the thought of his having the pick of any woman he chooses, while you'll be stuck with some broke divorcé or some Mama's boy who's not fit for anyone.' Mum helps herself to the tin of biscuits. She starts to nibble a digestive. 'Trust me,' she says as she wipes the crumbs from the corners of her mouth, 'it's awful out there.'

I wince at the thought of my mum experiencing 'out there' – does she date? Did she try to find herself a lover after Daddy died? She has looked the same for as long as I can remember: a soft brown bob that frames her remarkably unlined face, brown eyes brought out with charcoal-grey eye shadow, a lipstick that is more wine-hued than scarlet red. Her clothes are always neat and feminine, not so much eye-catching as a perfect complement to her trim frame. She is still, I realise for the first time in years, attractive.

'Now, the thing is not to traumatise the children,' my mother is saying decisively as we retreat into the sitting room. 'We really need to show them that you will all do fine without Daddy, and that no one's cross with anyone, and no one's playing the blame game.' She settles in the armchair, and takes out her crossword. 'We'll reassure them with a cosy family weekend. You'll see.' She tucks her feet under her legs and starts nibbling on her pencil. 'Two across: "Hellish time . . . seven letters . . ." Hmmm . . . Divorce?'

3

I fetch the kids from the tennis club. Feeling guilty about Devon, Jonathan has enrolled them for expensive tennis lessons. He should feel guilty, because although it's true, as I told Mum, that we've done our best to reassure the children that relations between us are good, they are showing signs of anxiety: Kat is texting furiously, day and night, and seems totally indifferent to everything around her; Freddy is still coming to my bed at dawn, and has to be led back to his room with whispered assurances of love and devotion. Both cling to me, whenever we're together: Freddy holds on to my skirt, clutches my hands, and climbs on to my lap the moment I sit down; Kat watched an entire episode of *Dr Who* with her head on my shoulder.

As I walk towards Haverstock Hill, I decide that I must enlist my mum's aid, so that together we can drive home the point that our separation is not an act of hostility. In fact, I'm beginning to wonder if I couldn't turn Jonathan's straying, and his guilt, to my advantage. Now that I'm being given time to review our marriage, I can think of a number of areas that need improving: Jonathan's workaholism, his hours on the computer playing Mensa brain games, his obsession with files, drawers, and boxes, his horrendous taste in ties . . . Yes, if we use this time of separation wisely, we can improve our life together.

Even the children will benefit from that. Meanwhile, Mum must help me cheer them up. We can take them to a movie, and maybe go for a meal at Gourmet Burger Kitchen, or that nice café in Regent's Park. Mum can do the granny routine and ask about friends and we could plan her stay at Christmas – she comes up every year, staying into the New Year – so that they know that some things are going to stay the same.

'Mrs Martin?'

I turn to find Mr Parker, the skinny little man who runs Belsize Parker Estate Agents. He stands, as usual, on the pavement outside his bright green office, Marlboro in one hand, mobile in the other.

'How are we doing?' He ends his call and stubs out his cigarette.

'Fine, fine.' I try to look like I'm in a hurry.

'I heard' – Mr Parker's eyes find his shoes, then my face again – 'about your circumstances . . . just wanted to offer my sincere sympathy.'

I wonder how news of our separation has reached the property world, but then I remember that Otilya cleans for Mrs Parker on Saturday mornings.

'Yes. Well, it's sad, but' – I try to look determined, in-dependent, business-like – 'we need a bit of time to . . .'

'I was just wondering if Mr Martin's found something to rent?' Mr Parker's little eyes sparkle with hope. I notice that his pinstripe suit looks too big for him, as if it were a hand-me-down uniform that he, or his parents, were hoping he would grow into.

'You'll have to talk to him.' I'm not going to find my husband a nice flat in which to nest, for goodness' sake. 'I'm off to fetch the children . . .' I try to walk on, but Mr Parker is at my heels:

'Nearby would be convenient, given the situation.' He coughs and splutters, out of breath. You can't smoke thirty a day and hope to keep up with a woman in a hurry. 'And I've got a nice little flat that would be just the ticket.'

'Do give Jonathan a ring,' I call to Mr Parker over my shoulder.

He is at a trot now, still pitching: 'Obviously I know this won't be for long, he's looking for a short-term let,' he splut-ters behind me, 'but they're hard to come by these days, and I think I could get him a good deal.'

'I'm sure he'd love to hear from you!' I shout as I sprint for the gates to the low-bricked buildings of Belsize Tennis Club.

'If you wouldn't mind giving me his mobile number . . .' I hear Mr Parker calling out as I enter the revolving doors before me. Before I can answer I'm being rotated into the warmth of the club.

* * *

41

The children let out a whoop when they hear who's waiting at home for them.

'Granny! Yippee!' they chant as we stroll back home – unaware that I've short-circuited England's Lane and Mr Parker's agency by going the long way round. 'Granny, hurrah!'

Jonathan's mum lives too far away, and is too reserved, for the children to feel totally comfortable with her, but my parents (and since my father's death, my mum) have always made them feel totally at ease. The criticism she cannot stop doling out to me is forgotten when it comes to her beloved grandchildren. I can do no right, they can do no wrong.

I let us in, and Kat and Freddy rush to the sitting room. As I watch the three figures wrapped in a hug, I smile to myself: yes, it was a good idea, Mum's coming down.

'Oh, my poor poor darlings,' my mother sobs as she wraps her arms around both children simultaneously. 'You are so precious . . . how awful for you to have to go through this! You'll have to be brave and strong, my poor pets, no matter how difficult it is . . .'

So much for not traumatising the children.

Mother's visit doesn't get any better. She finds dust behind her cupboard and tells me that losing a husband is no excuse for becoming slovenly; sees Freddy glued to the telly and whispers to me that he's retreating into a kinder world; and, after skimming through my copy of *Good Housekeeping*, begins, 'Men need sex once a week, do you think that's why . . .?'

'Mu-um!' I cry, exasperated.

* * *

On Monday, I receive a letter from the Marlborough Centre: they're interviewing me next week for a place on the Counselling for Life course which starts in September. I study the letter, wondering if I should even attempt the interview at this point. Will my life become clearer over the next month? Do I commit to a course while holding down a job, re-assuring the children, and trying to get my husband back? How can I think of helping others, even listening to them, when my own life is full of indecision?

'What do you think?' I ask my mum over tea and digestives.

'For goodness' sake, Rosie, what are you thinking of ?!' Mum shakes her head. 'You really need to concentrate now, put all your energy into getting Jonathan back home. You don't have time for more work when your life is going down the plughole.'

Worse, on Wednesday when I come home from Dr Casey's, I find her and our next-door neighbour, Carolyn Vincent, sitting in our kitchen having tea. Molly Vincent may sport black nail polish and three studs in her ear, but her mum is all Boden catalogue. Carolyn always manages to look pretty and peachy, with perfect creases on her trousers and nicely polished ballerinas and a girlish ponytail she swings over her shoulder when she wants to think things through.

'Hullo,' I say as I walk in on them.

Carolyn starts: 'Hi, Rosie, how *are* you?' She looks guilty and I can practically smell the pints of pity they have poured all over the subject of our s-p-l-i-t. Carolyn and

Louis's marital harmony is always on show – or at least within earshot, their cooings and tweet-tweets loud and clear beyond the wall that separates us.

'Hullo, darling. Carolyn dropped by for a cup of tea.' My mum looks totally unembarrassed.

'Er . . . yes.' Carolyn grows the colour of her beautifully cut pink linen dress. 'Just seeing if the children wanted to come over for supper tonight. Louis is doing a barbecue.'

It's a double whammy: first, Carolyn obviously suspects I no longer feed my children proper meals; second, she is letting me know that her husband hangs about the place lighting charcoal bricks and getting splattered by burgers and sausages while mine has made tracks with a sexy American.

'That's sweet of you, Carolyn, but I've bought lamb chops already,' I lie.

Mum and Carolyn share a look of complicity.

'Oh, and also . . .' Carolyn begins, as she swings her blonde ponytail over her left shoulder and lowers her lids shyly, 'I thought you might like to meet my friend Vanessa. She's a brilliant therapist. Specialises in relationships and . . . sex.'

'I thought' – my mother looks from Carolyn to me and back again – 'it sounded just the ticket. I mean, our subconscious does very weird things. And we all know how important bed is for the boys.'

'Hmmm . . .' I try to smile but my teeth feel set in stone – and misery. 'I believe in therapy – though maybe it's not the sex kind we need.'

'Well, let me know if you change your mind. Louis and I just want to help.' Carolyn sets down her mug, only half finished, and with a reproachful look makes for the back door: 'Nice meeting you, Mrs Walters.'

'A lovely girl.' My mother watches Carolyn's slender figure retreating across our garden. 'And I like the look of him, too. You couldn't hope for better neighbours, really.' Then she turns to me. 'Isn't it extraordinary, how different marriages can be?'

In between such helpful comments we play Monopoly, Risk and Racing Demon, and Mum wastes a lot of time trying to teach the children bridge. We watch a DVD of *High School Musical*: Remix, sing along to the lyrics, and call in a pizza. The children relax, and the familiar routines of Mum's stay – the questions about school which prompt her own, rather long-winded, reminiscences, the crossword, the Earl Grey tea and ginger biscuits for elevenses and 5 p.m., the insistence on a long walk after lunch – reassure them that all is as before. Almost.

Once the children are tucked up in bed, Mum and I sit reading in the living room.

'Freddy's such a star, did you see how he's been running errands for me, fetching glasses, books, my crossword?' Mum looks up from her Jeffrey Archer to smile at me. 'And our little girl, she's all grown up: do you realise what all that texting is about?' I shake my head, no. 'A boyfriend!'

'A boy who is a friend, you mean?' I look up, worried, from *The Times*.

'No, no, Mungo is an official boyfriend. She says so on Facebook.' My mother smiles, pleased. 'I think it's marvellous.'

'Do you?' I sound sceptical. Is my mum on Facebook, I wonder? I'm not.

45

'Yes.' My mother nods her head vigorously. 'It's a sign that she hasn't been put off men by your split.'

'Oh . . .' I breathe deeply, guiltily, and hide behind the newspaper: I hadn't considered that our separation could turn my daughter into a man-hater.

'It's not puppy love as we know it,' Mum continues, fingers tapping on the Jeffrey Archer. 'They've only met once, and their whole relationship is about texting.'

I set down the newspaper, feeling left out and slightly put out: first, my daughter chooses to confide in Mum rather than me; second, my twelve-year-old is beginning a relationship just as mine threatens to end. *Kat, Kat* . . . I want to take my daughter in my arms and whisper a warning: *Be careful, my love*. But even as I think the words, I know not to ever utter them; I don't want my daughter to be scared of love.

It's as if Mum reads my thoughts: 'I wouldn't worry about Jonathan, you know. These . . . sex things don't usually last more than a few months.'

Immediately I start imagining all kinds of scenarios: Jonathan weeping, on his knees, begging me to start again. Jonathan ringing on the door in the dead of night telling me that he's made a terrible mistake. The children and I coming back from tennis camp to find Jonathan on our doorstep . . .

From the depths of the chintz armchair, she gives me a long look. 'Would you have him back?'

Would I? I've gone from being shocked to being furious, to wanting some control over our relationship, to wishing him back. So would I have him back? Like a shot. Separation sounded like a good idea: a pause in which to review, regroup.

But nothing had prepared me for this loneliness. Jonathan and I have always been friends, after all. I won't be able to survive much more of this.

Out loud I say, 'For the children's sake, yes.'

My mother's hope becomes my certainty. Every time I hear a car park outside or a cab pull up, I'm convinced it's Jonathan. Whenever Jonathan rings to speak to the children, I'm sure he is about to plead to be taken back. And when Kat complains that her computer's acting up, and Jonathan offers to come by and look at it, and ends up also fixing the dripping tap in the downstairs loo, I read in these DIY efforts an attempt to worm his way back into our affection.

'Don't be pathetic,' Jill scolds me when I tell her. 'Men love playing at Mr Fix-it. They'd fix a tap for Myra Hindley if they got half a chance.'

I don't listen. He's left his electric razor behind – he wouldn't do that if he thought he would be gone for long. His post continues to come every day, as do the *International Herald Tribune* and the *Financial Times*.

'Don't read anything into it,' Jill warns. 'When they're in the throes of sex they don't remember their own name. When Ross was cheating on me he was always getting locked out because he'd forgotten his keys, and showing up late because he'd lost his watch. Multi-tasking is for women.'

'Hmmm . . .' I murmur, unconvinced. Ross and Jonathan have nothing in common. Ross is still getting handouts from his parents, whereas Jonathan prides himself on being a caveman provider. Ross is bohemian, while Jonathan's idea of being creative is thinking up names for pharmaceutical patents. Ross never wanted children, Jonathan adores his.

Which is another reason for my optimism. Kat and Freddy are my most powerful weapons against the American. I have to hide my smile when I hear Kat on the telephone to Molly, describing 'what a pain' Linda is. I feel a little thrill of victory when Freddy refuses to go to the Science Museum with his father and 'her'. And I'm secretly delighted when I overhear the children telling their father that they want to be with 'just you, Dad', when he offers to take them out for lunch on Saturday.

Jonathan is sheepish when he comes to pick up or drop off the children. He tries to worm his way back into Otilya's good graces by taking out the rubbish piled up in the kitchen. He offers to lend me the car so I can get to John Lewis to pick up the curtains I'd ordered. And he offers to help Freddy with his back stroke for hours on end. Between us, though, conversation has become impossibly stilted. We may be only separated, but we speak like a couple in the throes of divorce.

A brief guide to divorce-speak:

1. He says: 'This is very painful for me.'
   He means: *This is going to be very expensive.*
2. He says: 'This is not doing either one of us any good.'
   He means: *I don't want to have sex with you any more.*
3. He says: 'The children are so grown-up.'
   He means: *Don't try a guilt trip on me.*

4. He says: 'You don't understand . . .'
   He means: *You'd better do what I want.*
5. He says: 'Linda understands me.'
   He means: *Linda's better in bed than you.*
6. He says: 'I want regular access to the children.'
   He means: *I want to see the children for fun outings on the occasional weekend, once you've fed them, bathed them, and made sure they've done their homework.*
7. He says: 'I want you to know I'm always here for you.'
   He means: *Don't bother me unless the house is burning down.*
8. You say: 'Everything will be fine.'
   You mean: *This is hell on earth.*
9. You say: 'Your father's wonderful, really.'
   You mean: *Your father's wrecked your lives and when you're older you can sue him for negligence.*
10. You say: 'This can be a new beginning.'
    You mean: *I'm so emotionally battered I wonder if I'll survive this.*

'I'm dead! I've had an electric muscle-stimulator facial, and you can't imagine how looooong that takes.' Jill drops by Saturday morning. Jonathan has taken the children for pizza ('With just you, Dad, right?'). It's a glorious day and I'm sunbathing in the garden, trying to ignore the Vincents' lovey-dovey duet on the other side of the wall.

'They say it takes years off your face.' Jill opens and shuts her mouth in an exaggerated sequence. 'You know, we're supposed to give our facial muscles a daily eight-minute workout.' She scrunches her face, then relaxes it. You'd never know this was a much-respected GP, a woman who is rational and ultra-sane about most things. 'Now, are you ready to meet other people?'

'I don't need to, Jill!' I'm on the chaise longue, and I need to shield my eyes to see my friend, sitting beside me. I've made us both iced tea. 'He's coming back.'

'What?!' Jill's look of astonishment is comical. 'Thrown over the Yank?'

'Shshshshsh.' I bring an index finger to my lips and nod in the direction of the wall. From the other side comes a steady stream of 'Sweety' and 'Darling', 'Treasure' and 'Petal'. 'No, he hasn't left her yet. But it's almost over.'

'What's "almost"? Almost as in, he's told you to pack your bags because the two of you are off to the Caribbean for a love-fest, or almost as in, your wishful thinking?'

'Neither. The children keep saying that he looks miserable when he's saying goodbye to them, and he keeps hanging about the house, and he keeps doing things to be helpful, like offering to look into my mum's prescription and find out why it's not working . . .'

Jill draws her chair closer to me. She looks stern. 'This does not mean that he's coming back, Rosie. It just shows Jonathan's not a complete bastard. He loves the kids. He probably even loves you – in a kind of fraternal, protective way. But I see no proof of a change of mind.'

'Jill, you're always so negative,' I burst out. Then, mindful of the 'petal' and 'treasure' on the other side of the hedge

I lower my voice: 'I bet you anything he comes back, apologises, and we start a whole new life together.'

I hang on to the vision of our family reunited. And when I come home from Mr Ahmed the dry cleaner's to find Jonathan's message on our voicemail, I'm convinced this is it. 'Rosie. It's me. Can I come by this afternoon? I'm unhappy . . . garble garble . . .' The tape becomes indistinct but I am sure of the sentiment conveyed: Jonathan is unhappy and wants to return.

I run upstairs to check my makeup. I hear footsteps outside the bathroom: I'm tempted to ask Kat what she thinks of my dress – scoop neck, cotton, light blue; but I don't want to get her hopes up.

'Mu-um!' It's not Kat, it's Freddy coming up the stairs. I lock the door: my nine-year-old still has only a nominal notion of privacy.

'What?' I try to keep my hand steady as I draw eyeliner on to my lid.

'I'm just going over to the Vincents' to play FIFA 08 with Oscar. Kat wants to come to see Molly.'

'Off you go.' For only a second I feel guilty that I'm allowing the children to miss one of their father's visits. If my suspicions are right, though, today marks their father's return. Just me and Jonathan, I think, and my heart thumps. I feel shockingly lust-filled when I think about my straying husband: maybe someone else needed to find him attractive before I could get excited about him again.

The door bell goes as I finish brushing my hair. I rush

down and let Jonathan in. Except I can't. The knob that is supposed to unclick stays rigid in my hand. I try desperately to turn it but nothing happens. It's an American-style, button-in-the-middle knob that Jonathan had warned was lethal for small children. He's been promising to change it from the day we moved in. My husband is coming back to me and I'm stuck in the loo!

The door bell rings again. 'Jonathan! I'm just coming!' I yell. But there's nothing for it: the handle resists all attempts to turn it. 'I can't!' I scream.

Helplessly I look around the bathroom for something with which to prise open the wooden door. Tweezers? Nail scissors? Razor? I try to poke the little button in the middle of the knob, but nothing gives. I look up at the skylight that is the only window. If I stand on the loo seat, and prise it open, I could shout out so that Jonathan (and anyone else in the street below) could hear me.

The door bell goes again, this time for longer. Then I hear my mobile ring next door: Jonathan obviously thinks I've forgotten our appointment. As if. I'm up on the loo seat, and I push open the skylight: 'Jonathan!' I call out.

'Where are you?' I hear from below.

'Up here! In the loo! I'm locked in!' I try to sound calm and in control, but you can't when you've locked yourself into a 3 × 5 room with your maybe-on-again-husband waiting on the doorstep below.

'Let me come in and see if I can let you out!' Jonathan shouts up. 'I've got the keys still!'

'Thanks!'

I press my ear against the door and hear Jonathan's familiar heavy steps climb the stairs.

'Here I am. Now how are we going to get you out of here?' Jonathan asks affectionately. He sounds like Christopher Robin talking to Pooh Bear. It's the manner I know well. 'How *do* you manage these scrapes?' he asked when I, in a coat with rabbit-fur collar and cuffs, emerged from his HQ to find myself in the midst of a dozen placard-waving anti-fur demonstrators. Or 'I'd better come home and see to this' when I rang in a panic because I'd forgotten my house keys when I'd nipped out to buy some dill and was standing there in front of our locked door, with six guests arriving in ten minutes.

'I don't know what happened,' I moan as on the other side of the door I hear my husband trying the knob. 'I just locked it!'

'We should have got rid of these stupid locks when we moved in,' Jonathan grunts as he keeps working on the knob.

'I know. Do you think you can get me out?' I steal a look at the mirror: I'm a bit flushed, but the makeup is still in place.

'Of course.' Calm, confident, in charge: oh, how I've missed my husband. 'I have to get into the bathroom come what may. I've got to get my electric razor back. I've been using disposables and they're killing my face.'

My heart lurches. Surely he doesn't need to take his electric razor if he's coming back?

'You said you were unhappy . . .'

'Hmm?' Sound of a screwdriver working at the knob.

'Oh, I know what it was. Kat told me you were having problems sleeping . . .' (Oh no, she shouldn't lay on the guilt trip, I'm sure that's counter-productive!) '. . . and I wanted to say that usually I'm unhappy with anyone taking sleeping pills, but if it's only for a short period . . .'

'Well, it *has* been' – *Don't sound bitter*, I remind myself – 'a bit difficult.'

More rattling of the knob.

'Bloody hell, this thing is difficult . . .'

I lean against the door, and feel as if I'm leaning against him. *I'll take you back,* I whisper, *I know we're no longer in love but we're so comfortable together.*

'Hmmm . . .? Did you say something . . . Hey!' The door handle falls on to the floor and the door opens.

'Bless you!' I cry and spontaneously (well, almost) throw my arms around him.

'No worries.' Jonathan gently unclasps my hands to free himself. 'I think, er . . . you'll want a stiff drink after your captivity.' His face lights up with a smile, but not for me: he goes straight to the electric razor in its vinyl case. 'Perfect.' He turns back to me, adopts a look of concern. 'Kat's right. You do look pale.'

It's all I can do not to scream, 'Because of this mad separation, you idiot!' Instead I say lightly, 'Let's have a drink.'

He follows me down the stairs to the kitchen. I open the cupboard, get out the bottle of Famous Grouse. Jonathan leans against the counter. 'Where are the kids?'

'Vincents. As per usual.'

It's as if he'd never gone, I think. As if this episode had

never taken place, Linda never existed. Then I notice it: the big green canvas weekend bag he'd packed that dreadful night. It's back! He's brought his things back and we're going to be together again. I sigh with relief.

Jonathan follows my eyes. 'I've brought my bag. I need to get a few essentials. In fact, Rosie,' he looks me in the eye, right hand warming the whisky in his glass, 'it really makes no sense procrastinating about painful decisions: I'm going to consult a lawyer on Monday and seek a divorce.'

My face must have given me away because he reaches out to touch my hand. 'Don't look like that. I care for you very much, I always will. But Linda and I . . . it's not a fling. It's for ever.'

4

Jonathan holds my hands in his. 'Rosie, we don't need to be enemies, you know. We've got two wonderful children. A million memories. A divorce doesn't need to be horrible and devastating. It can be an arrangement that suits us both. I'll be with Linda, you'll find someone too, the children will still be the centre of our lives.' He studies my face for a reaction. 'You can still do your counselling programme, I'll pay for that. And the three of you can stay here, no problem.'

I shut my eyes: separation is for now, but divorce is for ever. I never meant to let this period drag on for more than a month or two.

Life without Jonathan for ever? I've never seriously considered it. Who else can find the shortest way from Belsize Park to Brixton? Or immediately guess what's wrong with Mum's prescription? We brush our teeth at the same time, check in with a telephone call at least once a day, eat supper together and, when it comes to the children, we lean on each other, like poles holding up the tent under which Kat and Fred can crawl and be cosy.

But then I look at my husband's expression of pity. Ugh! I can't bear the thought of him and Linda shaking their heads over my lonely disappointment. *Hey, you!* I feel like shouting, *You don't need to feel sorry for me. I can build a new life, find a new love.* I breathe in deeply: if I need directions, I can get myself a sat nav. If I need help with prescriptions I can ring Jill. And I'll always protect the children, Jonathan or no Jonathan.

I can do this. I toss my hair and stand up straight; yes, I can. I'm going to explode every prejudice, and turn all preconceived notions on their head. I'm going to think the unthinkable and do the impossible. I'm going for . . .

'A good divorce!' My voice rings with conviction. 'We'll make this a good divorce. A civilised split.'

'The most civilised divorce in the annals of break-ups.' Jonathan gives me a lopsided grin.

'Pain-free.'

'Humane.'

'Generous-spirited.'

'No one will be able to say that we traumatised our children, or ruined each other's lives.'

'Everyone will congratulate us on how brilliantly we've managed a difficult process.'

'Ours will be the most constructive collaboration ever.'

Then, with a look of concern, 'Hey, sweetheart' – Jonathan takes a tissue from the Kleenex box on the mirrored shelves above the toilet – 'you're crying!'

What not to do when you're considering a friendly divorce: tell anyone.

I'd prepared my speech, and repeated its promises of 'civilised separation . . . mutually convenient arrangement . . . friendly division of spoils . . . best for the children . . .'

Somehow, though, nobody heard these reassuring pledges, and the reactions to my announcement are the same as if I'd said Jonathan and I were fighting to the bitter end, no holds barred, until no one was left standing and the children were covered in our blood.

Kat: 'How can you DO that to us?! We'll have to see a therapist for the rest of our lives!'

Freddy: 'I'll be like Justin! His parents are divorced and he says he spends every holiday in the car, going from one to the other!'

My mum: 'What?! No . . . you can't be . . . Oh my God!'

Otilya, our Polish daily: 'My husband' – she pushes the mop across the kitchen floor – 'he divorce me for new girl too. She not pretty, she not clever, she not rich. I ask him, "What she have?"' Otilya leans her bulky frame on her mop. 'He say, "She not you."'

Dr Casey bestows upon me the look he usually reserves for patients whose excessive use of Botox has frozen their face into a mask. 'Chin up, my girl! You know what they say: better unaccompanied than shackled to a bad 'un.'

And I overhear him telling Mrs S: 'Do be gentle Lavinia – she is obviously near breaking point.'

Strolling down the stretch of Haverstock Hill where I normally shop feels like running a gauntlet these days.

Mr Parker, smoking outside Belsize Parker Estate Agents as usual, is always on the look out for me. 'Ah, Mrs Martin, how are we doing?'

'Wonderful, Mr Parker, thank you.' I don't want to stop.

'I understand' – Mr Parker stubs his cigarette butt on the pavement – 'things have become more . . . permanent.'

Otilya and her big mouth.

'Yes.' I sound as casual as I can. 'We are making it as sensible and friendly as possible.'

'Of course, of course.' Mr Parker's pinstripe suit smells of nicotine, stale and fresh. 'I went through a very hard time just after my own divorce . . . but' – here he beams again – 'I then met Mrs Parker, and now my life couldn't be better.'

'Hmmm . . . wonderful . . .' I try to walk off, but Mr Parker keeps up with me until after a few paces I stop: I don't want him following me home.

'I just thought that you should know we have worked with a lot of couples through . . . difficult times.' He gives a little cough. 'Divorce means two households. Two properties. I could help.'

'We already have our property – and Jonathan has –' I begin.

'There's some wonderful flats out there,' Mr Parker interrupts me, taking a step closer. I wince at the stench of cigarette; standing this close to him is like passive smoking. 'Really wonderful, if you and Mr Martin wanted to downsize. You should consider two flats. Or maybe you and the children could look at a maisonette and he could stay in a flat – with his friend.' I scowl and Mr Parker hurries on, 'And even if the market is soft at the moment, I think we could get a good price for your house.'

'Our house?!'

'I know it's a bit tired – you remember when I sold it to you ten years ago I warned you that the kitchen and bathrooms would need redoing – but it has those original features, and plenty of light, and people place a premium on high ceilings and a bit of outside space . . .'

'Our house,' I hiss, 'is not for sale.'

Mr Parker stretches out his hands to reassure me. 'No-no-no, Mrs Martin, this is just in case. What often happens is that the original home can be associated with . . . strain, stress . . . and a new environment is seen as conducive to a fresh start . . .'

'Mr Parker, our home is full of very happy memories, for us and for the children.' I sound glacial, and Mr Parker shrinks further into his suit. 'Jonathan is adamant that we stay put.'

'Of course, Mrs Martin.' Mr Parker nods eagerly. 'I saw him the other day. I thought I could help him get something nearby – you know, makes it convenient for visiting the children . . . He told me he's already got something in Bayswater with his . . . er, he's got a place already . . . still, it's just a rental property. We may be able to convince him that there's better investments to be made.' Mr Parker won't draw breath.

'Divorce means you have to be so careful about money . . . and if they can be had at a good price, two homes can mean two very profitable ventures.'

'Yes, but . . .'

'There's a maisonette around the corner from you, thirteen hundred square feet. At £950,000, it's a bargain.'

'Mr Parker, I'm not interested; we're not moving.'

'Maybe you don't like maisonettes?' Mr Parker extracts his packet of Marlboros, taps them nervously with his left hand. 'There's a nice little mews house up at Belsize Village, spanking new interior, got a designer in who really gave it the wow factor and –'

'We're NOT moving!' I can't help shouting.

For a moment, Mr Parker looks properly cowed. But then he springs back to his salesman life-form: 'I know this is probably not the right time, you're still very raw, but I can tell you there's a block of flats in St John's Wood' – I start walking away, shaking my head – 'that would be just the ticket for you and the children. Nice and quiet, very safe and a lovely garden out back . . .'

Mr Ahmed, our dry cleaner, is not much better.

'You washing Mr Martin shirts at home now? You try to do my job for me?' Mr Ahmed throws his hands up in the air when I bring in only a silk blouse and my ancient woollen jacket.

'Mr Martin no longer lives at home,' I tell Mr Ahmed without looking at him. Behind him, Mrs Ahmed's eyes grow round and she stops unfolding clothes.

'Oh, I'm sorry, I'm sorry, Mrs Martin . . .' Mr Ahmed tugs one end of his thick grey moustache.

Mrs Ahmed draws up to the counter, a jumper in her hand. 'These English men. No sense of family. The Queen's children, look at them: they too, all divorced.'

'It's not quite like that.' I find myself trying to defend Jonathan, and the Windsors, to our dry cleaner and his wife.

'Tchtch!' Mrs Ahmed shakes her head woefully, and her plump body beneath the red and yellow sari jiggles. 'They want fun and new things all the time.'

Mr Ahmed leans over the counter. 'You need an Asian man.' He takes my blouse and jacket and hands me a receipt for them. Then, taking one of the lollies he keeps for his customers' children, he holds it out to me. 'Here,' he says, 'you take this.'

Nadine, my hairdresser, is also full of sympathy. 'What?! With whom?! What a bastard!' She tugs at my wet hair with a comb.

'That hurts,' I protest.

'I know, I know. Trust me, I've been there. Me, it happened six years ago, and let me tell you, I lost two dress sizes, I cried so much. You know what makes it so hard?' she asks my reflection in the mirror: I shake my head, no. 'That he's doing it to you at our time of life.' I flinch: surely Nadine is a good ten years older than me? 'It's hard to get dates at our age. Show me a man who notices you when you're over twenty-two,' she goes on, addressing the woman with the stringy wet hair and pink towel on her shoulders. 'But I've got a good book for you.

In fact two: *Couple Uncouples* and *Split Does Not Mean That's It*. Really deep stuff. Written by psychiatrists. Take up yoga, too; it really helps with the pain. It's all in the breathing.'

'This won't do.' Jill shakes her head as she undoes my top three buttons. 'It's not Sunday school, you know.'

'What's going on?' I look from Jill to David as they draw me into their smart, ultra-modern sitting room. Black-and-white photographs decorate the walls, tall white orchids sit on window sills and mantelpiece. Jill ignores my query as she pushes back the hair from my face. David smiles mysteriously.

The door bell rings. Jill brings her index finger to her lips. 'Not a word,' she hisses over her shoulder at her partner as she opens the front door.

'How funny!' Jill trills as she walks back in, a handsome man in her wake. 'David and I were just telling Rosie how wonderful your *Romeo and Juliet* is, and here you are, in the flesh. What a coincidence!'

'Well, you did invite me,' the new arrival replies, puzzled. He's youngish, copper-haired and white-skinned, tall and wiry. He wears a purple velvet jacket and his hair in a ponytail: I take it he's one of David's friends – they're all theatrically turned out.

'Must be fate!' Jill drags the ponytailed man to where I'm standing. 'Orlando, Rosie. Rosie, Orlando.'

As I smile up at him, Orlando looks at me expectantly: I wonder if we've met before and I've forgotten.

'You may recognise Orlando,' David explains while his

friend smiles modestly, 'from his theatre work. He's been in some very famous productions.'

'Uh . . . I wonder . . .' I try to rack my brains about the plays I've seen, but the only recent production I remember is the panto, *Aladdin*, when I accompanied Freddy's class last Christmas. I sit on the huge grey silk sofa, wishing that I wasn't wearing my most comfortable and least attractive jeans and a boring button-down shirt. Couldn't Jill have given me some warning?

'Did you see *The Importance of Being Earnest* last May?' Orlando asks hopefully as he sits on the zebra-skinned stool in front of me. 'I was Algernon's butler.' I shake my head.

David hands me a glass of wine. 'Fabulous, he was, too. The *Ham and High* said he was "a scene stealer".'

'What about *Oliver!*?' Orlando tries again. 'I was one of Bill's boozing buddies.' I shake my head guiltily. 'OK, you must have seen *Wuthering Heights* two years ago, with Heathcliffe as a Shia Muslim and Cathy as a Hasidic Jew? *Everyone* saw that!'

'No,' I confess. Then, seeing Orlando's dejected expression: 'But *everyone* did say how marvellous it was.' Orlando shakes his head forlornly over his glass of wine. 'It's me,' I try to console him, 'I've been going through a philistine patch lately.'

'Nonsense, Rosie!' Jill interrupts me. 'You're very artistic. She once made me a lovely Christmas card – a collage of wrapping paper, really striking.' She sits beside me on the sofa, nudging me with her elbow. 'And she studied Shakespeare, didn't you, Rosie?'

'Well, yes, but only for A Levels.' My admission earns a furious scowl from Jill. And her elbow in my side.

'Tell Rosie about *Romeo and Juliet*.' Jill smiles encouragingly at Orlando.

'It's a fab adaptation.' Orlando bobs up and down enthusiastically, and some long copper curls slip out of the neat ponytail. 'We've got an all-male cast. So it's homophobia not a family feud that keeps the lovers apart.'

'How interesting . . .' I try to imagine the balcony scene between Romeo and Jules? (Julian?) and fail to. David holds up the bottle, enquiring if I'd like some more. 'Thanks, yes, it's delicious.' I might as well get drinking at this point.

'Hmmm, lovely, vino.' Orlando holds up his own glass for seconds.

'You both like Sauvignon Blanc: you've got so much in common!' Cringing at Jill's indefatigable matchmaking, I try to draw away from her on the sofa, but she goes on, heedless: 'Like – divorce.'

Orlando's eyes grow wide and round and interested. 'Really? You too? I've just come out of three horrible years of it.'

'Marriage?'

'No. Divorce court. The harpy was determined to get her mitts on the Hall and I wasn't going to let it happen.'

'Northlay Hall is Orlando's ancestral pile,' David explains. 'Adam. In Wiltshire. Stunning.'

'Once she landed a role on *EastEnders* she got ideas above her station,' Orlando explains. Then, in a high-pitched whine, '"Orlando, if I can't have you I want your house."'

Now he lowers his voice back to normal, "'Look, Violet, it's been in my family for centuries, it means nothing to you but everything to my father.'" He switches to the high-pitched voice: "'It means a lot to me, too. It means I wouldn't have to slog all day and all night.' 'You're being unreasonable!' 'You're being mean!' 'I need closure!' 'You need a shrink!'"

I watch, baffled, as Orlando alternates his wife's voice with his own. When Jill goes to the kitchen to fetch some nibbles, I follow her.

'Why didn't you tell me to expect a ventriloquist show?' I whisper, cross.

'I wish you'd get into the spirit of it,' Jill scolds me as she opens the bag of handmade potato crisps. 'Orlando's gorgeous.'

'He's also bitter about his divorce and horrid about his ex.'

'Everyone's bitter about their divorce.'

'Not me, and not Jonathan.'

'Your attitude to this divorce is just not healthy.' She fills the square glass bowl with crisps. 'Divorce is as close as two people can legally get to murdering one another.'

'It's not true, I don't want bitterness, recriminations, huge maintenance . . .'

'Stop!' Jill drops the empty bag of crisps on the counter and puts the back of her hand against her forehead in a dramatic gesture. 'Stop right there. No to huge maintenance? What's the point of divorce then?'

'I don't want Jonathan suffering. He's a good man. An excellent father. A better husband than most.'

'You can't be nice about your ex when you're in the middle of a split. It's perverse.' She grabs my hand. 'Now, get back in there and strut your stuff,' she barks.

In the sitting room, alas, Orlando's one-man show continues: '"You're a harpy!" "You're an idiot!" "May you rot in hell!" "May your scrotum itch you for seven years."'

The worst, though, is next door. Carolyn Vincent cannot resist a few words of concern every time our paths cross: 'Oh, poor you!' she intones piously when she sees me struggling under the weight of carrier bags. 'Do you want a hand?' she calls out from her doorstep. And then, over her shoulder: 'My love, will you help Rosie with her shopping?' And husband Louis, a square-jawed and handsome knight in shining armour, materialises to help me with the bags.

'Well done, angel.' Carolyn rewards her husband with a big smack of a kiss, right on the doorstep for everyone to see.

Worse, it seems as if whenever I stand at my window, lost in thought and wondering about what life will bring next, I am subjected to a sighting of the happy couple hugging, kissing, rubbing noses (nothing seems beyond them). These little vignettes of marital harmony have me reaching for the curtain cord and longing to move to Nuneaton.

Not that the Vincents are unkind. Carolyn is constantly inviting us over for a 'kitchen supper', or tea, or Sunday lunch.

Into the bright yellow kitchen we troop. Carolyn, in a pretty pale blue Cath Kidston apron, stands at her stove, stirring some delicious but non-fattening sauce. Louis springs up from the table where he was reading out loud, presumably for Carolyn's amusement, the *Daily Mail* Richard Kay gossip column.

'Hullo! Carolyn, Rosie and the children are here!' He offers me a glass of Bordeaux, and an expression of condolence fills his face.

'Kat, Freddy, will you fetch the children?' Carolyn turns from the Aga, wooden spoon in hand, a perfect homemaker's smile on her face. 'It's supper time. And wash hands.' Then, when Kat and Freddy are no longer in earshot, 'They're being so braaaave, you must be so prooooouuuud.'

At table, Molly immediately sits beside me. She has not, I've noticed, been seeking my advice lately: she has obviously drawn her own conclusions about my ability to navigate emotional life. Louis, on my other side, keeps my glass and plate filled and makes kind suggestions like, 'You will let me know if I can do anything, won't you? DIY, dig you out of the snow, cart down any heavy rubbish . . .'

Worst of all is watching Carolyn and him perform a perfect duet as they move back and forth from kitchen table to sink, from stove to dishwasher, enviably in synch with every step and look. Were Jonathan and I ever like that?

'Sweetpea, will you pour me a glass of water? Thanks, darling one. Rosie, are you and Jon . . .' Carolyn stops in her tracks, flushes, gives a little embarrassed cough, then resumes, 'er, I mean, are you going off somewhere nice before term starts?'

'Nah,' Freddy answers before I can.

'We aren't either,' Molly scowls. 'Dad just wants to be near a golf course so he can disappear for hours. Holidays are supposed to be, like, spent with the family all together and . . .' A look from her parents sends her into manic back-pedalling: 'I mean, er . . . Actually who needs fathers on holidays?'

The children and I seek refuge in Carolyn's tender roast chicken and comforting mash. We eat silently, leaving our hosts to find another subject of conversation.

'Mum, did you get Oliver's birthday present?' Freddy asks me.

'Oliver? . . .' I ask blankly, wondering in a panic who Oliver could be and when this shock birthday party is to be held.

'Oh, Mu-um!' Freddy groans. 'I to-old you!'

'Well, your mum has had a lot on her plate,' Carolyn says hurriedly. Then, trying to turn the conversation away from odious comparisons: 'Oh, Kat, that is the prettiest pendant!' Carolyn smiles. 'Matches your eyes.'

'Dad gave it to me,' Kat sighs. 'Hush money, I suppose.'

5

Babette Pagorsky's smile casts the soft and comforting glow of a child's night light. I feel as if I am sitting on Kat's or Freddy's bed, waiting for them to fall asleep. 'What brings you here?' Babette asks in her deep man's voice. I'm brought back to reality. I'm not with my children in their cosy bedrooms but with my soon to be ex-husband in a marriage counsellor's room. In the month between Babette making her assessment of us, during which she asked a million questions – how had we met, what did we do for a living, where did we live, how many children, and when had our 'problem' arisen? – and her managing to slot us into her busy schedule for our first appointment, Jonathan and I have started proceedings on our friendly divorce.

'So,' Babette repeats as she looks across to us, 'what brings you here?'

Jonathan and I sit side by side (but at least two feet apart) on a capable brown leather sofa. Babette sits in a squat armchair across an Oriental carpet from us. The room, painted the palest shade of green, looks elegant rather than cosy: antiques and silver ornaments, silk throw cushions, and two lamps on side tables rather than overhead lights. It's brilliant sunshine outside, but heavy green curtains are drawn against all that.

Babette had already briefed me over the telephone about the 'counselling process': we could have several joint sessions and then, if desired, we could meet with Babette one on one. Every case, she'd warned, is different, and she could give me no guarantees, or even time frames.

Jonathan looks at Babette. I look at Babette. Babette smiles at both of us. She is an elegant plump woman, in her fifties, with soft dark hair and eyes. She has a colourful silk scarf draped over her shoulders, in the continental fashion.

Jonathan clears his throat. 'We're getting divorced, and want to make it as painless as possible.'

'Oh?' Babette looks a bit put out. 'People usually come here because they want to avoid divorce.'

'Well, we know what we want.' Jonathan gives me an encouraging smile. 'We just want to take all the proper steps.'

'So you know what you want . . .' Babette echoes Jonathan, and her tone is ever so slightly ironic. Her dark eyes settle on me: 'You too, Rosie?'

'Yes,' Jonathan interrupts. 'The divorce is a mutual agreement.'

'Mutual?' Babette raises a well-arched eyebrow. 'You rolled out of bed one morning, one on the right, the other on the left, and said, "Hey, let's get a divorce"?'

'Well . . .' Jonathan begins.

'This divorce,' Babette's voice is warm and intimate, 'is your idea, Rosie?'

'No . . .' I sound uncertain. I shoot a look at Jonathan beside me on the couch. He smooths down the linen of his trousers. I'm suddenly conscious of feeling uncomfortably hot in this elegant but airless room. 'But . . . but the separation was!'

'I see.' Babette grants me a smile so small you'd think she had to pay for it. 'And so the separation didn't work and you now want to go down the divorce route?'

'I . . . agree that this is the best way to go.'

'Best for whom?' Babette asks, readjusting her silk scarf.

'Best for . . .' I begin lamely, looking around for Jonathan's support.

'Best for us,' Jonathan weighs in, 'best for the children.'

'You think so, Rosie?' Babette again looks at me. She's spotted the weakest link.

'Hmmm . . .?' I'm scared of being caught out.

'Are you succeeding' – Babette speaks slowly and articulates carefully – 'in keeping your divorce painless?'

'Oh yes.' I try to sound enthusiastic, but it's difficult when Kat's sobs last night woke me up and brought me to her bedside: 'Oh, Mummy, will Daddy and you really never be together again?'

'Not together as before,' I attempted to comfort my daughter. 'But still friends.'

But my twelve-year-old kept sobbing.

'Yes, we're making great progress.' Jonathan's optimism

sounds forced. His mother hung up on him when he announced he was moving out, and she's refused to speak to him since. When he told the children Linda would be coming along to Dim Sum last Sunday, Freddy kicked him in the shins, screaming 'I hate her I hate her I hate her!' And Kat very ostentatiously hugged and kissed me on the doorstep, in full view of the car waiting down below.

'Amicable divorces rely on both parties feeling that their needs are being met equally.' She smiles, pauses, turns to me again. 'You, Rosie: you don't feel bounced into the decision to split?'

Do I? I ask myself, almost surprised by the question. Babette Pagorsky's put her finger on what has been bothering me all along. I may no longer be in love with my husband; I may no longer see my future in terms of his; but the timing of this divorce is not of my choosing. We're not moving towards a parallel situation: Jonathan's moving straight to Linda; I've got no one of my own. If I'd been able to choose, we might well have parted – but not until the children were grown up.

'No one,' Jonathan volunteers before I can say anything, 'is putting any pressure on Rosie.' He crosses his arms. I can see from the slight flush that has spread over his features that he's annoyed.

'That's true.' I nod. I give Babette a quick, uncertain smile. 'I agree with Jonathan that there was something missing in our marriage.'

'What's missing, then?' Babette gives a little tug at the scarf round her neck. 'Have you identified the problem area?'

I sit, completely silent. I'm stumped. What was the problem? We agreed on how to raise the children. We agreed on how to spend our money. We had great sex once a week . . .

'We' – Jonathan gives me a quick look – 'don't have the same sense of fun.'

I'm stunned by Jonathan's betrayal. 'OK, OK' – I hold my hands up – 'I admit it, making a list of all our DVDs – alphabetically – is not my idea of fun.' I shake my head. 'But apart from Jonathan, is it anyone's?'

Jonathan looks shocked. 'I thought you found it amusing!'

'What about talking?' Babette seems to be studying the oil painting of a vase of roses behind our heads. 'Do you talk in your marriage?'

We answer in unison.

Me: 'Always.'

Jonathan: 'Never.' Then, with a sheepish look in my direction: 'I mean, of course we communicate at *some* level.' He shifts uneasily in his chair. 'Rosie and I talk about the children, about the house, DIY, the garden . . .'

I feel a lump in my throat. It sounds so banal, so dreary, so boring.

'The problem is,' Jonathan won't look at me, 'Rosie's never been able to understand what I do. Which makes our relationship rather limited. I can't discuss a lot of things that are important to me.' He is looking only at Babette. 'It's frustrating.'

Babette raises an eyebrow. 'Please can you give me an example? We have to learn not to generalise but be specific.'

'I love reading – proper, serious books. About my work – or general knowledge. Rosie doesn't.'

'I do read. Just not about hair follicles or the height of the Himalayas.'

'You feel your interests are being ignored?' Babette is asking Jonathan.

'He ignores me ALL the time,' I snap back.

'Only talk about "I" not him,' Babette chides me gently. 'Remember that "he ignores me" is not the same as "I feel ignored".'

'I feel ignored, too, you know,' Jonathan mutters.

'You know what I'm hearing in all this?' Babette tucks her legs to one side, and clasps her hands as if about to start storytelling. 'I hear: "I want attention!"'

I open my mouth to deny this, but then I shut it again. Because maybe she's right, maybe that's what I feel Jonathan has been withholding: he's good at noticing what I wear, the scent I've got on, the new haircut. But when did he last *notice* what I say – and what I don't say?

'When did you last notice me?' Jonathan asks. And suddenly he turns directly to me. 'Really notice what I'm up to, or what I'm saying?'

Hold on a second. I've played out the whole of my life reacting to, or predicting, Jonathan's moves. I didn't leave HOME for the course on substance abuse at Bristol because he said he couldn't bear the thought of commuting to see me. I didn't go with Jill on her round-the-world, year-long trip because he kept hinting that he was about to propose. I put my training as a counsellor on hold when he convinced me that to leave the children when they were young would jeopardise their well-being. It seems to me I pay very close attention to his needs.

But what about *him*?

'What about YOU?' I cry out. 'You don't notice anything any more. I had to remind you that we'd sent our deposit for the cottage back in February, that I changed my office days from Tuesday to Wednesday and that your mum not mine was hoping to come at Easter. You've been sleepwalking for months now. Sleeping with her and walking away from us.'

'That's not true.'

'Are you going to lie about this as well?'

'Am I' – Jonathan is suddenly furious – 'supposed to spend £100 an hour to listen to your insults?'

'No, the insults are free,' I shoot back.

We both take a deep breath, look away, then back to one another. Somewhere a clock chimes: 5.30. We've been with Babette Pagorsky only half an hour and already we're getting hot and cross and forgetting all about our good divorce.

'This is not very constructive,' Jonathan says in a meek, low voice.

From her chair across the room, Babette shakes her dark head wisely. 'I think airing issues like this is always constructive. You can see what you need to work on.' She folds her hands neatly in her capable lap. 'Look at the way you're sitting!' She raises both hands in our direction. 'What does this say about you?'

I look down at my arms, and then at Jonathan's, crossed protectively over our respective chests.

'Oh dear.' I feel miserable.

'Defensive,' Jonathan mutters, with a half-smile of recognition.

'Yes. That's a good word: "defensive".' Babette nods. 'Why are you defensive with one another?'

Silence. I squirm on the sofa.

'I feel uncomfortable,' I manage to say. I do: this room is suddenly oppressive, with its plump inquisitor, subtle lighting and drawn curtains. I had wanted to study Babette Pagorsky and take some tips from her counselling style. I had planned to learn from her, professionally even more than personally. Instead, I'm finding the whole exercise intimidating, as if someone were pinning me down in order to examine me carefully. Counselling may lead to a better understanding, but getting there is awfully painful. Am I going to be capable of guiding someone else through this process? Am I going to be capable of doing anything at all, after more gruelling sessions like this one?'

'You feel uncomfortable,' Babette is repeating my words. 'Uncomfortable because of Jonathan, or because of this meeting, or . . .?' Babette's gaze rests on me. Why does every sentence of hers hang in the air?

'Well . . .' I feel at a loss. I'm out of synch with everyone these days. I keep mistaking people's intentions: the driver of the Chrysler Grand Voyager in front of me was not turning left, as I presumed, but trying to park; Lech the plumber was not trying it on as he pressed against me in the tiny guest loo – just trying to manoeuvre his way to answer his mobile; Dr Casey was not cross with me when, as I sloped in late after taking Kat to the dentist, he asked me what time I thought it was – he'd simply forgotten his glasses on Mrs S's desk and couldn't see his watch.

'I'm not feeling my usual self,' I explain to Babette. 'Awkward.'

'When did you start feeling awkward in Jonathan's presence?'

Was it when he explained to Kat and me that Prada came from *praeda*, the Latin word for loot, and she and I burst into disrespectful giggles? Was it that night at the dinner party of some old school chum of his, when he wouldn't laugh at my joke about how do you recognise a blonde at a car wash? (Answer: She's the one on her bicycle.) Was it when he told me that he really didn't want my shepherd's pie for supper and that actually, if he was being truthful, he'd never liked it . . .

'I don't know,' I answer, eyes picking out the vine-and-flower pattern on the carpet.

Babette turns to Jonathan. 'Can you see why Rosie might feel uncomfortable with you?'

'It's not me. It's that' – Jonathan moves forward on the sofa – 'from the first, Rosie has never fitted in my world. Do you remember when I took you to our office party?'

I wince at the memory of the wine-soaked Christmas party, when Jonathan's 'team', as he likes to call his colleagues, stood about stiffly under festoons of holly and mistletoe, looking awkward and impervious to seasonal cheer. The conversation moved from what mead did to our ancestors' liver to whether the side-effects of Rollowart warranted an FDA ban. At ten o'clock, just as I thought it would be perfectly acceptable for me to ask Jonathan if we could go home, I was cornered by some bearded professorial type banging on about how German pharmaceutical companies were beating British ones in R&D. After 35–45 minutes of his monotonous monologue, and after four glasses of Rioja, I yawned: 'What about some party games to liven this lot up? Sardines? Charades?' The prof gave me a vicious look and turned on his heels. A moment later, Jonathan came up, ashen-faced: 'What did you say to Emory Watson? He's my new boss. He organised tonight.'

Why would I wish to fit into this world? I ask myself now. Eggheads, formulae, labs, white smocks and smoking glass vials: Jonathan's work has always struck me as an extended chemistry class. And I never did do well at chemistry.

'The children,' Babette interrupts my musings, 'how are they taking your separation?'

Again we answer in chorus:

Him: 'They're fine.'

Me: 'They're gutted.'

'Explain.' Babette turns her gentle smile on me.

'They' – I gulp, cross my arms again – 'seem in a daze. They don't believe that their father is really leaving. They keep asking me if there is something we can do to get him back.'

'Rosie, they are perfectly fine when they're with me,' Jonathan interrupts, scarlet with indignation. 'Honestly, Dr . . . er, Mrs Pagorsky. They are quite old enough to take on board that grown-ups can change their mind about whom they want to spend the rest of their life with.'

The rest of their life. Till death us do part. I can almost hear the officious vicar at St Swithin's intoning those words in the flower-filled church near Castle Cary where we were married. It had seemed so certain back then, among family, well-wishers and lilies. My father had had tears in his eyes, as did Jonathan's parents. My mum had spent most of her time elbowing her sister Margaret, trying to direct her attention to the groom's pews, where not one ('not one!' she would repeat later at the reception, fuelled by a few glasses of champagne, to anyone who would listen) of the women wore a proper hat. But even Mum had proclaimed us a perfect couple, that perfect spring day. 'They're just so much in love,' she had sighed, dabbing prettily at her eye with a white hanky.

'People change. They grow apart . . .' I listen to Jonathan's platitudes, watch him shrug off our twelve-year-old marriage as if it was the wrong beach towel. 'I'm not the only one who knows we need to move on. Rosie's heart hasn't been in this for years.'

'Maybe not, but I'm not the one sneaking around with a lover from work!' I jump up from the sofa, grab my handbag.

'I wasn't sneaking around! I was going to tell you everything!' Jonathan jumps up too.

'Only once I caught you!' I try to stomp off, but Jonathan grabs my arm.

'Please, Jonathan, Rosie, sit down.' Babette's dark eyes grow round in alarm.

'Will you stop picking a fight?!' he's yelling. 'What are you fighting for? We haven't had a real marriage for years.'

'What's a REAL marriage?!'

'We weren't in love. We hardly ever had sex . . .'

'Last time I checked, once a week was considered pretty normal!'

'Please,' Babette calls out again from her armchair across the room, 'will you sit down? The session is not over –'

'Oh yes it is!' snaps Jonathan as he stomps off.

I wake up and stretch out my left arm and leg, and feel the rest of the large double bed is empty. I take a minute to adjust to my new circumstances. It's been like this every morning since Jonathan announced he wants a divorce. The little armchair in the corner of the room is half-hidden by only my clothes – not layers of his and mine. The bathroom door is ajar, but Jonathan is not standing there in his striped pyjamas brushing his teeth as he methodically adjusts the shower jet, lays a towel on the radiator to toast it, and hangs up a clean shirt on the back of the door.

What is he doing, this Sunday morning? Do he and Linda have leisurely lie-ins, when they have sex non-stop and then eat a huge breakfast and read the papers and then more sex? Or does Linda get them up and out for a brisk run and then a joint shower that leads to hotvol-canicsex?

I try to picture the room my ex wakes up in – spotless and spartan, or is Linda into Disney princess pink, with a bit of ruffle on the dressing table and a four-poster bed as big as this one? Stop it, I tell myself. Because I can spend hours, in fact have done so, trying to picture their room, and what they do and say. This divorce may be a mutual decision, but how can I help being jealous when my husband of twelve years lies in someone else's bed?

I hear Kat moving about next door. I look at my alarm clock: 9.20. As I stir and peep over the white cotton waves, I see an unfamiliar red light blinking at me: I forgot to switch off the DVD player after watching *When Harry Met Sally* last night until 2 a.m.

I stir myself, and notice other unusual sights: clothes strewn across the chest of drawers and even on the floor. Jonathan would have gone mad. The curtains only half drawn and, on the bedside table, yesterday's mug of tea. It's as if every bit of our bedroom announces that Jonathan's gone.

It's the same downstairs. In the sitting room, the book-shelves look like an elderly East European's teeth: rows with huge black gaps where Jonathan has pulled out his must-have volumes: *Hair Growth*, *Folliculitis Prevention*, *Baldness is Not for Life*. In the kitchen, the Sabatier knives are missing, and half the Le Creuset set. Newspapers and tins and glass bottles spill out of the bin in one vast, unecological jumble.

I'm thirty-eight next year. I feel as wary of time passing as I do of crossing a motorway: I've made enough mistakes already, I daren't trust my instincts to get me safely across. I want to see the break-up of my marriage as a beginning; but right now I feel it only as an end.

I turn on my other side: my gaze meets Jonathan's in an old photo. It's taken at uni, he's nineteen, maybe twenty, and staring with a solemn expression into the camera lens. I know that expression so well: full of determination. Jonathan was the first Martin to finish school, the first to go to university, and the first to make any money. His parents were incredibly proud, and Jonathan could do no wrong in their eyes. Well, except marry a London girl from an uppity family. Thankfully, my dealings with the in-laws were limited by geography, so that I only had to hear about 'Mary Mullin up the road, she always had a soft spot for you, Johnny' every now and then.

My own parents' reservations that Jonathan was not one of us – comfortable middle class – were carefully concealed behind polite smiles and dry little coughs.

'Your parents,' Jonathan would say the moment he was behind the wheel and we were pulling out of their gravel driveway in Somerset, 'think you've married beneath you.'

'They don't,' I lied. 'What did they say to make you think *that*?'

'They look at me as if I were the gamekeeper and you were Lady Chatterley.'

My parents' class-consciousness melted in their enthusiasm for Zelkin, Jonathan's profitable venture; but maybe their son-in-law never forgot it, or forgave them – or me.

Perhaps, I muse, Jonathan's humble beginnings have played a role in his infatuation with Linda. My ex-husband has complete faith in meritocracy, and thinks that Britons have a great deal to learn from their American cousins. 'If you're bright, ambitious and hard working you can do anything there,' he would enthuse after his professional trips to the States. 'No questions asked about who your family is or what school or university you went to.' Perhaps he sees Linda in the same way: someone who offers him a chance to be anything he wants to be. I, on the other hand, remind Jonathan of where he came from and what is expected of him. Linda is the stars and sky above, I'm a glass ceiling.

The door squeaks open: 'Mum?' Kat looks in. One day she almost looks grown up; the next, like this morning in her pink pyjamas, she looks like a baby. 'Are you awake?'

'Hmmm . . .' I nod my head against the pillow.

'Shall I make you a cup of tea?' My tousled-head daughter peers at me anxiously.

'No, yes, I mean . . . I should get up now.' I stretch, and smile to reassure her.

'No, you stay there, Mum.' Kat tucks me in as if I were an invalid and she a nurse.

'Sweetpea, sit down.' I pat the bed beside me. 'Did you sleep all right?'

'Hmmm . . . n-n-n-ot really.' My daughter's pretty face crumples. 'Mummy, it's all so terrible!' She dissolves in tears.

'Come here, my darling.' I take her in my arms, and Kat, now sobbing uncontrollably, slips under the duvet beside me. 'Don't cry, my little Kat . . .' I try to comfort her by stroking her back; ever since she was tiny this would calm her down. I feel her silky warm skin, and keep up a soft soothing murmur.

'Mummy, is Dad never coming back?' she sobs, and presses up against my T-shirt. I've taken to wearing Freddy's, now that Jonathan's are in some flat in Bayswater, and today I'm in a Spiderman red and blue: it rides up, so that I can feel her against my naked stomach almost as clearly as when I carried her twelve years ago. 'It's really over?'

I stroke her hair. 'Yes, if you mean is my marriage with Daddy really over. No, if you mean fun, and good things, and our family and friends.'

'Mum, if break-ups are this bad, I don't want a relationship, ever!'

'Not every relationship breaks up. Not every relationship breaks up badly.' I lift her hair and kiss the back of her neck: a hot sleepy spot that I always go back to. 'And a good relationship makes you your best.' I stroke her back again. 'Are you thinking about someone in particular?'

'Mungo.' She nods shyly, looks away from me. 'We've been texting.' I can't help smiling: as if I hadn't noticed. 'When he doesn't get back to me immediately, I'm scared it's because he's broken it off.'

'You can't run a relationship worrying about it breaking up,' I murmur into her neck. 'You mustn't think like that.'

'The great thing about texting is you don't have to say anything to their face.' Kat's voice is low and soft. 'It's not as scary.'

'But not as satisfying either.' I ruffle her hair. 'Sometimes you have to take risks.'

'But if you do, you get your fingers burned.'

'You mean – like your father and me?' Kat nods. She is crying quietly, pressed against me. Did I take a risk with Jonathan? My mum would argue that choosing a man from a different background was a risk. My dad worried about our different interests. But to me, our love was an insurance policy: there might be a setback along the way, but the outcome would always be in our favour. 'Some risks are worth taking. Anyway, you can limit it to texting for now. But after a while you really need to be in each other's presence . . . nothing else will do.' I shut my eyes, and remember Jonathan's daily letters to me over that first summer, when we were apart, me in Somerset, him in Edinburgh because he'd found an internship at a big hospital lab. *How can I survive without you?* Jonathan's letters always began. *I feel as if I've been asked to do without an arm, or a leg. I can't work, I can't sleep, I can't eat: everything is pointless without you.*

'Mummy . . .'

I look up to see Freddy. My son, in his pyjamas, blinks with sleep.

'Mummy,' he whispers, and then, as he realises his sister is lying beside me: 'me, too.' He climbs into bed on my other side.

'I feel like crying . . .' Kat sobs.

'Mummy,' Freddy looks up at me, 'it's not something we did, is it? It's not our fault?'

I hug him tight. 'No, Daddy adores you. Absolutely adores you both.'

'Will Daddy have other children with . . . with *her*?' my son chokes on the word.

'Everything will be all right,' I promise them.

'Do you hate him? Does he hate you?' Freddy sobs.

'No!' I almost shout. Then, softly, 'No. And shall I tell you something? Not all divorces are nasty and full of arguments. There are plenty of families that stay together even though the father's moved out. Daddy and I are going to

87

have a friendly divorce and we're going to manage everything smoothly. Wait and see.'

At noon Jonathan comes to pick up the children. He sports
a new haircut and a new leather jacket. I put this hip new
look down to the American.

'I'm sorry about the other day.' He looks suitably sheepish.

Upstairs the children are rushing about trying to find what
to bring 'to Dad's': fleeces, DVDs, books, half of which will
be left behind, of course, requiring countless follow-up phone
calls by them; by THEM – because I certainly don't want to
risk talking to HER.

'It's OK.'

'I had the distinct impression that Babette whatever-her-
name-is was egging us on.' Jonathan's mouth is set. 'And I
guess that, at £100 a session, you can see why it's not in her
interest to promote goodwill between her clients.'

'On the other hand, she raised some interesting issues.' I
sigh. 'I had never thought that you might need more attention. Or me, for that matter.'

'Mum! I can't find my scarf!' Kat leans over the banister.

'If it's the pink one you're looking for, it's down here!' I
call over my shoulder. Then, turning to Jonathan: 'Do you
think we should go for any more sessions?'

'Lawyers will cost an arm and a leg' – Jonathan picks a
long, dark hair off his new jacket, looks at me, then lets it fall
on the doorstep – 'but at least we'll cut to the chase. I feel
we're wasting time with Babette, because her goal is to keep
us together, whereas ours is to be apart. In a friendly manner.'

'It will get so expensive. You're sure we can afford for me to hand in my resignation? I mean, I want to do the counselling course next spring, but I could continue to work at Dr Casey's. For the first few months at least.'

'Ooooo . . .' Jonathan frowns, smiles, then clears his throat. 'We-ell, actually, if it isn't a problem . . .' He looks up and down, to the left and the right, anything but looking at me. 'I'd really appreciate it if you didn't stop working quite yet. I mean, I'm sure you can really soon, eventually, but . . .'

My husband looks in such physical discomfort I feel moved to pity. 'Look, don't worry.'

'Oh, that's really helpful, Rosie.' Jonathan beams me a grateful smile. 'It's just, with the two households and the children's school fees and maintenance . . .'

'It's OK.' But I can't help wonder how much he contributes to Linda's lifestyle.

'Mum's still not speaking to me.' Jonathan looks miserable.

'She'll calm down. Remember how cross she was when we didn't christen Kat and Freddy? She almost mowed us down with her zimmer frame.'

'Last time I rang her' – Jonathan shakes his head disconsolately – 'she told me I was a cad and you were the best thing that had ever happened to me.'

'Last time she was here she said you were a genius and I was lucky you'd deigned to marry me.'

'Well, now you're a martyr and I'm a satyr.' He sighs. 'She just can't believe that a divorce can ever be a mutual decision.'

'I wouldn't worry.' I shrug, but then, seeing his expression: 'Look, do you want me to have a word with her? I mean, we've never been close, but . . .'

'Oh, would you, Rosie?!' Jonathan beams with gratitude. 'It would be amazing if you would.'

'She's bound to be worried about the grandchildren. Once she's reassured that life is relatively normal at home, she'll be fine.'

'If you could . . .'

'Don't worry. You will make sure that they're back in time for supper at seven, won't you? They're still not used to school after the summer.'

'I'm ready!' Freddy rushes down the stairs.

'Back by seven.' Jonathan opens his arms wide to embrace his son. The kiss he plants on his curly head brings tears to my eyes; a shock of hatred for Linda courses through me. How could she break up this happy little nucleus?

'Daddy!' Kat throws her arms around her dad. Then, having looked at me over her shoulder, she releases Jonathan and comes running back to me. 'You'll be OK, Mum? We'll be back for supper.'

'You're a star!' Jonathan calls out as, flanked by the children, he walks towards the car.

A star? As I stand here on my own, with the prospect of Sunday stretching ahead with only the papers and possibly a repeat of *Strictly Come Dancing* to cheer me up, I feel a loser. Like a forty-something who has to wash her clothes at the launderette.

I shut the door. I'm making things so easy for him. Yet, surely this is the best policy: with no bickering between us, the children will gradually adapt to the notion of two homes.

I ring my mum before tackling Jonathan's.

'We can congratulate ourselves,' I tell her, 'on having managed this very smoothly and with the least upset to anyone.'

'Don't even think of congratulating that man!' my mother is spitting. 'He's got it all his way – the woman, the children, even you. Don't be so accommodating, Rosie. Because I tell you: you'll be the first person he'll sacrifice when the going gets rough. All this talk of a "nice divorce" and a "perfect split" is total rubbish. A break-up is like a break-in: you lose what's most precious to you.'

What I have lost, actually, is my peace of mind. Like a hormonally-charged teenager, I grow tearful at the slightest provocation. Since Jonathan's departure I've had tears in my eyes when a telly actress begged Dr Casey to rid her of an unsightly rash left by a new foundation cream. I started weeping when Otilya told me for the umpteenth time that 'Women in my country, we have to be strong. Men all the same, all after one thing. After they get that, they kick you like a dog.' And sobbed when Freddy told me we could give away Badger, his favourite soft toy, because 'I'm not a baby any more.'

I'm fed up with it. I know I can't be happy for a while yet, but I'd like to be open to the possibilities out there. As Jill puts it, 'Don't let that Yankee hussy get you down!'

Let a new life begin.

This resolution has led me to get three books on substance abuse out of the library; volunteer to leaflet the neighbourhood for Help the Aged, and volunteer my house for a tea party for eight OAPs. I go and see a scary exhibition of German contemporary artists at the Tate Modern and a Japanese art house film so explicit I have to walk out halfway through the third lesbian sex scene.

6

It is only when I do a head-count of her guests that I realise
Jill is at it again. The fiasco with Orlando has obviously not
put her off matchmaking – though goodness knows, it's put
me on my guard. I'd come over thinking that it would be
just the three of us, a laid-back catch-up with a bit too much
drink, as the children are with Jonathan.

Instead here are two other couples and a lone man (the
give-away), sipping wine and listening to one of Jill's amusing
anecdotes about the latest medical fads her patients ask her
about, while David hovers around the table. David does the
cooking – and I suspect most of the grocery shopping and
cleaning. But then, his photography can't bring in very much,
while Jill's GP practice is lucrative.

'How do you know Jill?' Laurence takes the bottle of Rioja
from Jill, who is busy talking, and pours me a full glass. He
has curly greying hair and bushy eyebrows that sprout over

his thick-rimmed spectacles. He looks like a kindly prof, I think.

'We were at uni together. And you?'

'My wife' – he nods his head towards Janet – 'is a GP in her practice.'

'Oh, I thought Belinda was a GP?' I vaguely remember some earlier encounter with the terrifyingly posh Belinda.

'No, she's a consultant. Ear, nose, throat. Bit of a name, actually.'

'Oh.' Every woman here has a great career. I feel an amateur in a room full of experts. With Jill, I don't mind that she is a super GP with a huge workload. It's the women who have both a model family and enviable career who make me feel inadequate.

'For God's sake, Rosie, you should feel superior, not scared,' Jonathan had laughed when I confessed to my inferiority complex. 'I bet they'd give their eye teeth not to have to slog the way they do. They'd jump at the chance of a husband who can afford for them to go part-time.'

Jonathan was tremendously proud of the fact that, thanks to him and the success of Zelkin ('the hair-regeneration treatment that will make a ping-pong ball sprout'), I could do just that. Most of the time, I *was* grateful to him for this advantage. As a part-timer, I still had to juggle with childcare and school, dropping everything at work and earning Mrs S's ire when the school called to say one of the children was ill. But my rush was punctuated by Tuesdays and Thursdays at home, which gave me time to get some paperwork done, cook a proper recipe (though never anything as ambitious as my husband's), or go to John Lewis for a lampshade.

'Hullo, darling.' Jill sidles up to me. She whispers: 'I know the actor didn't do it for you, but this one could be good. Behave. Badly.'

'*A tavola*.' David, bearing a huge leg of lamb, approaches the table while Jill bosses us to our places.

'Belinda on David's right, with Laurence beside her, Rosie you there, no Max, you're next to Rosie.'

It takes ages before we're all settled round the refectory-style table laden with flowers, carafes, glasses, and over-sized hand-painted plates.

'We've met before, haven't we?' William hands me the bread basket.

'Yes, I think so.'

'I'm trying to remember when and where.'

'Isn't your husband' – Belinda leans across the table in my direction – 'Jonathan Martin, the trichologist? The Zelkin man?'

'Her *ex*-husband,' Jill contributes, with a meaningful look at the man on my right.

If she had said ex-convict, she couldn't have caused more of a stir. The women look at me as if I'm sitting naked, fondling their husbands under their eyes. The men inch closer, as if I have been exposed as a sex-crazed personal fan of theirs.

'I know where we met!' William's thigh rests against mine. 'With Jill at that cancer charity cabaret. Great stockings you girls had on!' he gurgles with a seedy laugh that earns him a ferocious look from Belinda.

'I keep meeting GPs who're giving up their NHS practice altogether,' Janet is saying.

'I keep meeting friends who're getting divorced,' Laurence addresses himself to me. He makes 'divorce' sound like a titillating lingerie shop or a lap-dancing club.

'Er . . . the statistics are pretty bad,' I squirm.

'Well, you know what they say . . .' William winks at me. 'Man was not made for monogamy.'

'Rosie's daughter is at the same school as Tessa, Janet,' Jill is trilling across the table.

Janet, whose long, stern face speaks of competence, confidence, and condescension, peers coldly at me. 'I'm very impressed by the new school counsellor. Have you met her? I'm sure the school will have recommended that your daughter see her.' She turns and says, by way of explanation, to the others: 'They're very good on the pastoral side of things.'

'Hey, is that you?' Laurence points to a nude among David's photographic gallery. He leers at me. 'I see a distinct resemblance.'

'N-n-n-no,' I stammer.

'Hmmm . . . I know what you mean.' The pressure of William's thigh increases against mine. 'Something in the curve of the . . .' lubricious pause '. . . neck.'

I look desperately at the man on my right for assistance, but he is engrossed in a conversation with Jill. I'm about to work up the courage to butt into their conversation, when I overhear Belinda, across the table:

'The thing is, most marriages end because one partner has a career that's going somewhere, while the other has opted out. Usually the husband's going strong in his chosen profession while the wife either stays at home or cuts back to part time. He is still learning, and being stimulated every day, and surrounded by really interesting women colleagues, while she's only been doing things at half-mast.'

I'm reeling from this direct hit, but before I can reply, the man on my right turns to me.

'Jill's just explained,' he whispers, 'that Belinda and her husband invited themselves to lunch, and she wants you to know that this is the last time they'll be gracing her table.' My discomfiture must be plain because he goes on, still in a whisper, 'Chin up. Nothing as threatening as an attractive woman who's just become available again.'

I smile gratefully, and notice his wide blue eyes and generous mouth. I notice too the pleasing warmth of his voice.

'You'd think,' he continues, voice low, 'given how many of us there are, divorcées would no longer be treated like lepers.'

'Maybe I should wear a placard like those men on Oxford Street selling cheap haircuts or all-you-can-eat buffets. "Beware: divorcée on the loose".'

'Loose' – Max shakes his head – 'is exactly what they think all divorcées are. Funny, how some stereotypes just won't fade.' He smiles, and holds out his hand. 'Max Lowell.'

'Rosie Martin.' I shake it. Then, as his name jogs my memory: 'Hold on a second. Max Lowell. I know that name.'

'Do you take the *Record*? I write . . .'

'Of course! You write the "Health Wise" column, don't you? My husba—, er, my ex-husband read it like it was the gospel.'

'Very flattering.' He grins.

'It must be great to have a column like that.'

'I don't think of myself as a columnist. More of a whistle-blower.' He smiles. 'Warning ordinary people about some of the quacks out there.' Max shifts in his chair to look at me full-on.

'Hmm . . .' I squirm uneasily at the thought of the Butcher of Belgravia. 'I suppose the temptation is huge. Medicine can be a very profitable profession these days.'

'I like to think of medicine as a field of science,' Max says dryly, 'not a bit of business.'

I have to suppress a smile: this couldn't be further from Jonathan's approach. 'Thank goodness doctors are so lazy,' he liked to say, a triumphant note in his voice. 'I stole a march on them. Zelkin was right under their noses. A great cash cow. But they didn't see the possibilities.' Out loud I say, 'My father was a GP. I grew up thinking of doctors as offering a service rather than making money.'

'Yes, those were the good old days.' Max laughs. 'Still, I suppose there are some pluses in the new attitude. Like the fact that, thanks to some of the profession, youthful looks are now much more accessible. Everyone' – Max raises his glass to me – 'can pay to look like you.'

I blush.

'Thanks. My self-confidence is at an all-time low.'

'I see every reason for confidence.' He grins.

I'm shocked by the realisation that I'm flirting. I thought I'd forgotten how to. I smile inwardly. Jill was right: Max Lowell is the first man I've found attractive since my marriage fell apart.

'But your' – here he gives me a mischievous look – '*ex*-husband is apparently in the business . . .?'

'Pharmacologist. He was . . . is.' I issue a little sigh.

'Very recent?'

His directness takes me by surprise. But his eyes are full of sympathy and I feel I can trust him. 'Yes. Not even formally divorced yet.'

'Mine was four years ago.' His face darkens, and his mouth sets into a firm line. 'Messy.' He lowers his voice again: 'It takes a lot out of you. I wonder how long it takes to recover. Sometimes I wonder if you ever really do.'

I feel a slight stab of disappointment. Jill was wrong after all. Max Lowell does not seem to be over his ex-wife. Was it a passionate, tempestuous relationship that went badly wrong? Was he traumatised at being left for another man, or did she drive him insane and he finally walked? I think how lucky Jonathan and I are that our divorce is proceeding so decorously.

We're eating the pudding now, a delicious apple cake from Paul's Bakery. Through the huge windows the afternoon light has grown softer, and half the table is now in shadow.

William, whose thigh is glued to mine, tries to pick up anew: 'So you live in Belsize Park? I'm up the hill. Hampstead. I write for "Plugged In" – you know, the website. I work from home.' He steals a quick look at his wife across the table. She's reassuring David about some symptom of his: as befits the husband of a GP, David is a hopeless hypochondriac. 'We should have coffee sometime.'

I nod without any enthusiasm. I wish I could go home now, I think as I look at the collection of animated faces around the table. I never did click with Jill's friends – high-flying, hard-edged professionals who voice their opinions with supreme confidence.

'Oh dear, it looks like it could rain! Max, could you give Rosie a lift – she came on foot.' Given that it's a golden October afternoon with not a cloud in the sky, Jill's exclamation sounds more than a little contrived. But Max Lowell looks as eager to leave this gathering as I am.

We set off in an old Volvo littered with sweet wrappers, two empty tins of Red Bull, a sports sock, and enough dog hair to stuff a pillow.

'Sorry, I didn't think I'd be driving a lady.' Max gives me an apologetic look. 'My usual passengers are the boys . . . as you can see.' He smiles ruefully as I peel a sweet wrapper off the passenger seat.

'No worries. This is the kind of car I'm used to.' I wonder how often he's allowed to see his sons.

'The children are with you?' Max casts me a quick look. I notice his hands on the wheel: large, capable hands.

'Yes.'

'You're lucky.'

'Sometimes that's the last thing I feel.' I bite my lip: don't sound bitter.

'I mean that I have to fight to see mine.' It's Max's turn

to sound bitter. I can't think of anything appropriate to say. But Max goes on, 'Some people are prepared to use their children to hurt their ex.'

I think guiltily of how I have been tempted to do this myself.

'The worst thing about divorce is the way that it turns even decent, civilised human beings into evil beasts baying for human blood.'

'It must be possible to have a good divorce. If two people work hard at it.'

'Sure. Anything's possible.' Max shoots me a sceptical look. 'Wait long enough, and two people can dig their way out of prison with a spoon.'

I shake my head, laughing. 'Seriously.'

'Maybe you'll be the one lucky exception.'

'All I mean is: divorce may be the end of one relationship. But it's also the start of a whole new relationship. And you have to work at it the way you work at a marriage or a friendship, or parenting.'

'Hmmm . . .' Max sets his jaw. 'You're trying to make divorce sound like something constructive. It isn't. It's the most destructive event in most people's lives.'

'Jonathan and I have decided to turn logic on its head.'

Max is not listening. 'The worst thing is the frustration. She gets to decide everything. From the split' – I steal a furtive look at the handsome profile: was he dumped? Was he devastated? – 'to where I live, when I can see the boys, for how long, and where I work.'

'Where you work?'

He turns to me briefly, a shadow clouding his blue eyes. 'I was offered a job with an NGO in Africa – just the kind of thing I long to do – but Ellie told me she'd never let the boys come and visit because it's too dangerous.' He pauses, steering us away from a bus that has stalled in the middle of the road. 'She's totally ruined any chance I have of doing what I want.' He turns to me with what I feel is a glacial look. 'Tell me how to turn *that* on its head.'

Misery fills me: I really, really didn't want to get off on the wrong foot with this man. Silence falls between us and it becomes so uncomfortable that I shift nervously in my seat. 'D-d-d-d-do' – I find myself stuttering – 'you live nearby?'

'No. Bath.'

'Gosh! You drive a long way for a Sunday lunch!'

'Well, Jill was pretty insistent.' He gives me a sideways look. I relish the feel of those blue eyes even as I feel myself blush.

We're climbing Primrose Hill, and then turn right on to England's Lane. We pull into Belsize Row and before we reach the house I ask:

'Can I offer you a cup of tea or coffee before your long drive?'

To my surprise he accepts. 'That'd be nice.'

He parks the car. I'm feeling nervous, and for a second an image flashes past me, of Jonathan walking me back to my room after our first date, and then planting a chaste kiss on my cheek. Then my ex disappears and Max Lowell takes his place beside me. This could lead to something . . . But as I reach for the door I start wondering if I've left a mess in the kitchen or if Jonathan's going to drop the children back early? Did I take out the rubbish or is it overflowing in the bin? Did I leave *The Sunday Times* scattered over half the sitting room?

I'm suddenly having difficulty with the lock.

'Nice pumpkin,' Max Lowell points to the pumpkin Freddy and I carved only yesterday for Halloween.

I sigh with relief when I push open the door and the house looks warm, inviting and almost tidy.

'Tea or coffee?'

'Coffee. I was so keen to leave Jill's that I only had a sip of the one she offered me.'

'I know what you mean.' I take out the Italian coffee maker, fill it and place it on the Aga. 'Jill's my best friend, but some of the people she's introduced me to . . . present company excepted, of course.'

'She's warm and funny and far too friendly. She should learn to be more discriminating.'

As he talks, Max strides about the kitchen. He is tall – taller than Jonathan by a head, I would guess. And bigger-boned. I quickly take in his thick country corduroys and the cashmere sweater which, despite the elbow patches, looks good quality: with a Labrador at his side and a pair of wellies, he'd look the archetypal country gentleman. Max finally sits on a chair at the table. 'This kitchen reminds me of mine when I was growing up.'

I take this as a compliment, and am immensely flattered. There's hope, after all. Hmmm, yes, maybe this Bath-based, bitterly divorced father of two could be just what the doctor ordered. I can see him winning over my wary children, I can see him accompanying me to the Vincents' party, and to an art house film that turns out to be soft porn and reduces us both to giggles. I can see us having dinner together and . . .

The coffee gurgles. I pour us two small cups. 'Sugar? Milk?' I set everything on the table, and sit in the chair opposite him. With every move I make, I'm conscious of that blue gaze following me.

'I didn't mean to give you a hard time, by the way.' Max stirs a spoonful of sugar into his coffee. 'Your attitude to divorce sounds a lot healthier than mine.'

'Oh, not always. When I discovered Jonathan was having an affair, after twelve years of marriage, I mean at first I was devastated – but out of hurt pride more than anything, if I'm honest. And then, well . . . then I found myself thinking that actually we had not been a proper couple for years . . .' I'm babbling, but there's nothing I can do to stop myself. Max Lowell seems to positively encourage me to go on, as his eyes crinkle and a half smile hovers over his lips. 'A new start didn't seem such a mad idea, especially as we both swore that we would make a superhuman effort to keep our relationship as smooth and friendly as possible.' I'm out of breath, and I have to push myself away from the table, as if to take in a big gulp of oxygen. 'I . . . I'm sorry. I don't usually burble on like this.'

There, I've done it, completely turned off the one man I've found attractive since Jonathan. He's thinking that I'm one of those motormouth madwomen you get on Jerry Springer or Jeremy Kyle.

'I think . . .' Max Lowell leans over the table, closer to me – so close, in fact, that I feel the warmth of his breath on my face, and breathe in the scent of the coffee he's been sipping '. . . I think that's rather wonderful.' And he beams a huge, inviting turn-on of a smile.

The door bell goes. I jump.

'It must be the children.' I go to the door, and for once I'm disappointed that they're back early. But it's not Kat and Freddy. Standing there before me are a dozen elderly ladies in hats, coats and scarves, smiling shyly in my direction.

'Mrs Martin, hello. I'm Janice Thane.' A sturdy woman in a bluish tweed coat shakes my hand. 'We're so looking forward to this.' I look on, bewildered, as she strides past me into the entrance, the elderly troupe in her wake. 'Ah, Mr Martin, I presume!' Boxy bossy tweedy woman marches up to Max Lowell. 'Janice Thane from Help the Aged. Your wife's kindly invited us for tea.'

7

Ladies of a certain age are not necessarily a passion-killer. But when they're clamouring for tea and biscuits and the loo, and you're desperately rooting about your biscuit tin and finding only a few chocolate digestives and Max Lowell offers to go out and get some crumpets and cakes, flirting goes out the window.

Jill's friend not only saved the day with his shopping expedition, and proved a surprise hit with the OAPs, he reminded me that I could still feel the stirrings of an attraction. But attraction for a man who lives in another city, is still obviously aching from the pain of his messy divorce, and is embroiled in fighting for access to his sons, is about as useful as a dust-buster in Jonathan's antiseptic office. In any case, he had to leave before the surprise guests did: 'I've got to be in Bath by dinner time,' said Max, smiling with what I hope was regret in his eyes, 'I'm taking the boys out so Ellie can do some work.' Despite Jill's encouraging noises – 'He definitely sparkled around you' and 'He took care of the old biddies, did he? That *proves* he's interested!' – Max hasn't rung. And it's now three weeks since the lunch.

But I can't concentrate on what might have been; there's too much on right now.

'So, what do we want? Child maintenance, the house, the lot? Did he beat you? Did he cheat on you? Did he make you give up a career to dedicate yourself to his? That gets us a packet for every year you've been unable to work, and of course we can argue that because your skills have grown rusty and because times are hard and, ehm, you're not twenty-one, re-entry in the job market will be difficult . . . yes I think we could get you a nice little sum.' Charles Mallaby-Steer's little blue eyes peer at me.

We sit at his wide mahogany desk, across from one another, in an impressive Regency oak-panelled office. Every inch of the walls has been covered: framed awards, photos, and certificates, all calculated to inspire trust in Mr Mallaby-Steer.

'We'll get him.' Mallaby-Steer's pink round face, beneath its thatched ginger hair, spreads in a wide smile. 'He won't get away.'

'But Jonathan doesn't want to "get away". He's promised he'll support me and the children. We're both committed to a very civilised divorce.'

'Oh, he'll have a nasty surprise!' My lawyer barks a laugh.

'Civilised divorces are for wimps. Brave boys go in for the kill.'

'We don't need to be . . . so aggressive. Jonathan's never been mean about money.'

Mallaby-Steer roars: 'Mrs Martin! – Rose! – you are being, if I may say so, a bit naïve. *Everyone* cares about money. Ex-husbands most of all.'

'No, honestly, Jonathan's not like that.' I shake my head stubbornly. 'He's always been generous.'

'That was then, this is now.' Mallaby-Steer smiles at my innocence. 'From what I gather, your husband's, uhm, friend, has a husband with money. Works for a big American management consultancy. But he's livid and he's told her he's not going to give her a single penny.'

I can't help savouring this news. Good: if they're going to have love, sex, and access to the children, let them at least have money worries.

'That means she'll be putting pressure on *your* husband to palm you off with the bare minimum.' Here he taps my papers with a big butcher's hand. 'We'll have to fight hard.'

I bristle at Mallaby-Steer's raised eyebrow and incredulous expression. 'Jonathan and I are determined to keep this friendly.'

'That, my dear Rose' – Mallaby-Steer taps his mahogany desk with his big hand – 'is an admirable goal. But in my thirty years' experience, it's never been achieved.'

'Jonathan's been very accommodating and . . . generous. He said we could have the house. He said he would support me if I wanted to stop work and do a training course I've been wanting to do for years . . . I can't tell you what that means to me: it's something I've put off for so long, but that I know would be just the right way to start a new life.'

'Mean?!' the word explodes like a gunshot. 'You don't know the meaning of the word, until you've seen me act on your behalf! As you will see, Rose, divorce is a complicated business.' Mallaby-Steer looks at me as if to size up the sheer scale of my stupidity. 'Let's test, why don't we, your hypothesis about Jonathan: has he been good about sticking to your schedule for children's visits, weekends, pick-up times, drop-off times, etc?'

I open my mouth to protest fiercely that Jonathan's been impeccable in his schedule-keeping, but then I realise he has been anything but. My normally super-responsible and schedule-conscious husband has shown all the punctuality and reliability of a sixties Flower Child.

Yesterday was typical.

'Hey, you're supposed to pick up the children at quarter to four.' I had to ring Jonathan's BlackBerry because Kat and Freddy were standing outside the school, waiting in the cold rain.

'The children?'

'Yes. A twelve-year-old and a nine-year-old,' I laid on the sarcasm, 'cute, freckly, one dark-haired, one brown-haired, called Kat and Freddy. You do remember them?'

'Oh God!' Jonathan wailed. 'I knew I had to do something! It's not in my BlackBerry. OK I'm rushing now.'

He was supposed to fetch the children on Saturday before breakfast, but turned up after lunch; was meant to pick them up for Sunday brunch, and arrived in time for tea. He seems incapable of remembering dates like Parents' Night (I go alone), or Freddy's all-important rugby match against Ellison School (I take the afternoon off at the last minute, and earn another reproachful look from Mrs Stevens).

Mallaby-Steer has a point. I study him now, across the desk from me. He looks as satisfied as a safari hunter who has collected some rare pelts. I feel myself sinking into gloomy visions of the road ahead: legal jargon, bureaucratic obstacles, forms to fill, phone calls to make, and above all money talk. That starts immediately:

'Divorce is about time and money. My time and your money.' Here Mallaby-Steer winks at me. 'Unless, that is, we're clever, and then it's your husband's money.'

'No, no, I'm really not interested in a bitter fight.'

'Now now.' Mallaby-Steer snorts impatiently. 'Buck up, dear girl. I know it's tough, but you're young enough and you'll get over it. I've seen hundreds of women through this. Look at the calendar' – he points, index extended, third finger on an imaginary trigger – 'the twenty-fourth of November. Now, if we don't waste any time, we'll have you sorted before Easter.' Here he shoots his imaginary target practice. 'Bang! Bang! You'll be free. Meanwhile we have to focus on extracting our pound of flesh. Make that several hundred thousand pounds.' He sits back in his brown leather revolving deskchair, and gives me a look. 'If we do this properly, you'll get away with a nice juicy package. Not as much as I could have got you, say, a year ago – before this financial crisis – but it's going to be fine.'

I feel slightly unnerved at all this talk of juice and pounds of flesh, not to say a little queasy. I'm finding Mallaby-Steer's hunting instincts a bit overpowering.

'Let's go in for the kill.' Mallaby-Steer grins. 'Remember, there's a woman out there who's got your husband, wants your money and probably the children too.'

'Cow!' I say, with a violence that surprises me.

'That's the spirit!' Mallaby-Steer gives me a wink. 'We'll skin him alive.'

What not to expect of your children in a divorce: any degree of understanding. I've bitten my tongue a thousand times. I've given them space and comfort. But Kat and Freddy can only see the 'have-nots' rather than the 'haves'. We have no father. We have no weekends with our friends because they're taken up with seeing said father. We have no proper family activities any more, like a visit to Alton Towers, or Bonfire Night.

Never mind that even when Jonathan lived with us, Kat and Freddy never saw their friends at weekends, never set foot in Alton Towers, and certainly never saw Jonathan build a bonfire in our garden. My children are determined to rewrite history: BD (before the divorce) has become a pink-hued idyll when we were one cosy, happy family, with never a raised voice and only a chorus of coochie-coos.

That idyll has been shattered, and guess who's to blame for it? Not the man who filed for divorce. Not the man who betrayed their mother and put his lust for some busty brain-box ahead of his love for them. No, they blame me.

'Mu-um! You're being so-o-o-o-o unreasonable!' Kat stamps her foot. I've just asked her to change her clingy lycra top. 'I bet that's why Dad's left us!'

Or:

'You don't understand, Mum!' Fred runs upstairs and slams his bedroom door shut. I climb up to knock on his door. 'You're so nasty to me! I want my daddy!'

Meanwhile Freddy's marks are suffering and when Mr Collins, the head teacher, bumped into me at the school gates he asked me with a look of concern: 'Everything all right, er . . . at home?'

As for Kat, she seems totally in control of schoolwork, but as she manically texts Mungo from morning till night, my daughter seems to be cutting herself off from everyone around her.

Someone had better remind the children that this is a *friendly*, non-traumatic divorce.

Jonathan brings them back Sunday night. He looks glum as they dart upstairs to their bedrooms. 'Your lawyer's a fiend.'

'He's just looking out for me.' Here I can't help a mean-ingful look. 'Someone has to.'

'Rosie, you know you don't need to say that.' Jonathan keeps his voice low. 'I'm not going to have the three of you wanting for anything. But your man doesn't get the picture.'

'He wants security for me. And for the children's future.'

'The children are being quite . . . hostile.' He keeps his voice low. 'They don't seem to understand that we're handling this in the best way possible.'

'At least you don't get blamed for Daddy leaving.'

'I get blamed for leaving Mummy.'

We huddle together at the foot of the stairs, in half-guilty, half-exasperated complicity while above us our children bump and stomp and bark at one another.

'We've been so clear with them,' Jonathan whispers.

'They find it difficult to adjust to change. They're set in their ways.' I notice he's wearing a new aftershave, something I don't know; and that his car keys hang from a new key-ring: a silver half of a heart. I bet I know who's got keys jingly-jangling from the other half.

'But I'm seeing them twice a week and it's proper, quality time. That's do-able, isn't it?'

'We'll just have to carry on reassuring them.' A heavy thud upstairs makes me call up: 'Careful, please, you two!'

'God, it's this complicated even without money problems!'

'Speaking of which – school fees due next week.'

'Bloody hell!' Jonathan's hand goes to his thick brown hair. 'I feel like I've just paid last term's! Thank God for Zelkin. Even when there's no money around, men will pay their last penny not to go bald.' Yes, Jonathan's miracle hair-regeneration treatment – a patent, it should be pointed out, he shares with three senior colleagues from the lab – has been a sturdy support down the years.

'Is your mum coming down for New Year's Eve?' Jonathan's mum had said she planned to come to see the grandchildren for a couple of days then.

'Nah.' Jonathan grows red and looks down at the floor in front of him. 'Mum's talking to me again now – er, thanks for making her see sense – But she refuses to have anything to do with Linda.'

I can't help a little thrill; I want to be friendly and accommodating, but I don't want anyone else to be. And certainly not with Linda.

'You know what's so maddening?' he asks as Kat comes slowly down the stairs. 'We are doing our best to conduct ourselves like proper human beings, but everyone else is buying tickets to watch two giant wrestlers tearing each other to bits.'

My lawyer will be buying front-row tickets.

'Your husband' – Mallaby-Steer is on the phone first thing Monday morning – 'and his paramour are fighting tooth and nail. Their lawyer rang me Friday afternoon to read me the riot act.' Mallaby-Steer chortles. 'I was on my way to a shoot in Gloucestershire, so I couldn't really deal with it.' Here Mallaby-Steer issues a long sigh. 'Fabulous place. The Taylor-Snells own one of the best shoots in the country . . .' Then, reluctantly turning back to my divorce: 'I just wanted to put you on your guard. Your prediction that he would be generous and relaxed about our demands was way off the mark.'

'Oh, I . . . I'm sorry.' I'm at work, on the mobile, struggling out of my coat, unwinding a scarf round my neck, while trying to gesticulate to Mrs S that, yes, I'll be there in one minute. 'I really believed he would be. He said he would.'

'Divorce is about breaking a whole series of promises.

Now,' Mallaby-Steer continues, 'about Zelkin. Quite difficult to determine how secure its future is.'

'Why?' My disrobing comes to a halt.

'Well, there seem to be some side-effects. People are becoming more litigious. Jonathan's never talked about the manufacturers being sued and the product being banned?'

'No. He never has.' I pause. 'Do you see cause for concern?'

'I wouldn't want to keep all my eggs in the Zelkin basket.' Mallaby-Steer draws in a long breath. 'I think', he tells me in a cosy, confidential tone, 'that I may get my man Tobyn to ring you. Great chap, big reputation in the City as a financial adviser. If you're going to live the good life after this divorce, we need to keep your money in a water-tight place. Tobyn will see to that.'

'Oh. OK. Thanks, Mr . . . thanks, Charles.'

I feel exhausted – and I haven't even started my day. There's a whole industry built on the carcass of my marriage: the counsellor, the lawyer, the estate agent, the financial adviser. And that's without counting the plumber, the builder, the handyman who will slowly but surely start filling Jonathan's shoes around the house.

One divorce, and dozens of people seem to have entered my life.

'Knock knock, anybody there?'

I blink and mumble, 'Sorry.' The red-faced man in front of me chortles happily: 'Oh, you city girls, you're always thinking of a million things! It's what you call multi-tasking,

I guess.' Another gurgle of laughter. 'I'm just a country boy, I can only cope with one thing at a time.'

I'm sitting in a gastro-pub in Fulham, under a skylight and Harry Black's pink, up-turned nose. Harry is a friend of Jill's from our university days. His beefy body is encased in a tight tweed coat, his fresh face speaks of country air, he has only a few tufts of blond hair left, and his eyes are small and round, like raisins. But he is, I remember, newly separated.

'Not to mention highly solvent,' Jill had underlined as she set up our date.

'Jill . . .!' I protest.

'Come along,' admonished Jill, wagging her finger at me, 'just because Orlando was odd and Max hasn't rung you does not mean I've failed at matchmaking. I get three strikes before I'm out, don't I?'

'We're not fighting crime, you know.' I was offended.

'No, but we *are* trying to get you an escort to the wedding anniversary party,' Jill said, triumphantly.

She's right: Carolyn Vincent has described, in lavish detail, the 'intimate – about three hundred guests, I guess' party she and Louis are planning next spring to celebrate their fifteen years of happy union. I will know many of those gathered to toast the happy couple and they will know me: they will have heard about Jonathan and Linda, about the impending divorce (will it be a signed deal by spring?) and many will have said with a little shiver of fear, 'There but for the grace of God . . .' I would really like to have someone fabulous on my arm as I stride through the room.

117

But I somehow doubt that Harry, who is now waving both tweedy arms to catch the waitress's attention, is the one. We sit surrounded by couples in pastel-coloured jumpers and tweeds and corduroys who place their fancy mobiles and the keys to their BMWs between them on the table: they're like the cowboys in Wild West films, emptying their pockets before a duel. The bright colours make everyone seem preternaturally happy, and through the skylight the sun winks at me: it's as if there is a conspiracy to rekindle my optimism – if not in marriage then in love.

'Anyway, as I was saying' – Harry takes a big gulp from his glass of beer – 'it's been a struggle with this year's crop. Last spring's hail storms practically ruined my apples . . .' I nod to show my interest in farming, Mother Nature, and Harry's crop. He rattles on about the best combine harvesters, the horror of windmills, the problem with rape seed, the future for farmers.

'My divorce was a picnic in comparison to what's going on now.' Harry shakes his head. 'I've had to lay off about half my men. There just isn't enough work to go around. Of course,' he crosses his arms on the table in front of him and leans right over, so he's only a few inches from me, 'I blame the EU.'

'For the farming crisis?'

'For the divorce. *She* went off with an Italian. Can you believe it? She was always doing these cheap Ryanair weekends to places like Pisa and Venice and Rome, and it never occurred to me she had a lover boy there . . .'

'That's hard.'

'Yep. And you?'

'We-ell, our marriage was beginning to . . . we were . . . drifting apart . . .'

'He had a lover, huh?' Harry's voice seems to have no level other than boom! and the word 'lover' brings the waitress, who was approaching us with a carafe of water, to a standstill.

'When I found out, I realised our marriage had no future.'

'It's hard, when they throw you over.' Harry massages his pink chin. 'And I bet it's a lot harder for women.'

Thanks, Harry. 'You make my prospects sound pretty bleak.'

'Chin up, old girl, who knows? You may meet the soul mate and – bingo!' He clicks his fingers. 'You'll be happy as a pig in shit.'

I wince at the image.

Harry misunderstands my expression of distaste for one of despair, and, suddenly concerned, reaches out to pat my hand with his. It's as big and floppy as a spaniel's tongue. 'I've been a brute, I'm sorry. But I promise, it does get better. I was so miz when she waltzed off that I drank myself silly every night for a month. But life does carry on, you know?'

I nod, trying to extricate my hand.

'You remember it, don't you?' Harry's little eyes fill with fond hope.

'Er . . . the pain? the disappointment?'

'The house. You came down to Leighbrook Farm when Jill and Ross were courting, didn't you? Before my divorce.'

'Ah yes, I remember.' I try to sound enthusiastic. What I

remember in fact is a huge, cold, sprawling building, surrounded by mooing cows, grunting pigs and neighing horses. The handle of the loo door came off in my hand, the sheets on my bed were damp, and Harry's chums' only topic of conversation was Harry's spectacular performance as Lady Bracknell at the recent village talent show.

'You must come down now that Belle is . . .' Harry catches himself, looks sad: Belle must be the ex-wife. Resolutely Harry ploughs on: 'You must come down. I've spruced it up a bit. Rebuilt the stable, mended the stone wall that runs . . .'

'I'm never happier' – I quickly stop the flow – 'than when I'm in the country.'

'Girl after my own heart.' Harry smiles appreciatively. 'Belle was like that: in her element in the country.' So much for 'moving on', I think. But I bite my tongue and start eating the warm chicken salad the Australian waitress sets down before me.

In keeping with the cheery-coloured Sloanes who fill its two capable rooms, the gastro-pub has music lite providing background to every conversation.

'Hey, "Dancing Queen"!' Harry, to my horror, starts dipping and swaying his arms and hands, in keeping with the beat. 'I've seen *Mamma Mia!* three times already!' He leans over and when he's only a few inches from my face he belts out: '"You can dance you can dance!"'

'Gosh, yes.' I blink, alarmed, pulling back from the table. 'What fun,' I say lamely.

'It's the best way to deal with divorce scars, isn't it?' Harry now tucks into his bangers and mash. 'Having a laugh, getting out and about. Let me tell you something . . .' He is still dipping and swaying. 'Three years ago I was a saddo with no life. But hey, look at me now!'

'Yes . . .' I murmur.

'Myum-myum-myum,' he lets out, followed by, 'Good sausages. Leek and garlic. Belle's favourites. She'd have some every morning for her elevenses . . .'

Still carrying a torch or what?! And how weird is that – sausages for elevenses?! I'm exasperated: Harry is no more over Belle than Max is over Ellie. Give it up, Jill . . .

'Didn't we meet in London?' Harry, a bit of mash in the corner of his mouth, leans forward to draw nearer. 'Remember – when Jill gave that drinks party last New Year's Eve?'

'Ye-es, I think so.' I recoil slightly.

'Of course we did.' Harry nods vigorously. 'You came with your children because you couldn't get a babysitter, remember?'

'That sounds right . . .' New Year's is the one time Otilya goes back to Poland.

'Sweet children. Do you want to see a photo of Belle's?' Before I can stop him, Harry dives into his trouser pocket and extracts a wallet. He flips it open: six Labrador pups yelp back at me.

'Belle is your *dog*?' I can't help screeching.

'Was, was.' Harry's face sags in mourning. 'Had to be put down last month. The vet said she was suffering . . . Horrible to watch . . . I buried her right by the house . . .'

8

I bury all thoughts of Harry and Belle and what I'd quite like to do to Jill by getting next year organised. I have decided that I must, for the sake of my sanity, enrol in the counselling training course. I don't want to put it off any more: the time has come for me to invest in my future, not just mourn my past. My decision involves a lot of careful planning: Otilya's hours have to practically double in order for me to be able to do the course as well as working; I'm going to fix my old bicycle so that I can cycle to the counselling programme at the Marlborough Centre and exercise at the same time; I'm going to organise our Easter break with Mum in Somerset. But before then, I have to somehow survive Christmas.

What is it about tinsel and 'Silent Night' and pine needles stuck on your upholstery that leaves you feeling like a sad and lonely reject unless you've got a man's arm wrapped round your waist and children munching mince pies at your feet? Officially, there may be twelve days of Christmas, but in fact I know there are many, many more, each one more painful than the last.

Already by mid-November, cinema queues, television, newspapers, and restaurants are transformed into one huge family album, brimming with snapshots of happy couples doting on loving children. Our home looks like a group photo where one of the figures has been ripped out. What's worse is that Christmas is a very Jonathan holiday: he's the one who put up the wreath, brought home the tree, and burst into carols at every opportunity. He drove us to Midnight Mass, carved the turkey and hurled endless logs on to the fire. The prospect of Christmas without him seems as dismal as Santa Claus coming to drink port and eat mince pies, then sneaking off without leaving any presents.

The children mope about the place with long faces and short tempers, and only the arrival of my mum on the eighteenth, for Freddy's starring role in the school's *Christmas Carol*, manages to lighten their mood.

After years of having played fluffy herbivores in a succession of Nativities, Freddy is to play not a sheep or a goat or a donkey, but – taaahdaaah! – Tiny Tim. I'm beside myself with pride and joy and have even volunteered to help the drama teacher, the highly strung Miss Dolcis, with the costumes.

I'm not alone. Under the careful tutelage of Miss Dolcis, three other mothers have been sewing a beard for Scrooge, turning sheets into ghosts, hemming skirts and underskirts, and otherwise recreating Victorian clothes.

When I arrive for a sewing session in the school hall at 9 a.m. on Tuesday, I see Alice Thomson: she is Joshua's mum and Joshua is Freddy's best friend. A long-limbed, horse-faced mother of three, she is very County and very in control; she seems to be involved in every school activity from costume design to field trips, from second-hand uniform sales to the summer fête. Every school needs one, I figure. And I'm grateful when, as I step tentatively into the freezing hall, she introduces the rest of us to one another.

'Your son's got the best role.' Mum Judy, round and rosy cheeked, with soft-toy brown eyes, sounds positively jealous.

'Joshua has more lines!' Alice Thomson stretches her long neck like an angry goose: I'm scared she might give me a painful peck. 'He's Scrooge!' Alice and I are in charge of stapling red berries on to a plastic wreath.

'But Tiny Tim is the one everybody loves.' Judy is at the sewing machine, working her way through patches to be attached to the Cratchits' clothes as a show of penury.

'He's so sweet, your Freddy.' A pale and elegant blonde called Beatrice patronises me with a smile. With her fragile slimness, made-up face and blonde curls, she looks like one of those porcelain figurines that my mum used to keep on her dresser. She is cutting out the pattern of what looks like a voluminous petticoat. 'It must have been very difficult for you.'

I wonder if even the dinner ladies at Westbury know about our impending divorce. 'Well, it was mutual, you know . . .' I say feebly.

'I think what's great these days is the way everyone can talk about it so openly.' Alice Thomson coils a string of red berries around the plastic wreath.

'Oh, I don't mind people knowing.' I try to sound relaxed, but I nip my finger with the stapler and my pained expression has Alice genuinely concerned:

'Poor you. It really is awful, isn't it? In a school like this one, it's somehow worse. I mean, no one would guess that out there one in two marriages end in divorce.' She frowns slightly as she says 'out there': it's clear the only place to be is 'in here', in Westbury's big happy family. 'Only a few children here come from broken homes.'

For a moment I see our house, with broken furniture and window panes, smashed pictures and torn curtains.

The other mums say nothing, as if to leave me to consider these wise words. I feel as self-conscious as if I were new to the school, even though the children have been here for the past four years. My new status has lifted me out of the category of average mum and dropped me into another, far more problematic: single mum. It means I see everything from a different standpoint. Other parents, their children, the teachers, seem suddenly enviable, confident, lucky and very much part of a whole – as in, a whole family.

And, I realise as I sit among these mothers, I must look different too. A mum on her own: others must think my life has been derailed into a bitter struggle for maintenance payments and access to children, disappointed ambitions and broken promises. I wonder if they feel uneasy in my presence, now that I'm an unknown quantity. After all, who knows why my marriage broke down, and what I might do because of it? I might have driven Jonathan away with my wicked tongue or unstoppable drinking; or I might have discarded him for a toyboy or an older and more powerful man. I might be out to avenge myself on all men, or be set on busting up other people's homes.

'Miss Dolcis is amazing, isn't she?' Judy, rearranging the multicoloured patches, tells us. 'Every year she manages to persuade us to come in and help out . . . I think this is my fourth Christmas production since the twins came to Westbury.'

'It's my fifth.' Alice sits up and looks around to see if anyone could question her superiority. No one does. 'I just wish some of the other teachers were as dedicated.' She shakes her head.

'I wish there were more male teachers.' Beatrice's clear blue eyes look up from the skirt she is cutting. 'Milo would really benefit.'

'I know. Male role models are es-sen-tial at this stage.' Alice nods forcefully.

'Ye-es.' I'm stung, but I try not to show it. 'Jonathan is determined to stay very involved with the children.'

'I do wish someone would tell these divorced dads that fatherhood is more than the odd football match.' Beatrice doesn't have the energy to look properly indignant, but a few delicate wrinkles cross her porcelain forehead. 'In the end, nothing makes up for the day-to-day presence, does it? I mean, children need to see you at meal times and on the weekend and just before they go to sleep and . . .'

'How many happily married fathers do that?' I can't help asking.

'Andrew does.' Beatrice gives me a cool look. 'I told him that having children is a 24/7 commitment.'

'Oh, Andrew is a model husband!' Alice issues a tight little laugh. 'The most important thing in the end is that the absent dad doesn't back-pedal out of paying the school fees.' She keeps twisting the wreath in her hands. '*That's* what's so scary about second families: more cost centres!'

'Jonathan doesn't have plans for a second family,' I say quickly. Jesus, I hadn't even considered *that* possibility. The thought makes my palms sweat. 'Lin— his new woman understands the importance of a good education.'

'Just you wait.' Beatrice shakes her head at my naïveté. 'Minnie Glover had to go to court every time the Westbury fees were due.'

'Thanks for the warning.'

Alice takes the wreath from my hands to study it better. 'You know, Rosie, if I were you I'd get them to see Mrs Schiffer, the school counsellor. She's brilliant with children – even the most damaged respond to her.' She rummages through the basket of accessories. 'Anyone see the super glue?'

Christmas draws near, and the costumes, it must be said, look fetching. My mother has come up a week earlier than usual for her annual stay; she has a keen sense of drama, and has been going through lines like 'God Bless you, Mr Scrooge' and 'Papa, isn't this a lovely feast?' with Freddy for two days solidly. By the big night he is word perfect, she is exhausted, and I'm in nostalgic mode: Jonathan is coming and he and I will 'ooh' and 'aah' in delighted unison at the sight of our son lighting up the stage.

And in fact, the moment we arrive in the crowded school hall, Jonathan's there, all smiles and warm hugs, and it seems as if we've stepped back in time.

'Jean, how lovely that you could come!' He wraps an arm around my mum. 'Can you believe he's graduated from beast to boy?'

Mum flashes Jonathan a big smile: one hug from him, and she's forgotten how cross she was about his affair and our divorce. In fact, while he explains to her that Dickens wrote his *Carol* in five 'staves' rather than 'chapters' – staves being a musical term more in keeping with the 'Carol' – she shoots me a look full of hope: maybe, just maybe . . . I can see her thinking that our split could turn out to be temporary.

'Honestly – they can't just say Christmas any more!' my mum snorts as she points to the festoons of crepe paper that decorate the hall. Golden letters above our head spell out *Happy Eid!*, *Happy Hanukkah!* as well as *Happy Christmas!*

'No,' Jonathan explains. 'Westbury makes a big thing of being multi-faith.'

Other parents push past us and children squeeze in between us to get to the rows of folding chairs. I spot Mr Rayne, the head, and Beatrice in a sleek black dress – she's standing next to a grey-haired man who looks a bit old to be her husband. The paragon of virtue that is Andrew. Close by stands Judy with her own husband attached to a considerable paunch.

As we follow the other parents in, Jonathan ruffles Kat's hair, which she hates. 'Hullo, poppet, how's tricks?'

'Fine, Daddy, just let go of my hair.' My daughter bats his hand away.

We take our seats, just as the lights dim: first Jonathan then Kat then Mum then me. With a little jolt I see that Jonathan has left the chair on his right empty. Does he want me to sit there? We can bask in Freddy's big moment whilst sitting beside each other like old times . . .

'I kept this for you,' Jonathan beams a smile in my direction.

I'm about to push past my mother and daughter when I suddenly see the shock on Mum's face. She is staring at something behind me, and trying to move her lips, but no sound comes out. I turn to inspect what could reduce my indomitable mum to rubble. Standing there in a mink coat, long dark hair tumbling down her shoulders, is Linda.

'I rushed as fast as I could.' Her voice is as low as her décolleté, as dark as her mink, as she addresses Jonathan. 'But I was looking over that Swedish research that came this morning . . . Hi, I'm Linda!' She lowers her face towards mine, and for a horrible moment I think she's trying to air kiss me. 'I suppose we'd better sit down.' She then sashays past my mother (still speechless) and Kat (who glowers).

The lights go down. I'm so angry and humiliated I want to scream. How DARE Jonathan bring HER to this? I feel as if my pleasure in my son's big moment has been spoiled. I feel robbed of my family's get-together, and of Jonathan's proximity.

130

'How could he?' my mother leans towards me and whispers.

'Don't,' I mouth. I don't dare reply, or look down the aisle at what Kat is doing, or worse, what they are up to. They may be holding hands or even smooching, for all I know. It is clear their sense of propriety is not to be trusted.

For months now I have been trying to be friendly, accommodating, civilised. *This* is my reward.

My anger is such that only Tiny Tim's appearance, with his little wooden crutch and woollen cap, calms me. Oh God, I think as my son hops from one corner of the fireplace to the other, what will happen in the interval?

What happens is that as we all troop out of the hall into the entrance, Linda, gorgeous and sultry in her splendid fur, attracts everyone's stare. I see Alice's eyes grow wide with curiosity, while a look of comprehension settles over Judy's small round face: Ah, of course, *that's* why the Martins' marriage broke up. I feel so tense, I'm pathetically grateful for my mum's presence, and Kat's. I find myself hanging on to both for dear life, as Jonathan hooks his arm into his lover's.

'Well, he's splendid, he's really prepared, you can tell.' Jonathan is handing round Styrofoam cups of mulled wine that are borne on a tray. He looks totally at ease, as does Linda, who offers me a Fishermen's Friend when I cough nervously.

'Here, I find these really help.' Her smoky voice is low and intimate, as if we were old friends confiding in one another. 'That little boy has talent,' she purrs.

I bristle.

'He-was-all-right-wasn't-he?' I say through gritted teeth.

'It's interesting to see how the genes turn up, isn't it?' Linda holds her Styrofoam as elegantly as if it were a glass of Bollinger. 'I mean, I can see so much of you in the children. Though I have to say, Freddy's more Jonathan, isn't he? Look at those eyes: dark and soulful. He'll be a real heartbreaker.' She curls her lips in a fond smile.

I give her a look: 'Just like his dad, then,' I say in a clipped, cold voice. And then, turning on my heel, I say wildly, 'Mum, let me get you another cup of this, it's delicious.' I make my way to the trestle table with its mulled wine and Christmas biscuits. Two sixth-formers stand there at the ready.

'Rose' – Jonathan is at my elbow: he calls me Rose only when there's something serious to discuss – 'I . . .' He touches my arm lightly. 'I just want to make sure you're OK with Linda coming here.'

'OK?' I look at him, disbelieving. 'OK? How could you?' I try to control my voice.

'She really wants to bond with the children, and she said that her being here in the audience, applauding Freddy, was really . . . "emotionally significant" for their relationship.'

'Spare me the psychobabble, please,' I snap.

One of the sixth-formers looks at us, curious. Jonathan notices, and motions me to the end of the table. We stand there, a few inches apart, surrounded by parents and students milling about.

'Look, Linda is a very positive person. She doesn't want any bad blood. She wants to be friends with you, friends with the kids.'

'Forget it.' I stab at him with my index finger. 'I've obviously made things so easy for the two of you, you think that you can just barge into every moment of our lives.'

'We're not barging in,' Jonathan hisses. 'That's my son on stage. And that's my partner.' He points proudly to Linda, who stands chatting to Mum. For once, I can see, even Mum is at a loss.

'Oh really?' I raise my voice.

'Linda is in my life now.' Jonathan keeps his voice low.

'She may be in your bed, but I don't want her here!' I realise that I must have started shouting because parents and children are staring at us. It is as if Jonathan and I were standing in an invisible circle: everyone else has taken a step back, frightened.

'You're a selfish bastard!' Our audience, now grown in number, stands completely still, and silent.

The bell rings to announce Act II. Our audience looks reluctant to trade this new entertainment for another, but slowly they go back to their seats, leaving Jonathan and me alone.

'You're being unreasonable,' Jonathan says.

'You're being insensitive,' I snap.

'I'm going back in.' Jonathan turns on his heel and leaves me.

I down the mulled wine in one go. I'm standing on my own in a huge whitewashed space beneath a vaulted ceiling, feeling like a freak because I don't want my husband's lover to play at being Mummy with *my* children. Doesn't anyone understand? I bite the rim of my Styrofoam cup.

'Well done you!' Alice Thomson comes out of the Ladies'. 'Men can be so in-con-si-derate. You should see my husband.'

'At least he's still yours!' I remind her, and stalk off back to my seat.

Tears fill my eyes so that I can hardly see the second act of *A Christmas Carol*. Scrooge, the Ghost of Christmas past, and even the Cratchits' threadbare little home hardly register as I think instead of the selfishness of my ex-husband and his new love. I've been trying so hard to be the perfect ex-wife, the capable, intelligent woman who has enough life and spirit in her to see when a relationship's dead and it's time to move on. But how can I make this a good divorce when Jonathan allows Linda to elbow her way into our family life? Surely a brilliant American pharmacologist can work out for herself that the school Christmas play is the kind of family-only ritual that new partners should steer clear of?

'Oh no!' Beside me, Mum interrupts my angry thoughts; I look at her, see her worried expression, and look at the stage.

Tiny Tim stands there, leaning on his crutch and looking truly miserable. His little face is quite pale and his eyes enormous with fright. I suddenly realise what my mum has already recognised: Freddy has forgotten his lines.

'Dear Papa, don't worry,' Mum whispers beside me. But it's no good: Freddy is not looking our way, he can't hear his grandmother's whisper. Where is Miss Dolcis, the indomitable drama teacher, always on hand as prompter? My son stares straight ahead, looking more terrified than at any time since he broke his arm and had to be rushed off to the A & E at the Royal Free three years ago.

'Oh gawd . . .' I hear Jonathan, two seats down, issue anxiously.

Still no sign of Miss Dolcis. Suddenly I know what I must do: crouching, I push past my mum and the groups of parents and siblings sitting on her left; I run down the aisle towards the stage to find a place only a few feet away from the ever-silent Tiny Tim. I look up at my little boy. And I'm just about to give him his lines, when, to my right, I hear: 'Dear Papa, don't worry, we will be fine.' It's a dark voice, distinctive in its American accent. I whip around: standing there, looking up at my son, is Linda, hands cupping her mouth, megaphone style.

'Dear Papa,' Tiny Tim begins in an uncertain voice, 'er . . . er . . . don't worry. We will be fine.'

9

'Mrs Martin, you've signed up to start the course on the fifteenth of March.' The woman from the Marlborough Centre has a freckled face and red hair tightly drawn back in a tiny ponytail. Eyebrows and lashes are sandy-coloured, almost transparent. She has the hurried, expressionless manner of someone who runs around with a clipboard. She's interviewing me to see if I'm a suitable candidate for the Centre's prestigious counselling course.

'A formality,' Jill had assured me when I rang her in a panic this morning.

'I haven't had an interview in five years, Jill! What should I do?'

'Be calm, laid-back,' Jill said soothingly. 'Look, you're the best listener I know. If you can't do this, nobody can.'

'The course is a big time investment. Four years – and we usually recommend staying on for a Master's.'

'Yes, yes, I realise that.' In four years I'll be forty-one. Will I be on my own? Will I be living in our home still? Will I be completely over my divorce and completely into my work?

'What we look for in candidates for this course is empathy . . .' I see no trace of empathy in my interrogator: with her cold eyes and unsmiling mouth she makes me uncomfortable; so does her furniture: I have to settle and resettle on the spindly metal and wicker chair. '. . . A readiness to engage your emotional imagination with the world around you.'

'Of course. Do I need to fill in a questionnaire? Give you a deposit?' I'm keen.

'No, that won't be necessary.' The woman swivels in her office chair so that she can pick up a file from her desk. She keeps it on her lap unopened. I notice that her tiny office is studded with photos of a poodle.

'It's just . . . I'm very eager.' Very: I want to leave Dr Casey and Mrs Stevens. I want to get my teeth into a proper challenge.

'Yes.' The woman sounds dubious. 'I do hope to see you – this time.'

'Wh-what do you mean?'

'Well, our records show that you enrolled in the Counselling for Life Training last September – but never made it to the interview.'

'I . . . I know,' I can't deny this; 'but we had a family crisis and the children were pretty miserable and I thought it best to be on hand . . .'

'Hmmm . . .' The freckled pale face registers neither sympathy nor understanding. 'Our records show that you were enrolled in the course the year before. You didn't come to the interview then either.'

'Oh gosh, yes, but that was when the childminder, who is also our daily, suddenly said she couldn't do five afternoons a week and, you see, I work part-time . . .'

'I see.' My interrogator jots something down on her brown file. Is she going to disqualify me as a flake who doesn't follow through with her plans, or a controlling hausfrau who can't give her children space? It's true that I've postponed this course more than once; but that's because I figured being a part-time professional is better than being a part-time mum. 'Are you sure you will be attending in March?'

I look around the room at the poodle in a tartan dog coat, in a pink ribbon beside a small birthday cake with two burning candles, chewing on a bone.

'Mrs Martin?'

'Yes?'

'You seem distracted.'

'I'm . . . I'm . . . sorry if I'm distracted . . .' I gulp, nervous and apologetic. 'You see . . . I'm going through a divorce.'

'Divorce?' It's as if I'd pushed a switch: suddenly the pale freckled face comes alive and the words pour forth. 'Really? Awful, isn't it? It's like a bomb going off in the middle of your home. And let me tell you, I've still got shrapnel inside me.' She narrows her eyes: 'I was so-o-o-o-o angry I could have castrated him right then and there. He'd been seeing her for four years! Can you believe it? Right under my nose, and I was so in love I didn't get it!' She stabs the pad in her hand with her pen. 'When I found him out, it was like some stupid stereotype: lipstick on the collar! The worst of it was, he could get away with murder because of this country's idiotic no-fault divorce. How can there be no fault when one partner cheats and lies, and the other gets hurt? What kind of justice is that? I'll tell you what kind: *man* justice. Which is *in*justice.' Her pen stabs the notepad in her lap. 'Seen how many lawyers and judges are male? There's Fiona Shackleton and that Serena Stewart – the one they call the husband beater – but apart from them it's men men men!'

I sit, silent and unmoving, and the woman before me doesn't seem to be aware of my presence any more. 'Bloody mafia, it is. If I'd had a proper counsel, I'm sure we could have bankrupted him. We've got two children, and he made me give up this' – she waves her hand to take in the office with its stick furniture and poodle photos – 'to be wife and mummy. *That* should be held against him, at least.'

I nod, in a genuine display of empathy. *Look at me*, I want to shriek, *I'm counselling right now!*

'You have to be really careful of how you do it, you know. There are people out there who get their divorce on the internet, just like' – she snaps her fingers – 'that. Lucky them, I say: because for us it took nineteen months and it got so bad I had a nose bleed every morning.'

I feel miserable now, and squirm again in the fragile chair. My movement breaks the spell, as if I've suddenly reminded my interrogator of her role here.

'Well, I'll put you down then.' She writes something in her notepad. 'I'll tell you one thing: divorcées understand first-hand the value of counselling.' She leans forward, pale eyes intense and scary. 'Don't let him squash you like mine did me.'

'I need this like a hole in the head' I mutter crossly through pursed lips as I follow my mum and the children to the Vincents' next door. They've invited us 'for mulled wine, mince pies and carols'.

'I really like your neighbours,' Mum tells us as I switch on the outside light and lock the front door. 'They're so wholesome.'

I grunt in acknowledgement. Carolyn and Louis are not our neighbours, they're a reproach. Every day, when I pick up the papers, I spot Carolyn standing at her front door in her cream silk robe, pecking Louis on the forehead to send him on his way to work. Often, if I've got a window open, I can hear the turtledoves next door as they coo over break-fast: 'My love, what shall we have for supper tonight?' or 'Petal, what do you think about having those nice Mallards over?'

'Mu-um,' Kat hisses as we march, crackling the frost that covers our little path, 'please could you not tell everyone that you and Dad have split?'

'Divorce is not that unusual, darling.' As I speak, my breath is white and visible in front of me. Mum's elbow digs into me, but I ignore it.

'I don't want anyone feeling sorry for me.' Kat's scarf muffles her voice. 'Especially no one tonight.'

'If you and Daddy had stayed together,' Freddy mumbles accusingly into his duffel coat, 'no one would call me a latch-key kid.' My mum's elbow repeats its sharp dig into my side.

'You're not a latch-key child,' I protest, speeding up so that I can get away from Mum. 'Otilya's here when I'm at Dr Casey's!'

'And I'm here until the twenty-seventh, poppet,' Mum pipes up.

'I know, Granny . . . But it's really difficult, you know,' Kat sighs behind us. 'I don't think Mum and Dad really understand . . .'

By the time I ring the Vincents' door bell – which sets off a tinny rendition of 'God Rest Ye Merry, Gentlemen', I'm wishing myself a million miles away.

Louis opens the door, big warm smile of welcome plastered across his face. 'Ah! Reinforcements for our carol singers!'

He waves us into the large sitting room where a gas fire burns bright. The Vincents have placed a huge Christmas tree in one corner of the room, and it hurts to see how all-embracing and steady it is, with its thick glossy green branches dangling a fetching combination of handmade ornaments and bright shiny balls. Ours, in comparison to this strapping great fir, is a poor spindly thing, unimpressive and unsteady, vulnerable to the slightest draught or knock.

Half a dozen people stand singing by the grand piano that occupies the west side of the room. The piano player, a handsome blond man with spectacles and a warm-hued baritone, is leading them into 'O Come, All Ye Faithful'.

142

Garlands of holly festoon the fireplace, the large paint-ings, the lamps. Carolyn must have been at it all weekend.

'Oh, Rosie, I'm soooooo glad you could come!' Carolyn's toned arms wrap me in a half-baked embrace. She air-kisses my mum. 'The *whole* family, how lovely! Now come to the piano, I want you to join in!'

Kat and Freddy, tears and accusations forgotten, run off to join Molly and Oscar.

'Joyful and triumphant . . .' I intone under Carolyn's beady eye. I'm pretty tone deaf and loath to inflict my voice upon unsuspecting strangers, but I can see my hostess will brook no compromise.

'O come ye, o co-ome ye . . .' Beside me, my mum belts out the lyrics with relish. I study the assembled carollers as I sing: I recognise the elderly widow who babysits Molly and Oscar; Mr Bolton, who used to teach Geography at Westbury; and Miss Stead, the archetypal sixty-something spinster, whom I've met before at a Sunday lunch here. The sight of Miss Stead jogs a distant memory. I frown in concentration: ah yes, Carolyn, after walking Miss Stead to the door, explaining in a loud whisper that 'Louis always teases me about my charitable cases, but I do so want to *help* her!'

I look around the group singing now, seeing if they prove my hunch is right: gleaming spectacles, grey hair . . . spin-sters, widows, lonely retired school teachers – and a mother of two recently abandoned by her husband . . . yes, yes, it hits me that we are all Carolyn's charitable cases.

I break off in the middle of 'Greensleeves' and make for the dining room, where a buffet gleams invitingly. Molly

143

walks past me: beneath the carefully messed-up hair she wears an expression of entrenched boredom. Her black tunic dress is torn and short, and her kohl-rimmed eyes match her black nail polish. I smile encouragingly: her dark and sulky figure provides a welcome relief amidst all this seasonal cheer.

'Hiya.' I lean forward to kiss her cheek.

But with a quick 'Yeah, hi' Molly stalks past me. I feel a surge of disappointment: she has obviously decided to discard me as her confidante, given that I haven't exactly made a success of my own relationship.

Freddy and Oscar are sitting under the table, giggling. I help myself to a mince pie. I spot Kat greeting a boy with blond curls and braces: the two look awkward, slightly out of breath. The boy moves off, into the sitting room. I study my daughter: she is pink-cheeked and bright-eyed, and on her lips I see a shy smile. Tonight she looks like a young woman. She extracts her phone from her jeans pocket: the smile grows wider, and she starts texting.

'You should be enjoying the party.' I step up to her.

'I am. Just texting Mungo.' She looks pleased and self-important.

'Oh? Who was that blond-haired boy you were just with?'

'Mungo.' Kat's blush deepens. 'He's gone to the sitting room to find Molly.'

'B-b-but . . .' I look confused '. . . why are you texting him?'

'It's too noisy to speak on the phone.' My daughter shrugs, as if this were boringly obvious. She turns her back on me so she can proceed with her texting in privacy.

Feeling slightly demented, I grab a tangerine from the

orange pyramid Carolyn erected as a centrepiece on the dining-room table. I peel it, slowly eat the juicy segments: even the Vincents' fruit tastes sweeter.

'That man with the hearing aid kept asking my name.' Freddy and Oscar emerge from under the table. 'Your mum and dad's friends are weird.'

'Oh no, Mum and Dad had their friends over on Monday night,' Oscar explains. 'This is their M & M party.'

'What's M&M?'

'Mince pies and misfits.'

I stalk back to the misfits, scowling, filled with an unseasonal rage. My mum is sitting beside the piano player, warbling happily. She is in her element, with her glass of mulled wine and lots of company, and even a good-looking man beside her.

'Come along, sweetheart!' She waves me towards her. 'This is Rob, Rosie' – she beams me a smile – 'the best piano player ever.'

Rob shakes my hand. 'Your mum's a great soprano.'

I look at him: he seems suspiciously normal. Maybe he has a wooden leg, a painful divorce, or a terrible addiction?

'Rob' – a petite blonde puts her hand protectively on his arm – 'I'm getting us a glass. But I want to go soon, OK?'

She is off before we are introduced, and I notice that my mum issues a little sigh of disappointment in her wake. She's incorrigible.

'You're a professional pianist?' My mum bats her eyelashes at Rob.

'Good God, no. Something far seedier.' He does a winning, self-deprecating chortle. 'I'm a divorce lawyer.' I gulp. Oh dear, not a Mallaby-Steer clone! 'But I've been roped in four years on the trot for this carolling. I suspect Carolyn doesn't know many piano players.'

Mince pies, misfits and musicians, I think to myself.

'Then on the thirtieth I'm off on my Saga cruise around the Med!' My mum has moved over to shout at the deaf man.

'She's amazing,' Rob says, admiringly. 'More energy in her little finger than most thirty-year-olds I know.' I watch my mother and can't help smiling: she is now acting out, for the sake of her deaf interlocutor, a boat on a cruise, waving her arms rhythmically and shielding her eyes with her hand. 'But you weren't singing very loudly.' Rob wags his finger at me. 'Letting the side down.'

'I'm hopeless.' I lower my voice. 'In fact, at the risk of sounding like the worst kind of philistine, I think I'm more comfortable with a divorce lawyer than a pianist.'

'Well, musicians are not comfortable with words.' Rob rakes a hand through his hair: he has a receding hairline, I think, set to soon get worse. I wasn't a trichologist's wife for nothing.

'My divorce lawyer certainly is.'

'Ah, you are consulting one of our tribe?' Rob the lawyer raises an eyebrow. 'Recent?'

'Seven months.' I feel a little tremor of relief course through me: saying it no longer makes me wince. 'I'm surprised how used to it I've become.'

'I'll surprise you further' – Rob smiles: it's a sweet, slightly shy smile, I think, warming to him: he is slim and good looking, and the spectacles lend him a slightly donnish air – 'there will come a time when you'll find it all boils down to arrangements about money and time.' Rob the lawyer crosses his arms and leans against the wall. 'A sad indictment of marriage.'

'I suppose we can't avoid the time and money. But the name-calling, the blame game . . . I hate it and I don't want to sink to that,' I tell Rob.

'You can get the name-calling and blame game in marriage as well as divorce.' And for an instant, Rob the lawyer loses his easy, self-deprecating charm and looks sad.

As if on cue, the petite blonde comes rushing in, holding two glasses. 'I cannot tell you the bore I met,' she tells Rob. 'A real horror, rabbiting on and on about her dentures.' She finally takes me in. 'Hullo, I'm Serena, Rob's wife.' Her smile is unconvincing. 'Did Carolyn get you on board to help out with her broken-winged friends?'

'No, I'm one of the broken-winged friends.'

Rob stirs uncomfortably. 'Don't be daft, er . . . I don't know your name.'

'Rosie Martin. I live next door.'

Christmas Day is a nightmare. It's not just the crooked tree that sways dangerously in its metal stand; or the turkey that, despite my patient bastings, tastes as if stuffed with sawdust. It's not even the fact that the children come running in on Christmas Eve from their afternoon with Jonathan, laden with presents of such extravagance that we could open a North London version of Harrods. Rather, it is the fact that from morning till night, Christmas Day is just a second-rate version of the past.

Scrooge, I think bitterly to myself as I lie awake at 5 a.m., would feel right at home.

I hope to get my mum to help me with the cooking, but she spends most of the time shopping online. 'I really need to get myself some new clothes.'

'Why don't you wait until the sales start, Mum?'

'Because I've just found out that my cruise is seventy:thirty.'

'Seventy:thirty? What's that?'

'Ratio women to men. I've got to get equipped for battle, if I'm to stand a chance. I don't fancy being a widow for the rest of my days.'

I jump guiltily: I'd never given my mum's widowhood a moment's thought. When my father died, five years ago, I'd assumed my mother would never look at another man again. They had been so happy together. And yet of course she must be lonely, now, in the house in Somerset. She has always been a sociable creature, and when we were growing up she was forever having friends round, and inviting us to do the same with ours. (I usually regretted inviting friends over, though, as Mum would inevitably collar them at some point 'for a chat' during which she would fish for information about their cigarette consumption, fumblings in the bike shed, and pot smoking.)

Why shouldn't Mum want a second romantic phase in her life? She deserves it. Although, I think desperately on

Christmas Day, I would dearly love a hand when it comes to cooking Christmas lunch. Mum thinks pouring the gravy into a gravy boat is enough.

'The thing about Jonathan,' she tells me as she wipes the boat with the corner of a J Cloth, 'is that he is so very particular. He likes things tidy and organised, just like me.' She sighs heavily. 'You don't think that's why . . . Americans are very neat and precise.'

'Oh, give it a rest,' I say crossly, struggling to move the turkey on to a platter to rest, splattering my hands and forearms with grease in the process. 'If he wanted neatness and organisation' – I tip the sprouts into the colander with unnecessary vigour – 'he could have bought a new filing cabinet. It wasn't better folders he was after.'

'Children, doesn't it look lovely!' Mum claps her hands as I place the enormous bird in the middle of the table. Then, as I start carving: 'Sweetheart, best start by taking off the drumsticks.' And, as Freddy beside her begins to eat, 'The stuffing looks a bit dry, why don't you pour a bit of gravy on it, darling?' Finally to Kat, who is holding her iPhone underneath the tablecloth: 'I'm sure Mungo can wait until after lunch.'

'He's your boyfriend on Facebook,' Freddy teases. Then in a sing-song voice, 'Kat and Mungo, sitting in a tree, k-i-s-s-i-n-g.'

'Loser,' Kat scowls at her brother.

'These sprouts could have done with a few more minutes, sweetheart,' says Mum, chewing a crunchy sprout.

'Yuck!' Freddy pulls a face. 'What's *in* this gravy?'

Suddenly I feel like I can't stand another minute. I want to shake my mum, followed by hurling the turkey on the floor and stomping on its dry carcass. Above all, I want to run upstairs and cry and bury myself under the duvet, and stay there until these ghastly forty-eight hours are over.

I grit my teeth, determined to make it a Christmas the children won't look back on with horror. I chat cheerfully about their forthcoming week in Courchevel with their father. Linda, he has assured them, will only be there for the first two days. But I feel as if I am holding my breath during the entire lunch, and by the time we re-group around the Christmas tree, to open the presents, I feel as if I'm going to burst.

'Oh, look what pretty wrapping paper!' my mum enthuses as she sits down in the armchair, a cup of coffee carefully balanced on her lap. 'Now first go for the children, because they're the ones who've had such a terrible time of it . . .' She ignores my murderous look and busies herself ruffling Freddy's hair.

Freddy's not listening, intent as he is on unwrapping his gift. 'A book . . .?' he sounds disappointed.

'A *special* book' – my mum won't be deflated – 'to cope with this difficult period.'

'Er . . . thanks, Granny.' Freddy sounds dubious as he holds up a copy of *Emotional Intelligence*. He hugs his grandmother, and she looks over his head at me:

'This will help with ironing out some of the d-i-v-o-r-c-e issues.' As if Freddy, aged nine, cannot spell.

'Oh, Granny, it's really pretty!' Kat holds up a skimpy satin top.

'Well, Granny knows that you're getting to that stage . . .'

I open my mouth to protest, but I have just unwrapped my own present from my mother, and all I can do is gawp like a goldfish. Lying there in folds of shiny gold wrapping paper is a DVD called *Divine Divorcée*. The cover, plastered with come-hither photos of a woman in a thong and nipple tassels, promises 'two consecutive hours of adult fun and games'.

'Mu-um! What is this?' I ask, outraged.

'I wanted you to see what fun you can still have – even if you're almost forty!'

10

What to pack for your children when they're staying with the ex-husband and his new love:

1. Primark jumpers, jeans, knickers, T-shirts, sports socks, to show that the children are not spoiled, but are now dressed in the cheapest wardrobe possible since their father set up *two* households.
2. Beautifully folded pants, knickers and sports socks that have been specially bleached to a perfect whiteness. This way *no one* can go around saying, 'Poor children, the mother is so depressed over the divorce that she can hardly remember they exist.'
3. A bottle of No More Nits lotion – that will have Linda worried.
4. A small framed photo of yourself, carefully placed

in the middle of their case, so that they can put it up; proof of their devotion to you.

5. A copy of one of those children's counselling books, such as *I'm Not Mini-Me: What Children Really Think About Divorce* to show that Mummy, at least, is trying her best to help the poor little creatures deal with the trauma.

6. A stack of CDs and audio-books so that the children can tune out whenever they want – especially, it is hoped, when it is most infuriating to the grown-ups. Like when they are supposed to choose from the dinner menu at the hotel. Or when Linda tries to embark on a getting-to-know-you session. Or Jonathan tries to explain 'blended families' and how a step-mum just means more attention and affection for the children.

7. Freddy's favourite alarm clock, the Donald Duck one that wakes up the whole household with its 'Quack! Quack! Quack!', pre-set to 6.30 a.m., so Freddy can catch his favourite Saturday-morning telly.

8. Homework – masses and masses of it. This has the children begging their father for help with maths, geography, history, etc; and means their father and Linda are not always associated just with Legoland, *Hannah Montana*, Pizza Express and all that's fun in life.

9. Lots and lots of packets of chewing gum: Freddy is still at the stage of sticking it under the table or a

chair when he gets bored of chewing. Why should the love nest be pristine?

10. Kat's recorder. Our twelve-year-old stopped taking lessons four years ago, when even determined Miss Blake failed to find any musical aptitude; but 'I know how much Daddy has always enjoyed your practising,' I fib, as I pack the instrument of torture. 'You should show him how much you've improved.'

Having packed all of the above, I wait for Jonathan with the children. Mum has gone, chirruping happily about her fortnight in the sun, oblivious to the devastation she leaves behind. Ever since Christmas Day, Freddy has been moping about the house, clutching his copy of *Emotional Intelligence*, explaining to me about how parents can crush their children and ruin their lives. Kat alternates between strutting about the house, parading her nonexistent bust in the skimpy satin top, and asking me if she can have a lock on her door because she needs privacy. Otilya has been off for a week now – but the last time she was here she looked like a dog who'd been whipped, as my mother had been at her about the dirt, mess and dust and general slovenly standard of our house.

'Well, your lawyer doesn't believe in holidays, does he?' Jonathan is at the door, in a bright red jumper I don't recognise: a Christmas present from the Yank?

'He doesn't want this to drag on.' I refuse to feel guilty because Charles Mallaby-Steer is proving as efficient as his reputation promised.

'His demands are totally unreasonable. If you're still

155

committed to a good divorce, I think we should opt for mediation. With Mallaby-Steer things are bound to escalate. We'll have a nasty fight on our hands.'

We can hear the children upstairs arguing about which DVDs they'll be taking to Courchevel.

'He seems to be under the impression that I'm some kind of millionaire and that Zelkin is a cash cow. It isn't. The FDA has turned us down. Some American study has found it causes constipation in too many men.'

'I'm sorry,' I say weakly.

'Yah.' Jonathan looks down, kicks his foot against our front door step. 'Look, I've heard this mediation thing works. We just need to focus on the area we're coming unstuck over.'

'You mean the children.'

'I mean the money.'

'Frankly, I'm much more concerned about Kat and Freddy being able to see you as much as possible – and without her.'

'Ah. I forgot to mention . . . Linda's staying for the whole week after all.' Jonathan looks down and kicks our welcome mat.

'What?' I cry in dismay. 'What happened to your "quality time" with them at Courchevel?'

'I know, that was the original plan. But then I thought, she is going to be a really important person in their lives' – Jonathan looks at me from under his brows – 'and they should have some exposure so they can acclimatise.'

'Acclimatise? We're not talking about trekking up the Himalayas,' I huff.

'Linda will give us our space.' Jonathan shakes his head. 'Besides, the three of them need to have some time to bond.' As if conscious that these American terms are not Jonathan-speak, he doesn't look at me as he adds: 'Linda's keen for us to try a family therapy session. All together. What do you think?'

'Absolutely not!' I pull myself up. 'That's the last thing I'd do. Are you mad?'

'Fine.' He raises his hands to fog-horn: 'Kat! Freddy! Let's go!'

'Bye, Mu-um!' 'Bye bye!' There is a scrum as the children hug me tight. It's the first time since the split that they'll be spending more than one night away from me and they know that I'm tense about it.

'Bye, have fun!' I bury my face in Freddy's hair.

I stand on the doorstep and watch them set off, Jonathan between them, one hand on Kat's shoulder and the other on Freddy's head.

The house feels instantly empty. I wander about, folding Freddy's 'I love Lara Croft' T-shirt, balled up in a corner of the sofa, putting away Kat's *Harry Potter and the Order of the Phoenix*, left open on the kitchen table.

What am I going to do with myself this week? I've finished the books about substance abuse I got out of the library. Dr Casey's practice is shut until the ninth. Everyone I know is away. The streets look as if they've been cleared of people and cars, and even the shops, though open, are deserted. Jill and David are in Suffolk with friends, and Mum is cruising for a second husband. Even Mallaby-Steer, with his constant queries and advice, is with his family in Scotland. The Vincents would make me suicidal.

I should have organised something ages ago, insured myself against the bleak wasteland now looming. But I have little practice as a divorced mum; I shall know better for next time. Because I know there are going to be many, many next times, until finally the children go off to university and I shall be left on my own.

At this prospect, I simply melt into tears. Sobs follow, so hard that I struggle to breathe. I lie down on the sofa and just give myself up to a crying fit.

I weep for the future I thought lay mapped out and secure. I cry because my family is no longer whole, and my work only a fraction of what I'd like to do. I cry because the counselling training which looms, in a fortnight's time, now seems an obstacle course rather than a challenge to be embraced . . .

I don't know how long I stay like this, face down, on the sofa. Suddenly I'm conscious of the telephone ringing. It's on a round table only a foot away, and I struggle to reach it. My hand fumbles among the silver-framed photographs and the magazines, and a hair clip of Kat's. Finally I reach the receiver and lift it: 'Hullo . . .'

'Is that Rosie Martin?'

'Ye-es . . .' I sound slurred and confused, even to my own ears.

'Oh, hullo. Rob Stewart here. We met at the Vincents' party the other night.'

'Hmmm . . . er . . .' My mind is blank.

158

'The one at the piano: do you remember?'

Yes, I do. Why is he . . .?

'I just thought you might be interested in a very practical guide to divorce?'

'What?' My astonishment makes him clear his throat in embarrassment.

'Er . . . It will see you through the legalese. It's written by a divorce lawyer – friend of mine, in fact – and aimed at clients going through it . . . Anyway, I just thought it might be helpful since . . . uhm . . . you said you were still in the process . . .'

'How kind. Yes, I'd love to have a look.' I'm hiccoughing as I speak. 'Thank you.'

'Are you all right?' Rob the lawyer sounds concerned. 'You're not crying are you?'

'Actually,' my voice trembles, 'I am.' And I promptly start sobbing again.

'Oh, Rosie, don't.' The lawyer sounds genuinely sorry. 'Honestly, it will pass.' He listens to me a bit and then: 'It's this time of year, isn't it? I mean, everyone is merry and cosy and playing happy families at home and . . .' This unleashes a new torrent of whimpers and sobs. 'Oh look, you mustn't cry. You're making me feel terrible. What can I do? Why don't I bring over this book? You'll have something to read over the next few days, to pass the time.'

'Oh.' I'm taken aback by this suggestion. 'Come here?' I look around wildly.

'Why not? You're on my way home and there's no traffic at the moment. Don't worry, I'll just drop it in your postbox, or through the door – you won't have to even open the door to me.'

'OK. Come over,' I offer tentatively; then, more decisively, 'Yes, come over.'

When I hang up the phone, though, I wonder what in the world I'm playing at. I hardly know this man and here I am, inviting him home. Well, not exactly, but I'm allowing him to drop off the book, and that's bad enough. With an effort, I stand up and slink over to the mirror in the hallway: I am a wreck, a mascara-splotched, red-eyed apparition.

The door bell rings. Omigod, I spin round to face the front door; how did he get here so quick? I must rub my eyes clean, find a comb, splash my face with cold water . . . 'Wait a second!' I cry.

'Hi, Rosie, it's me, Carolyn!' a cheerful voice calls out.

Arghhhhh . . . the last thing I want is that vision of perfect womanhood on my doorstep.

'Oh, Carolyn!' I walk towards the door. I can't open it, looking like this. Clutching my hair in dismay, I grab Freddy's black woollen ski mask, which he forgot to pack, from the coat rack in the hall. I slip it on. She recoils involuntarily at the sight of me, as I open the door.

'Ros— help!!!!' Carolyn yelps. 'What *are* you wearing?'

'This?' I say breezily, as if wearing a black woollen ski mask indoors is perfectly normal. 'I'm cold.' Then, rubbing my arms in an exaggerated fashion, 'Brrr . . .'

'I hope you're not coming down with something, on top of everything else.' Carolyn gives me a pitying look. She is wearing, I'm depressed to see, a perfectly matching and very flattering skirt and jumper set in creamy cashmere.

'I feel slightly awkward,' Carolyn says. So do I, in my woollen mask. 'It's my friend Rob Stewart. He asked me for your telephone number and I' – she shoots me an embarrassed look – 'I gave it to him. And then I got worried that maybe, as a woman alone, you might feel vulnerable and . . .'

'Oh, don't worry' – the wool tickles my nostrils slightly, and I adjust the holes to fit my features better – 'he's already rung. He's coming over with the book.'

'He's rung already?! He's coming over?!' Carolyn looks taken aback – and a little suspicious.

'He wanted to bring me a book about divorce,' I explain, wondering if I need to invite her in or can dispatch her quickly.

'Oh.' Carolyn gives me a long look that strikes me as vaguely familiar. 'You do know he's married, don't you? Serena is a very high-powered lawyer too.' I recognise the look now: it's the one the women at Jill's Sunday lunch gave me. A look that spells out clearly that I am the predatory divorcée who cannot be trusted with other women's husbands.

'I know he's married, yes.' I smile to myself. 'I'd better go though, Carolyn, I really need to see what's wrong with the heating. Need to fix it before' – I pause for emphasis – 'I entertain your friend.'

With that, I dispatch my neighbour.

*   *   *

161

By the time the door bell rings again, I've washed my face and put some fresh makeup on, I've undone the top three buttons of my Cath Kidston tea dress, and casually un-buttoned the cardigan. I open the door to Rob Stewart.

'Oh!' he exclaims, caught in the act of pushing a carrier bag through our letter box. 'I didn't think you'd be up to seeing anyone...'

'No, come in. I could do with some company.' I let him in.

'Well, if you're sure.' Rob eyes me warily, as if scared that I might burst into tears again.

I lead him into the sitting room. After my flash tidying session before he came, the room looks warm and inviting. I've hurled all evidence of the children into cupboards and turned on the gas fire.

'What about a drink?' I go to the drinks cupboard. 'It's not six yet, but it's dark and it's the season to be jolly. Gin and tonic, vodka and tonic, red wine...?'

'Wine would be lovely, thank you.' He is still holding on to the carrier bag he has wrapped around the book. 'And here's the book. Everyone tells me it's helpful.'

'Thanks!' I hand over a glass, take the book. 'Hmmm... *For Richer But Not for Poorer: How to Keep Divorce from Bankrupting You* – Snazzy title.' I sound dubious. I start leafing through it, eyes lighting upon the chapter headings: 'Don't Be a Softy: Why Playing Hardball With Your Ex Will Set You Up Nicely', 'The Spy Who Went for the Gold: When Divorce Espionage is Necessary', and 'Plundering the Wreckage: How to Claim Your Possessions in a Split'.

'Well, it covers all the main areas, doesn't it?' I raise my glass in a toast: 'Cheers.'

I sound cheerless, but Rob the lawyer doesn't mind. He looks around the sitting room, taps his fingers on the crystal coffee table, and nods. 'The house is nice. Could be' – he blushes and looks uncomfortable – 'well, in the trade we'd call this a great asset.'

'We've paid off the mortgage.' I feel slightly crass to be discussing my finances with a stranger. But he's a pro, after all.

'If you can walk away with this, plus something for bringing up the children, you'll be fine, Rosie, seriously.' Rob gives me an encouraging smile. There's something soft about him that is very appealing, I think, something about the kind brown eyes behind the spectacles, and the way he doesn't jut out his chin when he talks. 'I know it's not something you're ready to hear at this point – but in a divorce money makes a huge difference. Walk away with an unfair settlement and, no matter how determined you are to make it civilised, the divorce becomes hell on earth.' Rob leans against the fridge with its school schedules and Kat's sticker of Zac Efron. 'Walk away with your fair share and you'll feel the pill is bitter, but it won't choke you. I never asked you who represents you . . .?'

'Charles Mallaby-Steer.'

Rob lets out a long whistle. 'He's tops. Our industry is filled with scavengers swooping around the carcass of a marriage. Mallaby-Steer is one of those who've grown fattest on it.' He laughs and I smile encouragingly. 'If his past record is anything to go by, you'll walk from this very comfortably off.' He shoots me a shy look. 'Your ex initiated proceedings?'

'Yes.' I am leading us back into the sitting room, where I sink into the sofa by the fire. Rob, I notice, sits down beside me. 'Fell in love with a colleague. An American woman. I was shocked because I'd never thought him capable of that kind of thing. But we'd grown apart – I just hadn't realised how much.' I have finished my wine before he's finished his, rather embarrassingly. As I get up to take the bottle from the kitchen, I feel pleasantly naughty: I'm sitting here, drinking before six with a stranger, discussing relations between the sexes. I fill my glass and then, as he empties his, Rob's.

'It's amazing how many men lead double lives.' Rob raises his glass in a second toast, 'I've got a client who claimed he was MI6, swore his wife to secrecy, convinced her that he was a hero battling for queen and country in hot spots around the globe, while in fact he was sneaking off for steamy sex with his mistress in Fulham.'

'Gosh,' I gulp.

'Another one made up a rich aunt on her death bed, who had promised him her fortune and made him dance attendance. So he'd be home late, go off on weekends and have endless long meetings with "Aunty", all with the wife's blessing.'

'Oh dear.' All this subterfuge for a bit of sex?

'I'd better stop,' Rob laughs, 'or I'll be putting you off men completely.'

'Don't worry. I won't be put off. I'll just proceed with

caution, that's all.' I give him a sideways look. He does the same, and we both immediately look away. The wine has put me in a good mood. Or is it a handsome man beside me on the sofa?

'The thing to remember is that, when it works, marriage is the best club of all. Think of all the nice people who really believe in honesty and loyalty and patience.' Rob smiles. 'People like you.'

I look away, embarrassed. We sit and sip in silence.

'But when it doesn't work – God, it's miserable.' Rob has settled back in the sofa with his glass of wine. 'You know, sometimes I get home to Serena and she'll be talking and talking and about an hour in she'll say, "What do you say to that?" and I realise I haven't been there at all. Just like a sleepwalker.'

I now realise Rob the lawyer is not talking about marriages in general but his marriage in particular.

'Yes,' I murmur.

'It makes me feel so guilty, you know, but I can't help myself: there she is, with her briefs and her Law Society dinners and her favourite judges . . . I know I should care, but I feel a million miles removed.' He looks at me, unseeing, and takes another big gulp of wine. 'I don't know why I'm telling you all this.'

'Have you thought of leaving? You don't have any children do you?'

'Basically, if I'm being honest, I'd get a divorce tomorrow if I wasn't so frightened of the expense. And of her.'

'I wouldn't worry about the expense . . .'

165

'You must be joking!' Rob blurts. 'Serena's known as "the husband beater" on the court circuit.' He pauses, shakes his head disconsolately. I realise his wife must have been Jill's divorce lawyer. 'She'd go for the jugular. I'd be ruined and a wreck.'

'Then I guess you'd better hang on in there.'

Rob the lawyer slips his spectacles off, folds them and sets them on the table in front of him. Then he gently takes my glass from my hand: 'May I do something? Just once, and we'll never refer to it again? May I kiss you?'

A kiss is just a kiss. Except when it is between a woman who's been left by her husband and a man too scared to leave his wife.

'I think we'd better stop,' I gasp when Rob has finally pulled his lips from mine.

'Not yet.' He grips my arms. For such a slim man he is surprisingly strong. His eyes have gone all gooey chocolate and I realise that Jonathan hasn't kissed me like this for at least five years. And there's nothing sexier than a proper kiss. This one is at once tender and rough, a getting-to-know-you exploration that leads to a gottahaveyou explosion.

He's only touching my mouth yet every part of my body is responding: my eyes, nipples, for God's sake even my nostrils. I feel fabulous, warm and slinky. Rob caresses my throat, my right breast, and I hear myself purring.

'I cannot believe anyone would leave you,' Rob whispers as he nuzzles my throat, then my ear. I feel sensations I'd forgotten, and am scared of how ravenous I am for IT. I feel as deprived of good old-fashioned sex as if I'd spent the last seven years locked up in a convent, surrounded by a shark-infested moat. Rob's hand works its way down my dress, then under it, only to swoop up again, and dive into my knickers, where it begins delicately but firmly to make me moan with pleasure. As Rob starts whispering 'God I want you' and 'Oh, you're gorgeous' I realise I haven't felt like this in years. Rob has me on the sofa, dress up around my hips, with him on top. I want this so much, my hands grip him as if he were saving me from drowning.

Suddenly I realise that if I don't stop I'm going to have an affair with a married man.

'Stop,' I whisper as I press my hands against Rob's chest.

'I can't,' his voice crackles with desire, 'I can't stop this. It's too good.'

I agree. I feel hot and light and positively tingling with electricity. But I won't play the Linda role.

'You'd better go,' I practically moan because it is so painful to stop. 'Rob, please!' I can barely manage to get the words out as I push his chest away from mine. 'You're someone else's husband.'

'Argh,' above me Rob issues a deep sigh of disappointment. He slowly tears himself away. 'I know.' He sits up, adjusts his sweater and shirt, which had come out of his corduroys. He is pink-faced and breathless. He sighs, and clears his throat. 'I know you're right. It's just that . . .' he takes my hand in his '. . . I liked you immensely, the moment I met you. You looked so sweet and cross and vulnerable.' He pecks my fingertips. 'You're lovely.'

We sit there, catching our breath, wondering at what might have been, in silence for a few minutes. Then Rob sighs, retrieves his spectacles, and slowly, regretfully stands. 'Rosie Martin' – he smiles down at me – 'don't worry. You'll get through this.'

I stand up too. 'Comb your hair,' I advise. Rob looks into the mirror above the mantelpiece, pats down his hair. Another sigh: I suspect regret over me has given way to regret over his incipient baldness. 'Men are obsessed with their hair,' Jonathan used to say, rubbing his hands with glee, 'which is why they'll spend millions a year to get Zelkin to grow it again.'

'If I promise never to . . . er . . . lay a hand on you, can we see each other again?' Rob's gentle brown eyes fix me through his spectacles. A sad little smile plays on his lips. 'I'll do lunch, or coffee.'

'Yes of course. But' – I wag my finger in mock-sternness – 'no more funny business.'

11

'Not a cavity in sight.' Dr Karovakis straightens up. I heave a sigh of relief and shut my mouth, finally. He's been prodding my gums and tapping my teeth for the past half an hour. 'But you've been grinding your teeth something awful.'

'Hmmmm . . .'

'Work stress? Credit crunch worries?' Dr Karovakis, a second-generation Greek with a mess of blue-black hair and tiny eyes behind thick glasses, crosses his arms and cocks his head to one side.

'We-ell . . . actually divorce.'

'Whew!' Dr Karovakis whistles. 'No wonder.'

'No wonder?' Am I that bad?

'I mean,' he beams me a big white smile, 'no wonder you're grinding. We'll fix that in no time: a plastic mouth-guard to be worn at night.'

Well, as there's no one to mind my plastic mouthful, I have little to lose.

'We'll get you in tiptop form.' Again the head to one side, as he studies me: 'And maybe . . . what about a perfect smile?'

'A perfect smile?' *What's wrong with mine?* I'm too proud to ask.

'White as snow!' Dr Karovakis beams at me again, and I notice that his own pearly-whites are really, really white. 'Bright as sunshine. Dazzling as diamonds.'

'You mean . . .?'

'I mean *that* –' he points to a bed in the corner of the room.

It looks like a sun-bed rather than a dentist's chair. Does he want me to get so super-tanned that my smile will appear all the more brilliant in contrast?

'What is it?'

'BestSmile. Absolutely guaranteed to get you a Hollywood smile in forty minutes. One session under this machine and – bleep!' He winks at me. 'You don't have to worry about acid solutions that leave your teeth so sensitive you can't enjoy a cup of tea.' There's a messianic gleam in my dentist's eyes. 'You don't have to go through two weeks of mouth-guards with itchy gels . . .'

'But I wasn't thinking of going through any of that.' I'm standing now, facing Dr Karovakis and noticing how little tufts of black chest hair peep up out of his white smock's collar.

'All my clients are doing it,' he purrs, eyeing me up and down. 'And most of my clients are like you.'

'Really?' I'm gathering my bags (Selfridge's for my control-top tights, Top Shop for Kat's jumper dress) and coat.

'Yes, all ladies in their thirties who want to go on looking great. Some of them are single, but most of them' – here Dr Karovakis's smile grows an inch at either end – 'are divorced, and dating again.' A pause. 'I'm divorced too, you know.' Here a hollow little laugh, followed by an injured tone: 'She said I was a workaholic. But does she think money grows on trees? I was supposed to keep her in a house in Primrose Hill, send our daughter to Godolphin, and drive a BMW. You can't do all that and work only nine to five.'

'I suppose not . . .' I try to sound noncommittal: I don't want another divorce story to listen to.

'She said I knew the insides of my patients' mouths better than hers. Which is *not* true, let me tell you. I know Sally's mouth like the back of my hand. Very pronounced incisors and one wisdom tooth that should have been pulled out but wasn't.'

'Oh?'

'It's awful, isn't it? They suck the life juices out of you, then spit you out and move on. Moved in with our vet – can you believe it? I was just beginning to get suspicious about Muffy needing so many injections, then she tells me. And she's taken my daughter as well.'

'Oh dear . . .'

Dr Karovakis throws his hands up in the air. 'I bring her up, I pay her bills, and now she's going to call another man "papa"!'

'No, no, I'm sure nothing of the sort.' Kat and Freddy would never call Linda 'Mummy'. Would they?

'I betcha.' Dr Karovakis shakes his big black head. 'What a life.' He sighs, look at me. 'Hey, you know, you're very easy to talk to.' Before I can say anything he turns back to his sales pitch.

'It's only £350. A bargain. One of my clients said it had completely restored her self-confidence after her husband left her for a twenty-three-year-old Russian model.'

'Hmm, £350 is a bit steep . . .' I'm not sure I can afford these kinds of expenses – especially given how much I'm having to fork out for Mallaby-Steer.

'You don't want to be caught off-guard now, do you?' Dr Karovakis takes a step closer to me. I can smell Calvin Klein aftershave: I'd bought some for Jonathan the Christmas before last but he never wore it. 'There's a lot of competition out there. And I don't know about you' – here he frowns – 'but I know that, after our split, I needed my confidence boosted, big time.'

I drop my bags and coat on to the chair I've just vacated.

'What's crucial' – Dr Karovakis can see that he's getting his message across, and his gaze and voice grow in intensity – 'is that when your friends see him with that new woman on his arm, you've got something else to show off.'

They won't see someone on my arm but they'll like what's in my mouth.

'Explain again how it works?'

'Oh, Rosie, what a big smile you have!' Jill teases me. 'You look a million dollars. Perfect for the Great Wedding Party.' We're having a coffee at her house, and sit on her black-and-white striped sofa, beneath David's elegant black-and-white photographs. Not for the first time, I ask myself how a child would fare in this pristine house.

'It's a wedding anniversary,' I remind her.

'How depressing to have to celebrate another couple's happy marriage,' Jill says archly. 'At least at a wedding, you know they've only got a fifty-fifty chance of staying together.' She lowers her voice in a conspiratorial whisper, as David is in the kitchen on the telephone. 'I have found you the perfect escort. He's nothing long term, but he's blond, bronzed, and frankly so sexy I almost fell for him before I'd properly committed to David.'

'Hmmm . . .' I remain sceptical: Jill's record in match-making has been pretty abysmal thus far.

'No, honestly!' Jill's voice crackles with a barely suppressed giggle. 'I know it didn't work out with Harry – though it was your fault: you could have made an effort instead of laughing maniacally while looking at those snaps of his pooches. He told me he was very hurt.'

'I really appreciate everything you're doing, I promise.' I try not to think of Harry's round pink face crumpling at my reaction when he asked me if I'd like one of Belle's perfect puppies. I try to forget Orlando's mad voices. And Max Lowell.

'I *am* trying,' Jill sounds miffed.

'So am I,' I tell her forlornly. 'So am I.'

'And it almost did work' – meaningful pause – 'with Max, didn't it?'

'I certainly liked him. But . . . he could have asked me out and he didn't.'

'Maybe he's biding his time . . .' Even as she says it, Jill sounds unconvinced.

'What? Waiting five months to ring me?'

'I just know that you and he would be great together.'

'I thought so too.'

'I don't suppose' – another meaningful pause – 'you'd dare invite him to the Vincents'?'

'Not in a million years.' My voice is steely with determination.

'Men like that – sometimes they need to be chased a bit.'

'I'm NOT chasing him,' I exclaim, cross. What kind of a desperado does Jill take me for?

I'm pacing the sitting room in my new shoes and an outfit that has seen me through half a dozen country weddings and one at Chelsea Town Hall. Where is Zac? I check my watch for the umpteenth time. The invitation reads 12 for 12.30, and it's already 12.15. Otilya has swooped up the children and taken them ice skating; Jonathan has rung rather surprisingly offering me a ride to the Orangery; and I've put on makeup and checked my reflection in the mirror several times already. I almost look the part, I think hopefully, but where oh where is my escort? 'Hey, I'll be at your place by 11.45. That gives us time to have a little drink before we take the taxi to Kensington.' Zac had rung me last night.

'Great,' I'd gushed, remembering the hunk I'd met at Jill's over drinks, 'but . . .' here I hesitated, hoping I wouldn't sound neurotic, 'don't be late.' I'd like to get as much bang out of my gorgeous buck as possible.

It has to be said that although Zac is indeed as gorgeous as Jill had enthused, he is also difficult to talk to – or so he seemed over drinks at Jill's.

'Anniversary party, huh?' Zac drawled as he studied me over the rim of his glass of Cava. He lay back in the chair, keeping his jean-clad legs wide apart, so that his crotch was very difficult to ignore. 'Any talent invited?'

'Talent?' I asked, puzzled: does that mean young pretty girls, in which case Zac is definitely the wrong man for this mission.

'Yeah,' Zac leaned forward, legs still splayed. 'I mean, anyone worth snapping?'

'Oh, of course.' Zac had been at pains to explain ever since he took off his Wild West-looking fringed suede jacket, that he was a hotshot photographer.

'Zinc Gallery, Oxo Gallery, Gem Gallery . . .' he rattled off the places where he's exhibited, 'and *Vogue*, *Harper's*, *Tatler*, Condé Nast, *Traveller's Interiors*, *Sunday Times* mag . . .' But doubting that the Vincents' guest-list included any celebs – even C-list ones – I shook my head.

'Afraid not, I think this will be pretty normal people.' I apologised, trying to keep my gaze eye-level. 'I hope it's not too boring for you.'

'Oh, Zac is never happier than at a party.'

Jill smiled benevolently at us both. She sat on the zebra-skin stool beside Zac, eyes shiny with excitement beneath her glossy black fringe: after the disappointments of Orlando, Max and Harry, I could see she thought things were going really well. She and David kept jumping up to check on the

175

ice in the kitchen, though we were not drinking cocktails; answered a phone I never heard ring; consulted one another on which tortilla chips to serve. You couldn't hope for keener matchmakers.

'Too true!' Zac ran a hand through his gorgeous locks and his drawl stretched each word like a criminal on a medieval rack. 'Par-ties are fu-un.' He placed his elbows on his knees. 'Best one I went to this year was the one Mick gave in Mustique for New Year's. Liz and Arun were there. So was Hughie.'

'Wow,' I said, impressed.

'Yeah. Amy was supposed to be there, but she never showed.' Zac rolled his beautiful green eyes. 'Probably done her head in.'

'Probably.' I tried to keep my end up, even though I had a flashback to sitting in the dentist's waiting room, which is where I usually leaf through *Hello!* and *OK!*

Something caught Zac's eye, and he stood up and peered at David's black-and-white photos decorating the wall. 'Hey, that's the Hotel Eden, isn't it? I shot Kylie there.'

'It's a great location,' David agreed.

'Rosie's got a great house for a shoot,' Jill winked at me.

'Yep.' David, sitting beside me on the sofa, nodded enthusiastically. 'Kind of traditional meets cutting edge, you know what I mean.'

'Cool.' Zac rewarded me with a sparkling smile nearly as white as my own. Then, to David: 'You ever take any photos there?'

'Er . . . no,' David admitted.

'But it might be worth checking it out' – Jill stepped in – 'for *Interiors* or *Elle Decoration*.'

'Fab. The last one I did for *Elle* was with Madonna and she saw this' – he showed me a thin red thread tied around his wrist – 'and just told me her whole life story, for hours on end.'

'What *is* that?' I asked.

'Kabbalah bracelet.' Zac moved it round and round his bronzed, manly wrist.

'Rosie's a very spiritual person,' Jill piped up from the sofa. 'She's really into . . . was it Yoga, darling? Or meditation?'

'Well . . . I . . .' I frowned, trying hard to please. 'Does Pilates count?'

I have all the confidence I need in this paragon being great arm-candy at the party today. If he shows up at all, I think grimly, as the grandfather clock on the mantelpiece sounds the half hour. Did I hear him right when he said we'd meet here? Should I ring his mobile and risk seeming neurotic? Should I text him? In the end, I decide I care more about what the Vincents' guests, and in particular Jonathan, think of me than about Zac's opinion and I ring his mobile.

It rings and rings, and I suddenly realise that the dial tone is foreign. Where *is* Prince Charming?

'Slushayu-vas?' The words are unfamiliar but the drawl is very recognisably Zac's.

'Hello?' I ask tentatively.

'Oh, it's you!' Zac reverts to English. He sounds rushed, impatient. 'Sorry, I didn't have a chance to ring you, but they've released Misha and I'm part of the only journalist team allowed here.'

'B-b-b-b-but where are you?'

'Where am I?!' Zac sounds shocked that I need to ask. 'St Petersburg, of course. Haven't you been watching the news?' He sounds almost outraged. 'Don't you know what's going on?'

Suddenly I'm the one in the wrong. I'm about to shout down the phone that I don't know who Misha is, or why he's big news, but that Zac is letting me down at a crucial moment in my life. Instead I hang up and gulp hard, as if I'm swallowing a huge boiled sweet rather than the bitter realisation that I'm on my own. Again.

I can feel tears welling. But I don't have a minute to lose. If I'm to go to this party, I've got to rush.

As I sit in the minicab, listening to the radio repeating 'local, local, local' and the Afghan driver swearing under his breath at every stop sign and red light we encounter, I tell myself that Misha is probably the most important political prisoner in the world, and really I shouldn't behave like a teenager ditched by her first date. But after telling myself to buck up, I dissolve in a panic as I realise I'm going to be late, and noticeable because of it. Everyone will turn to see me walk in on my own, the loser in their midst.

I don't notice St John's Wood High Street, or Maida Vale, or even the Canal, as we hurtle towards Kensington. The driver has sensed my anxiety and is driving like a fiend, sending the worry beads and the glass evil eye beating against the windscreen.

Poor Rosie, how sad, I can hear everyone say. And they're right.

The Orangery is a pretty conservatory of glass and mirrors and potted miniature orange trees. The midday sun fills it, as do about three hundred guests, scores of waiters, and round white tables, each with the initials C and L entwined in silver as a centrepiece.

I venture forth warily into this sunny space. Thank God I got my teeth whitened: everyone looks so perky and bright-eyed, wearing their best clothes and their party attitude. I walk in, and it looks like Noah's Ark, with everyone in twos; I help myself to a glass of champagne. Quickly I down half the bubbly, then tentatively, as the new shoes are unusually high for me, I approach the hosts.

Carolyn Vincent looks fabulous in a pale blue floaty number that manages total elegance even though it stops well short of her ankles; Louis looks dashing in an Italian-looking suit. Both smile and nod in acknowledgement of my appearance, and Carolyn peers over my shoulder, looking for my escort.

'You came on your own?' she whispers, then looks so sympathetic I bite my lip hard to stop the tears welling up again.

'He's a photographer. Had to fly to St Petersburg for Misha's release.' I try to look relaxed, as if in my new life this was par for the course. 'Only a few journalists have been allowed access,' I say importantly.

'Well, that's put us in our place then,' Louis laughs lovingly as he raises a toast to Carolyn. 'We come second place to a Panda.'

'Poor Misha,' Carolyn shakes her head. 'He did have bad indigestion. The vet said it was very painful!'

The Vincents laugh, while I reel from the realisation that I've been trumped by a bear. I watch my hosts move on to mill about with their guests, stopping at now one group, now another. I can't help feel a stab of pain: *they* managed to stay together, why couldn't we? Maybe it's all down to sex. You can tell that the Vincents still fancy each other like crazy: look at the way Louis pats his wife's bottom, the way she gives him a knowing look, as they pose for a photograph with arms wrapped around each other's waists. Jonathan and I still had the occasional wow sex – but usually it was more like a chat with your BF rather than a spontaneous combustion.

'Well, look who's here, Philip!' It's Ginger Simpson, looking enviably slim in a tight turquoise dress. 'Rosie Martin. We haven't seen you in ages . . .' Then, with a smug smile: 'On your own?'

'Yes.' I almost hang my head in shame.

'You look well,' Leo says kindly, clearly seeing how nervous I am.

'Yes, considering . . .' and Ginger again gives her patronising little smile.

'Oh, I think I see the Websters!' I utter an exclamation of false excitement. Anything to get away from her. I wander off, wishing I were anywhere else on earth.

'Hullo, hoped you'd be here.' Rob the lawyer sidles up to me.

'Hullo.' How could I forget that he would be invited! Thank goodness for Rob!

'You look pretty in pink.' For a moment I think this is a sly dig at my flush, having emptied my first glass already, and well into my second. But Rob's admiring eyes sweep my palest of pink dress. I feel a little secret thrill at his proximity and, as if he's read my thoughts, Rob draws closer and whispers, 'I know we did the right thing, but I still fantasise about what could have happened, you know . . .'

I blush, look down into my glass of champagne, and feel a stab of regret: why does he have to be married? This is one man who'd rather spend the day with me than with some animal in the zoo.

'You have no business looking so delectable.' Rob has moved close enough to look down my décolleté. Again, I feel that charge, and wish he were unattached and we were in a bedroom rather than the middle of a reception for three hundred.

'Don't be naughty,' I whisper back; but I grin, and I realise I'm not saying 'no', but 'if and when . . .'

'They look beautiful, don't they?' Rob looks at our hosts as they pose for yet another photo. 'The perfect advertisement for marriage.' He raises his flute at me. 'A divorcée who looks like a damsel in distress any man would wish to rescue.'

'Cheers.' We clink glasses.

'I'm so glad you're here.' Rob smiles and his soft brown eyes twinkle behind the spectacles. Hmmm, I think wistfully, does Rob have any idea just how welcome his attentions are?

'Me too.'

'Have you found someone suitable to sweep you off your feet?' Rob asks, eyes fixing me.

'Not yet. There's been the farmer who was obsessed with his Labrador and the photographer who went AWOL at' – here I cough – 'the wrong time . . . It's a desert out there.' I pull a face.

'Internet dating. That's the ticket.' Rob laughs, slightly sheepish. 'At least, that's what I hear.'

'Maybe that's my next step.' I sound unconvinced.

I look at the nice blondish hair, nice firm lips, nice nose. It's not just the memory of our hot and heavy session that draws me to him. There's an endearing whiff of melancholy about Rob, a little sigh of regret that life hasn't quite worked out the way it was supposed to. In comparison to the overpowering self-confidence of men like Jonathan, it's refreshing to meet someone who obviously has self-doubts.

'I wish you'd let me take you out to lunch,' Rob is whispering.

Out of the corner of my eye I spot Serena Stewart staring in our direction. I take a step back from Rob and am about to issue a warning, when Jonathan approaches us.

'I'm late. Couldn't find a cab.' He runs his fingers through his hair. 'God, I need a drink.' I see Rob the lawyer staring enviously at Jonathan's thick head of hair, then offering his hand. 'Hullo. Rob Stewart.'

'Jonathan Martin.' Jonathan shakes the hand and looks at Rob's hairline. I recognise the messianic glint in his eyes: he has spotted a potential Zelkin customer. 'I'm hot!' My ex-husband cunningly wipes away a sweaty lock. 'I must look like a pig, sweating like this . . . All this hair is such a nuisance.'

'I wish I had such worries!' Rob's sigh is absolutely genuine – and gives Jonathan the opening he had sought.

'You haven't heard of Zelkin then?'

I wince at the heavy-handed approach. I stand by and watch the two men sniff each other.

What not to do with a prospective love interest: compare him to your ex-husband. I can't believe I'm doing it, but here I am reviewing my impressions of Rob the lawyer, simply because he's standing beside Jonathan. The slim body suddenly looks slight, the firm lips part to show teeth that are far from white, the eyes look small behind his spectacles, the perfectly formed nose seems a bit girly when compared to Jonathan's larger manly features. Stop! I tell myself, and leaving the two men engrossed in their follicly-centred conversation I wander off for a look around the party.

Hats off to Carolyn: she's done this beautifully. The flowers give off a sweet scent, the waiters purr their offers of refills, the silver gleams. I can't think of many weddings that have been as perfectly orchestrated as this anniversary party.

The row of floor-to-ceiling windows trap the sun, turning London in March into midday in the tropics. The men hold their jackets over their shoulders, while the women have discarded their wraps.

A murmur from the guests makes me look up: the wall at one end of the conservatory is being used as a giant screen upon which a projector is casting a succession of images of the happy couple. Carolyn in a low-cut summer dress, stepping out of Louis's sports car. Carolyn, as a bride in white, and Louis, dashing in a dark suit, kissing under a rain of confetti. Carolyn – this one draws wolf whistles and claps – in a teeny bikini, being chased by a laughing Louis. Louis washing baby Molly in the bathtub. The whole family in what looks like an al fresco restaurant . . . I gulp. There, sitting at a table next to the Vincents', are a man and a woman, elbows on top of the table between them, right arms entwined as they drink from their wine glasses. They are young, smiling, with eyes only for one another. It's me and Jonathan. We had gone to Aix-en-Provence for our first weekend away from the children (toddlers, at the time). We had booked into the most marvellous inn, and had exhausted one another in lengthy and loud sessions of sex; the kind that were no longer possible at home. When we'd come down to dinner, hair wild and legs trembling, we'd been stunned to find the Vincents from next door sitting at a long table just in front of our inn. We spent almost ten minutes trying to explain that no, we didn't want to join them for a drink. By the time Carolyn had finally understood, we were too tired to go hunting for another restaurant and had crashed on to the chairs at the nearby table, giggling and whispering to each other throughout the meal.

I feel a knot in my throat. We look so perfect, sitting there, oblivious to the photographer, the table beside us, the waiter approaching . . . what went wrong? There was so much good there, so much love and lust and the children . . . how did our marriage fail?

'Madame, please find your place . . .' A waiter holds up a board on which a dozen round tables are drawn, with name tags for each table. I scour the tags, find mine – mercifully three down from Jonathan – and before I can study the names on either side, the waiter's off.

I make my way to table number 6.

'Rosie Martin – what a surprise!' I turn to find Max Lowell smiling at me.

12

I am so taken aback I gawp: what is Jill's attractive friend,
the man who never got in touch with me again after being
roped into giving tea to a dozen OAPs, doing here?!

'You're a friend of the Vincents?' I look so bewildered,
Max Lowell laughs.

'Small world, isn't it?' When he laughs his blue eyes crinkle
up in the nicest way. 'I've been looking after Carolyn's parents
for years. They live in Bath and are in my practice. How do
you know them?'

'They're my neighbours.'

Max pulls out a chair. 'Please . . .' he beckons to me. As I
sit down I'm about to ask him where he's sitting, when he
pulls up a chair beside me. 'You're here?' I squeak with delight.

'Yes. Carolyn has very cunningly placed the only two
singles in this room next to one another.'

I want to say that Jonathan is floating about somewhere

(on his own – Carolyn had told me proudly that she had 'banned that American from our do') but something checks me: I don't want to bring up my ex-husband with Max.

As Max introduces himself to the woman on his left, a red-haired stunner with an amazing cleavage, I realise that he is even more attractive than I remembered, taller and more striking. I like his deep voice, which instantly gets your attention; and his blue eyes have humour and warmth. I remember the way he had tried to raise my spirits after Jill's guests had been so hostile.

I remember the drive home, and the bitterness that had crept into his voice when he talked about gaining access to the children. And how he'd jumped into action over the OAPs' surprise visit; and the ease with which he made a dozen white-haired women feel like treasured guests. Yes, I think, I would like to see this man again. And again.

But Max Lowell obviously has this effect on quite a few women. I watch through narrowed eyes as the redhead leans towards him in flirtatious mode, placing her breasts right under his nose. He seems to be having a good time, I think jealously as the man on my right, a septuagenarian with an earpiece, slurps his sea bass and spinach while shouting at me about the appalling echo in the room, the disgusting things on telly these days, and the ludicrous women priests who're running and ruining his parish. I smile and nod, and feel the delicious sensation of Max Lowell's elbow sometimes inadvertently touching mine, and of his foot once tapping against mine, and then quickly retreating. I can hardly touch my food, I'm so excited.

'I feel like we never got a chance to finish our discussion properly last time around.' The waiter whips away my half-empty plate and Max leans over. 'Your surprise visitors took over, rather.'

'Yes. But you were perfect with them,' I beam, and hope against hope that there's no spinach caught between my teeth.

'Bedside manner. Years of practice.'

My thoughts go to the bedside, the bed, Max beside it . . . I blurt out:

'Those women loved you.'

'I think they loved YOU. And the scones. It was a very nice afternoon.'

So why did you disappear from my life? I want to ask him.

'It looks like you've figured out how to cope with the post-divorce blues.'

'Oh really?'

'Yes. Getting out there. Doing things. Not wallowing in self-pity.' Max smiles. 'Which, I must admit, was my way. I moped for four years. Even my sat nav sounded like she felt sorry for me.'

I laugh, prod the fish with my fork. 'Don't talk to me about sympathy: everyone decided that, if there was a divorce, there must be a victim. And that victim was me.'

'True: I don't think anyone's prepared for your version of divorce – no tears, no mess.'

'We-ell . . . it hasn't been quite as pain-free as I'd hoped,' I admit. 'For one thing, everyone's investing so much in our divorce that they can't bear for us to be friendly. It's like being in a pool, and someone dunks you, then you pop up, then someone else dunks you again. A few more times, and by the end you're exhausted. And you don't think you can do it any more.'

'Sorry.' Max frowns, pats his jacket, extracts his mobile phone, looking at once pleased and embarrassed. 'A message. This is rude, I know, but . . .' He looks down at the screen and his face lights up in a huge grin. For a second I feel a stab of jealousy: Please, please don't let it be another woman! 'My sons are apparently having a whale of a time.' He looks up from his phone: 'I parked them with Oscar and Molly Vincent.'

I smile back, supremely relieved.

'Getting better access?' I ask, after dessert as the waiter pours coffee into our cups.

'Still a struggle. But she's happier because of the move. She hated Bath.'

'What move?' I sound almost panic-stricken: he's just the type to be off to Africa to help out on some leper colony.

'I've been looking for you everywhere.' Jonathan materialises beside me. 'Do you need a lift home?' He leans down, hands on the table beside me, and says in a voice just loud enough for Max to hear: 'I'm ready to go. I had a right bore beside me.'

'N-n-n-no I'm fine.' I wish I could blink him away.

'Oh, hullo . . .?' Jonathan peers at Max as if he were a specimen under observation. 'Jonathan Martin –' He stretches out his hand.

'Hello. Max Lowell.'

190

I shut my eyes tight, open them again and issue a huge sigh of relief: even next to Jonathan, Max looks great. I needn't fear odious comparisons.

'Max, this is my ex-husband.' For the first time, I can say those words without oozing regret. 'Max,' I turn to Jonathan, 'is a GP –'

'Hold on a second,' Jonathan interrupts me. 'Did you say Max Lowell? *The* Max Lowell?'

'Well,' Max looks slightly embarrassed, 'that's my name.'

'You're the one who writes in the *Record*, aren't you?' Jonathan beams. 'I read you every week. I love your stuff. Spot on, every time.'

'Glad you like it.' Max looks positively uncomfortable with the praise.

'Yes, well, er, Jonathan, don't you think you should . . .' I try desperately to catch my ex-husband's eye and make him understand that his presence is unwanted.

'Have you ever done a column on trichology?' Jonathan ignores my raised eyebrows.

'No.' Max looks irritated. I can see he's not in the mood for this.

'Max,' I break in hurriedly, 'has been Carolyn's parents' GP for years. In Bath.'

'Yes. Carolyn's making me feel guilty about the move. She says she really wants me to look after them still, long distance.'

Again, the move. 'Where are you moving to?' I ask, tense.

'We're coming to London.'

Yippee! Not Africa. Is Ellie included in the 'we' who're

191

moving? I want to know. Or is there a new woman on the scene? And why won't my ex-husband get the hint and buzz off?

'I don't know if you've ever written anything about baldness cures?' Here, Jonathan gives a little chuckle. 'Not that you need it, of course . . .' And he gives Max's dark and very full head of hair an approving look.

'Jonathan!' A sleek, slim man with a shaved head and round red spectacles interrupts my ex before he can embarrass me further. 'You sly old dog, you!' The man's booming voice is slightly slurred, and he sways as he waves Jonathan to his table. Jonathan hesitates before leaving his favourite columnist, then, with an amiable pat on Max's shoulder, joins the red-spectacled man at the nearby table.

'I think I'll be off.' Max finishes his coffee.

Oh no: I don't want him leaving, when I've just found him again!

'Do you want a lift home?' He turns to me with a smile. 'I've got to pick up the boys from the Vincents'.'

Yes, please! I want to clap my hands. But the beam is wiped off my face when I overhear the bespectacled man saying loudly to Jonathan:

'I hear you've got yourself a real looker! A Yank, isn't she?'

I see Jonathan cringe, and Max set his jaw. 'Look, why don't we go? I've got the car parked around the corner.' Max stands up and pulls out my chair. Swiftly, and without a look in Jonathan's direction, he escorts me past the other tables, towards the cloakroom, then out into the sunshine.

'I'm sorry. Some men are idiots.' Max takes great strides

down the drive. I wonder if he includes Jonathan under that umbrella term. I'm in no doubt when he goes on:

'What was a nice girl like you doing with a man like that?'

'Put it down to inexperience.'

'That's my line. One day I was inexperienced, the next I was in hell.'

Max is walking so fast, I'm finding it difficult to keep up on my high heels.

It takes us only a few minutes to find the Volvo, and then I'm back among the sweet wrappers and sports socks and another Red Bull tin (this one unopened) as well as a map that looks as ancient as the car. I feel incredibly tense.

'Are the boys staying in Bath?' I need to know, urgently, who is the 'we' moving up to London.

'No.' Max is grinning as he drives. 'Ellie jumped at the chance of moving with the twins back to London. She always resented my taking her away from here. They're ten, so they were changing school in any case.'

I'm still in the dark about Max's set-up, but I don't dare probe any more. We're driving towards Marble Arch, and the usual Saturday afternoon traffic slows us down.

I steal a look at Max's profile. Despite the congestion, and the pressure of running late, he looks relaxed. I like the way he sits back in his seat, hands lightly resting on the wheel before him, taking in the scene of buses and cars and cyclists, shops and hotels. I like the way he doesn't flap when a cyclist tries to cut in just in front of him, swerving dangerously as she does so. And I really like the way he looks.

Stop! I chide myself. *You're getting smitten about someone who so far, has not exactly exhibited a huge amount of interest in you.*

'I'm looking forward to a change.' Max looks straight ahead as he manoeuvres us between two taxis. 'Anything must be better than the past four years. I feel like I've been in a GP's waiting room, waiting for my turn to have the drug that will get rid of this pain.'

'Four years,' I say quietly, 'is a long time to be in pain.'

'Yes. And it's a long time to sit around waiting,' Max agrees. He turns to look at me. 'Though you know what they say: It's not how long you wait, it's who you're waiting for.'

I feel a surge of optimism and lust.

We drive on for a while in silence. I wonder what Ellie is like. A striking natural blonde who could pass for Elle Macpherson? Or maybe an exotic brunette with a feline expression and a sinuous body? Has she let go of her ex, or is she determined to stay at the centre of his life? Is she grasping? Is she meddlesome? Does she hound him every day with phone calls and emails?

'Moving back here will be good for Ellie too. She's got friends here, contacts, buyers. And' – here he shoots me a quick look – 'the man she's seeing lives here.'

Then Ellie is not interested in Max, she's taken, she's no threat . . . I sigh with relief.

'Poor guy,' Max shakes his head, 'I almost feel I should warn him. She's ruthless. Sweeps you off your feet – and then leaves you lying on the floor.' Max turns into the Edgware Road, avoids running over a pedestrian who suddenly decides to cross the road, looking neither left nor right. 'Sorry,' he suddenly gives me a long look, 'other people's divorce stories are a bore.'

'Not necessarily.' I pause. I want to say, *Not when I'm so interested in one half of the couple*; but Max interrupts me:

'Did you go in for marriage counselling?'

I shake my head. 'Not for long. By the time we got there, we'd made up our minds to go through with the divorce.'

'Ellie and I did it for a few months. By which stage, we'd raised so many painful issues, I felt emotionally exhausted.'

How long will it take him to get over that?

'I have a confession to make.' Max steals a sideways glance at me. 'You were one of my New Year's resolutions.'

I'm so struck by this disclosure that for a while I can't speak. Then, when I trust myself not to squeak with delight, I utter a long, 'Ohhhhhhhh . . .?'

'I told myself that you were a great opportunity that had come my way. And that I was an idiot to let you slip through my fingers.'

I sit, stunned, as we suddenly lurch forward. Max Lowell is saying that he thinks I'm worth his while. Max Lowell is letting me know that he has been thinking about me. I try to stop the smile that wants to take over my lips. While Max changes lanes, I study the man beside me. Long lean thighs. Muscular arms. Beautiful hands. Handsome profile. A mouth parted in a half smile so suggestive that I feel like a shy virgin. *I-want-this-man*, I silently spell out *my* resolution.

'It will be easier now that you're in London,' I venture.

'Yes. Camden.' Max grins. 'A bit of a come-down from

Bath, but when you've got to keep two households, you can't be precious.'

I will him to ask me out. *Do it, do it, please, Max, say the words. Give me a date – before we get home and you have to deal with your children and I with mine.*

But he's silent. I see the Edgware Road disappear behind us, tourists, down-at-heel locals, and long-robed men spilling out of its cafés, hotels and twenty-four-hour shops. I notice with regret that we're gaining on the cars in front, and rumbling towards Swiss Cottage all too quickly. I secretly wish the traffic would bring us to a standstill again, forcing Max and me in close proximity, in this car, for another hour or three.

Instead it seems a matter of a few seconds only, and then we're in front of my house – and the Vincents'.

'Thank you so much,' I murmur. 'For . . .' here I pause, and I hope he notices '. . . for everything.' I mean it: I want to tell him how much I like him.

'Well . . .' Max turns to me, 'I'm glad we met up again. I didn't think I'd enjoy a wedding anniversary.' Happiness fills me, and then, as he lightly taps my forearm with his index finger, lust. In fact, lust doesn't just fill me, it throbs, sings, bursts inside me. I feel light-headed and suddenly incredibly confident: I'll tell him how much I too have enjoyed this, how much I would like to see him again, and how . . . The Vincents' door flies open and two curly-haired boys run zigzagging towards us.

Max, unaware of his sons' approach, gives me a warm smile. 'We should . . .'

Get together? Get to know each other? Go out tomorrow night? I want to fill in the blanks but just as I prepare my answer – the quickest most resounding YES ever – 'Daddy!' the first boy flings open the car door and throws his arms around Max.

'Daddy!' the second tackles his twin from behind in order to burrow into his father. 'Was it fun?!'

'Yes, er, yes.' Max hugs them both then gently peels them off. He gets out of the car, stands on the pavement beside it. 'This is Rosie Martin, boys.'

'Oh?' They peer at me suspiciously.

'Hullo?' One, in a black fleece, addresses me grudgingly, after Max prods his back.

'Manners, boys, manners. Introduce yourselves, please.' Max is sweetly anxious that they should make a good impression.

'I'm Will.' The one in black proffers a limp paw.

'Sam.' The other one, in a red puffer jacket, gives me a dirty look from beneath his brown curls.

'Hello.' I try a friendly smile. The boys scowl. 'I live next door,' I try again. I really do like children, and I usually get on very well with them. 'I've got a boy and a girl of about your age. They've gone ice-skating, but they'll be back soon. How about some tea?'

'What do you say, boys?' Max turns expectantly from one to the other of the identical boys. 'Sounds good, eh?'

'Nah . . .' Will kicks against the pavement, not deigning to look my way. 'You promised we'd go see a film when you got back.'

'Please, Daddy!' Sam sounds incredibly cross. 'We haven't seen you all day!'

'Of course we'll go to the film.' Max, eyebrows raised in despair, looks at me over the boys' heads. 'I just thought a cup of tea to revive your poor old Dad . . .'

'Come,' I tell the boys who stand on the cement path that leads to the Vincents' house, blocking me. I sidestep them by cutting across the grass. 'A quick cuppa for everyone.' I must take the situation firmly in hand, I tell myself as I try to march confidently, head back, chin up, across the grass. I don't want my love life scuppered by Max's twins and . . . For a moment, I feel as if my right foot is being pulled, and I am losing my balance. Then SPLAT! I trip, and land so hard on my knees and hands that I'm on all fours, the breath knocked out of me, unable to so much as twitch.

'Rosie!' Max's cry reaches me as if from a great distance.

A mischievous 'Ooooops!' resounds somewhere near me, and I spot one of Max's little horrors biting his lip so as not to laugh.

'Oh no!' The other one comes to stand beside me. 'Our trap!' I notice he does not volunteer to help me up. I also notice that my pink dress is torn, and my coat muddy at the knees.

'You've ruined it.' Sam (or is it Will?) looks down accusingly.

'Here, Rosie, let me help you up.' Max holds out a hand, then pulls me up. 'Are you all right?'

My knees ache, my coat is muddy, my dress is ripped: I feel like an idiot.

'Here –' Sam or Will says as he hands me something shiny. I recognise the heel of one of my brand new shoes. I breathe in deeply. I say nothing. I've seen the look of pride on Max's face and I don't want to alienate him by letting him know what I think of his offspring. I struggle to smile. 'Don't worry, I'm all right . . . Sorry to have ruined your trap, boys.'

'Let me get you home.' Max's hand is under my elbow, and I lean against him more than I need, limping so that he wraps his arm around my waist and holds me tight. Fifteen all, I mentally address the twins, as they tag along sulkily to my front door. 'Will, give me a hand here, hold her bag.' Max, all concern, ignores the boys' black looks. 'Can you manage with the keys?'

'Dad, she's fallen on her knees, not broken her fingers, you know,' grumbles Will, my little handbag dangling from his hand.

'I think you should go back to the Vincents', boys, and tell Molly and Oscar and the babysitter where we are. I'll just make a cup of tea for Rosie here.'

I try to conceal my delight as I see the boys slowly make their way next door.

13

'Thank you for being such a good sport.' Max sounds genuinely grateful as he pilots me into the sitting room. 'They don't mean any harm, they're just a bit rambunctious . . .' He deposits me carefully on the sofa. I hold his arms as I lower myself slowly on to the cushions. Who cares about a bit of a bruise and a few rips in a dress when they earn you these precious attentions from Max Lowell? As I settle back in the sofa, I look up and meet his eyes.

'Does it hurt?' he asks me, his face a few inches from mine.

'No,' I whisper. I want to wrap my arms around his neck. I want to kiss him.

'I've spotted the kettle.' Max stands up abruptly and shatters my romantic fantasy. 'If you tell me where you keep the tea . . .'

To hell with tea, kiss me! I want to shout.

Instead, 'In the first cupboard above the sink,' I reply,

trying to keep my voice light and devoid of disappointment. I check my watch: I have an hour, maybe a bit longer before the children and Otilya come back from the ice-skating rink in Bayswater.

'You know,' Max is talking as he fills the kettle, then rustles around the cupboard for the tea bags, 'I owe our mutual friend.'

'Carolyn? Louis?' I call out from the sofa.

'Jill.' Max comes to stand in the doorway. 'She told me about the job at her practice. And I'm pretty sure she's the one who swung it for me. She convinced the other partners to get me on board.'

'Jill? You're going to be working in Jill's practice?!' I can't believe my best friend never told me. 'When did all this happen?'

Max approaches me with two steaming mugs. Jill's machinations have taken me so much by surprise that I hardly register his sitting beside me on the sofa.

'She asked me back in October when Janet left the practice. But I didn't know if I'd be accepted by the others . . . I think that's all her work.'

'She never breathed a word . . .' I murmur. Why didn't she tell me? Didn't she think I might be interested? I'm at once cross and curious.

'She probably didn't think she should until it was signed sealed and delivered.' Max sets down his tea on the little table beside him.

'Maybe' – I look him straight in the eye – 'she didn't want to get my hopes up.' He's given me some encouragement, after all.

'Or mine,' and Max takes both my hands in his, draws them to his lips.

I hear a tremendous thump, and at first I think it's my heart registering all this excitement. Then, as I see Max look up, frown, and pull away immediately, I realise the sound is of someone knocking on the French windows. Not someone, in fact, I discover as I turn to see behind me, but two small and very cross identical boys.

'Oh . . . bother!' Max springs from the sofa like a jack in the box. I bite back far ruder words.

'I'm coming, I'm coming,' Max is telling the boys as he rakes a hand through his hair. 'I'm sorry,' he whispers to me. He reaches the door, then, hand on handle, he turns: 'I'll . . . I'll be in touch.'

'Why didn't you tell me he was coming to work with you?' I hiss into the phone, trying not to let Mrs Stevens over-hear me.

'Until about a fortnight ago I didn't think it was going to happen,' Jill explains, defensive. 'Janet was leaving, but I wasn't sure that Max was going to get the other partners' thumbs-up.' Jill chortles with pleasure: 'It's great, isn't it? And you know, I think he *is* interested in you, because he told me he'd been a fool not to follow up with you.'

'Well, I hope he follows up now.' I see Mrs Stevens peering at me over the folder she holds. 'And why didn't you warn me about how possessive his sons are?'

'Uh-uh, you've met the terrible twins!' Jill laughs. 'He adores them and is so worried they are damaged by the divorce. I suspect they're very good at manipulating poor old Max, and keeping interested women at bay.' She sighs. 'If they take after their mum, you're in trouble. Ellie's one of the hardest, most demanding women I've ever met. I know divorce is no picnic, but Max should be glad he got away.'

'I thought she was the one to get away . . .?' I can't resist probing.

'Well,' Jill lowers her voice, 'she suddenly decided she was a great artist, and that marriage was bourgeois and conventional. Kicked him out. She makes quite a lot of money from her painting, but she still got him to pay her a huge maintenance. He was very bitter about it.' Jill's voice fills with pity, then panic: 'Help! Gotta go, I'm seeing my IVF man!'

'You *are* talking to Mrs Kenyon, aren't you, Rose?!' Mrs Stevens bears down on me. 'I thought I'd made it clear that we needed to reach her this morning!'

'Er . . . yes, Mrs Stevens, yes, of course.' Do all jobs reduce you to feeling like a schoolgirl?

'Mrs Kenyon,' Mrs Stevens huffs beside me, 'has been a client of Dr Casey's for sixteen years, and expects us to remind her of her appointment the day before.'

'It's a Botox treatment, not open-heart surgery,' I can't help muttering.

'Did you *say* something, Rose?'

I give up.

By the time I'm walking home from the tube station, having first done my usual grocery shop, I've written half a dozen differently worded letters of resignation. I can't keep working like this, being scolded by Mrs Stevens, worrying about Dr Casey's integrity, and dealing with women who are obsessed with their wrinkles and age spots.

But once I step through the door, all thoughts of the job fly out the window.

'Mummy!' Freddy ignores the carrier bags in my hand and hugs me tight. 'I need to find a big map of Britain.'

'How was your day?' I try not to trip over him while lugging the bags into the kitchen.

'OK.' The voice sounds unconvinced. And the hand that has kept hold of my skirt gives it a little tug. 'Missed you.' It breaks my heart to see him so clingy. He has a new game these days: 'If Kat and Granny and I were trapped in a burning building, Mummy, and you could only save one of us, who would you save?'

'Freddy! What a silly question!' I chide him. It upsets me to think of him working out these horrible hypothetical situations.

'Mummy!' Kat comes running down the stairs in tears. 'I have to have a new PC – mine's crashing all the time!'

'Yes, darling, yes,' I murmur, wondering how I can possibly fix my daughter's PC when mine is still an inexplicable maze to me; and how I can possibly get her to stop texting Mungo during school, as it infuriates her teachers.

Otilya only now surfaces from sitting in front of the telly. She starts helping me unload the carrier bags.

'This country full of animals,' she tells me as she stacks tins in the cupboard. 'Murder, robbery, rape.' At this she raises her eyebrows at me. 'I leave my country and come here to look for gentleman. My friends, they tell me English men have good manners. Good clothes. Good sports. But it's not true. Men here like in Poland.'

'Hmmm . . . yes, Otilya.' I nod, distracted. The children ignore their babysitter's musings: her view of men, English as well as Polish, is by now familiar.

'Mummy!' Freddy is at my elbow still. 'What are we having for supper?'

I'm opening cupboards and the fridge, Freddy sticking to me, Kat still talking about her computer. I pick up a tin of tomatoes and one of baked beans distractedly, then leaf through the Yellow Pages for a local computer fix-it man, and listen to Otilya explain why tomorrow she will need to go home early (again).

In the midst of all this, the door bell rings.

'I asked Daddy to come round and mend my PC.' Kat smiles weakly at me. 'I hope that's OK.'

I want to scream: the last thing I need this evening is my ex surfacing. And yet, I look into my daughter's smile and I read the hope there, and I look into her eyes and see the fear.

'All right, darling.'

In the event, Jonathan is relaxed and cheerful, and charming to Otilya (who growls at him nonetheless, as he has proved himself to be no better than her Polish ex-husband). He basks in Kat's total conviction that Daddy will fix her computer, and in Freddy's cheers when he hands him the signed poster of the Arsenal team.

'It's a doddle, Kat, really.' Jonathan has brought our

daughter's PC down to the kitchen where he is patiently trying to fix it, brow frowning in concentration. 'She's got a perfectly good machine you know' – he turns to me – 'we needn't rush out to buy another one.'

'Do you want tea?' I ask casually. I feel ridiculously self-conscious about unpacking my groceries in front of him (what if he notices I've gone soft on what the children eat, and am allowing Coke, frozen chips and Rice Krispies? What if he realises I've started buying myself SlimLine ready-made range) but I am not really bothered about his approval; Max Lowell's, that would be another matter.

'Oh, Daddy, you're a star!' Kat claps her hands, kisses her father and runs upstairs with her PC.

'Arsène Wenger! Arsène Wenger!' Freddy chants happily to himself, staring at the line-up on his new poster.

'Why don't you take the poster up to your room?' Jonathan pats his son's bottom and turns him in the direction of the stairs. I can see my ex wants to discuss something: money? The weekend? Half-term?

'Linda really, really wants us all to see a counsellor.' Jonathan keeps his voice low. 'She thinks Kat can only handle virtual relationships and Freddy is regressing into babydom.'

'I won't hear of it.' I block my ears with my hands.

'Our daughter thinks she's "going out" with some pimply teen she's met *twice*! That's not normal, Rosie!'

'Would you rather that she was having a hot and passionate affair with him?'

'Linda's noticed that Freddy is lapsing into a baby voice the moment he leaves this house.'

'Has this woman thought about her role in my children's distress?' I'm furious.

'Well, I don't want them to feel they have no one to talk to.'

'No one to talk to?! Speak for yourself. I'm here, on call, 24/7, thank you very much.'

'If you really want the best for them' – he points upstairs – 'you cannot ignore the signs they're giving us of being . . . unsettled.'

I'm about to retort that if he'd been worried about the children feeling unsettled he would have made do with our marriage, just as I did, when Jonathan's mobile goes. The ring has changed: it used to be a gentle Chopin. Now it's the bullish, he-man Toreador song from *Carmen*.

'Hullo, darling . . .' He's talking to Linda, I realise. He sits up, half-smiles, concentrates on the voice in his ear.

'Everything's fine . . . yes, I've fixed it and I can be home soon . . . Can't talk right now . . .' Here a quick look in my direction. 'Whatever you like. Chinese, Indian, Japanese – you know I'm easy.' I cough in protest: when I *think* of the fuss my ex used to make every time I cooked for him. Jonathan frowns at me, then coos, 'Me too. Lots.' He presses the off button and turns to me with a smug smile. 'Linda is so punctual, she always worries when I'm not home by seven.'

His phone goes again. I groan: can't she leave him alone?

'Sorry about this –' he reaches for his jacket pocket again. But I see immediately it's not Linda.

'Yes. No. What?' He frowns in concentration. 'What?! Oh no . . .' My ex-husband's face sags into an expression of such anxiety that I feel an involuntary twinge of compassion. 'There's no way we can fight that. They're exaggerating, but in essence they're right. Damn it.'

He hangs up and turns to me. 'That was Miles.' Miles has been in charge of the production of Zelkin since its discovery. 'The *Medical Record* has just published a news story about Zelkin's side-effects. It's only a small item, but Miles is worried that there's more on the way.' He sinks his face in his hands. 'It could ruin Zelkin's reputation.' He brings away his hands. 'And then what happens to us?'

Jonathan's right. Within weeks of the *Medical Record* article, Zelkin sales plummet. Our nest egg has gone splat! and Jonathan and I are forced to reconsider our lives.

Our financial loss hits my ex-husband like an expert shot from Charles Mallaby-Steer's hunting rifle. It sends Jonathan reeling, trying desperately to protect our savings and save his professional reputation. He rings me two or three times a day with endless alternative plans: we have to sell the house, we can get away with not selling the house if I take in lodgers, Linda and he should find a cheaper place to rent, we should consider my going full-time, we should put the children in a state school . . .

'I won't skimp on the children's schooling.' I put my foot down.

'You're right, of course . . .' Jonathan's voice is broken.

'How did Linda react to your suggestion about moving out of the mews house?' I think I can guess.

'Linda is in shock. I don't think she has ever had to deal

with belt-tightening measures.' Jonathan pauses. 'In fact, she won't discuss money things with me.'

'That's not very helpful.' I can't help savouring my ex's mournful tone.

'I know. I'm going to sell all my shares: it's not a brilliant time, but I think it will bring in something.'

'I'll take a rain check on the counselling course and tell Dr Casey that I'd like a full-time post.'

'I'm sorry, Rose . . . I know how much you want to do the training. I'll make it up to you . . .'

In the end, we do have to put the house on the market, Linda and Jonathan have to move out of the mews into a flat, and I postpone my counselling course to work full-time.

'Rosie, you're being marvellous,' Jonathan repeats every time we speak. 'I cannot tell you what a relief it is to be able to count on you.'

'The only way we can get this right is if we work together.'

'You've been so understanding.'

'My lawyer won't be. He wants his pound of flesh.'

'Arghhhhhhhhh . . .' Jonathan wails into the phone. 'Can't you call off that hound?'

'The children are my priority.'

I doubt that I could have called off Charles Mallaby-Steer, in any case.

'Jonathan is in a bad way.' I could swear as I look at the walls that another trophy has been added to Charles Mallaby-Steer's collection.

'He should be,' my lawyer purrs like one of those great

cats he's probably shot on some safari. 'But he'll get over it. He's a bit stunned right now – I got him right between the eyes.'

'He says we're skinning him alive.'

'His ego's wounded. He'll drag himself away for a while, and lick his wounds.'

'You keep seeing him as the enemy.'

'Of course. And this enemy knows he's beaten,' Mallaby-Steer crows triumphantly. Then, lowering his voice: 'I had one of my chaps investigate the whole Zelkin saga. You're lucky you only have to sell the house. It's amazing no one ever brought a lawsuit against the company before. Some baldy' – Mallaby-Steer grins the superior grin of the man in full possession of his own hair – 'whose stomach cramps got serious.'

'Poor Jonathan.' I see my ex with a fox's pointy ears and thick tail, cowering before my lawyer in a hunter's get-up.

'Don't worry. He's a big beast. He'll survive.' Mallaby-Steer beams at me. 'And you will, too. Though it's sad about the house, and it might take a few months to sell it – it's a bad market out there.'

'Don't go losing your new kite!' I cry out in warning as Freddy runs out of the house. It's Sunday morning, and I'm taking the children to Primrose Hill. Jonathan is off to Lausanne for a pharmaceutical conference and can't have them this weekend.

'Kat! Come on!' I call upstairs: these days my daughter can take up to half an hour to find the right cap to wear with her shoes, or the scarf to match her hoodie.

'Coming . . .' My daughter comes down as if in a trance, hypnotised by the mobile in her hand.

'Oh, for goodness' sake, Kat!' I snap at her as she stumbles slightly on the last step. 'Can you just stop that texting!'

My daughter gives me a long hurt look. 'Mu-um, you're being really un-fair . . .' Her expression turns cross. 'Mungo and I are just deciding when we'll get a chance to text again, since he's off to Cornwall next weekend and apparently the signal's really bad there.'

'Good. Then we can have a normal conversation for once.'

'You just don't understand . . .' my daughter huffs, flicking her hair over her shoulder. 'Just because *you* don't have a relationship . . .' I hear her mutter under her breath. She saunters out the front door, head held high.

I bite my tongue: my daughter sees me as a failure in the relationship stakes. I wanted to be her role model, instead I serve as a warning. I, who wanted to spare her all unpleasantness and wrap her in loving memories, have shown her an experience she never wants to repeat.

'Kite! There's just enough breeze, Mum!' Freddy zooms about the garden, clutching the kite my mum sent him. 'Consolation prize, poor darling,' she had cooed over the phone to me this morning.

'Consolation?' I echoed.

'Yes. For being forced out of his home.'

I'm not sure even this thermodynamic Technicolor wonder will make up for the loss of Freddy's home, but I know better than to tell my mum that.

'How are *you* feeling about it all?' she asks.

'Pretty upset.' It's true: I feel vulnerable, frustrated and angry. Not only are we losing our home, but I'm having to postpone my life plans. Jonathan's appreciative of my sacrifices, but Linda has had such a fit about moving from the mews, he spent last weekend not, as scheduled, with the children, but at a spa in the Cotswolds to calm her down.

Above all, I'm upset for the children's sake. They keep telling me that they don't want to leave and that nowhere else can be their home.

Our home: I look around our sunny sitting room, with its ornate wooden mantelpiece over the large fireplace, the comfy armchairs, the long sofa we had to have cleaned two years ago because it had become so grungy with sticky finger-prints. Above it a large mirror twinkles; no matter what time of day, this room is always filled with sunlight. I remember bringing Kat as a baby here in the winter, in a Moses basket we set at my feet while I lay in the armchair pretending to read but in fact daydreaming about my wonderful new life. She learned to walk in this room (from Jonathan, squatting with camera in hand, to me, standing, arms outstretched by the door). Freddy, instead, took his first steps up the stairs: head down, shoulders up, little fists thrusting forward as if to push through some imaginary obstacle course.

This home has withstood children's birthday parties and sleep-overs; an adopted cat who for a summer clawed on every inch of wooden skirting she could find, only to ditch us for the neighbours down the road; and Freddy's Reception class, who came after a snowstorm cut short a visit to the Zoo and I, who had accompanied the trip, volunteered to make hot chocolate for everyone at home since we were only up the hill. Thirty five-year-olds with cocoa whiskers on their bright little faces filled kitchen and sitting room, clamouring for more biscuits.

'Run where I can see you!' I call out as the children rush down the hill. It's a breezy day but sunny, although on the news last night they promised showers: what else can you expect, in April? I'm at the top of Primrose Hill, London's skyline stretching beneath me. I see St Paul's and the Eye, the Gherkin and the BT Tower. Closer in, there's Regent's Park, and the extravagant nets that cover the bird cages of the Zoo. It's a view that never fails to raise my spirits, and that has become wonderfully familiar during the twelve years we have lived here. Below me, the grass that dips down the hill and then stretches all the way to the children's playground is dotted with families with young children, teenage couples, mums pushing prams, a father chasing two squealing, shrieking sons. I see Kat and Freddy running down with the kite floating between them, and when I hear their laughter I can't help but smile: they may have been shaken by the past year, but they haven't been blown off course.

But my happy relief evaporates when I ask myself once again the question that, despite the Zelkin bust, and the house for sale, has been at the back of my mind for days now: Why hasn't Max rung? It's almost three weeks since our near-kiss was rudely interrupted by his boys, and I have been tempted, at least a thousand times, to ring him. He had promised to get in touch but he never did.

I've been so desperate, I've sought Jill's advice.

214

'Ring him, you idiot!' my best friend snapped, impatient. 'You've got his number, or at least I do.'

'If he wanted to see me again, he would make an effort, Jill.' I shake my head, despondent.

'You're a grown-up. *You* want to see *him* again. Make it happen!'

But I can't: first Jonathan preferred Linda to me, then Zac preferred the Panda. ('I'm mortified: how do you get to thirty-five with priorities like that?' Jill had been appropriately contrite when I told her.) How can I expose myself again to a disappointment? It's no use explaining this to Jill, a go-getter whose self-confidence revs up after every disappointment like a sturdy dodgem car after a crash.

'Oh no!!!!!!!' The scream pricks my thought bubble. Instinctively, I know it's one of my children, and I raise a hand to shield my eyes from the sun. Yes, there they are, Freddy and Kat, a few hundred yards directly below me, looking up into the tree where their kite hangs forlornly.

I rush to join them, and as I do, I see the father and sons I had noticed earlier approach the tree. It takes me a second to recognise them.

'Max!' I wave. Then, more hesitant, 'Hi!' This chance encounter may be the last thing on earth he wants.

'Rosie!' Max comes over, beaming. 'It's great to see you!' He looks like he means it. I notice with relief that his boys are too busy trying to climb the plane tree to free the kite to bother with me. Kat and Freddy stand by, looking impressed, as Sam and Will tackle the impossibly smooth trunk.

'Kite yours?' Max points skyward. 'And them?' He smiles. He wears a crumpled and worn flannel shirt and jeans. He looks gorgeous and happy and extremely relaxed. I feel none of these things.

'Yes.' I try not to let on that I've been willing him to call for at least two weeks.

'I've been meaning to ring . . .' Max draws closer, his eyes on the children: his two are disentangling the kite, while my two whistle and clap appreciatively. 'But Ellie suddenly drove up one night and dumped the boys on my doorstep. She said she's got a commission to finish and no time "to be mumsy".' He rolls his eyes here. 'Thank goodness it's their half-term so I don't need to worry about school.'

'Gosh, you've had your hands full.' I look at the boys as they patiently explain to Kat and Freddy how to keep their kite from crashing into trees. 'Kat and Freddy are lost in admiration,' I whisper.

'Your lot look nice.' He grins. 'Your daughter's very pretty: like mother like daughter.'

I blush at the unexpected compliment. 'They're a bit shaken because it suddenly looks like we'll have to sell the house.' I don't want to go into the whys and wherefores, and Max doesn't probe. He merely raises an eyebrow.

'It's been your home for long?'

'Yes. It's the only home the children have ever known.'

'Poor things.' Max shakes his head sympathetically. 'My children went through the same thing when we moved to Bath. Ellie insisted that the boys see a child psychologist at that point. She said no one could expect children to cope with divorced parents *and* a new home all in the space of a few months.'

'You split up, and you can end up spending all your time and money seeing a catalogue of experts.'

'There's a whole raft of people who've made money out of my divorce.' Max's eyes turn sad. 'Doesn't bear thinking about.'

'I know.' I nod. 'It's the same with me and Jonathan. Far more people have a stake in our divorce than ever did in our marriage.'

'Mu-um!' Fred runs across the grass, the kite high behind him. 'Look!'

'Come on, let's do it from up the hill!' Sam or Will yells. I'm delighted to see the terrible twins seem far more relaxed about sharing their father with me now that I'm sharing my children with them.

'Isn't it great?' Max stops and looks up at the four little figures as they run back up Primrose Hill. 'They're so easy to please.' He smiles at me. 'Don't you wish grown-ups could be like that?'

Some grown-ups would be very easy to please, actually: just a word from you, or better still, an invitation for a date, and I'd be over the moon.

But 'You're right,' I say instead. 'Although,' I proceed cautiously, 'I find a great deal more pleasure nowadays than I did just a few months ago.' I wave back at Freddy up at the top of the hill.

'That's good.' Max gives me an encouraging pat on the back. He might as well have pushed me on the grass and forced his lips on to mine: I feel a tremor and a kick of adrenalin. 'So tell me: how are your plans for a good divorce coming along?' The voice is gently teasing, but the blue gaze is caressing.

'The selling of the house has raised the stakes. The children and I hate leaving, and Jonathan's feeling guilty and depressed because he can't deliver on his promise to keep everything as it was for them.' I look up. 'Money makes it really difficult not to get acrimonious. My lawyer wants to make sure we're going to be OK and he doesn't give a damn about hurting Jonathan in the process.'

'Divorce lawyers are the worst kind of vultures.'

'Not all divorce lawyers are the same.' I think of Rob Stewart. 'Some hold out hope. Like the one who told me that, after a while, divorce boils down to simple transactions: you get the children on the weekend so I can get a lie-in; I'll do Easter with them so you can go on the business trip . . .'

'Let me get lunch.' Max turns around, whistles and waves his arm. 'Boys! Come along! We're going to get a bite to eat!'

14

I turn down Max's offer of the little bistro round the corner: 'Let's go home. It's only a five-minute walk, and I've made a big lasagne.'

I insist, and Max gives in. I'm suddenly eager to show how spontaneous I am, how cosy our kitchen is, and how good my lasagne. I want him to see that I've managed my divorce in a way that means my family has survived despite everything.

The children run ahead, and as Max and I stroll up the hill, we fall into step.

'It won't be a traditional Sunday lunch,' I apologise. 'I love a good roast with potatoes and the works, but the children are usually with Jonathan on Sundays.'

'The boys will be delighted to have a proper meal at all.' Max kicks the football that rolls towards us back to its owners – a group of teenagers and a sweaty father. 'Ellie says she's a free spirit and she doesn't want to force a rigid schedule on the children.'

'Meal times are sacred.' I speak with conviction. 'It's the best way to make you feel you're still a family.'

'Agreed. Food glorious food.' Max smiles.

'You sound like the children!' I laugh. Then, growing serious: 'I do worry about them. Freddy's a bit clingy, Kat spends an inordinate amount of time texting a boy she's met twice in her life.'

'They look absolutely fine to me.'

'I hate being paranoid, but since the divorce everyone's been pointing out how damaging it is for my children.'

'I still dread the boys' reports.' Max nods. 'I'm so scared some teacher will say that they are struggling with French or the volume of a cube, because they are so scarred by the split.'

'I'm glad you think like that, too. Jonathan says I'm a drama queen when I do.'

'It's just what Ellie tells me.' Max laughs and I join in, delighting in yet another area where we can be complicit. 'I was a paranoid parent' – Max ticks off his fingers – 'a workaholic, but a dreamer. Oh and I haven't got a clue about how to make women happy.' This last is delivered with such a mischievous grin, I find it difficult to believe anyone in their right mind could find Max Lowell anything except every woman's dream come true. I don't know how to respond, so I don't.

'I think my biggest flaw in Jonathan's eyes' – I blow out a sigh – 'was that I didn't care who invented the telescope or the telegraph or . . .'

'He was a trivia buff, huh?' Max shakes his head, laughing. 'I shared a flat with a medical student like that. You couldn't mention anything without Michael droning on for hours about dates, facts, numbers.' Max looks at me, 'I bet he listens to *Brain of Britain*.'

'You guessed it!' I giggle.

'You giggle just like a little girl.' Max's hand rests lightly on my forearm. *This is really good,* I think, thrilled; *we're making progress.*

We walk up the steps to the house and in through the front door, left open by the children. Kat's playing hostess, pouring orange juice for the four of them. My eyes quickly scour the white tiled room with its elderly appliances and school schedules and artworks Blu-Tacked on every cupboard. The sun streams through the window, through which we can see an unruly patch of garden. The kitchen suddenly seems perfect, with Max here, ruffling his sons' hair, pecking Will on the forehead when the boy wraps his arms round his father's waist for a hug, taking a glass of Chablis from me with a big beam of gratitude.

'Mum, we're going to show Sam and Will our rooms,' Kat says as she leads the boys upstairs.

'I *like* this kitchen.' Max leans on the counter to watch me place the lasagne under a loose sheet of foil. 'I think I told you – it reminds me of my mum's.'

I remind him of his *mum*? OK, Sigmund, I ask an imaginary Freud, does he think me staid and old fashioned, or cosy and cuddly?

'It's so cosy and welcoming,' Max answers my silent query.

'Reminds me of watching her at the Aga while doing my homework.'

Oh good, I've struck just the right note then, and I take a big gulp of the Chablis, relieved.

'It must be heart-breaking to leave a place like this.' Max looks around the wooden cupboards with their childish artwork, the white tiles, the bay window.

'It's really hard,' I admit, and I have to squint in order to keep the tears from my eyes. 'Thirteen years. And most of them very happy.' I extract plates, glasses and cutlery from the cupboards behind us and start setting the table.

'That's probably what's helping you now.' Max lowers his voice, and draws closer. 'You have good memories. It means you have some idea of what a good marriage can be like.' He looks into his glass, and for a moment falls silent. 'But me . . . I don't know anything about good marriages. I just know that Ellie and I didn't have one.' He pauses, looks around the room again with a faint smile. 'When I was growing up, home was lovely, but Mum was a widow and I never knew what her relationship with Dad was like.' He looks up at me. 'Maybe it's because I never knew a good marriage that I can't conceive of a good divorce.'

The oven timer rings. I don't answer, but don my white and blue striped oven mitts and extract the lasagne. 'Will you call them, Max?'

'Boys! Kat! Freddy!' Max stands at the bottom of the staircase shouting up. 'I'd better fetch them, they can't hear me with all that racket.' Max goes upstairs.

For a brief exhilarating moment I picture us all living

222

together, in a house like this one, Max and I busy mending our hearts and the children's world. There's something so reassuring about Max's presence, as if nothing bad could ever happen again with him around. I used to feel the same with Jonathan, in the old days, but I realise now that he was more interested in protecting his routine and his interests. And Max makes me feel like talking – without fear of being found a bore or stupid. Despite his constant heartfelt praise for my listening skills, Jonathan never showed any such skills himself. Perhaps he thought mine made his redundant; or perhaps he never found my talk very interesting.

I look down at the table, and suddenly realise Max has been gone an awfully long time. I stand at the bottom of the stairs, ready to call out, when I spot him, stock still, on the landing above me. He motions me to join him and as I climb up, he brings a finger to his lips: the children have congregated in Kat's room and are discussing life. Or rather, divorce.

'The thing is,' one of the twins is saying, 'Mummy really *is* nice. Just not when Dad's around.'

'I know. Divorce brings out the dark side in everybody.' Kat puts on a lugubrious voice, sounding like the trailer of one of those teen vampire films she and Molly love.

'Don't you hate the way, when you mention one parent, the other gets all tense but pretends everything's normal?' the other twin asks.

'The worst thing is when one of them finds someone else but the other one doesn't . . .' With a jolt I realise Kat's talking about me. 'Makes you feel all protective, but also that you can't go out of the house or have a relationship. Otherwise they'll feel left behind.'

I make as if to speak, but Max's hand shoots over to cover my mouth. The touch of him shocks me into silence. Then, gently, he leads me down the stairs. We stand in the kitchen and I feel guilty at having secretly listened in on our children, feverish with the memory of Max's hand on my mouth, and totally devastated by the realisation that, after all our efforts, Jonathan and I have not managed to protect our children from the trauma of divorce. I don't want Kat to feel protective about me, or sorry for me. I don't want my babies to think that their father and I have a dark side that has surfaced with our split . . .

'It hurts, doesn't it, to hear them speak like that?' Max stands very close, and looks down at me with eyes full of sympathy.

I nod. 'I was hoping we'd managed to avoid it. We've been trying so hard . . .' I stand very still. Max is standing so close to me I can feel his breath.

'At least they don't blame themselves. And they don't hate us.' Max's hands are on my arms, and he pulls me towards him.

'Lasagne!' The children come rushing in.

Max and I step apart. I have to bite back the moan of disappointment as I serve everyone from the large terracotta dish. Max sits down in silence, looking as awkward as a twelve-year-old caught smoking in the school toilet. The children, impervious to the grown-ups' embarrassment, squabble about who is sitting where, make a lot of noise; the twins elbow each other in the ribs over some cheeky remark one of them makes.

'Yummy!' Freddy smacks his lips with gusto as he tastes a bite of lasagne. Then he turns to me, eyes wide with excitement. 'Will and Sam want us to go visit them when they move up here. Their mum is really nice and the two of you could become friends.'

'Hullo, Rosie, Jonathan, come on in.'

Julian McIntyre ('everyone calls me Jayjay') stretches out his hand to us in turn. He is, according to the pamphlet Jonathan handed me ten days ago, an accountant by training. But he looks like no accountant I've ever met; a personal trainer, more like. He's a very fit thirty-something and, in his sweater and jeans, extremely laid-back. He'd instructed us to dress in a similarly relaxed fashion: 'Please dress comfortably: mediation can be hard work,' read the pamphlet. I've obediently donned jeans and a cotton jumper from a mail-order catalogue. Jonathan, though, is wearing work clothes – navy linen jacket, beige linen trousers. No tie: nobody at the lab wears one.

'Look,' Jonathan had said two weeks ago on our doorstep (our every encounter seems to take place on our doorstep, with my ex-husband framed in the doorway, and the children either running in or out between us), 'it's getting too bitter with Mallaby-Steer. I think we could cut down our lawyers' fees. We agree, in essence, about what we want, what we're prepared to give up. We don't need these men in suits. I think we should sign up for mediation.'

Charles Mallaby-Steer was, predictably, furious: 'You're wimping out, Rosie, and frankly you're making a mistake. We can get him on his knees.'

'I'm sure, Charles, but it's not what I want. I want to try to settle this in as friendly a manner as possible . . .'

'"Friendly"? Who's ever made money out of being friendly?' my lawyer snorted. 'I don't approve.'

'I know. I appreciate your support, Charles, but I really want to try the mediation.'

'I hope you won't regret this,' his voice was resigned. 'And of course I'll provide you with all the relevant documents.' He paused. 'Just remember: the moment you want to stop the mediation stuff, I'm here.'

There are plenty of documents. Every financial transaction I've ever made seems to be crucial to Jayjay's work: bank statements, credit-card bills, pension plans, stocks and shares certificates, statements from Jonathan's health insurance – Jayjay needs them all. His office takes up the ground floor of a Victorian house in Hampstead. A tapestry in earthy greens and oranges – two hands, one female, one male, clasped – hangs above the fireplace. The woven rug repeats the motif of friendliness: two profiles touch foreheads. There are three armchairs and not a desk in sight, though a computer and a photocopier and a fax machine fill one corner of the room.

'I want this place to inspire positive feelings,' Jayjay almost drawls, he speaks so slowly. 'Couples uncoupling can be so bitter. I want to show it doesn't have to be this way.'

'Yes, yes . . .' Jonathan nods approval. When Jayjay turns to me, Jonathan gives a thumbs-up sign behind the mediator's back: finally, here is someone who agrees with our view of divorce.

'Can I offer you tea? Green, ginger, mint? The mint's special because my partner grows it in her garden.'

Her garden? Does our mediator keep marriage, or at least communal living, at arm's length?

'That sounds lovely.' I smile while Jonathan shakes his head. I watch Jayjay go to the kettle in the corner of the room and fix the tea. I notice he wears those ungainly MBT trainers, and that his jeans are Armani: mediation must be thriving. As he sets out a tray, every move is silent, measured, as if he's under water.

'Hmmm . . . the scent of mint makes me so happy. Jonathan, you sure I can't tempt you?'

The clock is ticking, but our mediator shows no sign of being in a hurry. On the other hand, at £100 a session, this is a bargain: Mallaby-Steer's bills are in the thousands.

'Here, Rosie –' Jayjay hands me a mug, keeps one for himself, beams us a well-exercised smile. 'I understand this whole process is a bit of a novelty for you, so I just want to explain what we're going to do. We'll meet for a couple – I *like* that word' – he winks at me – 'of three-hour sessions. Usually I can wrap things up in three. We'll focus on the two areas you and Jonathan have brought to the table: children and' – here he turns to Jonathan – 'money. This means full disclosure of assets, liabilities, income and expenditure. We're comfortable with that?'

Jonathan and I nod in unison. 'We've brought our documents' – Jonathan raises his thick manila folder for Jayjay's approval. I bring mine out of my canvas bag.

'Good.' Jayjay sips his mint tea, gives a satisfied smile. 'There may be times when I will call for a "caucus". That's when I meet with each of you separately to clear up any issue you have problems with. I'd like to make it absolutely clear that whatever information you share with me in caucus will not be reported to the other partner without your permission.'

Jayjay pauses, turns from me to Jonathan and back again. Again I notice how everything is in slow motion in this room. How relaxing. How disarming. Maybe this mediation is the answer after all.

'I'll prepare successive drafts of computer spreadsheets and a Draft Settlement Agreement and distribute copies to both of you at the end of each mediation session. At the conclusion of the mediation process, I will provide you each with a copy of the Draft Settlement Agreement. You will be free to review the Draft Settlement Agreement with your lawyers before we finalise it.'

'Sounds good.' Jonathan sits forward in the blue velvet armchair, expression full of hope.

'If you're happy too, Rosie, we can start.' Jayjay drops into the leather armchair, his mug on a writing pad. 'In today's session we'll do money.'

'Here are my documents.' Jonathan holds out his manila envelope again.

'And mine.' I hand over the long, tiresomely detailed forms I was up late last night filling out.

Jayjay has been forced to set down his mug in order to take our forms. 'Jonathan, you've done your calculations, and figured out how much you'll be owing Rosie in terms of child maintenance?'

'Of course I have!' Jonathan snaps impatiently. Then, almost embarrassed: 'The problem is, we separated when I was in a better financial position than I am now. That means I made some promises I may not be able to keep. And I hate that. But I know Rosie understands.'

'Do you, Rosie?'

'Well,' I concentrate on the woven rug, the two profiles that have come together, hers, framed with yellow yarn to her pink shoulder, his, framed with black curls, 'it's true that Jonathan's safety net has been taken away. It's not his fault. But' – I try to keep my voice steady and quiet – 'it is quite hard for me and the children to be turfed out of our home.'

'That's not fair, Rosie, I'm trying so hard to keep everything as easy for you as possible . . .'

'Jonathan, I agreed to the divorce because you'd found Linda. I agreed to keep things friendly. You should have access to the children. The one thing I asked was that you should help me keep the children's world intact. You've let them down.'

'Zelkin going bust is out of my control. Don't you think the children's welfare is one of my priorities?'

'I just think that they don't come first any more.'

'OK, the children are not my only priority. But do you really think I care less for them because of Linda?'

'I think you've got a limited budget and you're having to share it among five people instead of four.' I am pleased with the way I'm holding my voice quiet and firm.

'Rosie, have you come up with a figure that you would be happy with?' Jayjay studies me over his scarlet mug.

'Well . . .'

'You've got to take into account what's happened with Zelkin,' Jonathan warns as he looks at me.

'Yes.'

'Let's calculate' – Jayjay is writing something on his notepad – 'how much it costs Rosie to run the household, transport the children, school fees . . .'

'Oh gawd, how will I ever manage everything?' Jonathan slumps forward in his armchair, elbows on knees, chin propped up by his hands. 'Sorry . . .' he looks up at me, red-faced, 'I'm just really under pressure. You have no idea how badly she's taken this downturn . . . everything has to be top quality, only the best will do. Last night she had a fit because I suggested we should cancel our reservations at that pricey French restaurant in St John's Wood.'

'Jonathan,' I can't believe I have to reassure my ex about his lover, 'give her time to adjust. She knows this is completely out of your hands.'

Jayjay has been turning from me to Jonathan and back again, ping-pong style.

'She doesn't seem to. She keeps badgering me . . .'

'She looks a very competent woman. She'll cope beautifully. Eventually.'

'Eventually' – Jonathan sounds lugubrious – 'may be too late.'

'"Let this blonde bombshell blow your mind."'

'No. Awful.'

230

'"Yummy mummy on her own."'

'Nah – at this stage of the game, children are liabilities not assets.'

'"Let me light your fire."'

'Oh, David, you *are* hopeless!' Jill explodes. 'Give me that!' My best friend snatches her laptop from her husband's hands and curls up with it on my sofa. It's almost midnight, the children are asleep, and the three of us are sitting by the fire.

'Can't you think of something sexy so we can sell you online?' Jill looks at me as if I were a ten-year-old irritating her mum by refusing to practise her piano.

'I'm depressed. I can't think.'

'Can't say I blame her.' David passes over a bottle of Prosecco from a trip to Venice.

'I know, I know,' Jill says, but she's distracted; she's already admitted that she's worried because she's doing yet another IVF cycle and she just couldn't bear it to end in failure like the others.

'Zelkin, the house – and that's just on the financial front.'

'Yes.' Jill casts me a sympathetic look. 'First the dog man, then the panda man, now Max.'

'Atishoo!' David's brought back a stinking cold from his trip, which, for once, is not a figment of his imagination. He's sniffling and constantly dabbing his nose with tissues. 'I'm feeling so low . . .'

Join the club, I feel like telling him: a dozen strangers have come plodding through our home, peering into cupboards, issuing warnings about how 'you can't expect to get asking price these days, of course' and making nasty little comments like, 'Oooh, this is NOT how I'd do things.' Jonathan is depressed because of Linda's inability to rein in her spending. Mallaby-Steer is cross because he feels I should have been a 'hunter and not the hunk of meat that he drags in.' And in a few months' time I turn thirty-eight. I'll face my birthday on my own, without husband or lover. And what will I have to show for my thirty-eight years? I work for a butcher I don't respect, with a harridan I don't like. My children haven't come to terms with our divorce, and I've had to give up once again any hope of training myself into another job.

And that's not all: after what I thought were some pretty meaningful glances, Max Lowell has yet to ask me out. Since our cosy, lovely lunch, we've talked on the telephone (once) and he's sent me a text (twice). But nothing as conclusive as a proper invitation to share a meal or take in a movie.

'Give me a flavour of your personality . . .' Jill puts the laptop flat on her legs so she can type more comfortably.

I gaze through the windows. 'Hmmm . . .' My mind goes blank.

'Don't take all night.' Jill impatiently taps her fingers on her laptop. 'Just give me a few clues and I'll write it up for you. Shoot.'

'OK. I love family and friends, reading by the fire, and walking on the coastal path.' I watch Jill type furiously. 'And – oh, I don't know, travelling?'

'What about throwing in cooking, too?' David suggests, as Jill bangs away at the keyboard. 'Men love women who nurture.'

'Let's make these interests sound come-hitherish.' Jill stretches her hands wide over the keyboard while David looks over her shoulder. 'Help me, David,' she orders her husband.

'Well . . .' David scratches his head. 'Family and friends . . . the sea . . . walking . . . cooking . . .' Then, suddenly beaming: 'Hey, OK, what about this: "I love cuddling by the fire, and walking by the sea, and if you like home-made cooking, look no further than me."'

'How *naff*,' Jill and I moan in unison.

'Not naff,' David pipes up, offended. 'It's Rosie to a T. The nice divorcée next door.'

I take a long sip from my glass, trying the label on for size. 'This divorcée is still scared they're going to find her hacked to bits in some serial rapist's freezer.'

'*Will* you relax?' Jill shakes her head. 'I know a billion people who've done Match.com.' She crosses her long legs in their over-the-knee black boots, looking the perfect Miss Whiplash, in Match.com parlance. 'In fact, I'm pretty sure Cora, the receptionist at work, met her husband through it. Look at this' – she reads the website's introduction – '"Hundreds of thousands of people found someone to keep them warm at night. That's four large football stadiums filled with couples who've been walloped by love."' She turns to me and David. 'That's our mission: we won't rest until you're walloped by love.'

My profile on Match.com (user name: Second-chancer) has received twelve 'winks' – sent by members who are interested in me. Despite my initial reservations (what madman can hide behind the weasel words of an email?) I have to say that I am intrigued. Thanks to the internet I am in touch with a host of men whom I would otherwise never have met: a baker from Manchester, a teacher from Kent and a 'very Christian professional driver' from Chiswick.

'It's wonderful,' I confide in Rob the lawyer when he rings out of the blue one day. 'You don't meet face to face, so you don't give chemistry a chance to confuse you. I've already figured out that the baker is a bit crass, the teacher a bit of a nerd, and the Christian is too Christian for me.'

'I told you, didn't I?' Rob chuckles. 'The internet is the key. What's your Match.com name?'

'Second-chancer.'

Rob whistles. 'Spoken with true optimism.'

The one winker I do start to like is called GentlemanJim. He writes that he loves good cooking, travelling, and his idea of heaven is walking in Devon. He even has a house there: I go there every August for the month. Devon: I look up from the screen. We rented a cottage there for years for summer holidays.

I love reading by the fire too. I play the piano so that's what I would be doing. Serenading you while you read, GentlemanJim emails me.

Sounds perfect, I write, and press reply.

I'm glad you're not laughing at my being a hopeless romantic.

I love romance. I sometimes think I could still believe in it. While I wait for his reply I study his photo again: a He-man with plenty of blond hair. He looks young – thirty at most. But I suspect this is an old photo, used as bait by a middle-aged man.

You don't sound bitter. I'm glad. Too many divorcées are ground down by resentment.

I'm determined not to be. I want a good divorce. For my sake and the children's.

Children? How many? I don't have any.

I wonder what his marital status is. Would it be too forward of me to ask at this point?

Two.

Nice. My wife never wanted any.

Wife? Not ex-wife?

That should read: ex-wife. It's so recent, I sometimes slip into the old lingo. Recent, but it should have happened sooner.

What happened in his marriage? Does he live in London or in the country? What does he do?

I resent having to resort to the internet to meet a nice woman. Whatever happened to social interaction and friends introducing you to the single women they know?

Matchmaking, I write back, went out with the dowry.

Another excellent tradition.

Our email exchanges become something I look forward to over the next few days. I like to sit at my computer on my free mornings, with a cup of tea, and exchange a few pleasantries. I only spend a matter of minutes on our communications, as does Jim, but I find it gets my weekday off to a fun start. We enjoy just enough of a flirtation to make me feel as if

I have an appreciative audience during a little parenthesis of my everyday.

Hey, how would you feel about meeting up sometime?

I think about this. A week in, is he being too pushy? Do I trust him? What do I know about this man, after all? I have learned that he is forty-two (or so he claims), a lawyer (ditto), living in London. He sounds perfectly rational, but . . .

The problem with this internet thing is that our imagination starts running riot. Because you're not there in the flesh, I'm starting to create you just as I would like you – an ideal woman who probably doesn't exist. I'd like to meet the real you.

Hmmm, yes, but . . . I think. And read on:

Look, see when it feels comfortable for you. I'm ready – but I'll wait.

'Hi, er . . . GentlemanJim. It's Second-chancer.'

A pause on the phone. Then a warm laugh. 'Ah, Second-chancer. Sorry, you caught me off guard. I'm glad you rang.'

He sounds nice: good voice, classless accent, maybe slightly older than I thought from the picture. Forty-ish?

'I wanted to get beyond the codenames and the winking, which makes it all a bit silly.' GentlemanJim is articulate as well as warm-voiced.

'It feels odd, talking to you.'

'What's your real name?'

'Rosie.'

'Lovely name,' Jim enthuses. 'I bet it suits you, too.'

'And you? What's yours?'

'Mine? Oh . . .' there's the briefest pause. And then: 'James Robin Stewart. Jim for short.'

I enjoy my telephone chats with Jim. He makes me laugh. We keep it bright and breezy, no sexual allusions, no pressure to meet up. I make sure I ring him when the children are at school: I don't want the children to overhear me talking to him. Linda and Jonathan, with their never-ending displays of affection, are bad enough.

'I'm sure the appointment was for this afternoon at five!' Mrs Bretton-Hall, tightly wrapped in a greyish tweed suit, puffs out like a boa constrictor.

For the third time, I look down in the appointments book, spot her entry and shake my head. 'I'm afraid you were booked for three, Mrs Bretton-Hall.'

'You've made a mistake.' She is out of breath, and trembling with indignation. 'I MUST see Dr Casey today.' She leans forward, small pale eyes gleaming crossly. 'I have to look my best for the wedding next Saturday. I the fillings done today.'

'Your daughter's wedding – Caroline that nice boy who studied forestry at win over the boxy, bossy lady before how we can fit you in today.' I father's clock in the wood-pan to get the six fifteen to Ch

Mrs Bretton-Hall rus a page from a magazi be a close-up of Den

231

unlined face. 'I had booked these collagen fillers. She has a round face just like mine, you see . . .' She holds out the page for me to see the remarkable resemblance between Demi and herself.

'Hmmm, I see . . .' I begin, doubtfully, 'but . . .'

'Anything the matter?' Mrs Stevens bears down on us. The look of tender concern she gives Mrs Bretton-Hall is replaced by one of cold contempt when she turns to me: 'Have we made a mistake in our appointment schedule, Rose?'

I open my mouth to answer, but Mrs Bretton-Hall gets in there first, launching into a long explanation of how crucial it is that she should see Dr Casey, and has Mrs Stevens ever seen her look so wrinkled, it's all the stress of the wedding, and the preparations, and hiccoughs like this over her appointment, and . . .

I listen in silence. Beyond Mrs Bretton-Hall I can see three other middle-aged ladies sitting in reception, leafing through magazines or talking on their mobiles, waiting to see the man who will push back time and its unwanted advances.

'Rose!' Mrs Stevens stands so close to me, I can see the beads of perspiration on her upper lip. 'I'm sure you can do something for Mrs Bretton-Hall.' Then, with a smile at her client: 'Don't worry, Rose will fix things.'

As I walk home from the tube it's already dark. A light rain falls and the wind blows it into my face. I feel slow and defeated, cast down with the burden of feeling that I play an important role in the unimportant world of what Mrs Stevens keeps stressing is non-invasive cosmetic surgery.

Thank goodness I'm off tomorrow, but I dread Wednesday already. I've been on my best behaviour for weeks – ever since Jonathan warned me about Zelkin's disastrous fortunes. I have not exchanged emails with GentlemanJim from the office, I have scrupulously filed and tidied and noted. I have beamed at Dr Casey whenever he comes in with his 'top o' the morning' greetings, and offered to make Mrs Stevens tea every morning at eleven pronto, and then again at four.

My mobile rings, and quickly I search my handbag for it: as ever, my first thought is that something's amiss with one of the children. But it's Jill.

'Hi . . .' I shout into the phone as the wind swells.

'Hullo,' Jill sounds faint. 'I have a proposal. What would you say to working here with us?'

I gawp at the phone, then look up at the sky: did someone hear me up there?

'Anita, our main receptionist, is leaving in June. We've got two others at reception, but we have seven thousand patients. It's full-time . . .' Jill pauses. 'You don't need to give Dr Casey more than a month's notice, do you?'

'I-I . . .' I splutter. I'm so winded by the coincidence of her calling me now.

'Oh, and don't think I'm trying to matchmake or anything, but Max Lowell asked me about you this morning.'

15

'Come and meet some of the other partners,' Jill clucks like a protective hen, arm around my shoulder. 'Alicia and Ben, this is Rosie Martin – I told you about her, our new receptionist. She starts today, so everyone's to be on their best behaviour.'

Alicia, who looks about my age, is a pretty, slender brunette. 'It must be very different,' her brown eyes narrow as she sizes me up, 'from a small practice.'

Ben, a small, slim man with thin hair and thick spectacles, is more welcoming: 'You've really saved our bacon. You're the gatekeeper between us and seven thousand patients.'

Alicia picks up some folders from the counter and starts sorting through them: 'I hope you won't find it intimidating.' She makes it sound like a threat.

'Yes.' I try to smile.

It certainly does seem a bit intimidating. I'm used to a

relaxed schedule, where I wander in at nine, fix a cup of tea, sort the post, take down the few messages on our answer machine, and then sit by the phone, which might not go off until ten. I'm used to quiet, wood-panelled interiors, and four hundred patients max, seeking attention for nothing more critical than spreading wrinkles or an ugly rash.

Here, by contrast, it's like being in a buzzing newsroom, with the phone ringing non-stop even though it's still only twenty past eight, strip lights overhead, a room with all the cosiness of a warehouse, and thousands and thousands of files parked in neat rows behind the horseshoe-shaped receptionists' desk.

For a moment, I'm scared: my idea of a GP's practice is what I experienced at my dad's: small and familiar, the pace as slow as a farmer's tractor on a winding country road. This is something completely different.

'Anyone seen Max?' Jill asks. I realise this is the moment I've been waiting for, ever since accepting Jill's offer of a job a month ago.

'Max? He insisted on doing a house call. Mrs O'Rourke, the one whose leg they amputated because of the gangrene.' Alicia shakes her head at the thought. 'He works too hard.'

How will I survive the suspense? When I accepted Jill's proposal, I told myself I was motivated by my desire to leave Dr Casey's practice, and my need for more money in view of Zelkin's disastrous fortunes. But, if I'm being honest, there was another reason: Max Lowell.

'All right then!' Cora, the plump twenty-something head receptionist, slaps down a fat folder on the counter. 'Better have a go at manning the phones.' She points to the seven thousand manila files behind me, then at the computer beside me: 'We're inputting the patients' records into the new computer system. We've done about three thousand.'

I study my new colleague with her orange streaked hair, the row of studs along her ear, and the Doc Martens, and remember that Cora found her husband through Match.com. Her recent marriage does not seem to have filled her with the joys of spring or the milk of human kindness, however. Indeed, I wonder if she is much of an improvement on Mrs Stevens.

'Well, I'm off then.' Alicia slips away, through a door marked 'Dr McDonald'.

The phone rings.

'OK, answer!' Cora barks.

I leap to attention, grab the phone and try out my new spiel: 'Good morning, Hill Street Surgery. May I help you?'

I feel a knot in my stomach: what if it's an emergency? What if it's someone listing symptoms I have no idea of? What if it's someone who's cut himself and is bleeding to death? What if it's a child who cannot describe what she needs? What if I can't cope?

'Hi,' I hear a sing-song woman's voice. 'Is your postcode NW1 4LM for Mary or 4LN for Nancy?'

Time passes: I begin to relax. A second receptionist has arrived, Premila. She's Pakistani, willowy, friendlier and more soft-spoken than Cora. The patients have been filing in, with nothing worse than the flu, a broken arm, strep throat, a badly cut hand. I can handle this, I think to myself. But where *is* he? Beside me, Cora and Premila seem relieved that I haven't botched things. 'Tea?' Cora asks.

I take it as a token of approval and nod happily. Patients on black metal folding chairs line the walls. Two toddlers are playing with Lego on a small plastic table in a corner. *Worried about your memory?* asks a poster above them. *What's your limit?* asks another. There are posters advertising support groups for breast-feeding, stopping smoking, stopping drinking, adolescent counselling. Where is the support group for divorcées trying to start afresh?

The in-house phone rings beside me: it's Alicia. 'Can you find me Mrs Marrouf's file? She's not in the computer yet. Her NHS number is . . .' I grab a pen to write down the number, drop the pen, search frantically for it under the desk, find it, sit up again, and . . .

'Hello, Rosie.' Max Lowell smiles down at me. 'I was wondering if you'd be here when I got in.'

I'm dishevelled, slightly out of breath and red in the face, but I beam at him. 'Hi!' I cry out inanely. 'Nice place!'

'A bit busier than your previous practice, I gather.'

'Ye-es.'

'I'm sure you'll cope beautifully.' Max gives me an encouraging smile, then leans over the counter, closer to me. 'You'll have them all eating out of your hand in no time.'

'Well . . .' I sound dubious.

Suddenly I hear Alicia's cross voice: 'Rosie? Rosie?!' I'd completely forgotten about her. I mouth 'sorry' to Max. 'Rosie, are you taking this down?'

I jot down the digits, then realise that Max has disappeared and that a man is pounding the desk in front of me, asking me why he's been kept waiting for so long to see Dr McDonald, and that Cora and Premila are nowhere to be seen, and one of the phones is ringing and ringing. I sort the man and the phone call, then realise the in-house phone is ringing again. Alicia sounds cross: 'Are you going to bring me Mrs Marrouf's file or do I have to come and fetch it myself?'

'Oh, of course!' I spring up and start looking through the manila envelopes behind me. 'Here we are . . . I'll be right back!' I shout at Cora.

When I hand her the folder, Alicia thanks me with such a glacial stare that Mrs Marrouf, a veiled woman in her twenties, looks curiously at me, trying to work out why I'm the black sheep in the practice.

But when I step out of Alicia's room, I'm rewarded with a sighting: Max Lowell grins at me from the water cooler: 'Why don't I give you a speedy induction course,' he asks, keeping his voice low, 'over a drink? Tomorrow, six-ish?'

'Yes!' I almost shriek, then, toning myself down, 'That would be so helpful.'

'Great. There's a wine bar next to the tube station. Stacy's. Meet you there at six thirty.' He winks and leaves me sipping the most delicious cool water I've ever tasted.

Back in the waiting room, Cora grabs her jeans jacket and rucksack. 'I'm off for lunch. I'll be back at one and then it's your turn.'

I wish I could have lunch with Jill or even – more improbable – Max. But I don't dare ask my best friend, who has already done so much to help me out; or Max, who has already volunteered some time with me tomorrow after work . . . I take my seat at the receptionists' desk, and listen to an elderly man who has come to pick up a prescription but wants to have a chat about his wife, Emmie, who passed away last winter, and complain about the noise on his estate at night, and moan about the post office being closed down when it was so convenient, just on the corner of Talford Lane and . . .

It is rewarding, I think as I see him hobble away with his cane, to be of use to people who are so obviously in need; a far cry from the well-off ladies who only sought Dr Casey to melt away wrinkles or fill in lines. But at the Hill Street Surgery, most patients do not expect me to listen to their life stories. They know that in the course of the day I, and my colleagues, and the GPs, will meet legions of other patients in similar or worse predicaments. When I show any interest in their circumstances – 'How old is your son?' 'Oh, you live on the Tress Estate: did you read about the new neighbours' helpline in the *Camden Journal*?' 'Are those orthopaedic sandals any good?' – they are humbly and pleasantly surprised, and their personal tales begin to tumble out as readily as water from the school-style fountain in our waiting area.

Yes, I look around the room at the down-at-heel men and women, the frail OAPs, the children with runny noses and hand-me-down clothes: this is real life, and I have a role to play.

Cora stands over my shoulder: 'There's a Tesco Express on the corner and an M&S up the street.'

I scuttle out without a word, and have a lonely sandwich on a bench on the pavement, watching the pigeons and passers-by, wondering if I'm ever going to feel at ease with everyone in the practice.

When I come back to the practice Cora gives me a cool, unfriendly look. A group of new faces sit in the folding chairs: an elderly woman in black, a teenager plugged into an iPhone, a golden Labrador sits beside a blind man. I won't be browbeaten, I tell myself. The best way to impress my new colleagues is to show them how capable I am. Show them that I may come from the fluffy end of the market, but I know what I'm doing. I sit diligently at my desk and open the directory of patients' files. Carefully, I begin to transfer the data on to the computer. It's laborious, painstaking, but if I'm to wow these people, I've got to pull it off.

My phone bleeps a text. I rummage in my bag and extract the mobile: How's first day nerves? from Mum. How sweet, I smile to myself.

'Personal calls on your first day? I don't *think* so.' And Cora fixes me with a look of disgust.

I retreat to the computerised directory. If this is what she's like on my first day, what hope is there for me? Only the thought of Max Lowell around the corner – literally – makes up for Cora's aggressive behaviour.

'I need to see Dr Shone NOW!' a woman pounds the desk in front of me. Her voice is loud and everyone in the waiting room looks up. She is obese, grey-haired and in her sixties. 'Princess' reads the pink T-shirt stretched over her too-ample bosom. 'Let me see him!'

'I'm sorry, please don't shout.' My voice trembles as I try to sound authoritative. Where is everybody, why am I on my own? 'Please sit down and wait your turn.'

'I'm not going anywhere but in there!' The belligerent 'Princess' points to the corridor with the four doctors' rooms. 'He told me to come see him at four and here I am. So where is he?!' A large hand, the size of a small ham, bangs the receptionists' counter. I wince at the noise and then gasp as the huge woman bolts for the door that leads to the doctors' rooms. She moves with surprising speed, and by the time I've managed to circumvent the desk and chase her down the corridor, her hand is on Dr Shone's door handle. Omigod, my first day and I let in a madwoman!

'Please!' I tap 'Princess' on the shoulder. 'You must wait your turn.'

Princess ignores me as she rattles the door handle. 'Wait my turn – what nonsense!'

'Please go back to your seat.' I'm trying to keep Dr Shone's door shut, and not to manhandle 'Princess', but the mammoth woman is now banging on the door, her arms wobbling crossly as she does so.

'I'm going to have to call for help,' I warn, trying to sound threatening. I make as if to pull her away from the door. 'Princess' whirls round and I fear she's about to slug me when the blind man's guide dog charges us both. Knocked sideways by the unexpected attack, the big woman falls to the ground. 'Beeeeeeeeennnnnnnnnn!' she screams as she comes down, 'Tim-ber!' fashion.

The door instantly opens. Dr Shone peers through his spectacles. 'Mum?'

Not a great start to my new job. I walk home feeling down-cast. Ben Shone obviously thinks I'm a nutcase, Alicia McDonald seems prickly, and Cora not at all friendly. My protector, Jill, seems to be permanently locked up in her room. As does Max. Though tomorrow evening, at least, he is making time for me. The prospect of our rendezvous is my only hope – I pray that Dr Shone doesn't put him off me by telling him that I flattened his mother.

A honk wakes me from my reverie. Rude driver, I think crossly, and walk on. The honking continues, as if it were directed at me. For a moment, I feel flattered: is this appre-ciation of my Jigsaw cotton dress and cardigan (carefully chosen for Max's benefit)? I walk on, more slowly, and very self-conscious. A red Mercedes kerb-crawls beside me. What in heaven's name . . .? The passenger window rolls down automatically. I feel a lurch: all I need is a stalker. And then I stop dead. I recognise Linda at the wheel. She leans across to me.

'Hi, Rosie, I know you told Jonathan you didn't want to talk to me, but do you think you could reconsider?'

No! My husband's lover is the last person on earth I want to see after a hard first day at a new job. I keep walking, as if she didn't exist. I want her to leave me alone. I'm sweating from the climb up the hill from Chalk Farm and she's sure to notice, then go back and ask Jonathan how he could have stuck by me for so long.

'Please, Rosie. I'm not asking you to be my friend, I just need a bit of your time.' The car inches beside me as Linda continues her pursuit: 'Come on, Rosie, draw the bolt. We need to be there for those kids.'

Draw the bolt? I want her locked out of my life. But she's brought up 'the kids': my Achilles' heel. I stop in my tracks.

'Rosie, give me five minutes. I'll make it worth your while.' This woman will not take no for an answer. I look down at her, at those wide green eyes and beautiful face set in a determined expression: she exudes self-confidence, undentable optimism, and youthful energy. Linda fixes me with a gaze so forceful and unblinking I feel as helpless before her as Jonathan must have done when she set her sights on him.

I stop walking and issue a long sigh. 'OK. What do you want? What about the children?'

'Hop in, I'll drive you home.' Linda flashes me an all-American smile. Even after my teeth-whitening session, I don't possess a smile as white as that. 'Just push that report off the seat, it's some nonsense research from Finland about protein and embryo cell regeneration,' she tells me with a light laugh, as if having a 100-page tome on embryo cell regeneration on your front seat was no more unusual than having an *A to Z*.

Silently I buckle my seat belt and watch Linda quickly turn the wheel to the left, narrowly avoiding an incoming lorry. 'Hey, watch it, buddy!' she calls out cheerfully, sounding more like the leader of the pack than a potential road-rage victim. 'There's only room for one of us on this road!' She is so damn sure of herself, I can't help think admiringly.

'I love your kids, you know, I really do!' She flashes me a huge grin then turns back to look straight ahead. 'But I think Kat is having a hard time adjusting to the new boundaries. Jonathan and I have to have "us space" as well as "us time", and she just doesn't seem to get it.'

I swallow hard. I hate the thought of my baby having to fit in with this woman's wishes, and I hate the way Linda manages to look at once glossy, desirable and fiercely professional in her silk shirt and pencil skirt.

'I think she is conflicted,' Linda goes on, flicking her long black hair back with an impatient hand, 'about whether she is a little girl or a woman.'

'A woman?!' I cry, genuinely shocked 'But she's only thirteen!'

'Rosie' – Linda shakes her head – 'thirteen is the new eighteen. Your daughter is wrapped up in a virtual love story and I'm not sure it's healthy.'

'What do you mean?' I cry, furious.

'I mean that 24/7 texting she goes in for. It's all very exciting, but it's not real, is it?'

'It's typical of her age group.' I defend Kat and all teenagers against Linda's scornful tone.

'She needs your help. You have to free her to be a woman. She feels confused by the way things are now. We treat her as a young adult, but you're still babying her.'

'I don't!' I snap at her. 'You don't know what goes on in our home. I don't baby Kat.' How can I, when she has had to learn grown-up truths like security doesn't last and families are not for ever?

Linda ignores me. She changes gear – literally, with the car, and metaphorically, with me. 'I'm only telling you because I think that she listens to you more than to anyone else. She really looks up to you, you know. Freddy is the same. You've done a beautiful job with the children.'

Linda sounds so genuine, I feel tears sting my eyes. I wish I could hold them close, now, pull them to me, feel their warmth. I wish they could barricade me against this woman with her uncontrollable go-getter's attitude.

'I really think it would be best for everyone if the children had a few sessions with a therapist,' Linda says, then, raising a hand to still my bubbling denials: 'I know that Jonathan's going through a bit of a financial crisis' – though she keeps her eyes fixed on the road ahead, I hear the dark warm voice turn steely – 'but there's some great children-of-divorce therapy out there and I think we could wrap it up in a few sessions.' Linda turns to face me, leaving me to worry about the oncoming cars. 'Look, I know we can't be friends. But' – Linda's eyes go big and round, as trustworthy as a spaniel's – 'I want you to know that I'm ready to reach out.' An oncoming car honks loudly. 'Aw, shut-up!' Linda replies with a giggle, though thankfully she turns back to the road. 'To your kids, to you. I want us to be a team. Team Martin.' She does a thumbs-up sign. I gawp at her, wordless.

'I appreciate that you're trying to help, Linda . . .' I find it difficult to get the words out. 'But I'm not ready to share my children's upbringing with you.'

'OK, OK, whatever.' Linda doesn't look cross or sulky, but immediately challenges me. 'There is one other thing I'd like you to do for me, though.'

'What's that?' I ask, feeling exhausted by this encounter.

'Can you give me your recipe for fish pie? Jonathan keeps saying it was absolutely the best. And since we can't go out every night any more . . .'

'Mummy . . .' Freddy and I stand at the school gates. Kat has run off, darting into the playground, where she stands now surrounded by friends. Freddy clings on, tracing and retracing a line on the tarmac with his heel. Then, eyes on me: 'You, Kat and I are on a sinking ship. You jump off into the only lifeboat. There's room for only one more on the lifeboat. Would you pull me or Kat in with you?' My son's expression is anxious as he fixes me with his gaze.

'Freddy' – I squat, lowering my voice – 'I don't want to play this game, I told you that. It hurts me just to think about you or Kat in that situation.'

'Yes, Mummy, but which would you choose?' Freddy persists.

'Stop.' I don't budge. I check my watch: oh goodness, I'll be late for work! 'You'll be late for school. Now, be good and have a wonderful day!' I kiss my son in a rush, and then give him a little push towards the children in grey uniform who flock towards the school doors. I turn back, as always, when

I have taken a few paces: and there he stands, my Freddy, looking sad and alone, turning to wave at me.

I walk away slowly, so downcast I almost cannot bear the thought of going to the office. Jonathan Martin, it's not the money I mind about, not the house. It's the knowledge that our children are unhappy because we're not together any more. I would have put up with all your silly annoying habits, with the lack of praise and the lack of cherishing. I would have tolerated the Mensa habit and the Sudoku at dawn: anything, for them. But you had to have Linda for your happiness and you were prepared to risk theirs for it.

My mobile goes off. I don't recognise the number, but then 'Mrs Martin?' I recognise Mr Parker's voice: no, no, no, please don't tell me he has sold the house. 'Great news!' the voice booms on. 'The Liptons, that family from Barnet, have made a fabulous offer! If you accept, we've got ourselves a sale!'

16

'It could have been really serious. She gave me the wrong file for Mrs Marrouf.' Alicia's cold, cutting voice paralyses me. I'm standing in the walk-in closet where the practice's stationery is kept along with some random pieces of medical equipment. A few yards away, the partners seem to be holding a meeting in Jill's room. They've shut the door, but I can hear every word through the thin wall.

'Can you imagine the consequences?' Alicia continues, voice strident. 'Mrs Marrouf has a heart condition – if I'd prescribed half the stuff I normally do, she would have died.'

'And what about when she practically fell on top of my mum?' Ben Shone's voice pops with anger. 'The woman's a menace.'

My legs start trembling and I lean against the shelf with its boxes of envelopes, headed paper and staples. 'It *was* her first day,' Jill intervenes, voice soft and soothing.

'Normally she has brilliant people skills. Let me have a word with her.'

'I think we should institute a three strikes and you're out policy,' Ben goes on, still cross. 'Cora is very unimpressed.'

'I'll talk to her,' Jill says firmly.

I tiptoe away from the closet. My new job is already on the ropes. They hate me. They think I'm useless, out of my depth. And I can't bear the thought of Jill having to talk to me. It will be wretched for her, and humiliating for me. My best friend, the one who stuck out her neck to get me this job, the one who all the years I've known her has believed in me more than I have ever done myself – is now going to have to wag her finger and give me a Giuliani-style warning. I know our friendship will survive, but even so . . .

I slip into my seat at the receptionists' counter. Premila is at the photocopier. She shoots me a quick look that tells me she knows I'm in trouble. Cora is out having another 'fag', I'm relieved to see: my heart beats so furiously I'm sure she'd snap at me for being too noisy. I sit at the desk and pretend to look over the post, while the whole time I wonder how much longer they're going to let me stay.

I relished the moment, a month ago, when I handed my resignation to Dr Casey; I loved every expression of shock registered on Mrs Stevens's face. But maybe I acted too rashly. I can cope with the old dears who cluster in Dr Casey's waiting room, clucking about Botox and fillers and wedding parties. But this big practice has winded me, and maybe, just maybe, my new colleagues are right: I'm not up to it.

And then my heart lurches: the one voice I did not hear

joining in the chorus of disapproval is Max's. Was he there, and kept quiet? Or was he absent from the meeting and will be told in due course and Technicolor detail? He may even cancel tonight's drink. No, please, no: don't let him do that. I've been looking forward to seeing him ever since we bumped into each other at the water cooler.

Bleep-bleep, my mobile goes off. Oh no . . . Max already pulling out? And despite my fear of Cora coming back from her cigarette break, I dive into the handbag to find my phone.

It's not Max. I breathe a sigh of relief. It's Jonathan: Sorry about ambush. Linda never takes no for an answer.

I want to scream. But I need him onside. I text back: Will email fish pie recipe.

I spend the entire morning trying to redeem myself. I've already offered to visit Mrs Shone at home, to do her shopping for her and keep her company. 'No thanks!' Ben Shone shuddered at the prospect of my proximity. I hand him the bouquet of flowers and box of chocolates as a 'get well' present for his mother. 'She's diabetic,' he sniffs as he takes the flowers and refuses the box of chocolates – but then adds grumpily: 'They're nice.'

I get Cora and Premila teas, make sure I get the phone before they need to and that they see me inputting a huge pile of medical records into the computer. I smile brightly at Alicia McDonald when she asks me to ring a minicab for an eighty-year-old woman with bad rheumatism.

Please, please give me another chance, I want to beg them all.

'Could you help me, Miss . . . er . . ?' the elderly woman before me studies the name tag on the counter, 'Khan?'

'No, that's my colleague; I'm Mrs Martin,' I speak loudly because I can see the hearing aid in her left ear. She was here yesterday, I remember, picking up her prescription.

'Jackie Wells. I've come for my prescription.' Mrs Wells seems to have forgotten that she's already come by.

'I seem to remember that you picked it up yesterday,' I say as gently as I can.

'Yesterday? Yesterday was dreadful,' Mrs Wells begins. We go through a catalogue of horrors: the post wasn't delivered, Meals on Wheels didn't come, no one phoned, and she almost slipped as she came down the stairs. I listen, nodding: this, I know how to deal with. Mrs Wells is a substantially less polished version of the Butcher of Belgravia's patients. At the end she cocks her head. 'You've let me ramble on. You're new here, aren't you?'

'Yes, she is,' Cora snaps from behind me. 'How *did* you guess?' Her voice is heavy with sarcasm.

'Nice girl,' Mrs Wells says kindly, before turning to go.

'Hmmm,' Cora twists her mouth.

I swallow hard. Mustn't crumble in front of the colleagues, I tell myself. But only a quick trip to the Ladies, where I can splash my eyes with cold water, prevents me from crying.

It doesn't help that I'm on tenterhooks, terrified that Max will ring or text to call off our drinks. I feel as if this is my last chance with him, the one and only opportunity left for me to wow him. Because, pretty soon, if he doesn't know already, he will be regaled with tales about my unprofessional conduct. I don't relax until it's almost six thirty and I'm on my way to Stacy's Wine Bar. And my first tête-à-tête with Max Lowell.

The wine bar has low lighting and a mixed clientele: urban young, with lots of tattoos and caps and jeans; and middle-aged locals with corduroy jackets and worn faces. I don't belong to either group, and wish that Max would appear.

Benches line the walls. The lights are feeble, and despite the smoking ban I feel as if the air is musky. I find a small round table in a corner, and sit on the rather unforgiving wooden bench. Near me hunky men discuss Arsenal and girls with sexily messy hair confide about last night. I hope Max will manage to spot me. I study the blackboard with its bar menu, the distressed oak floors and ancient wine carboys on display. I look at the newspaper rack and decide that I may have to take a paper if Max doesn't hurry up.

My mobile bleeps again. I hold my breath as I check it: no, it's Mr Parker letting me know I can view the flat in Gospel Oak once more, on Saturday morning. It's the only time I can make it, now that I've gone full-time, and I want the children to see it again so they feel that they have a stake in our new home. The children hated it, last time, predictably. At my shock announcement last night that the house had been sold, Kat ran weeping up the stairs, and Freddy threw his arms round my waist and buried his head in my tummy. I haven't been so cross with Jonathan since that night when I'd discovered Linda's hotvolcanicsex text message.

I wince at the thought of last night's tears, then set my jaw and try to be calm. The flat in Gospel Oak is the best property I've seen so far. It's the ground and first floor of a large house, with three bedrooms. It's not even half the size of our old home – but beggars, or divorcées, can't be choosers.

I should probably get myself a drink to feel less conspicuous, but I'm scared that would mean losing my place. I'm not good on bar etiquette – in fact, I wasn't even when I was a single undergraduate. Jill loved the thrill of going out, being ogled by strange men and sized up by competitive females, drinking a glass or two and letting the conversation flow and the flirtation heat up. I, on the other hand, always felt uncomfortable and tense, hoping that I wouldn't attract anyone's attention, like a student who doesn't know the answers and sits squirming in her chair, hoping the teacher will not call on her.

The old familiar feeling fills me now. I'm about to make for the *Evening Standard* when I see him. Max walks in, looks around, frowns, can't spot me. Frantically, I wave and when he sees me my heart just stops: his whole face lights up. I watch him weave his way past shoulder-to-shoulder football fans, girls with hands on hips, a weary waitress.

'Hullo! Sorry I'm late.' Max pulls out the chair in front of me. 'My last appointment couldn't hear a word I said and in the end I had to write everything down on a pad – and my handwriting is the archetypal illegible doctor's . . .' He runs a hand through his hair apologetically. 'I hate making anyone wait.'

'No worries. I only got here a few minutes ago.' I smile and try not to purr with satisfaction. This is it: it's me and him, no children, no exes, no colleagues. Well, it's me and him and about seventy others including, I notice grimly, a group of men by the door determined to deliver a deafening rendition of 'Here we go, here we go . . .'

'What can I get you?' Max is up again, and has to lean forward across the table to catch my order.

'White wine?'

I watch him approach the bar counter, place his order, count out the bills. There is something pleasingly measured about him, something very grounded.

'It's not my favourite spot, but it's very convenient for work.' Max apologises about the rowdy singing from the corner. He sits on the stool in front of me. 'How was your first day then?' he asks as he sips his beer. 'Or rather, your first two days?'

So he doesn't know! I practically sob in relief. 'OK. Though I'm not sure' – I proceed cautiously – 'that Ben Shone thinks I'm cut out for the job.'

'Oh, Ben.' Max shrugs his shoulders. 'He's always difficult at first. But he's a softy underneath, don't worry. Hear you gave his mum a fright!' Max can't help a grin.

So he knows, after all. My heart sinks and I look down at the table.

'Don't worry,' Max laughs. 'I figure that Mrs Shone's, er, padding' – here he winks – 'protected her in the fall.'

'Do you think' – I can't help a worried look – 'they'll want to kick me out?'

'I won't hear of it.' Max again gives me a big, encouraging

261

smile. 'You're just the kind of friendly, sympathetic presence we need at the practice.'

'Hmmm . . .' I'm not completely convinced. 'I'm not sure they see it that way. But I really am enjoying seeing the patients and trying to help them out. It's like when I was helping out in my dad's practice. I noticed that half the time they weren't ill so much as lonely. It's the same now. A few of the older ones really, really need to talk. And I love seeing how much they enjoy just the opportunity to have a chat, or tell someone about their children.'

'A practised listener. No wonder I'm getting so much less of that at my end' – Max is laughing, but the look he gives me is so affectionate, I feel a surge of happiness – 'they've told you everything already!'

'I think seeing their GP is the only socialising some of them do.'

Max sips his beer, then the blue eyes fix me. 'It sounds to me like you're fitting in beautifully.' I blush hotly. 'Where did you use to work?'

I should have known I couldn't avoid the question for ever. I take a deep breath, then: 'Dr Hugh Casey's, in Hans Crescent.'

'Ah, the Butcher.' Max shakes his head. 'I'm glad you got away from him.'

'Me too!' I almost squeak with gratitude: my association with the Butcher of Belgravia has not tarnished me in his eyes. 'I'd much rather be doing what I am doing for you.' I smile and he smiles back. I look down immediately, so he can't read the longing in my eyes. I pretend to study my glass, the grooves in the pine wood, the red wine stains. I feel breathless, with his knees an inch from mine beneath the table, his hands near mine above it.

Now what? I wonder. We've done work, are we going to move into more dangerous waters?

Max crosses his arms on the table, leans closer towards me. 'How are the children? Sam and Will asked me to book you for the next weekend they're up. They really enjoyed our Sunday together.'

'Just name the date.' I smile. But he doesn't take his cue.

'Have you found a new place?'

'Nothing that the children like.'

'I can see that would be difficult. Your place is very welcoming. But you've got the gift for making people feel at home. I bet you could turn a beach shack into a home.'

'Nice of you to say so. But I'm slowly realising that somehow I've handled my life so badly that I'm left without a husband or a home.'

'But with, as those self-help books say, your self-esteem intact.'

'Sometimes I'm not too sure about that.' I take a large sip of wine. 'We went to a mediation session.'

'Wow, I'm impressed.' Max nods slowly. 'That really does mean you're trying hard!'

'We are. But Jonathan keeps worrying about how Lin—, his lover is taking their new straitened circumstances, and doesn't seem to understand that it's the children who are shell-shocked.'

'Are you?' Max leans towards me as he poses the question.

'I can't afford to be.' I pause, give him a half smile. 'But I *am* cross with Jonathan for being such a selfish wimp.'

'Glad to hear you're cross. Means you are human, after all.' Max holds up his beer and clinks his glass against mine. He speaks in such a suggestive tone that I draw closer to him: *Go ahead, kiss me,* I will him. *Find out just how human I am.* But Max is frowning, and I see him pat his jacket pocket. Oh, not the damn phone!

'Sorry, it's my phone.' Max looks rather gratifyingly annoyed at the interruption as he extracts the throbbing mobile from his pocket. 'Oh no . . .' His annoyance has given way to concern. 'Ellie? What's up?' I study his expression: regret at the interruption? Frustration at being always at the end of a chain she can yank because of the children?

I decide it's the latter, as I watch Max look pained. 'Please, Ellie, couldn't we discuss this some other time . . .?' He gives me a quick glance of apology, and I nod to show that I, as a divorcée, understand all too well.

'What . . .? Oh, please, Ellie!' He winces, removes the phone from his ear, snaps it shut, and pockets it again.

'She can't seem to finish a conversation without shouting.' He shakes his head. 'I'm so sorry . . .' he mutters, but I shake my head.

'Don't worry. I really understand.'

'Thank goodness you know what it's like. Some of the women I've seen' – Max rolls his eyes – 'have no idea.'

My heart thumps. What women? Who has he been seeing? Is he a 'winker' on Match.com? Why in the world did I take it for granted that he was not enjoying a busy social life?

There I was, thinking myself the sole object of his attention. I was acting like a self-satisfied idiot.

With a huge effort I pull myself away from the ghastly thought of Max being courted by a posse of long-legged beauties back to what he's actually saying:

'Sometimes she makes it so difficult for me to see the boys that I feel like giving up. I could go off to Africa after all. In the end, if she poisons the atmosphere like this, I'm not sure my seeing them is more damaging for them than not being here.'

Oh no. Having nearly lost him to a host of long-legged single women, am I about to lose Max to his do-gooding instincts? I swallow and try not to look too upset: 'Is this how you see your future?' I ask in a timid voice.

'Hmm . . . sometimes.' He takes a long sip of beer, stares into the glass before him as if he could read some import-ant message there, and then he turns to me with a serious expression: 'It's a struggle not to feel bitter and defeated.' He gives me a sad look. 'Healing takes longer than one thinks.' Here he pulls a comical face. 'Oh gawd, that's one of the worst aspects of this whole business. Half the time I catch myself speaking in cod-psychology.'

I laugh. 'Me too. I've even used expressions like "move on" and "the children have issues".'

Max nods, 'Yes. I suppose given that most marital break-downs are blamed on lack of communication, we are all desperately trying to talk talk talk to show we can. And ready-made formulae make it easier.'

He takes another long sip of beer, a bit of foam stays on

265

his lips, and then I see him discreetly licking it off. The sight of the tip of his tongue makes mine practically hang out. I feel hot, shivery, incapable of speech, and a strange humming noise takes over my brain. This is l-u-s-t, and a very bad case of it. I haven't felt like this since . . . since Max Lowell almost kissed me in my sitting room more than a month ago. *That* didn't lead to anything – will this?

'Now I get it!' Max beams and nods vigorously. I look puzzled, so he explains: 'I couldn't place that girl.' Which girl? I follow his eyes to the pretty brunette in a corner. 'She's the actress in Vassar's new play. She's had fantastic reviews. If that's the kind of thing you like, maybe we could go one of these nights?'

'I'd love that.' I smile. Yes! He *is* interested! Enough to ask me out – again!

'Another?' Max gets up, glasses in hand. I nod and watch him go to the bar. I steal a glance at my watch: Oh lord, it's almost seven and Otilya is expecting me back. But . . . I can't cut this short. Quickly, I extract my phone from my bag and text Otilya: Will be 1 hour. SORRY! Pizza in freezer.

Max comes back to the table with our drinks. Then, slowly and very deliberately, he sets the glasses on the table and sits beside me on the bench. My whole body grows tense. My heart starts racing and I freeze.

'I really wouldn't worry about those doctors . . .' Max mistakes my silence for concern about the practice. 'They're a funny lot – *we* are a funny lot.' He gives a self-deprecating smile. 'We have to be. We play at being God, but all the while we know that we get things wrong.' I try to concentrate on what Max says as opposed to what I feel.

'It's a huge responsibility,' I offer lamely.

'It's an honour, too: so many people trust us automatically.' He looks me in the eyes. 'That's why I have no time for people like the Butcher. They don't just betray their profession, they betray the most vulnerable and innocent.'

I nod slowly, but I think guiltily of the various double-barrelled ladies of a certain age whom I probably had not taken seriously enough.

'But maybe' – Max takes another sip of his beer while looking at me intently – 'it all looks different from where you're sitting.'

'No. I think you're right. It's one of the reasons I wanted to do something related to medicine.'

'Did you ever consider becoming a doctor like your dad?'

'No, a counsellor.'

Max beams. 'You're a natural.' Then, voice and gaze gentle as he probes: 'What made you stop?'

'Jonathan,' I say immediately, then check myself: I want to sound like a woman in charge of her own destiny, not a wifey pushed around by the husband. 'Well, and being pregnant with Kat. I suddenly realised that being a full-time mum was the most important thing to me.'

'You could have done the training part-time.'

'No. Yes. I mean, my life was so full.'

Max draws closer. I concentrate on his lips, try to avoid his searching gaze: 'You'd be brilliant at it. Talking to you is dangerously easy.'

The pleasure of his approval makes me smile.

'I'm glad we've been introduced. Twice.' Again, that heart-stopper of a smile.

I laugh. 'Yes.' I am terrified that he can hear my blood rushing, my temples beating. I wish I could turn the volume button down, to control my body – but every bit of it seems to be humming and throbbing. 'We've had the blessing of two matchmakers.'

'What? What did you say?' Max turns to catch what I've said, and in so doing he brushes against my left thigh, my left arm, part of my left breast. We both sit bolt upright, Jack-and-Jill-in-the-box, and I feel as if I'm slowly melting on to the hard bench before his very eyes. Max links his fingers through mine, rests our joint hands on the table in front of us, proof that we have at last come together. He turns to me: 'I'm so glad I found you, Rosie Martin.'

I hear Bach. Suddenly, out of nowhere, I hear a faint but familiar tune. Am I in heaven? No, I realise with horror: it's my mobile. *Not now, not now,* I will it away.

'What do you say to a quick supper?' Max is saying.

The Bach has grown insistent. 'My phone . . .' I groan, rummaging through my bag at my feet, feeling angry, impatient and totally aroused, when Otilya's voice, shrill with fear, brings me to my senses:

'I don't know where Freddy is! He had football after school but he hasn't come back. Kat rang Joshua's mum and she said the football game ended at six!'

17

I don't know exactly what happens next. I think I tell Max that Freddy is missing, and then he's hailing a taxi, and insists on coming home with me. By the time we get there, Otilya is standing in the doorway, crying, Freddy's hand in hers. My son hangs his head low, refusing to say anything.

'Freddy!' I scream. I rush to him and hug him hard. He looks at me, then down again at his feet.

'You'll be all right?' Max is beside me.

'Yes.' I can hardly speak, I'm at once so relieved and angry and happy at the sight of my ten-year-old safely back home.

'I think this may call for a family summit,' Max whispers, then squeezes my hand. I'm not aware of his departure, but only of Freddy in my arms, body racked with dry sobs.

'Where were you?' I ask as I stroke the dark curls, the neck and shoulders. 'Where did you go?'

'I didn't want you to be cross with me,' my son manages

to tell me when Otilya, wiping her eyes with the back of her arm, has led us both inside, and his sobs subside. 'I thought you'd be angry . . .'

'Angry? but why?' I am trying hard not to shout. Kat is standing by, round-eyed with shock, and Otilya, bless her, wraps her big muscular arm around my daughter's shoulders. 'Why would I be angry?'

'I thought that Mr Collins had written to you.'

'Mr Collins? What about?' I haven't received any letter from the headmaster.

'Bullying.'

'Oh, Freddy!' I'm trembling with a mixture of anger and fear. Who has been picking on my little boy? I feel like a tattooed, ear-ringed man in a wife-beater vest, ready to punch the lights out of a young thug. *Don't mess with me or mine,* I want to hiss.

'He wants you to meet Sebastian's parents.'

I start: does Collins want me to meet the savages who can't teach their child to show respect? 'He wants me to meet them?!'

'Yes.' Freddy's lower lip trembles.

'Freddy, what's been happening?' I motion to Otilya and Kat to go through into the kitchen, so I can be alone with Freddy. I sit on the sofa, and keep hold of his hands as he sits beside me. I wonder if I should ask him to roll up his sleeves or trouser legs: I haven't noticed any bruises or cuts when he's been getting into his bath, or out of his pyjamas.

'It's not that bad really,' Freddy says without conviction.

'Oh, my brave, brave boy!' I hug him tight. 'You've been going through hell. You should have told me . . .'

'Oh, Mummy . . .' Freddy rubs his face against me. 'You're really not cross then?'

'How could I be cross?' I shake my head. 'I'm only cross with myself, for not spotting that you were having a miserable time.'

'And you think Dad will be all right about it?' Freddy pushes me away and looks at me earnestly, big dark eyes full of tears still. 'I'm just scared Sebastian's parents will be so angry . . .'

'How old's their boy?' I huff.

'Er . . .' Freddy looks uncomfortable. 'Eight. But a TALL eight, Mum, really.'

'Little beast. I cannot believe Mr Collins will give the parents the time of day, frankly.'

'Oh, Mu-um . . .' Freddy looks shocked. 'You don't understand . . .'

'Of course I do.' I pat his thigh reassuringly. 'Now, let's get you into a nice warm bath and then we'll have supper together and I'll ring Mr Collins tomorrow and tell him that Dad and I are ready to speak to the little bully and his family . . .'

'Mum, Sebastian's not the bully.' Freddy bites his lip. 'I am.'

'Obviously no one can be judged on their first two days,' Jill tells me crisply. 'But you should be warned that the partners are a bit concerned. They think that perhaps the increase in workload from your last job is proving too much for you.'

I look across at my best friend. Jill appears suddenly fierce, green eyes narrow and bright, red mouth set. 'Is it?' she asks, eyebrow raised.

I'm taken aback by the cool, unfriendly figure facing me down. 'No, no, it's fine. I was just . . . a bit nervous. And honestly, Ben's mother did look . . . well, odd . . .'

'All right. No more to be said.' Jill lifts a pile of papers on her desk, holds them up as if to prove to me that really, this is not a brush-off. 'Now I'd better get on with these.'

'Oh . . . of course.'

I try not to look cowed as I emerge from her office and regain my seat between Cora and Premila: it was absolutely clear in our brief exchange that Jill was Boss and I was very far down the pecking order. I spend the rest of the day trying not to resent Jill for issuing her warning. Talk about not letting personal relations colour your professional life! You would never have guessed that Jill and I have been the best of friends for almost twenty years, or that she's godmother to Kat, or that I helped her through her divorce and she mine, or . . . I want to plead with Jill that I'm living in difficult circumstances: Freddy's a bully, Kat's an obsessive texter, and Jonathan's blissfully happy with someone else. Plus, we're about to move, and my one date with Max Lowell was cut short by a family emergency. I'd like to tell her all of this, but I know that special pleading doesn't work with Jill.

But, if I'm being honest, Jill's manner upset me for another reason, too: I felt her subordinate. I felt the difference between the woman who has planned her career carefully and the one who simply went where life took her. And life had taken me to Jonathan and the children first, and only then to whatever part-time work I could fit around my core job – as wife and mum. If I could take it all back, though, would I forgo the pleasure of having the children? Of being with them when they were little? Never. What I do wish I could change is my return to work: I should have waited, enrolled in a training course, laid the foundations for the counselling work I'd always yearned for. Instead, I plunged in without thinking of anything except the manageable distance between Hans Crescent and Belsize Park, and Dr Casey's relaxed attitude to which three days I took on.

Jill would have done it differently. In fact, she did. And she is reaping the rewards. Whereas I am back to square one. But I can do something about that: once we've got Freddy sorted out, once we've found and moved into our new place, once Kat gets some perspective on Mungo, I can concentrate on a proper counselling course – though, perhaps, not at the Marlborough. There, they will never believe I'm in earnest.

In the meantime, I must make a success of this job. I sit at the receptionist desk, and tell myself I cannot afford to make a slip. I input more names, I volunteer eagerly for every request made, I listen with the utmost concentration to everyone from the OAP on his way to Dr Shone's room to the teenager with the hoarse voice picking up his prescription. By the time I see Max, emerging from his consulting room, I am dizzy with suppressed emotion.

'Morning.' Max comes to pick up his post and messages from the reception desk. He must have come in late this morning, because I didn't see him before I went to Jill for my dressing down. I watch him, expectantly. I'll take my cue from him: either last night was the beginning, or the end, of something.

Premila sits beside me, on the phone. Cora, thank goodness, is in with the man from Canon, fixing the photocopier.

'Everything all right last night?' Max keeps his voice low. He keeps rifling through his post as he addresses me, not once looking up.

'Yes. No.' I'm trying to sound calm and not as if my entire emotional life hangs on his every word. 'Turns out my son has been thumping an eight-year-old. He was scared of the consequences.'

For the briefest moment Max meets my gaze. 'I guess when one has children this vulnerable, everything else goes out the window.' He sounds resigned, and nothing in his expression leaves me to hope that he seeks to re-play our encounter.

The man who only the night before had linked his fingers through mine and practically levitated with desire seems to have come crashing down to earth.

'What does this say, Rosie?' He peers closely at a Post-it slip. 'Mrs Wand or Miss Wood?' He's more interested in my handwriting than my heart. The moment has passed.

At least we tried.

'Mr and Mrs Martin' – Ms Schiffer, a skinny young woman with dramatic kohl-lined eyes, shoulder-length dark hair and glasses pushed back on her head Alice-band style, looks at us sternly – 'Westbury takes bullying extremely seriously.

274

We don't play the blame-and-shame game.' We are seated on orange metal folding chairs, arranged in a circle, in the school counsellor's office. Two empty chairs beside us await Sebastian Wytcham-Best's parents. Above us a rainbow of feel-good posters stretches on the pastel blue wall: *Different is another word for interesting* (beneath a childish image of the ugly duckling) and *Talking makes it better* (beneath a cartoon of a motor-mouthed teen deafening his mother).

'We go for total interaction: both boys will come to me for counselling. Until the end of term. If they make progress, I won't need to see them in September.'

Jonathan is nervously cracking his hands, I am studying my feet. It's not easy being the parents of a thug.

'I see from your files' – Ms Schiffer shoots us an enquiring look – 'that you are divorced.'

'Yes.' Jonathan and I go puce with guilt.

'Did the children take the break-up in their stride, or . . .?' Ms Schiffer pauses diplomatically.

'They're OK.' Jonathan and I answer in unison. Freddy's plight has triggered an avalanche of telephone calls, mutual assurances, plans to heal the children's psychological wounds . . . we've seldom been more in agreement, we jokingly agree, as Jonathan drives through the school gates.

'OK?' Ms Schiffer nods, as if this is precisely how all divorced parents talk. 'Children of divorce' – I bridle at her doom-laden voice: *Divorce is not murder or rape,* I want to object – 'often store tremendous anger. They can't help but resent those around them who, they think, have the kind of happy family life they themselves feel robbed of. You understand the psychology? They are so angry that they need to lash out, verbally or physically . . .'

'Mrs . . . er, Miss Schiffer . . .'

'Ms, actually.' Ms Schiffer's eel-like body pulls itself up high in her chair.

'Yes, Ms . . . anyway' – Jonathan ignores the counsellor's indignant look – 'I don't think divorce automatically turns children into bullies, or victims.' I shoot my ex-husband a grateful glance. 'Given the statistics, you'd have a lot more trouble on your hands if it did.'

Yes, I think. Things are different from when Samantha Cross was the only girl in my sixth form with divorced parents, and although our parents told us to be extra nice to her, she was the instant suspect when Mrs McCabe's purse went missing. 'Children of broken homes . . .' the grown-ups shook their heads, 'you just don't know what they could be doing.'

'You're careful how you speak about each other when you're with the children?' Ms Schiffer asks, suspicious.

'Yes we are,' we answer in unison.

'I've never said anything nasty about Rosie.' Jonathan smiles at me. 'It would be a lie if I did. We are' – here he gives a little cough and looks somewhere above my head – 'fond of each other still.'

'We are,' I repeat with conviction. And I realise it's true. Freddy's difficulties have renewed my ex-husband's efforts to keep the children's world steady. We are once again in synch about Kat and Freddy coming first. We've fought off the spectators who wanted a conflict, not a collaboration.

And now we can settle into a new, post-divorce phase where we can troop in together to the Christmas play or the counsellor's office, ready to support and cheer on the children we had together.

'What exactly' – Jonathan leans towards the bony woman before us – 'did Freddy do to the boy?'

'He threatened to punch his lights out if Sebastian didn't keep him supplied with copies of *Nuts*.' Even Ms Schiffer has to smirk at this point.

Jonathan snorts with laughter. 'How in the world does an eight-year-old get hold of that trash?'

'I expect Sebastian has an older brother.' Ms Schiffer rolls her kohl-rimmed eyes.

'Either that' – Jonathan grins – 'or Mr Wytcham-Best has an interesting collection of magazines.'

A knock on the door restores a serious expression on Ms Schiffer's face.

'Come in, come in . . .' She opens the door. In file a blonde, pink-cheeked couple. He wears a Barbour and cords; she, a Barbour and corduroy skirt. A silk scarf tied under her chin makes her look like a royal at a polo game. They look at us – and do a double-take, as if surprised that the bully's parents are not nose-studded, gum-chewing, rough trade. For a moment I'm paralysed. I'm not really sure what is expected of me, as the mother of the attacker. Do I hug the victim's parents? Do I drop to my knees, prostrate with grief and guilt, begging forgiveness?

Beside me, Jonathan jumps up, hand outstretched, face sheepish as he approaches the Wytcham-Bests. 'Jonathan

Martin. My wi— ex-wife and I are extremely concerned about this.'

'So are we.' Mrs Wytcham-Best looks close to tears. She holds her head down as if she cannot bear to see the parents of the monster who has been inflicting such pain on her innocent little cherub.

'Yes, well . . .' Mr Wytcham-Best struggles awkwardly for words. 'An odd situation to be in . . . I'm not sure . . . er . . . how we can resolve this . . . er . . . problem.'

I sit down. So do the Wytcham-Bests.

'I'm here to help.' Ms Schiffer locks her skinny fingers. 'Westbury has a four-point strategy for dealing with bullying. We call it the four Rs: remorse, retraining, respect, review. The onus' – here she fixes first me then Jonathan with her very intense black eyes – 'is on the aggressor – and his parents, of course.'

Jonathan and I humbly nod, criminals awaiting sentence.

'Remorse' – Ms Schiffer turns from us to the Wytcham-Bests – 'is the first step. We encourage the aggressor to accept total responsibility for his actions and ask forgiveness. Freddy will write a letter to Sebastian apologising for what he's done.' A loud sniff from Mrs Wytcham-Best. Ms Schiffer hands her a tissue from the pink heart-studded box on the desk behind her. 'Retraining: both aggressor and victim examine their behaviour. Does Sebastian regularly wind people up?'

'Steady on . . .' Mr Wytcham-Best interrupts crossly.

'Does Freddy always react violently to situations? If so, we need to stop this pattern and retrain them to adopt a new one. Respect is self-explanatory,' Ms Schiffer continues.

'Westbury wants our children to treat one another with respect at all times.'

'Yes . . . er . . . of course.' Mr Wytcham-Best gives an embarrassed cough. He looks as if he wished himself a million miles from Ms Schiffer's office – preferably on a grouse moor.

'Finally' – Ms Schiffer crosses her hands on her lap – 'Review. We will review this situation at the end of term. With all parties involved.' Ms Schiffer breathes in deeply. Mrs Wytcham-Best issues another little sob.

'Any questions?'

'J-j-j-j-just' – Mrs Wytcham-Best still won't look at us – 'shouldn't their son be on some kind of drug to calm him down?! I mean, just while he's getting over the divorce.'

'Drugs! Can you believe it?' I'm still angry twenty-four hours later, when Max asks me how the meeting went. It's after work, and we're both working late at the practice. In fact, I'm pretty sure we're *alone* at the practice. The thought sends a little shiver of excitement through me; as does the realisation that, despite that first stand-offish encounter when, admittedly, we were surrounded by colleagues, Max has been asking me regularly about Freddy. So regularly that I'm beginning to flatter myself that he really does care.

'Little boys are at their most vulnerable at this stage,' he tells me as he stands by the receptionists' desk, briefcase in hand. 'Sam had such a difficult time when we divorced that he used to come home from school almost every day with a black eye – he'd pick a fight, get into any scrap going, and then Ellie and I had to fuss over him. Which was precisely what he wanted.' Max gives me a big grin of encouragement over the counter that separates us.

'I've been blaming myself. I can't help wondering whether the children would be acting up if I gave up work and gave them my full attention?'

'You'd go mad,' Max says with conviction. 'You need a role that has nothing to do with Rosie the ex-wife or Rosie the doting mum.'

'Hmmm . . . you are good at giving unhappy women advice.'

'Dispensing advice is the easy bit.' Suddenly I feel him staring at me. 'I've got something . . .' Max stops, embarrassed. 'A pamphlet' – he rustles through his briefcase, takes out a thin booklet. 'Has an interesting-sounding counselling training course.' He hands it to me. 'Camden Council. Around the corner.'

'That's so kind!' I'm genuinely touched – and thrilled that Max Lowell took in what I told him about my unrealised ambitions.

'Damn, I've left my reading for the column in my room.' He looks up at me, expectant. 'If you wait here a second, I could drive you home . . .'

'Yes, I'd love that!' As always with this man, I have to make sure I keep my voice calm and steady. How does he manage to make a ride home sound like a moonlit stroll on the beach?

I slip his pamphlet into my bag and start tidying my desk. My mobile goes off. As I extract the phone from my handbag I see Jonathan's number on the display screen.

'You'll never believe what's happened.' Jonathan sounds almost breathless with anger. 'The latest Health column in the *Record* is dedicated to "vanity medicine" and does a hatchet job on a whole load of products. Including Zelkin.' He pauses a second, then: 'It says Zelkin's side-effects should not be under-estimated. It talks about that American study that found some men who'd taken Zelkin suffered stomach cramps. We're royally screwed. Zelkin is not only over – the column practically invites people to sue us.' Jonathan's voice sounds furious. 'Do you know who writes that column?'

Of course I do. Max Lowell.

18

'I don't believe it,' I whisper into the phone. And then switch it off.

Traitor. How could Max do this? The good mood that I'd slipped into thanks to him – his concern about Freddy, sharing his experience with Sam, the offer to drive me home – evaporates. Max Lowell has made sure my husband's professional success is over, and his brainchild busted. And my children and I will suffer as a result.

How could he?

'Rosie, are you all right? You look as if you've just had a shock.' I look up to find Max, in the doorway, studying me quizzically. I swivel in the chair so as to give him what I hope is a long, hurt, accusing stare.

'I have,' I reply icily.

'Oh?' Max raises an eyebrow. 'Something up?'

'Yes, something is up,' I hiss. 'Just the small matter of my future and the children's legacy.'

'Has Jonathan done something?' Max draws near, looking concerned – or is it hypocrisy mixed with guilt that I read in his expression?

'No. *You* have.'

'What?' Max looks genuinely confused.

'With your column.'

Max frowns and stares at me as if he's trying to gauge whether I've gone completely mad. 'What on earth are you talking about?'

'I'm talking about your column on Zelkin.'

'Zelkin?' Again Max looks puzzled.

'Yes. You remember: my ex-husband's invention. The baldness cure.' I speak slowly and patiently, as if teaching a child. 'You wrote that it leads to severe complications.'

'Oh, the American study!' Max exclaims.

'Yes, the American study. Pretty devastating.' I am working myself into a rage. 'You've made sure that no one will ever buy it again. And that anyone who's ever had any side-effects will try to sue the manufacturers.' I've been sitting at my desk, but now I draw myself up to face him over the counter that separates us.

'Rosie, I think you're exaggerating . . .' Max begins.

'No. I'm not. Why did you have to pick on Zelkin?'

'I –'

But I don't let him speak, I'm so angry. 'Were you always like this?' Max watches me, arms crossed, without saying a word, or moving an inch. 'Or is it since the divorce?' Max flinches. 'All you do is criticise and destroy!'

'Rosie –' Max tries to interrupt me.

'No, don't interrupt. You've been wallowing in your – what is it? Grief, shame, fear – ever since I met you. You paint your ex-wife as a monster but you allow her to run, no, RUIN your life still.'

'Please . . .' Max looks angry now too, but I can't be stopped.

'She rejected you. That's sad, but growing up means learning to accept someone somewhere may reject you.'

'Is that so?' Max's voice trembles with anger. I refuse to meet his gaze, but go on:

'Why don't you break away?'

'I can't break away as long as Ellie has the boys.' Max stands there, voice cold, arms crossed.

'Stop being so passive! You're not a victim. DO something. Don't just stand there, waiting for Ellie to take all the decisions.'

'Not everyone can have the kind of divorce you've pulled off!' Max's eyes flash furiously. 'You and Jonathan fell out of love, and when he found someone else you decided to be magnanimous and civilised. Well, hats off to you.' He is almost shouting. 'But when Ellie decided it was over, she didn't have an affair and waltz off. She kicked me out of our home. She tried to ban me from seeing the boys. She threatened me with a restraining order. It got ugly, Rosie, really ugly. You can't expect someone who's lived through that to feel like you do.' He stops to catch his breath and I read anger and pain in his expression. 'My boys are heartbroken and they need me there for them. The only thing I can do is give in to their mum all the time so that she never makes it impossible for them to see me.' He pauses, breathes in deeply. 'And giving in to her without a fight – that, I can tell you, makes me feel bitter.'

I'm still trembling with rage, but Max looks so raw, so hurt, I'm not sure how to proceed. And what about Zelkin?

'What about Zelkin?' I cry. 'Did you have to ruin our future?'

Max sets his briefcase at his feet and holds on to the counter. 'Look,' he fixes me with angry blue eyes, 'do you really believe that of me? That I'm only interested in destroying and criticising? I'd love to be positive and optimistic. About quacks, and snake oils, and yes, even divorce. But I can't. I can't approve of people who make a quick buck by exploiting someone's weakness. I can't stand by while a miracle cure leaves the patient worse off – and a lot poorer.' He draws breath, stops, as if to allow me to counter his argument. I don't, so he resumes: 'I'm not how you think. I don't see everything in the gloomiest possible terms. I chose this profession – in fact, I like to still think of it as a vocation – because I want to help build, not tear down. I want to cure, heal, make right and whole.'

'That's why you lay into someone else's invention?' I burst in impatiently.

'You're right, I have little time for vanity medicine. You can't expect me, as a doctor, to ignore a cure that has serious side-effects.'

'N-n-n-no . . .' But even so, didn't he understand that by attacking Zelkin in print, he was ruining Jonathan, and by extension me?

'In any case . . . how was I to know that Zelkin was your husband's patent?'

'He told you himself!' I'm practically shouting. 'At the Vincents' anniversary!'

'No, he didn't. He asked if I had ever written about baldness cures.' Max shakes his head slowly. 'But I never knew he was involved with Zelkin.'

Max draws closer. He places his hands on the counter that separates us, and looks straight at me. 'In fact, I don't remember what he was saying, or what he looked like. I know that he wanted to get me to promote something in my column. But the whole time I was just thinking that this was the man who'd made you suffer, the fool who'd let you go. I wanted to punch his lights out.'

I look at Max. Then down at the patients' files I've tidied, the diary I've shut, the yellow Post-its I've left on my desk. I wasn't ready for this. I breathe in deeply, to calm myself. Is he telling the truth? Can it really be that he didn't know . . . I look up at the determined face before me.

'You . . . you never knew about Jonathan's patent?'

'I only knew about Jonathan's betrayal.'

'Oh,' I manage to utter, after a long silence.

'I thought he must be mad.' Max reaches out and with his finger lightly brushes my hair away from my face. I shiver. I don't dare meet his eyes, I'm so ashamed of my recent outburst.

Max slips his hand in his pocket and extracts his car keys. 'Please, now, will you let me take you home?'

Handbag in hand, I come around the counter to stand beside him.

'Come on,' Max smiles. 'I'll forgive you for thinking the worst of me.'

'You' – I look up at Max – 'have every right to leave me here.'

'Hmmm . . . I think I'd rather give you a lift. I don't usually bring the old thing to work, and I might as well get some mileage out of it.'

'I'm . . . I'm so sorry. About what I said . . .' I'm standing so close to him I think I can hear his heart beat. I realise that I'm trembling again, but not out of anger. Max looks at me, and there is something serious, sad, but also yearning in his expression.

'Rosie,' he takes my hand, 'you think so little of me.'

'No!' I cry passionately, and lace my fingers in his. 'No, I was angry, shocked.' I pause, then: 'And of course, you're right about every divorce being different. I forget that I've had it easy, relatively speaking. I was upset about the affair with Linda, and I was shocked that Jonathan broke off our marriage so easily once she came along . . . but if I was being honest, I knew there wasn't very much life left in our relationship.' I feel his warm fingers tighten round my own, and a thrill of lust, and genuine affection, courses through me. 'Planning an easy and friendly divorce seems pretty logical when neither of you is devastated.'

Max moves his hands to my shoulders. 'It's a marvellous project.' I feel the pressure of his hands on my shoulders, and the warmth of his breath on my face, and I wonder if I dare give in to my impulse and draw that handsome face towards my lips, place a kiss on the forehead, eyelids, cheeks, on the beautifully drawn, generous mouth.

'I think we should discuss this over a drink,' Max is telling me. 'We need to have a pretty in-depth conversation, don't you think?' His half smile overwhelms me. I want to shout, 'Yes!' throw my arms around his neck, and bury my face into his chest.

A door bangs loudly behind us. We both start: I'd taken it for granted we were on our own. But here, in a pale green jacket and matching skirt, a huge grin spread across her face, comes Jill. My best friend, who has kept a scrupulous distance from me since she warned me I had to improve my office manners, is practically skipping towards us.

'Hullo, you two!' she sings. Max shoots me a look that shows he is as surprised as I am by this transformation.

'Well, what do you know' – Jill starts giggling – 'two hard-working souls.'

Again Max and I exchange a look: is my best friend tipsy?

'We were just . . . er . . . going,' I stammer, rather warily.

'Everything OK?' Max asks, uncertain.

'OK?' Jill repeats the question in a light, girlish voice I've never heard her use before. 'OK? It's more than OK! It's absolutely bloody marvellous!' She pauses, looks from one to the other. 'I'm pregnant!' she shouts.

I stare at her, disbelieving. 'What?'

'I-am-pregnant!' Jill enunciates each word carefully for our benefit. 'Doctor's just confirmed. I'm going to have a baby!'

'Jill . . .' I practically squeak in delight. 'A baby!' I rush to hug her, and such is the impact of my embrace Jill is forced to take two steps back.

Max approaches us too and when I've released my friend, he squeezes her in a quick hug.

'Congratulations!' He pecks her cheek affectionately.

'Can you believe it? Can you?' Jill is clapping her hands like a little girl.

'I'm so glad . . .' Her happiness is infectious.

'You will help me, won't you?' Jill reaches out to me, taking both hands in hers. 'You'll coach me through all those horrible bits like morning sickness and looking like a hippo and the natural birth and the breastfeeding . . .'

I look at Jill: she's transformed from her quick, sharp managerial self to a wide-eyed beginner longing to be initiated into the mysterious world of motherhood.

'I'm no expert,' I tell her. 'I sometimes think I'm not a good mother at all. I haven't even been able to keep the children's home for them – or their father.'

Jill doesn't listen. 'David is going to decorate the nursery, he's got a fabulous eye, and he's been longing to try his hand at a mural. But I don't think I can knit, do you?' She giggles again.

'We should celebrate . . .' Max meets my glance over Jill's shoulder.

'I'd love to, but I can't do that to David.' Jill's glorious beam seems to light up the entire surgery. 'He's got a bottle of bubbly on ice. Although' – she winks – 'I'll only have a sip.'

'Point taken.' Max nods. Then, with a look at me: 'I should, er . . . go, I guess.'

'Yes . . . me too . . .' I agree, reluctantly.

Jill, normally so sensitive to any situation, and especially to a potential matchmaking one, stands between us, looking pleased with the world at large and herself in particular.

'We-ell,' Max begins again. And then – as Jill turns to pick up the latest leaflet from the council on child vaccinations with an excited, 'Look, this is the kind of thing I'm now going to have to pay more attention to!' – he bends over me and whispers, 'Meet you at your place in half an hour.' And before I can reply he picks up his briefcase off the floor and strides through the revolving door.

'What a great man!' Jill watches Max's retreating figure. 'Enough pussy-footing, woman: you must go out and get him!' She wags her finger at me. I daren't inform her that she has just stopped – OK, postponed – my doing just that. But as I follow Jill through the revolving door and try to keep up with her as she practically skips down the pavement, I feel as if my heart might burst with happiness.

What not to tell children when you are about to go on a date after your divorce: ANYTHING.

'Mummy, where are you going?' Freddy's voice sounds accusing. 'You've just got home!'

'Mummy, why are you changing?' Kat, mobile in hand, lays across my bed and watches me go from cupboard to mirror to cupboard again. 'The pink's prettiest,' she shoots from the bed. 'But who are you seeing?'

'Oh, just going out to dinner,' I answer the children as elliptically as possible. But I can't help a smile. Max's message reached me even before Jill and I separated on the pavement:

How bout dinner not drinx? 8? Yes! I had exulted. Perfect, I'd texted back.

I'm so excited I have forgotten to check whether Freddy has written his apology to Sebastian, Kat has done her homework, and Otilya is sulking because I've once again let her know at the last minute about babysitting. I look at the woman in a pink dress who stares back from the mirror, and pucker my lips in a kiss which has Kat in a fit of giggles and Freddy scowling. I spray Diorella into the air and then walk into it, like I read I should do in *Vogue*, at the hairdresser's.

'Yu-uck, Mum, that's gross!' Freddy holds his nose.

I brush my hair while the children go on with their guessing game: 'George who fixed the sink!' 'Your lawyer!' 'The cabbie who said we were lucky to have a mum like you!'

By the time the door bell rings, everyone except Otilya, who sits in front of the box, with a set expression on her face, is in a state of such excitement we all run to the door. I take a deep breath, suck in my stomach, and then open it.

'Ohhhhhhh . . .' Louis Vincent is greeted by three people's disappointment.

'Gosh, what a reception. Shall we try again?' He laughs ruefully. 'Who were you waiting for?' he asks, eyes on my dress and high heels.

'Oh, no one,' I answer airily. 'Just out to dinner with a colleague.' I smile and usher him in. He is still in his City suit, and looks polished if a little weary. 'What brings you here?'

'Didn't Kat tell you?' Louis turns to my daughter.

'Oh, sorry, I forgot! I'll go get them!' Kat disappears upstairs.

'Kat borrowed Molly's Tai Chi things, and now Molly's got a lesson tomorrow.' Louis flashes me his smooth charmer smile. 'So I was told to pick them up on my way home . . .' He gives a little nod in Freddy's direction. 'Anything you'd like me to hand over to Oscar while I'm at it?'

Freddy waits a fraction of a second and then 'Yes!' he runs upstairs.

'Just call me the go-between,' Louis jokes.

We're still standing by the door. Behind us, we can hear David Attenborough explaining to Otilya about the cheetahs' mating patterns. Louis's dark eyes sweep my dress and he whistles softly. 'You look a million dollars.'

I'm pleased because I have confirmation that Max Lowell may like what he sees tonight; and embarrassed because Louis's eyes linger a little too long on my breasts. 'You've lost weight, haven't you?' Louis continues, and this time his right hand goes on my hip. It settles there lightly, but just long enough to send a tremor of alarm through my body. What's he up to? 'I hope whoever's taking you out appreciates you . . . hmmm, Rosie' – and Louis suddenly grabs my shoulders and pushes his tongue inside my mouth.

I'm so taken aback, at first I don't fight him off. *Hold on*, I want to say, *you're one half of a perfect couple. I've just celebrated fifteen happy years of your marriage. I see your wife almost every day and* . . . Instead, I can only flail my arms while he continues to prise apart my lips with his tongue.

'Stop, stop!' I try to issue the words, but it's difficult when

Louis's tongue is tunnelling its way inside my mouth and down my throat.

For an instant, Louis seems to glow, incandescent, as he bends over me: the flash of a light dazzles me – it's a car turning in the drive.

'Don't push me away' – Louis is trying to hold down my hands while nuzzling my neck. 'I know what you divorcées are like. Always hot for it.'

Outrage gives me the strength to finally push him away. 'Stop it!'

This time I don't try to keep my voice low, and 'You call?' Otilya shouts from the sitting room.

Louis doesn't know that shouts of 'fire!' wouldn't prise Otilya from her Attenborough animals, so I whisper my warning, 'She's coming.' Then, as I rush upstairs, I call over my shoulder, 'I'll get Molly's things!' and leave Louis looking no more put out than if I had rejected his offer of a seat on the bus.

How dare he assume I'd welcome his advances? I step into Kat's bedroom, shaking with rage. As if going through a divorce had turned me into a desperado without scruples. Disgusting hypocrite! When I think of all the cooing, twitterings, and pats on the bottom I've witnessed. He played his perfect hubby role to a T – although looking back, I now wonder if all those offers to help me out with the DIY were attempts to corner me for a pounce? If it weren't for the children, I'd give him a piece of my mind. Poor Carolyn, I think, suddenly protective: she looks up to him, trusts him, loves him so obviously. How could he cheat on her – and with a mutual friend?

Kat is folding her friend's white tunic and trousers on her bed.

'I've got a DVD for Oscar –' Freddy bursts in.

'Take it down. Louis is waiting for you.' Even though my legs are trembling and my breathing is shallow, I act as if nothing had happened between me and their best friends' father.

Freddy thunders down the stairs, while Kat slips the Tai Chi uniform into a carrier bag. As she does so she steals a glance at the mirrored door of her wall unit.

'Mum,' Kat whispers, eyes on her reflection, 'do you think I look like you?'

I stand beside my daughter, place my hands on her shoulders. 'You'll be far prettier.' I smile into the eager, innocent face. A burst of inarticulate love explodes inside me: *Kat, my darling little girl, I want you to be not only prettier but more confident, more determined, more sophisticated and . . . a lot wiser.* My eyes fill with tears as Kat stands on tiptoes, peering into the mirror as if in it she could read the future. *What will life bring you?* I wonder. *May you be happy and fulfilled – and shielded from unpleasant encounters like the one I've just had.*

'Mungo says girls grow up to look like their mums.'

'Mungo this, Mungo that . . .' I shake my head, smiling. 'I think it's high time Mungo came over for supper.' I peck my daughter's ear. She looks pleased, then anxious.

'Oh, Mummy, I don't know if I'm ready . . .'

'Well, it's been daily texts since before Christmas, pet: if you're not ready now, you'll never be.' My eyes fall on

295

the Tai Chi uniform Louis is waiting for. 'Better go down.' And I follow her downstairs.

I don't meet Louis's eyes, and keep a few paces from him as he bids us goodbye. I shut the door firmly behind him.

I check my watch: Max is late. Louis's visit has distracted the children from my 'hot date' and they're flanking Otilya, watching some exotic snake do its thing. I draw the curtains in the entrance and wonder if I should tell Max about Louis's extraordinary behaviour. No, better not: he's obviously known Carolyn for ages, and is very protective of her . . . I don't want him worrying about the state of her marriage while we're exploring our own new relationship.

I check my watch again: half past! I resist the urge to ring him and ask if everything's all right, and pace up and down in the small entrance. I wish he'd hurry, I want to enjoy the luxury of many, many hours in his company. I want to get to know Max Lowell, to peel back the thousands of layers I know he wraps himself in. I want to see if the warm, intelligent, caring man I have caught glimpses of is as attractive close up and personal as he is at a distance.

But where is he? I shake my head at my watch: 8.40. I straighten the photos of Freddy and Kat on the little side table. We're asking so much of you: to survive our divorce, the move from here; to learn lessons about love and marriage without being put off either. Are we asking the impossible?

Jill said she wanted to learn about motherhood from me – but am I really in a position to teach her anything?

Jill! Jill and her momentous news! *How could you?* I scold myself as I catch my reflection in the round mirror in the entrance: *Your best friend has just shared the most wonderful news with you – and what do you do? Forget all about it to concentrate instead on a date.* Jill as Mum: I can't picture my friend with milk stains on her silk-lined Agnès B cardigan; or coochie-cooing into a beribboned crib; or in support tights and Birkenstocks. The thought makes me smile – until the sight of my watch showing nearly nine makes me jump.

Why is Max so late?! I wonder if I should put on more lipstick, and toy with going back upstairs – but I don't want the children to open the door when Max comes. I want to let him in and dazzle him with my charming hostess act. He must see me at once easy and relaxed; I'll introduce him to Otilya, who looks appropriately solid and maternal; and the children will rush to greet him and ask about his boys, which will put him in a good mood. I shall remind him that I'm capable of making a warm welcoming home – and to prove that there is not even a shadow of Jonathan left. I shall kiss the children goodbye and then sail away with Max, a woman in complete control of her household and her life.

Bleep! I rush to my handbag at the sound of the text message. Him? I check: Sorry can't make it family emergency.

I stare at the little green telephone screen, read again and again the words that shine there. What family emergency? Is it really something that can't wait? It's like a tragic echo of my own family emergency – Freddy's disappearance – which cut short our intimate drink the other night. Or is Dr Lowell, I suddenly worry, giving me a taste of my own medicine? Letting me see that in his life too the 'children this vulnerable' take precedence?

Whatever is going on, the let-down is so great I'm near bursting into tears. Instead, I swallow a couple of times and tiptoe into the sitting room, where I perch on the arm of the sofa beside Freddy and watch a lioness lick her wounds.

19

'Hi, Rosie, it's Linda . . .' I gulp as I recognise the American voice over my mobile. 'Jonathan is going on and on about your crumble. I can't find an old-fashioned English recipe for apple crumble, so I just thought it would be a lot simpler if you shared yours when you have a moment . . .'

I stare at my mobile in disbelief: 'Look,' I hiss, 'I'm not allowed private calls during working hours.'

'OK, OK' – Linda doesn't sound the least put out – 'it's just that your fish pie recipe was great, and he really loved it. You know how men are, he just wants someone to cook for him.'

'Listen, Linda,' I hold the receiver right up to my mouth, so I can keep my voice low, 'I'm going to let you into a little secret: Jonathan is a gourmet cook. He can make better fish pie than I ever could, and his apple crumble is a thousand times better than any recipe I could share with you.'

'B-b-b-but . . .' Linda splutters. And, after a moment's pause: 'He's never set foot in our kitchen!'

'Maybe he's testing you,' I snap, and hang up the phone.

It's been a grim morning. I've been opening post, answering telephones, explaining the English on forms being filled out – always on the alert for Max. But no sign of him. Hasn't the family emergency been resolved? Is he having a showdown with his ex over access to the boys? Or maybe one of the boys is in trouble, à la Freddy? Or Max's ex has had an accident? Or . . .

Suddenly there he is. He comes in looking terrible, pale and drawn, huge dark circles under his eyes. He looks as if he hasn't slept a wink.

'Hullo, Mrs Eden rang for you twice already.' Cora, normally so brusque with everyone, adopts a soft feminine voice.

He nods but doesn't reply.

'And here's your post, Max.' I hold up a pile of envelopes. I hardly dare look at him: he mustn't see the disappointment, mixed with curiosity, that fills my face.

'Thanks.' He doesn't glance up, just takes his post through to his room.

I'm left sitting there, feeling totally baffled: does Max Lowell really not think I deserve some kind of explanation? The face he wore as he came in tells me something serious has happened, something to really upset him.

Be patient, he'll tell you when he's ready to, I remind myself as I wait on the line for the receptionist at the Foot Clinic to answer: Mrs Simons, elderly, portly, and blighted by terrible bunions, stands before me, explaining for the umpteenth time about the pain in her feet.

Be patient, I repeat as I help a Somali mother fill in her registration form. She is beautiful, young, and with huge black eyes full of fear at the unfamiliar registration process, and pain – her stomach has been hurting for the past week.

Max knows he owes you an explanation. All in good time.

But by 6 p.m. I'm packing up my things and wondering whether he has snuck out of the surgery when I was at lunch: I haven't seen him since his arrival. And then suddenly he's there, standing beside my chair, obviously waiting for me to finish packing up my things. I look up from my basket, and meet his eyes.

'I . . . owe you an explanation.' Max looks quickly away.

'Yes?' I straighten up, and try to sound encouraging.

'Last night . . .' His voice is so low I need to strain to hear it. 'Ellie . . . ehm . . . needed me to help out with the boys . . . ehm . . . a babysitter didn't show . . .'

I look at him, disbelief plain on my face: Ellie and the boys live in Bath. Not even the ex-wife from hell would expect her ex to drive down from London for a spot of babysitting.

'Really?' I sound totally unconvinced.

'Ehm . . . yes . . .' So does Max. He won't meet my gaze, but just stands there, hands twitching around his briefcase, looking as nervous as Freddy when he had to explain that he was the bully not the bullied. I find the sight of the big man suddenly reduced to schoolboy nerves oddly touching, and I'm moved to offer an olive branch.

'I was sorry' – I check to make sure neither Cora nor Premila are listening: in fact, they've gone – 'about the dinner. I was looking forward to it.'

There, I think, heart beating furiously, I've given him the chance to make amends: Max can stop apologising and ask me out again instead.

'I'm sorry too.' Max shakes his head, and then leaves.

I stand, silent and immobile. Is that it?

'Frankly I don't think motherhood is meant for women over thirty.'

It's Saturday morning, the children are playing tennis with the Vincents at their club, and I've just picked up Mum from Paddington. We're sitting with a cup of coffee in our new kitchen. Mum's already had a go: 'It really is a seventies nightmare, isn't it?' she sniffs, nose wrinkled in disapproval.

She's come down to 'help', whatever that means. In fact, we've already done most of the unpacking and the re-arranging and the discarding of boxes and boxes of things that only a week ago I could not live without. They say that moving is the most stressful event in your life, after a divorce. In fact, I haven't had the time to be stressed, as I've had to pack us all up, helped by removal men who looked like an identity parade, without taking time off from the practice in case they think I'm unreliable, needing time off so soon. Otilya overcame her misgivings about working cheek to jowl with 'animals' and proved a star – even though she did use it as lever to hold out for a rise.

The purchase, the exchange, the move: we managed it all in six weeks. No wonder I feel exhausted.

'And Jill's a professional woman, so I bet she will be parking the baby with the nanny before it's weaned properly.' Mum shakes her head. 'IVF, divorce, mums who spend more time at the office than at home: what are we doing to our children?'

Guilt engulfs me: there's no denying that Freddy and Kat are feeling uprooted and adrift. They find the new place cramped and dingy, and the new neighbourhood 'too far from home'. Home being Belsize Park, still, with Primrose Hill down the road and the Vincents next door.

I, on the other hand, see the absence of the Vincents as one of the most important advantages of our new home.

'Well,' concludes Mum, emptying her mug, 'I'm just glad it wasn't like that when I was raising the two of you . . .' Then, after looking left and right in our new tiny kitchen: 'It's certainly no palace. And the neighbourhood looks dodgy. Did you see those two hoodies hanging about the off-licence round the corner?'

'Mum,' I say quietly, 'you're supposed to help me make the children feel at home, not point out everything that's wrong with this place!'

'I hope Jonathan feels properly guilty.'

'Mum, please.' I open the wrong cupboard to extract the tin of biscuits. It's still so new here that I get things wrong all the time. 'I quite like it, actually. Small but cosy. And Jonathan actually can't afford to give us more. His savings have been wiped out with the Zelkin crash, poor man.' I pick out a digestive. 'He's really depressed about it all. He's constantly on the phone making sure we're all right. He would never try to cheat his children.'

'Just his wife,' Mum says archly.

I ignore her. 'Otilya has gone to fetch Kat and Freddy from the Vincents'. I really want you to make an effort when they're here.'

'Of course. Poor poppet' – Mum shakes her head – 'he's obviously having such a tough time of it. Imagine our little boy bullying someone. Though, frankly, I'd much rather that he was doing the punching rather than being the punch-bag.'

'The counselling seems to be going well.' I munch on a digestive.

'What about Kat and her boyfriend?' Mum pretends to study her mug of coffee.

'She's absolutely fine, Mum,' I answer quickly, then guiltily realise that, what with the new job, and the move, and Louis Vincent's pass, and Max Lowell's cold silence, I'm not up to date with my daughter and her text-buddy.

'Well, I hope so. She sounded confused when I last spoke to her.' Then, before I can probe: 'And before they get here' – she gives me one of her knowing looks – 'what about *you*? Is there a new man on the scene? You look much better, so I imagine there is.'

'Oh, Mum . . .' I sigh. 'I was quite interested in someone, but . . .' I shrug, pretending that I don't really mind. In fact, I'm still smarting from Max's no-show and his determined pretence, when our paths cross at the surgery, that I'm a potted plant or one of those jolly-coloured posters. Whatever there was between us – and maybe I had blown it all out of proportion – Max Lowell is no longer interested in me. But I don't want to discuss this with my mother: I'm not used to confiding in her. I shiver at the memory of the last time I did. I was seventeen and mad about my next-door neighbour, Felix Barrett. I admitted as much to Mum – only to overhear her sitting with Felix at our kitchen table: 'She's a nice-looking girl, Felix, just a bit shy. Why don't you take her out for a meal? My treat.'

'Nothing happened?' Mum continues to probe.

'I have a nice new friend, thanks to one of those internet dating things.' I throw her a red herring. Though it is true that GentlemanJim's cheeky emails have shed a bit of light in an otherwise pretty dark month.

'Oh, I was thinking about trying that out myself.' Mum pats her bob with a smile. 'I mean, I've had some very nice evenings with one of my chums from the cruise, but I've heard that internet dating is worth a go.'

'Oh?' I have to force my mouth shut. My mum with a MAN?!

'I have to say, it's all a bit exhausting.' Mum smiles again, coquettishly. I gulp. 'But I believe everyone deserves a second chance, don't you?'

Maybe it's my mother's words that prompt me to do what I do next. Feeling incredibly self-conscious, I sit at my computer, scanning every email I've ever received from GentlemanJim, until – bingo! – I find the mobile number he'd once sent me – on a dare.

With a gulp, I dial the number.

'Hhhhhullo?' Another gulp. 'It's Second-chancer.'

'Hey! Rosie! How's it going?' GentlemanJim sounds genuinely happy to hear from me – and somehow wonderfully familiar.

'I . . .' I can't believe I'm doing this '. . . I'd love to meet up for that drink we keep postponing.' There, I've done it.

'The drink *you* keep postponing, you mean!' GentlemanJim laughs. 'I've been trying to get you to accept for about a month now.'

'I know, I know, but the new job, the new home . . .' I try to defend myself.

'Of course. It would be great. Monday, Tuesday – when suits?'

'Tuesday.' Mustn't seem too keen.

'Perfect. I know a nice little wine bar near your office. Stacy's . . .'

'No, no, no,' I interrupt him immediately, 'I don't want to go there.'

'Tell you what, if you don't think it's too compromising, why don't you come to me?' He senses my reservation and laughs. 'Don't worry, I'll meet you downstairs. There's a little bistro round the corner. I'm just very proud of my new pad – I moved in a month ago.'

'Oh, you've moved . . .' I can't remember if he'd told me of a move. 'I've been so wrapped up in my own move, I . . .'

'Hey, I don't mind. Around seven, then.'

The dinner with GentlemanJim becomes something to look forward to over the weekend and the very long, dreary

306

Monday at work. Since my non-starter with Max, I dread every moment I spend at the Hill Street Surgery. Ironically, I seem to be much more appreciated now that I loathe coming in rather than in those first two days when I was so delighted with my new job: Cora seems to consider me a worthy third receptionist, Premila is always cheerful, Ben Shone manages to be civil and even Alicia doesn't scowl every time I walk into her line of vision. Jill pointedly avoids me at work, and as for Max Lowell, he's scrupulously friendly and noncommittal when we see each other on either side of the receptionists' horseshoe desk. I haven't felt this lonely since Jonathan first left home. I long to find someone – someone who does not work with me, who does not have 'vulnerable' children, who is not overburdened with emotional baggage.

I smile, despite myself: I remember Max's horror at coming out with those psychobabble expressions. Yes, I must, must get to know Jim. The thought of Max Lowell and of our budding relationship cut short acts as a spur rather than a brake: I'd better turn to new pastures. And given that even my mum has some romance in her life, I think I do deserve *someone* in mine.

On Tuesday, I arrange for Mum to babysit, put on a strappy cotton dress (Jigsaw, about five years old), a matching blue cropped cotton cardigan, and bring my prettiest sandals in a carrier bag to work. By six I've changed out of my plimsolls into my sandals, squirted a puff of Diorella and I'm sauntering out of the Hill Street Surgery.

GentlemanJim's address is a five-minute walk from the

St John's Wood tube station. It's an impressive red-brick mansion block, set back from the road behind a small tidy green lawn. Number 24, he'd said.

I press the buzzer and a crackling voice answers almost immediately: 'Hi, Rosie, I'll let you in. Down in two seconds.'

The door buzzes and opens automatically. I step into the very swish reception. The parquet floor is beautifully polished, the walls a soft peach, small chandeliers hang in a row from the high ceilings: yes, I can see why GentlemanJim is pleased with his new posh place. I stand by the door, in full view of the lift. After the last two exchanges, what will we make of each other? Will we have something to talk about? Will he find me prettier than he'd expected, or plainer? Will he think me too old or too young? Will he look exactly like his photo or bear no resemblance? Will he give me the goose-bumps or the creeps?

The lift doors open. Rob the lawyer saunters towards me. Oops: I'm here for one man and another surfaces. I smile, a bit embarrassed. I don't think I'll explain to Rob the circumstances of my rendezvous. 'Rosie . . .' Rob comes towards me, looking pleased. He looks different, I muse: somehow bigger, and more self-confident.

'Hullo.' I smile, too, and hold out my cheeks to be kissed. It's when he comes up close that I realise what's different: Rob's not wearing his spectacles. He looks even handsomer than before: no bad thing if GentlemanJim finds me being kissed by this good-looking stranger. 'Fancy meeting you here!'

'Yes, fancy that, Second-chancer,' Rob whispers into my ear.

*   *   *

I gawp, mouth open, eyes blinking.

Rob the lawyer laughs: 'Didn't you realise . . .?'

'N-n-n-no. It never oc-c-c-c-curred to me,' I stammer. 'You're married, for a start.'

'Not any more.' Rob beams at me. 'I've been dying to tell you: Serena left me. She's found herself a judge. Older, wiser and with pots of money.' He winks. 'She is being incredibly civilised about it. Very keen that I should not go around bad-mouthing her and His Lordship. Our divorce will be far easier than our marriage.'

'I . . .' I'm still reeling from the shock that GentlemanJim is Rob the lawyer. And that he is FREE. 'I just can't believe it . . .'

'Start believing it. Because I've organised a lovely evening and it would be a shame to waste it by staying here and trying to decide whether this is a figment of our imagination or the real thing.'

'Ye-es,' I manage, in a daze. And still in a daze I follow him out of the grand entrance of his mansion block into the street.

'I've booked us into a great little restaurant around the corner. Hope that's all right?' Rob gives me a solicitous look. I notice again how well, and how much younger, he looks without his spectacles.

'You look . . . different,' I venture.

'It's a new me!' Rob chuckles happily. 'Contact lenses and – don't laugh – a personal trainer. He's got me doing weights, and it makes all the difference. I've gone from zero to hero in two and a half months.'

Again he beams. This is one man, I muse, for whom divorce has been truly the beginning rather than the end of something wonderful. Gone is the faintly melancholic manner, the self-effacing ways and shyness. This Rob is in high spirits and in control. 'Do you approve?' He looks down at me with an expression of such pride, I can't help smiling back.

'Yes. You look really, really well.' I take the arm he proffers, and suddenly feel a little shock course through me – excitement? Lust? – as he announces 'We're going to have fun!'

We do. Over the scrumptious French dinner of snails, sea bass and the most delicious crème brûlée, Rob talks animatedly about everything from his new neighbourhood ('it's just fab') through the last time he saw the Vincents ('they really miss you and the kids, you know') to work ('keeps me busy and out of trouble – for *now*'). He makes me laugh with his impersonation of the judge, a posh widower in awe of Serena.

'The thing is,' Rob tells me, his brown eyes round and pleading as those soft toys Freddy claims to have outgrown, 'I really never realised how much I resented her. When she told me about the judge I was almost crying. She thought I was upset – which in retrospect is very useful, as she feels obliged to be generous. But in fact I was just experiencing the most incredible relief.' Rob rakes a hand through his hair (which, unlike the rest of him, shows no sign of post-marital improvement). 'God, my marriage was like being stuck with

310

a really irritating back-seat driver. She knew better, at every turn. Drove me mental.'

'She certainly looked like a . . .' I conjure up the vision of Serena with her narrowed eyes and set mouth '. . . er, determined lady.'

'It's bliss, to be shot of it.' Rob raises his glass to me. 'I'm now in the land of the free.'

'Well' – I can't help laughing – 'you certainly put a positive spin on divorce. Most people think of it as horrific.'

'Actually, I was terrified at first.' Rob draws closer across the peach-coloured table cloth. 'I was scared that it had all come too late for me. That for instance you' – he runs a finger down my arm; I shiver with pleasure – 'had found someone else.'

I flinch, a vision of Max Lowell suddenly looming. I banish it, shaking my head as if to rid myself of an annoying gnat.

'Thank goodness.' Rob reads a 'no' in my head-shaking. 'I couldn't have borne it. I thought about you so much after we . . . er . . . kissed.' We both blush and look down. 'That was why I logged on to Match.com. Once you'd told me that you were looking for a date on the internet, and using Second-chancer as your name, I knew there was hope!' Again his finger lightly touches my arm. Again I shiver with pleasure. 'I know it wasn't terribly honest to keep my identity from you – but I hope you don't mind.'

'Not for a minute.' I shake my head. 'It gave us a chance to get to know each other.'

'Rob'n'Rosie . . . oooh, it has a nice ring.' Rob winks as he raises his glass in toast.

We drink a bottle of something heavenly and golden between us, then Rob orders 'a little Sauterne' with our pudding, and by the time we're walking out of the restaurant, I am easily persuaded that, really, we could have a nightcap at Rob's. I allow him to wrap his arm around my shoulders, then allow his hand to caress my hip as we stroll back to his mansion block.

We start kissing in the lift: Rob nuzzles my neck, murmuring something about 'finally together'. He lifts my face to his and begins kissing my eyes, my nose, my lips. He parts them with an eager tongue that tastes slightly of Sauterne.

Somehow we manage to get out of the lift and into his flat, and the moment he kicks the door behind him his hands are on my shoulders, sliding off the straps of my sundress. 'Hmm . . . lovely, lovely,' he whispers before tracing the outline of my right breast with his finger. 'You're so beautiful,' he continues, as his blond head draws close to my breasts. He unhooks my strapless bra with an expert hand. My heart thumps beneath the breast he starts manipulating. I feel as if I'm melting and burning at the same time, then let out a moan of pleasure as he urgently pulls off my dress. 'We have unfinished business,' he tells me in a breathless voice as he looks up for air, after kissing my breasts, my belly, and now pulling off my knickers. 'I can't believe how long I've had to wait for this . . .' he moans, and then takes me up in his arms and carries me to his bed.

Later, I can barely make out the furniture in Rob's bedroom, but I see his newly muscular body naked beside me. Rob snores gently, on his back, and it's all I can do not to kick him gently to make him roll on his side, as I always did with

Jonathan. My eyes light upon the clock radio on the bedside table, and I practically yelp at the time. It's one o'clock and my mum is bound to be furious, given that I told her it would be just a quick drink. But then, who was to know that GentlemanJim was to transform into Rob the lawyer?

I gulp. How do I get up? Do I wake him now or when I'm dressed? Do I prod him in the ribs, or do I kiss him? Do I murmur 'darling', or do I act business-like and matter-of-fact? I test my reactions gingerly: I don't feel totally comfortable – but then again I don't feel completely uneasy either. The closest I get to describing my feelings is 'confused'. Here I am, thirty-seven years old and completely knocked sideways by the fact that I've woken up next to a man not my husband. Or ex-husband. Or boyfriend. I don't do casual sex, I explain primly to some invisible jury. I believe in responsibility, and genuine emotions, and romance, and . . .

'Hello!' Rob blinks open his eyes, and reaches for my shoulder. 'You're so beautiful.'

'I fell asleep,' I tell him softly. 'I . . . must go. Children. My mum.'

'I won't let you go' – the hand grips my shoulder firmly – 'until you've promised to see me again.' Rob sits up, and modestly pulls a corner of the off-white linen sheet over himself. 'Promise.'

'I promise.' I slip off the bed, and run on tiptoes next door. 'I promise!' I repeat, as I rush about the sitting room looking for knickers, bra, dress and sandals. Oh goodness, did I have a pashmina with me? Or just the cropped cardigan? I tiptoe around the elegant off-white sitting room, looking behind silk cushions and bending to check under the leather sofa, desperately trying to retrace our path from the front door to the bed. 'Hey you!' Rob lets out a wolf whistle. 'Come back to bed!' he calls out.

'No-no-no,' I cry, at once amused and anxious, over my shoulder.

'I mean it, Rosie Martin . . .' He crosses his arms behind his head. 'I want to see lots and lots of you.'

Ten rules for carrying on an affair after your divorce:

1. Do not ring him every five minutes just to make sure he hasn't gone off you.
2. Do not plan your holidays together.
3. Do not give him hell when he absent-mindedly refers to his ex-wife as his 'wife'.
4. Do not give him hell when he absent-mindedly calls you by her name.
5. Do not talk about your ex.
6. Do not compare him to your ex.
7. Do not compare notes on lawyers, marriage counsellors, pre-nups, settlements, etc.
8. Do not tell everyone who'll listen that you're having an affair.
9. Do not take out the family albums and expect his riveted attention.
10. Do not try to introduce him to your children too soon.

No matter what I tell myself, I seem to be in a permanent whirl of comparisons between Rob, Jonathan, and Max; plans to introduce Rob to Kat and Freddy, projects for this summer, Christmas, next year. At home, the children manage to keep me focused on them most of the time, but the moment they are out, or asleep, I find myself reliving every minute of my passionate encounter with Rob the lawyer: his lips on my skin, his tongue inside me, the way we moved in perfect synchronisation on his linen sheet. The memory makes me blush, and at least three times, Otilya has asked me, eyebrow raised, eyes beady, 'You OK?'

At the surgery, I have to concentrate very hard in order to hear anyone above Rob's breathless, 'You're so beautiful', which swirls round and round my head. The only time the memory of our encounter fades into the background is when Max Lowell comes up to my side of the receptionists' counter and asks to see his messages. For a few seconds I feel frustrated and cross: this could be YOU and me, I want to shout. But the moment passes, and I simply look up at the man who only a few weeks ago seemed a wish come true: 'Here, Max,' I hand over the four Post-its. When our fingers touch I refuse to feel any tremor of excitement and when his blue eyes look into mine I refuse to feel that shock of recognition that once sent me trembling. *I'm over you,* I want to tell him. *Totally over you. And you'll never know what you're missing.*

Having silently addressed him in this way, I flick my hair back with a hand, and saunter past him to the photocopier. I have work to do, and a life to live, I want Max Lowell to understand.

And life, thanks to Rob, has become a lot more interesting. He regularly rings, texts or emails me, sprinkling little messages like 'I miss you' and 'what r u wearing?' over my day, cheerful confetti on drab municipal steps. He sets up dinner dates at his flat, where, immensely house-proud, he shows me his latest purchase – a rare lithograph or an ultra-modern coffee table ('La Palma, you know: a great investment') – before seducing me on the double bed. We never even taste the Moroccan couscous he bought from the upmarket deli around the corner. We go on film dates that find us making out like teenagers as soon as the lights go down. And on Sundays, when Jonathan takes the children, we go for a walk round Regent's Park that has us frolicking in the grass like Bambi in the Disney forest. I buy four new dresses at the Whistles sale. I get a pedicure and manicure, and opt for 'Fiery Red'. I smile mischievously when over my haircut Nadine remarks, rather sourly, that I look well. And I discover that, despite no gym and no diet, my jeans are loose and my stomach almost flat. Suddenly, turning thirty-eight does not fill me with fear.

I haven't had this much attention since I was on honeymoon in Italy with Jonathan, this much fun since I was at uni. Our lust fest makes everything bearable: our cramped new quarters, Freddy's tantrum about having to attend yet another 'anti-bully' session, Kat's blues when she discovers Mungo's parents have confiscated his iPhone for a fortnight.

I buzz. I sing. I giggle. I hum. I glow. I'm so irritatingly cheerful that I overhear Otilya telling someone over the mobile phone that I have 'gone crazy, like an animal' and at the office Cora rolls her eyes when she thinks I can't see her. I feel like the star in a film of my life, after years of having been the bit player everyone could overlook.

For about a month, my affair takes over everything I see or do. I'm unstoppably happy at work, and so determined to share my good mood with every patient that I pay even more attention to their complaints, pleadings and anxieties. The children see me with a perennial smile on my face, and I overhear Kat tell Molly Vincent that 'the best thing that ever happened to Mum was going full-time – she feels so guilty she's really, really nice to us all the time'.

Incredibly, given that when I was twenty-one I used to analyse every look of Jonathan's, every intonation of his voice, every step he took, I don't try to read too much into my time with Rob. I seem to have reverted to my seventeen-year-old self with these flirtatious phone calls, steamy texts, and breathless romps. I'm light-headed and carefree, unhurried and unstressed. I realise that I don't feel an all-devouring need to own, or even know, Rob. I sense that he feels the same: he's not interested in my children, not at pains to know about my work life, he looks positively pained when I mention my mum . . . it's as if I'm a product he has thrown into his shopping trolley without wondering about the ingredients – or, I hope, the sell-by date.

20

My elation is only surpassed by Jill's. My best friend walks, talks, breathes Baby. When Cora asks her for a signature on a document for the practice, Jill trills, 'Of course', signs, and then, head to one side, asks, 'Scarlett or Angelina? Oscar or Otto?'

Standing by the photocopier, I hear Jill welcome a youthful patient: 'Now, what seems to be the pregnancy – I mean, the problem?' I overhear her ordering a minicab ride home: 'Could I have a pram to go to Wimpole Street, W1, please?'

Gone is the sharp and hard-nosed pro, totally on top of every situation; in its stead I see a gentle figure wafting through the surgery wearing a permanent Laura Ashley smile, her voice soft and melodious as a lullaby.

'I think we should look into replacing the fax machine.' Premila shakes her head over the ancient white box in a corner of the reception.

'Oh? I bet it's twins,' Jill mutters softly as she strokes her invisible bump.

'B-but,' I splutter crossly into the telephone, 'I've never asked you to have them for a weekend before!'

'Sorry, no can do.' Jonathan sounds clipped, cold. 'I cannot be expected to pay through the nose and throw in extra babysitting at a moment's notice.'

'Jonathan!' I explode. 'It's not a moment's notice: it's two weeks down the line. I'm invited for a weekend and . . . I don't think it would be . . . appropriate for the children to come along . . .'

'"Appropriate"? Why, what's going on, an orgy on the beach?' Jonathan almost snorts his derision.

'I mean . . . they . . . don't know the host . . .' I weakly reply.

'Oh really?' Jonathan sounds surprised. There's a long pause, then he asks, 'Who *is* the host? Someone I know?'

For a moment I'm about to tell him, and then I realise it's none of his business.

'I mean, of course you don't owe me an explanation, you're your own woman, it's just that there are some real cads out there,' Jonathan rambles, then coughs self-consciously, and starts anew: 'Is this serious?'

'Jonathan! It's none of your business!' I cry – and then realise, with a flicker of pleasure, that my ex-husband is jealous.

'No-no-no-no-no, of course not. Just think you should be careful, that's all.'

'I'm not getting a chance to be anything but.'

'It's not Mallaby-Steer, is it? I've heard about lawyers like him. They zero in on the divorcées who get a fat alimony, and then pounce.'

'Mallaby-Steer? What a thought!' I can't help laughing at the vision of my savage lawyer being amorous. 'He's still angry with me for opting for mediation.'

'Well, I'm relieved: he was hell to work with . . . Hey! I hope it's not Max Lowell? That man killed off Zelkin!'

'Jonathan, it's not, and I wish you'd stop this guessing game.'

The little smirk I allow myself at the notion of a jealous Jonathan fades immediately at the prospect of my weekend with Rob the lawyer being ruined. It was supposed to be a forty-eight-hour sex extravaganza, with a bit of beach and a lot of 'bouncy bouncy', as Rob had explained with a twinkle in his eye.

Now it looks set to be spent playing charades, or looking for the frisbee that Freddy somehow always loses, or picking up wet towels from Rob's no-doubt-immaculate wooden floor boards.

I adore my children – but I feel stuck. Otilya has bought her ticket to Krakow and won't be budged, even with my offer of paying for the alternative Ryanair flight.

'No,' she shakes her head and sets that indomitable jaw. 'My niece has baptism. We have big party. All the family there.'

I try my mum, but she too has a celebration: 'Sorry, pet – I'm off to Nice that weekend with a new friend. I'd love to help out, but . . . I can't afford to pass up this chance . . .'

I sigh: Rob the lawyer isn't a children-person. He's never

showed an ounce of interest in Kat and Freddy. He acknowledges them politely when he comes to pick me up, but it's with a sigh of relief that he shuts the door behind me and whisks me away from the domesticity he's caught a glimpse of.

'Oh . . .' His reaction to my announcement that Jonathan won't take the offspring confirms my suspicion: if I had asked whether I could bring leprosy and dysentery he couldn't have sounded less enthusiastic.

'Don't worry, they're easy, really,' I try to persuade him. 'And I'll bring lots of DVDs . . .'

'Oh dear . . . er . . .' Rob sounds unconvinced. 'I've just had the cottage redecorated . . .'

'They're good like that.' The blatant lie issues forth before I can stop it. 'There's no need to worry.'

'Does he want to marry you, Mum?' Freddy shouts over the *High School Musical 2* CD.

'He doesn't seem very friendly.' Kat manages to be audible above 'You Are the Music In Me'. 'Do you like him, Mum?'

'Does he have any children?'

'Is he rich enough to buy our home back?'

We're speeding down the A303 and the children haven't stopped bombarding me with questions since we left Gospel Oak. A weekend in Devon, which was how I presented it to them a fortnight ago, was greeted with howls of delight and a little hopeful query: 'Will Dad come too?' Devon, after all, had been our favourite family holiday destination for years.

'No, we're not going to Rose Cottage,' I explain with what I hope is a casual air, 'we're staying with a friend of mine.'

I only reveal the friend's identity on the morning we set off.

'He doesn't like me,' Kat protests.

'He always looks at me like I've just farted,' Freddy echoes.

'Freddy!' I reproach him. I look in the mirror and catch his eye. 'I don't want language like that when we're Rob's guests, OK?'

'Yes, Mum,' Freddy mumbles.

'Whatever,' Kat sulks.

'Don't let me down,' I warn.

'So you DO like him!' Kat says triumphantly.

'Oh pahllllllleeeeeeeeeeeeease,' I cry, exhausted. 'I just don't want you to embarrass me, that's all.'

We drive on in silence for a bit. I wish for the umpteenth time I had a fall-back to count on when Otilya is unavailable; I think again how lovely it would be if my mum could be a granny minding my two instead of someone's girlfriend off on a sun-and-sex break. I wonder how Rob will cope with two pre-teens and whether Jonathan really minds that his ex-wife has finally found herself someone. And above all I wonder how difficult it will be to snatch some moments of grown-up intimacy under the beady eyes of my charges.

Then, at the thought of my poor children having to cope with yet another grown-up relationship in their lives, I offer: 'Shall we get an ice cream at the service station?'

Squeals of happiness and a wolf-whistle transform the atmosphere and have me smiling: Kat and Freddy are in fact still innocent, manageable and easily pleased. But as I follow them into the crowded service station with its sunburnt, overweight, ungainly throng, I overhear Freddy say to Kat: 'Do you think they will be at it the whole time like Dad and Linda?'

'Look, I'd really appreciate a little co-operation here,' Rob the lawyer talks through gritted teeth. 'I said wet towels in the wicker laundry basket on the landing upstairs, PLEASE.'

'Yessir,' Freddy answers, surly and scowling.

'Whatever,' mumbles Kat, avoiding my gaze.

My children slope out of the all-white, avant garde designer sitting room. I hold my breath: I can see Rob throbbing with indignation beside me. It's been a tough day. His cottage is absolutely perfect – for a label-conscious, child-free, pet-free, tidy couple. Preferably blonde, as even one dark hair on the white sofas and armchairs would mar the look.

The 'look' – variations on the theme of white and off-white perfection – features designer chairs, sofas and lamps. It might have survived children – even *my* children – if everyone had spent the entire day out in the sun on the beach, and only passed the immaculate sofas and armchairs on their way to their bedroom.

Alas, this has not been the case, quite. It's been raining since we arrived. Sometimes it has come bucketing down; sometimes it has been fine and steady. Sometimes there have been distant rumblings, at other times gusts of wind. Throughout, the impenetrable grey sky above shows no sign of clearing, and the rain no sign of letting up.

We are stuck inside, and no matter how often I whisper,

'Mind those hands,' or 'Watch where you sit,' the children leave imprints on cushions, wooden surfaces, and glass tops.

'What about a nice game of charades?' I try hopefully, feeling like the moderator in a particularly angry debate. The children sit scowling on one side of the room, while Rob, pretending immersion in a book, sits on the other.

'Nah . . .' Freddy yawns without covering his mouth.

'Nah . . .' echoes Kat, pulling a face.

'Oh, come *on*,' I urge, and give Kat *The Jungle Book* to act out. But after a few more tries – *Tess of the D'Urbervilles* and *High School Musical* – I have to bring the game to an end when Rob starts gyrating obscenely, pumping an imaginary partner as he tries to act out the Kama Sutra, which Kat mischievously set for him.

'I wish we could have spent the entire day in bed.' Rob presses against me in the kitchen while the children watch *The Bourne Identity* in the sitting room. Quickly his hands slip inside my shirt and cup my breasts. But before I can respond, a plaintive call reaches us: 'What about the popcorn, Mum?'

'Bloody hell!' Rob snaps, hands dropping. And that was at the beginning of the day, when he was still in a good mood.

He has cause to be cross, I can see that. There is the elaborate wicker and steel chair that Freddy decided to test by bouncing up and down on it, repeatedly, until a white-faced Rob rushed to shove him off it, shouting 'Tom Dixon!'

'Who's he?' Kat asks, vaguely curious.

'Designer. World-famous.' Rob spits out the words with effort. 'This is a one-off.'

There is my glass of wine, which Kat accidentally tips over as she reaches across my place setting with a loud 'sorry'. 'That wine,' Rob practically sobs, 'is a Meursault-Charmes. Only four hundred bottles are produced each year.'

He is so heartbroken he can only cover his face with his hands, while I use my napkin to mop up the golden puddle on his white and hitherto pristine Scandinavian table. Then there is the coffee table.

'Rosie!' Rob points an accusing finger at the low-legged glass table, now foggy with finger prints and – oh no! – one short, very definitely Freddyish footprint. 'I thought I'd explained,' he hisses, 'about this table. It's a Marc Newson design and one of a kind. Pleeeeeeeease can you have your children take care?' He frowns and looks at me not as the woman who lights his fire but as the bearer of the two juvenile delinquents bent on destroying his designer haven.

'They're only children, Rob,' I begin, weakly protesting their innocence. 'And it seems a bit daft to have a white sitting room.' I'm wearying of his perfectionism and clear dislike of my flesh and blood.

'Not if people treat their surroundings with respect,' Rob snaps.

Rob's nerves remain on edge throughout the day: he darts about the cottage with a dusting rag and a spray, trying to remove the marks my two leave in their wake. He is so busy polishing, rubbing, wiping and buffing that he hardly casts a look in my direction. Our dirty weekend is suddenly a cleaning-up marathon. Sadly, instead of running after me,

326

my lover is running after my children, hoping to erase all evidence of their existence.

In fact, Kat and Freddy are so objectionable, I can't say I blame Rob. They whine, they moan, they sulk, they skulk.

'Please,' I hiss when Rob is in the kitchen cooking supper, 'I know it's not great being stuck in here, but Rob is trying so hard to make everything nice for us and you are being extremely spoiled.'

'Mum, he's awful.' Kat shakes her head, disapproving. 'He's a real hygiene queen.'

'I like him,' I say defensively, placing index finger on lips to remind them to keep their voices low.

'He keeps pretending we're not there.' Freddy curls his lip. 'He makes Linda look good.'

'If you marry him,' Kat narrows her eyes threateningly, 'we'll book ourselves in with Social Services.'

'Shh! Don't wake them, whatever you do!' It's past midnight when Rob sneaks into my bedroom. He has cunningly placed the children in the guestroom downstairs, while we are on the first floor, next door to one another. Outside it's still raining. Somewhere in the distance a low rumble breaks the monotony of the drip-drip.

'Are you sure this is a good idea?' I whisper.

'I can't think of a better one.' He slips into bed beside me, and within a second has peeled off my nightgown and clamped his mouth to my right breast. 'Hmmm . . .' he moans with pleasure. 'I want you.'

'Oh yes . . .' I begin to relax, forgetting about Tom Dixon

and Marc Newson, Kat and Freddy, and the lot of them downstairs. Rob's fingers are beginning to part my legs and I hear my own deep intake of breath: the expectation is delicious.

Crash! Bang! Rob sits up as if electrocuted. 'Owwwww!' I hear Freddy's wail. 'Mu-ummmy! Owwwwwwwwwwwww! It hurts . . . the glass lamp's broken!'

Our exit from Rob's cottage is hurried and rather sooner than anticipated. The children pretend contrition, but I can sense their delight in having scuppered the weekend. I'm furious: but not just with them. How *could* Rob be so damn precious about his cottage, and all that designer furniture? The children might have been less than angelic, but he was worse than pedantic. How can I hope to have a relationship with a man who views my children as a vampire views garlic? Rob is fun. Great fun. And I owe him for waking me up again. But I'm a mum, not just a bed bunny.

'Mu-um!' Freddy calls from the back. 'I'm sorry I broke Rob's lamp.'

'It's not really your fault.' I continue driving and then look at him in the mirror: he is smiling his widest, most winning smile.

'He's not good enough for you, Mum.' Kat extracts the iPod from one ear and beams me a great grin. 'You can do better.'

We drive on a while in silence. Then, 'You know who was a lot nicer, Mum?' Freddy asks.

'Who?' But I know immediately.

'Sam's and Will's dad.'

*　　*　　*

328

It's all very well for my children to express their opinions about the men in my life, but what am I supposed to do when they are off with their dad and Linda? While they spend the whole of the following Saturday at Jonathan's, I'm left on my own in the new flat I still cannot call home. Every room is a poor replica of its counterpart in our old home: the kitchen is smaller and sunless; the children's rooms seem shrunken and dingy; the sitting room squashed and oddly shaped.

Same as my life, I realise as I sit on my bed, still in Freddy's Spiderman T-shirt, drinking my second cup of coffee. It's as if I've taken the perverse decision of down-grading everything: the house has become a flat; the husband a series of un-satisfactory love interests (even after I made the children write him thank you letters for their stay, and left him two affectionate voicemails, Rob has yet to be in touch); the safe and easy part-time job for a full-time one where they may yet get rid of me. There's downwardly mobile, and then there's plunging down the well – and that's me.

All of this, plus my thirty-eighth birthday looms.

The presence of Rob the lover in my life gave me the self-confidence to face my birthday. Whatever else I lost or was about to lose – husband, home, flexibility, X factor – I was getting so much wonderful carefree sex that I felt wanted, if not loved. Rob's constant attentions reassured me that I was still desirable. Now the texts have stopped and the phone is mute, and I'll be on my own most of next Sunday while the children see Jonathan. I know I could ask Jonathan to swap weekends, but I don't actually want the children to see, or sense, their mother's misery. I'll probably receive a couple of cards – the children will hand me something homemade and adorably sweet that will bring tears to my eyes; Jill will send me something funny, Mum something girly. And then that's it: I didn't feel I knew Rob well enough to confide in him my fear of getting older, so he doesn't know about my birthday.

And Max Lowell . . . has washed his hands of me.

Monday morning, at the surgery. I was staggering under the weight of a carton of the heaviest books I'd ever carried, and the one person who noticed was Max Lowell.

'Can I give you a hand with those?'

'Er . . . thanks . . .' I turned bright red, and not just with the effort of the load. Max took most of the books from the carton and silently followed me into the walk-in closet where the stationery and other surplus matter is kept. As I watched him set down the pile of books, I wondered if he'd stepped to my aid because his gentlemanly instincts couldn't bear to stand by and watch a damsel in distress – no matter who she was – or because he wanted to rekindle our relationship. I guessed the former when he turned on his heels and, stony-faced, tried to walk past me out of the closet.

But I couldn't waste this opportunity, and tugged at his sleeve. 'Thanks for that. No one else seemed to notice.' I positioned myself so as to stand between him and the door.

'I'm grateful that it's *that* kind of a place,' he said, without looking at me. 'I mean a place where people *don't* notice everything about you, don't snoop . . .' Then, with a pointed look at me: 'I'm sure you feel the same.'

I felt like protesting that I had nothing to hide, but I was suddenly defeated by his cold expression, and the indifference in his gaze. I breathed in deeply as if to steady my nerves. 'Max,' I began, and as he took a step forward as if to rush off, I took one backwards, to block him. Instead, the door banged shut behind me. *Oh gawd – he'll think I did that on purpose.* I winced at the thought. 'I'm sorry, I didn't mean to . . .'

As if in spite of himself, Max cracked a smile. 'I don't know your intentions, but I have quite a busy schedule today.' He didn't move though.

My palms grew sweaty, my heart started thumping, and I felt dry-mouthed. Max stood less than a foot away from me. I could reach out and touch him: stroke his face, or his hand; maybe even shock him by planting a kiss on the lips that were set against me. All regrets about Rob, all thoughts of Jonathan – or anyone else, for that matter – evaporated. *This* was the man for me. I must somehow overcome his hostility.

'I'm sorry . . .' I whispered. I felt like confessing how much I'd missed him, how wrong everything felt in my life because of his silence, how wonderful it was to snatch a few seconds together . . . Nothing came out though.

'Are you?' he asked, his expression giving nothing away. The blue eyes fixed on some spot on the floor. I felt paralysed by the cold disapproval I could sense in him. But I couldn't give up like this.

'Look,' I tried to sound calm and coaxing, 'I'm sorry if something's happened to upset you, Max . . .' I stopped, my hand on the brass knob. 'If you wanted to tell me about it . . .?' I pleaded.

But Max just shook his head. 'No. Thanks. I've got to go.' And with a quick turn of the knob he let himself out.

We haven't spoken since.

Now I sit here wondering what to do on my birthday. If it were not on a weekend, at least I could go to work. My status at the practice is still insecure, yet I enjoy the patients, as they troop in with different ailments to cure and different stories to tell. I enjoy the thought of belonging to a team that is determined to help people get better. Max Lowell may no longer show any interest in me, but his words about building, and restoring, and being constructive, keep echoing in my head. Maybe because, like Max, I'm a divorce survivor, maybe because I too have lived through disappointment and emotional destruction, I want to do the same: help cure, rebuild, regenerate.

The phone interrupts me. When I hear Jill's cheerful voice ask, 'So how's it going?' I have to gulp in order not to weep.

'Uhm . . . fine . . .' I say, though my voice doesn't fool my best friend.

'No, you're not. Come on, tell me everything.'

'I . . . uhm . . . oh, Jill!' A tidal wave of woe bursts forth: 'The weekend at Rob's was a disaster. You remember, he was the one I had been –'

'Yes, yes,' Jill interrupts, 'at it like rabbits.'

'But he hated the children, and they hated him and and . . . and I'm thirty-eight next Sunday!' I sob.

'Yes, of course you are.' Jill sounds wonderfully in control. 'Which is why I'm calling. You and I are going to Ludo.'

'Ludo?' I break off from my dry sobbing.

'Yup. The new super-luxurious day spa in Mayfair they've just opened. I need some antenatal massaging and pampering, and you need cheering up. We'll have a ball.'

Thanks to Jill's treat, my mood is much improved during the rest of the week. By the time we don our white fluffy towelling robes at the Ludo Spa, I'm thirty-eight but coping.

The spa shines: polished beechwood and polished pebbles, sparkling glass and brass, not to mention the glowing complexions of the staff in their white cotton uniforms, and the guests, mainly female, in their fluffy robes. Ludo is elegantly minimalist, with exotic flowers shooting out of crystal vases, and scented candles floating in white bowls. A fountain outside trickles over white stones, and clouds of smoke roll above the hot tub. A restful quiet fills the rooms: everyone speaks in whispers, and dons white slippers.

'Heaven . . .' Jill rolls her eyes with delight as we troop into the Wellbeing Centre and are greeted with a low bow by a handsome young Japanese.

'Bliss,' I agree.

I'm even more enthusiastic when we are presented with a dream menu of saunas, facials, salt-water swims, massages (antenatal, postnatal and Swedish), hot-stone therapy, aromatherapy, stretching and mud baths.

By tea time, we've spent the afternoon ambling from seaweed wraps to Hungarian facials. Jill has enjoyed an hour and a half of antenatal massage with a beefy Polish twenty-something, while I've been pummelled by a swarthy Russian who looks like her second job is as a mud wrestler.

'I think a birthday glass of champagne is called for,' Jill announces as she emerges, hair in a turban, face pink with heat, from her 'Cleopatra's milk bath'. 'After all our exertions, you deserve one. I of course' – she gives me a radiant smile – 'will stick to OJ.'

We make for the Juice Bar, which despite its puritanical name promises not only every berry juice possible, but also Moët et Chandon and Dom Perignon. The Bar is in a blue-domed room, with art deco lamps and mirrors, and a sad-looking bartender behind the counter. We settle on a pillow-stuffed sofa in a comfy nook.

'Happy birthday, darling.' Jill clinks her tumbler of orange juice against my flute of Moët.

'You're the reason it's been happy rather than hellish.' I smile at her.

'I know what it's like.' Jill shakes her head. 'Remember, I've been there. The fear of getting older. The worry about being on your own for the rest of your days. The terror that actually the divorce was all your fault, and if you don't iron out your tragic flaw quickly, no one, ever, will commit to you again.' She sighs. 'Phew, it's a struggle being a grown-up woman.' Then she strokes her protruding tummy. 'But now . . . nothing seems quite as important as this. Them.'

'Them?' I blink in surprise.

'Yes!' Jill trills and now both hands fly to her stomach,

holding it on either side. 'Doctor says it's twins!' she gurgles happily.

'Oh, Jill, this is so exciting!' I hug her. 'Double whammy!'

'Yes, but I have to be careful.' Jill's face, framed by the white turban of her towel, grows serious. 'I mustn't get tired. David and I have decided I'll start my maternity leave next month. Max agrees.' She says the name, and watches me jump. 'He's been such a support, you know.' Jill's index finger traces the rim of her glass.

'He's your friend,' I say, keeping my voice devoid of emotion.

'He could be yours.' Jill's green gaze pierces me. 'He was telling me how well you've done in the past two months. He's not the only one' – she flashes me a big, generous smile, 'all the patients spend the first five minutes telling us how marvellous you are.'

I glow with pleasure.

'Max is really impressed.'

'Impressed, but not interested.' I shake my head. 'This is one thing' – I smile and raise my flute at my best friend – 'that even you can't arrange.' Jill says nothing and I take a sip. 'I'm really, really appreciative of your introducing us. Max Lowell is . . .' I turn red '. . . perfect. What I needed. But it's not going to work.'

'I just *know* he thinks about you a lot.' Jill crosses her arms, frowns. 'If I ask him about you, he goes puce; if someone else mentions you, he pricks up his ears. And he studiously avoids you at the practice.' Jill pauses, to see if her words have sunk in. 'I mean it: that man likes you.' Now she turns to face me, and her hands forget the vulnerable balloon of her stomach and clasp mine instead. 'And he's the right man for you. I can see it, even if you can't. I agree that he's not playing by the rules . . .' Jill pauses, studying my hopeless expression. 'There's only one thing for it. Go get him. *You* make the next move.'

'I can't!' I burst, and the bartender looks up, his mournful face even sadder than before, as if fearing a complaint. 'I don't have the guts.' I lower my voice. 'Don't have the confidence.'

'Stop being pathetic,' Jill barks. 'Max is as scared of rejection as you are. So what are you going to do? Not move, not say anything and let the chance of a lifetime just slip by?'

'I can't approach him when he's made absolutely no overture.'

'So that's that?' Jill's voice rises in disbelief. 'You're giving up on the future?'

'I need to focus on surviving the present,' I say softly. 'Trying to work out a good divorce –'

'Oh, pahhhllllllleeeeeease!' Jill snaps impatiently. 'You're pouring all your energy into having a good divorce. What about a good relationship?! The children are fine – mostly. Jonathan's not bitter – mostly. But what about YOU? Do you want to go through the rest of your life making sure you manage what's wrong, or do you want to go get something that's right?'

'You don't understand. I can't get on with a good relationship if my last one is a wreck. A good divorce is not just about what's best for the children. It's also about me, and realising that I don't want unfinished business, bitterness and anger.' I finish the champagne in my glass. 'And there's no one out there ready to help.'

'I've tried . . .' My friend looks hurt.

'Yes, you have. What I mean is that the experts are only useful if you care about money, not emotions. If you want a civilised split, you're on your own.'

'Well, you've done your bit. By now' – Jill wags her finger – 'you should be ready to go after something new.' Then, more gently, 'Come along, you wimp, let's have some more pampering. You don't deserve it, but I do.'

We both have a manicure and pedicure, and then, for my final treat, I venture into the hot tub.

It's a huge hexagonal wooden tub that sits in the middle of a mini jungle of potted plants, within earshot of the tinkling fountain. Small palms, tall cacti, waxy Aloe Vera surround us in wide and ornate terracotta pots.

'Can't join you, because of the twins.' Jill stretches out on the lounge chair beneath a palm.

The hot tub already has one inhabitant: a woman with her hair wrapped in a towel, turban-style, and cucumber discs on her eyes. She doesn't budge when I join her in the hot bubbling water.

I rest my arms on the wooden rim and concentrate on not touching my fellow guest with my feet. I shut my eyes and relish the feeling of my entire body being massaged by the hot water.

Jill's right. I must do something about Max. If I look back

337

over our encounters, I recognise signs of interest, affection – even desire. Surely I could build on these encouraging overtures? Maybe I *have* spent too much time worrying about the divorce and not enough time thinking about the one relationship that can heal me. I've been too shut off from him, clammed up too much. I should be more open, more accessible, more . . .

'There you are! That aromatherapist is fab!' A plump blonde comes bounding into the tub. 'Ooooooh, isn't it lovely,' the blonde purrs as she settles into the bubbles. 'Sorry!' she calls out cheerily as she steps on my feet. Then, turning to her friend, 'Isn't this perfect?'

'It's great.' The turbaned face speaks, the cucumber discs tremble but remain in place. She has a low, sultry voice with an American accent. 'Oooooooh I needed a break from that family.' The cucumber discs tremble slightly as she speaks. 'You know, it's very full-on, this stepmother business.'

The voice sounds horribly familiar, I realise.

'I think he's worth the sacrifice,' the blonde sighs enviously. 'I mean, how often do you see the brats – once, twice a week?'

'They're cute kids really. Even if they cost an arm and a leg.'

I'm transfixed, as if in a nightmare, yet I can't find the strength to move.

'What do you mean?'

'School fees. Your English schools – I don't know how anyone manages to survive.'

'I thought he had bags of money?'

'It's all gone pear shaped . . .'

I can't bear to hear any more. I stand up and clamber out of the tub.

'And let me tell you, counting your pennies is a real bore . . .'

I wrap the towel tightly round me, praying that Linda will not take off her cucumber slices until I'm safely far away.

21

'You know what else really gets me?' the cucumber-lidded Linda goes on, unaware of my rush to the chaise longue beside Jill's. 'He's always going on about ME spending money.' A huge sigh, then: 'I knew he'd never have Richard's money. I mean, Jonathan's big thing was Zelkin, and even *that* patent was shared . . . but I did think we'd have FUN.'

Even as I bend to whisper to Jill that we must go, I can't help noticing the sharp note of criticism in Linda's voice. 'And right now it's not fun.'

I'm signalling to Jill to get up, hurry up, but she ignores me and only when I hiss 'Jill' and she still doesn't move do I realise my friend's fallen into that deep, impregnable catnap characteristic of pregnant women.

'Plus, get this' – Linda goes on, laughing – 'he's obsessing about his ex-wife's cooking. He wants sausages and mashed potatoes, fish pie, chicken casserole, cauliflower cheese . . . I mean, carbo-charged or what?' Linda whistles her disapproval. 'So I've been trying my hand in the kitchen, bought pots and pans, that new Jamie Oliver book, got the ex-wife to email me some recipes . . . And after all that, do you know what she tells me?'

Linda's friend giggles. 'What?'

'That *he*'s a great cook.' I hear Linda's resentful voice over my shoulder as I rush from the hot-tub jungle. 'I've been wasting my time in the kitchen!'

'Yes, Mum, what is it?'

I answer the landline while I rummage round the papers on my desk for today's post.

'I just thought you should know that Kat's very upset.'

'Kat?' I immediately stop sifting through the letters in my hand.

'She rang last night. She's going through a bit of a hard time. Mungo's stopped texting.'

'What?' I start guiltily: I haven't noticed a thing. 'But why is she telling you this?' What I mean, of course, is why isn't Kat telling *me* this? I'm her mother, after all. And I don't live three hours away in Somerset, but right under her nose.

'She likes to ring me every now and then. She always has.'

'She does? She has?' I can't believe my daughter has been confiding in my mum – and I've never known about it.

342

'I know you find this hard to believe, but there *are* people who confide in me.' Mum adopts a hurt tone. 'Kat's always done it, ever since she was in Year 3 and that Williamson girl used to pick on her. Now she's very upset about Mungo.' Mum pauses. 'Haven't you noticed?'

No, I haven't. Obviously I am the most insensitive, most unsympathetic mother around. Not to mention daughter. 'No,' I mumble.

'I've given her a few pointers. How to get him back. But she needs monitoring.'

'What . . .'

I hear a door bell ring: it's so clear, I think it's ours and jump up.

'Oh, it must be Peter.' My mum issues a little giggle. 'Got to rush, darling, we're going to that new fish restaurant tonight. In Bath.'

'That's a long drive. You'll be back past midnight . . .' I can't help being concerned.

'Oh no, sweetheart – Peter's got a house there. We're staying the night.'

I have to sit down. I need to unpick my conversation with my mother slowly and carefully, and I feel as if it will take all my energy and attention to do so. I'm still reeling from the knowledge that Kat sees my mum as a confidante; one, it would seem, she prefers to me.

Doesn't she know how my mum used to share with her friends everything I ever had the misfortune of telling her, even though I'd sworn her to secrecy? My crush on my neighbour, my worry about my breasts not growing, my difficulty with tampons and with Mlle Jeanne the French mistress – my mum served them up as if they were canapés to accompany her bridge evenings. Later, when I knew better, I never told her a thing – though even that didn't protect me from Mum's attempts to sabotage my sentimental life. I brought Jonathan home to meet Dad and her, secretly hoping that he would propose during the visit. Jonathan was a bit shy, obviously rather in awe of my parents' easy lifestyle. 'Rosie's home from university with her first boyfriend . . .' I overheard Mum's loud telephone voice when I came down the first morning. 'Sweet, really, if a bit, you know, awkward. I always suspected she'd like a bit of rough.' It was only because Jonathan was singing 'You Are the Champion' under the power shower in the guests' bathroom that he didn't run out of the house.

Yet here is my thirteen-year-old daughter choosing this same woman as the repository of her secrets. I feel all protective: I don't want Mum to betray my lovely little Kat. And I don't want Kat to go through a heartbreak when she is just mending from her parents' break-up. I feel guilty, too: I had no idea that things with Mungo had ground to a halt. And I never guessed that Mum and Kat were so close. Their special relationship seems so unlikely.

If this new character, my mum as confidante, strikes me as improbable, what of my mum as 'friend', 'partner', or God help us 'mistress' of some man called Peter with a house in Bath?

I check my watch: 7.30. Otilya will be bringing the children home any moment now, and I have yet to get supper under way. In the kitchen, I root around the fridge and freezer for something suitable. I can't help a smirk as I spot the Tupperware with the fish pie I made last week: I wonder whether Linda has managed to get Jonathan to cook for her. I wonder, too, as Linda's sharp words echo in my head, whether Linda and Jonathan have many cosy suppers any more. She didn't sound like she welcomed the down-shifting she's having to deal with.

As I set the table for three (by now I always get the number right), I relive the timid little overture I made to Max today again. Jill's words at the spa had struck a nerve.

'You've got a huge package from Synter Pharmaceuticals.' I smiled cheerfully as he walked in through the revolving door. 'Do you want me to bring it through?'

'Thanks, but better not. I send all those free samples straight back.' Max didn't meet my gaze. 'They hope for a plug in the column.'

'I thought your demolition of the anti-MMR lobby last week was brilliant . . .' I tried, rather desperately, to appeal to his vanity.

'Oh? Good.' Max sorted his post. He stood only a foot or two away from me, and I tried to muster all my courage to say:

'That pamphlet about the drug counselling training scheme is really, really helpful.' I checked to see whether Cora and Premila were listening. 'I'm going to enrol in September.

They offer night classes, plus one Saturday in two. It'll take time, but it's worth it.'

Max looked up, unsmiling. 'Well done.' He retreated to his room.

Not a flicker of interest. Jill was wrong – and so was I. I feel a pang of disappointment: Max Lowell, a man who has everything to give, has allowed his bitter divorce to constrain him. He won't give a new life – or at least a new person – a try. I don't see anything I can do to change his mind.

The phone rings as I put the fish pie into the oven.

'Hullo, Rosie.' I recognise Rob's voice and I feel a little twinge of relief: OK, Max is never going to work out, but someone, somewhere, cares about me. 'Sweet of you to send me the thank you letters.'

'Heart-felt.' I sound a bit nervous, and I clear my throat. 'I'm so sorry again about the Tom Dixon –'

'La Palma. Hey, it doesn't really matter.' Rob sounds unconvincing. There's a brief pause. 'I just wanted to let you know that you left your rather beautiful pale blue pashmina here.'

Oh, how sweet, I can't help smiling into the phone: the old, 'you left some item of yours here, why don't I bring it over?' routine. It touches me to think that Rob doesn't have the gumption to ask me out without resorting to such a silly excuse.

'I couldn't for the life of me figure out what had happened to it,' I begin, sounding, I hope, pleased and open to all possibilities.

'Shall I leave it downstairs with the doorman?' Rob sounds in a hurry.

'Oh . . .' I do everything I can not to show my surprise and, let's be honest, disappointment. 'Of course.'

'I would bring it over myself, but' – here he coughs self-consciously – 'it's just that I'm in training right now and between work and running and . . .'

'Training?'

'Yes.' Rob laughs at my surprise. 'I'm going for the Triathlon. My, er . . . personal trainer is putting me on a gruelling schedule. In fact, Mimi's even put me on a muscle-building diet.'

'Mimi?' A memory stirs.

'Yes. Australian. She's . . .' a catch in his throat tells me Rob is smitten '. . . rather wonderful.'

The children and Otilya find me subdued as I set the table: 'Otilya, will you have supper?'

'No thank you, I go dancing.' Otilya smiles smugly.

'Dancing?' I can't help ask.

'Yes. Ballroom dance.' Otilya kicks up her heel as she says 'ballroom' and her eyes light up.

'I see.' And suddenly I feel lonely: even my nanny/cleaner has a nightlife. 'Hands!' I call to Kat and Freddy while Otilya stands in front of the mirror in the hall and puts on lip gloss. *What happened to the animals?* I want to know: who's turned this man-hating snarler into a smiling, lip-glossed dancing queen?

'Hmm, fish pie!' Freddy rushes to his chair.

Kat, instead, takes her seat half-heartedly. Without her iPhone.

'Tell me about your day . . .' I begin the familiar ritual: it's the only way to keep me from sinking into miserable thoughts about losing my lover to my ex-husband's personal trainer. The children immediately start, with descriptions of favourite tennis pros, complaints about the canteen food, enthusiastic exaggeration of their prowess on the court. I let them talk and smile, keeping the conversation going with now one question now another. Maybe this is it, then: the self-sacrificing mum who looks after her two children, with no man on the scene. I will work hard at the surgery, then dedicate myself to the counselling, modestly accepting the gratitude of countless addicts who will put their victory over drugs down to me. This will be my role in life – and actually, is it such a come-down? It leaves no room for broken promises and broken hearts, grand illusions and hopeless daydreams. It may not offer the thrill of passion, but it will grant me the security of standing on my own two feet.

'More, Mum, please.' Freddy holds out his plate, Oliver Twist-like.

'Of course': even after thirteen years, my desire to feed them is positively primitive. 'What about you, Kat?'

But Kat has barely touched the plate before her.

'Kat's broken up with Mungo,' Freddy says in a singsong voice.

'Sneak!' Kat bursts, then pushes away from the table and

jumps up. She throws down her napkin and bounds up the stairs. I watch her retreating figure.

'Is it true?' I whisper to Freddy, who seems unperturbed by his sister's dramatic exit.

Freddy cocks his head to one side and looks at me over his forkful: 'Mungo stopped texting her.'

'I see.' I sigh. 'You know, sometimes I wish I could be around you 24/7 so I could protect you both.'

'She'll be OK, Mum.' Freddy chews on, a placid expression on his face.

'I know, but it hurts when someone's gone off you.' I pause. Then, putting on a smile: 'I have some experience of that myself.'

'Yeah.' Freddy nods matter-of-factly.

'I'll go up to her.' My son makes as if to follow me, but I restrain him, hand on his shoulder: 'No, darling. I need to talk to Kat on her own.'

'Kat!' I call up. Silence. I climb the stairs: 'Kat?' I repeat, as I rap lightly on her door.

Silence, still. I open the door: my daughter lies sprawled across the bed, face down. Her shoulders are shaking. 'My darling' – I sit down on the bed beside her – 'what's wrong?' I stroke her head. 'Baby, baby, what's up?'

Kat shakes her head into the pillow and I hear a strangled: 'Don't! I want to be alone!'

I wait, stroking the dark head, the shoulder-length hair, the shuddering shoulders in the khaki green T-shirt. Slowly, Kat calms down.

'Mu-um,' she looks up, the tear-stained face all pink and wet, the mouth, down-turned. 'We've broken up! Mungo stopped texting me last week.' She wraps her arms around my waist. 'He didn't say why. Just stopped.' The sobs start again, and it's with a huge effort that she manages to say, 'I'm never going to trust another boy again!'

I let her sob into my arms. 'You will. But it will take some time.'

'I don't think he ever really cared.' Kat dries her tears with the back of her hand. 'If he did, he wouldn't be able to just stop like this.'

'I know how much that hurts,' I whisper. 'And no one can say anything to make it better.' I stroke her head.

'My heart's broken.' Kat's voice quivers.

'Hopefully it's just bruised. Painful, just the same. And I'm an expert.'

Kat sits up, looks at me. 'But you're all right now . . .?'

'I'm all right now.' I hug her tight again.

'Mum,' Kat breathes into the nook of my arm, 'do you think I'm scared of being a woman?'

'Oh goodness, is that what Granny says?' I'm outraged.

'No, Linda.'

What?! Am I third in the queue when it comes to my daughter's confidantes?

'I think that's rubbish,' I say decisively. 'Being a woman is a lot easier than being a girl. So much of what happens to you is not of your choice, at your age.'

'But, Mum . . .' Kat sits up, leaning against me, 'when Dad left to live with Linda, that wasn't your choice, was it?'

'No,' I admit. 'That was not my choice.' I test my voice for bitterness, and am pleased to find none. 'But how I reacted was.'

'Poor Mummy . . .' Kat wraps her arms around my waist, leans her head on my shoulder.

'Poor Mummy nothing!' I smile. 'I knew the marriage was not giving either me or Daddy enough. And I decided, with him, we would make our split as painless as we could. Which, I think, we've pretty much managed . . .?' I look down at her tear-stained face and hold my breath: what will she say, what does she think?

'Yes.' Kat dries her eyes with the back of her hand. 'I mean . . . You don't quarrel. And Freddy and I get to see Dad a lot . . . and . . . Linda's OK, I guess.'

'I'm glad she's understood how special the two of you are. And how devoted your father is to you.' I look at Kat: it's my turn to confide in her, I decide: 'Remember that counselling training course I wanted to start last year?' And the year before, and the one before that . . .

'Yes . . .?'

'I'm going to start in September. It's dealing with drug addicts.'

'Wow.' My daughter's eyes grow wide and round. 'That's cool.'

'I hope so.' I push the hair from her eyes. 'One thing: next time you're down, will you please tell me about it? Even if it's just to keep me in practice.'

'I thought you had enough on your plate.' Kat squeezes me tight. 'And Granny was brilliant.'

'Was she?' I try to keep the scepticism from my voice.

'She gave me some really good tips about playing it cool. I mean' – she laughs as she wipes her face with the back of her arm – 'cool with *him*.'

'Really?'

'Yeah.' She rubs her cheek against my shoulder, an affectionate little cat. 'Mum, will I ever be happy?'

'Yes, of course you will.'

'Are you?'

'Am I?' I hesitate. Max Lowell, Jonathan, Linda, my mum, Rob the lawyer, Zac the photographer, Harry the farmer, Orlando the actor, Cora, Ben Shone's mum, Louis Vincent: they flash, in quick succession, across my mind. They're replaced with Kat and Freddy, the patients who come to the practice, the patients I imagine I'll be helping once I've qualified. 'I am, yes, I am.' I squeeze my daughter's hand.

'It's certainly . . . cosy.' Carolyn Vincent sits gingerly on the edge of the chintz armchair in our sitting room. She looks peachy-perfect in her orange pastel sleeveless top and matching three-quarter-length trousers. Through the window, the sun catches the highlights on her glossy blow-dried hair, which today falls loosely but neatly to her shoulders. Her plum-coloured toenails peep through the golden sandals, her French manicure shows off her tanned hands.

'It's August already, and the Liptons still have tons of building work going on. Your house won't be recognisable once they're finished with it!'

I wince at the thought that the nice family from Barnet who bought our beloved home have not stopped knocking down walls, inserting windows and rearranging the layout of the rooms since they moved in.

'We're thinking of not coming back until the Tuesday after the Bank Holiday, is that OK?'

The Vincents have invited the children to their cottage in Cornwall for a fortnight. Kat and Freddy are over the moon, and I'm incredibly grateful: Jonathan told me categorically that he can't afford to take the children on holiday this summer. Because of the Hill Street Surgery, and because I'm not too flush with money myself, I had already written off as impossible any dream of going away with the children on a little trip.

'Of course. I'm so grateful, Carolyn, it couldn't come at a better time . . .'

'It's a pleasure.' Carolyn beams her sweetest smile. 'And you know the children . . . Whoa, what's this?!' She pulls the pamphlet on drug counselling training from behind a sofa pillow where it must have ended up after I'd re-read it a few nights ago. An expression of alarm fills her face. 'For Kat? Freddy?'

'No, no, no!' I rush to explain before she cancels the holiday, lest my children corrupt hers. 'That's for me.'

'You?' Alarm, followed by vindication, register on Carolyn's pretty face. I've lived up to her worst fears: divorcée seeks refuge in crack, coke or heroin.

'Me, as in, I'm going to enrol in a counselling training programme. I've always wanted to do it – helping drug addicts. And someone' – I don't want to tell her that it's her friend Max – 'gave me this. I'll start in September.'

'Goodness!' Carolyn's eyes grow big. 'You don't think you have enough trouble to deal with? I mean, with the divorce, and having had to sell the house and . . .'

'I think I need a challenge.' Here Carolyn looks at me in surprise: how could anyone ever find a challenge anything but trying? she seems to ask. 'And by the last year I get to actually meet with my own clients – under supervision, of course.'

'Well . . . if you're sure . . .' Carolyn looks around the cluttered sitting room. Children's shoes, Kat's hairbrush, my sunglasses, the drug pamphlet: she takes them in and I can see she thinks I'm overwhelmed by life as it is, without any need of a coke-snorting, ecstasy-tripping druggie clamouring for help.

'Drugs . . .' she shakes her head. 'Louis says there's so much of that going on in the City.' She rolls her eyes. 'That and lap dancers.'

I wonder if Louis ever drops in on lap-dancing bars. Nah, I bet he prefers hitting on divorced friends: less dangerous, more hygienic, and more gratifying, as they would be immensely grateful. I study Carolyn while she skims the pamphlet: has she any idea of her husband's straying?

'Yikes, reading this just makes me feel so grateful.' She looks up at me. Then, deciding that I probably have a lot less to be grateful for, her expression turns serious once again. 'What I mean is, I think if I *had* to work, I'd do something like this too.'

I can't help a smile. There was a time, many months ago, when I would have given anything to have Carolyn's easy life. Now, though, I feel differently. My life has its disappointments, but no deceptions. My children are not yet completely out of harm's reach, but we talk openly with one another, and they have realised that Jonathan is devoted to them, with or without Linda. I'm working more and harder than I ever thought I would, but I find satisfaction in the work – and suspect that this will be all the more so once I start the training next month.

'I think it'll be interesting.' I take the brochure she hands back to me, and set it among the magazines on the coffee table. Carolyn immediately tidies the stack, so that for a minute or two my coffee table can look as neat as hers.

'Well, I know Molly is always saying how much she misses you living next door because she found you so easy to confide in.' There's no jealousy in Carolyn's voice, and I feel suddenly mean for having resented the way Kat talked to my mum. 'I think she's got a new boyfriend . . .' she smiles at me, 'so she may well be booking an appointment.'

'She's pretty and lively: I predict she'll have men swarming round her for the rest of her life.'

'You know, sometimes I do think I should take up something.' Carolyn examines her perfect nail-polish. A slight frown mars her unlined brow: 'Something that I can do when the children are at school and Louis is at work. He's working such long hours these days.'

'Is he?'

'He is so ambitious for us. He really wants only the best.' Carolyn shakes her head sadly. 'I think some people misunderstand him. They feel resentful when there's someone who's so happy and hard-working and . . .' Carolyn can't help smiling fondly, 'so lucky.'

'I suppose some people do have more than their fair share of luck,' I begin cautiously.

'That's what I like about you, Rosie. You're not bitter. You didn't let it get to you.'

'Jonathan and I did try hard to keep it civilised. We had some bad moments, but on the whole, I think we worked it out.'

Carolyn looks around the sitting room again. 'Have you had to let Otilya go?' she asks. I follow her critical gaze: my desk is invisible beneath a pile of books, papers and bills. On the armchair there's a letter from Charles Mallaby-Steer recommending the services of a financial adviser 'to help you invest your alimony prudently and profitably', and a brochure for a new Couple Therapy Centre headed by Babette Pagorsky. On the squat footrest I can see the card Dr Karovakis sent me, advertising a veneer that will turn my teeth 'whiter than white and more even than even'. I'm surrounded by the relics of the divorce industry.

'I know it looks like it, but no.' I shake my head, smiling. 'She's still with us.'

'Better go, I've got my bridge lesson at three.' Carolyn

stands up to go. She smooths down her peach-coloured trousers. 'I hope you can rest without the children about.' She peers at me with concern. 'You look like you could use a proper night's sleep.'

22

I've only time to go back to the kitchen and start on a salad when the door bell goes again.

'Hi . . . just dropped by with that Mac catalogue I promised Kat. I know it's a bit reckless at this point, but she does so want one . . .'

I'm so surprised at the sight of Jonathan standing in the doorway in the middle of the day, without children to drop off or pick up, I don't even think of inviting him in.

'Shall I, er . . . drop it off, or can I come in . . .?' Jonathan looks down, laughs self-consciously.

'Come in, come in.' His awkwardness has infected me, and I feel suddenly as if we're being watched. We head into the kitchen, where the chopping board on the counter is piled with a small mound of cucumber, spring onions and tomatoes.

'Hmmm . . .' Jonathan breathes in as if I'd left a handful

of rose petals on the board rather than a few vegetables. 'I really miss those big salads you used to do in the summer. Perfect with the soufflés I'd whip up – remember?' I do: tall, fluffy concoctions full of cheese or spinach, and Jonathan grinning, satisfied with the success of his elaborate dish. 'Hey' –Jonathan's expression changes when he sees the two mugs left from Carolyn's visit – 'guest already, this morning? A gentleman caller?' His voice sounds strained.

'You really think we can afford a new computer for her?' I pretend not to have heard his question. 'Her marks *have* been really quite good this year, so maybe . . . you could present it as a reward as well as a birthday present?'

'The children told me Devon was *not* a great success.' Jonathan cannot keep the note of satisfaction from his voice.

'No, not a success. Would you like a salad? I've got enough for two.' I keep my back to my ex as I mix the dressing in a bowl.

'Well, if you do have enough . . .' Jonathan perches on the stool. 'It's a shame, really, that they didn't get a chance to do Devon properly this year.' He watches me set the table for us, and springs up to get two glasses. 'Hey, these are the tumblers Uncle Nick gave us when we got married!' He holds up the glasses to the sunlight. 'I was thinking about maybe seeing if Rose Cottage is still available for the end of August. It's late in the day, I know, but I bet a lot of their regular clients are having a hard time in this financial climate . . .' I sit down across from him, and hold the salad bowl for him to help himself. 'What do you think?'

'The children would love it, but . . .'

Jonathan looks me full in the face: 'I didn't mean just the children. I meant you, too. Linda won't be coming.'

I sit, the salad bowl in my hands, and wonder how to react. What is my ex-husband proposing? A seaside holiday with me and our two children? The four of us splashing about in the waves, collecting seashells, taking long walks on the coastal paths – just like old times? What would the children make of these holiday plans? Watching me and their father side by side for seven days, won't they be lulled into thinking things between us are back to BL – before Linda?

I can't look at my husband, I'm so confused by his suggestion. Jonathan's invitation is certainly a tribute: more than one year on, we've handled the divorce so well we can contemplate a holiday together. But is it also an overture? I can feel my ex-husband's eyes on me, can feel the heat of him sitting across the narrow table. If I stretch my legs ever so slightly, our knees will touch under the table. I feel, as I haven't felt for over a year, the object of Jonathan's sexual interest; which is pleasurable but ultimately, I decide, inappropriate.

'We can't, Jonathan.' I spoon some tomatoes on to my plate, give him a quick look and smile to keep the conversation casual. 'The Vincents have invited the children to Cornwall that same week.'

'Aw, what a shame.' My ex-husband sounds genuinely disappointed. 'Well . . . it would have been fun. Like old times.'

'Er . . . yes . . .' We eat in silence for a while. It's warm in the bright kitchen, and I want to peel off my cotton cardigan

– but somehow I daren't: my ex-husband looks too . . . well, hungry.

'You've been marvellous, the way you've handled this divorce.' Jonathan is wolfing down his salad. He reaches across the table for the bread basket, and as he does so he brushes my forearm with his outstretched hand. We draw in our breath simultaneously, and I look away. Oh my god, this can't be . . . I mean, I can't be . . . I practically drop the fork in my hand. The shallow breathing, the feverish trembling feeling, the blood rushing to my head: am I feeling a lust attack for my ex? 'We've proved them all wrong, haven't we?' He gives me a big grin. Yes, I think, and my mind fills with images of Nadine my hairdresser, and Mr Ahmed, the dry cleaner, both dripping with sympathy; Mr Parker the estate agent and Dr Karovakis the dentist, scenting a profit; the interviewer at the Marlborough Centre and my mum, predicting unending trauma and bitterness. No, thank goodness, our divorce has not sunk to their expectations.

'You've been so patient . . .' Jonathan is talking again, 'and so generous. I really appreciated the way you traded in vicious old Mallaby-Steer for mediation.' I don't answer, thinking of how disgusted Mallaby-Steer must have been that I kept my promise and pursued the mediation with Jayjay. Still, I think with not a little bitterness, my lawyer did manage to extract a tidy sum from me until then. 'The children' – Jonathan goes on, sipping water and looking at me over the blue tumbler – 'seem unscathed.'

'They are doing well.' And I realise as I say the words that

I truly believe them. 'Kat's still upset about the break-up with Mungo, but I notice she's no longer locking herself in her room every afternoon. And Freddy's counsellor says he's very good at chess, and so is Sebastian, and they spend a lot of time playing together.'

'You've managed it so smoothly. And the new job. And . . .' Jonathan sighs, sets down his glass, pushes away his plate, crosses his arms on the table and looks straight at me. 'In a weird way I think I've appreciated you more as a result of this.'

'Divorce makes the heart grow fonder?' I look back, sceptical. The waves of lust I'd been feeling disappear.

'Well . . . what I mean to say is that you've managed a good divorce so well, I think you could manage a good marriage too.' Jonathan shifts in his chair, looks sheepish, then reaches for my hand. 'I am . . . I'm beginning to wonder if we shouldn't give it another go?'

'Another go?' I snatch back my hand. 'What?' My voice rings with disbelief.

'Yes, I've been thinking,' Jonathan explains, as if I hadn't understood the meaning of his words, 'that I should come back.'

'You want to come back to live here?' A thousand memories of the past year explode dizzyingly in my mind: the children climbing into my bed for a cry and a cuddle; Max confiding his bitterness over his divorce as he drives me home from Jill's after Sunday lunch; my mum stunned into silence by Linda's appearance at Freddy's Christmas play; my weeping all alone at home when he took the children skiing.

I've been through a lot, over this year, I want to shout at the man who sits, quietly confident, before me.

'I realise we've made a mistake and I'd like things to go back to how they were . . .'

'YOU made a mistake.' I speak slowly, trying to keep all expression from my voice. 'I didn't.'

'You didn't?'

'You remember – the divorce was both our idea.'

'I thought . . .' Jonathan looks genuinely shocked.

'You thought it was only your decision?'

'Well, I had Linda, you had no one . . .'

'I didn't need anyone to see that you and I were not working.'

'B-b-b-b-ut . . .' I note with some satisfaction that my ex is spluttering.

'You thought it your prerogative to move on – and now to come back? I suppose I just stand by patiently and wait for you to make up your mind?'

'No, of course not. But . . . the divorce was my idea. I naturally assumed that you would have preferred to stay married. You never gave me reason to think otherwise.' Jonathan sounds almost petulant.

'The marriage was over for both of us. As you pointed out yourself, I hadn't been in love with you for years.'

'I didn't mean . . .'

'You were right. I wasn't trying. I was taking you for granted, and that's unforgivable.'

'I suppose I was guilty of that too . . .'

'I was prepared to keep things the way they were because

I was scared of what a split would do to the children. You were convinced that you couldn't wait because you'd lose Linda. I accommodated you.'

'I appreciated it . . . which is why I worked so hard to keep our divorce so friendly.'

'YOU worked so hard?' I laugh. 'What about me?' I'm scared I'll shout at him. 'I held back, bit my tongue, made sure the children never heard me say a cross word about you.'

'Well, yes, you too, I know, but . . .'

'I thought this divorce was a partnership. The two of us working together to prove that it was possible to split up without hurt.'

'Well, yes, in a way it was, but I was the one who chose the divorce and I was the one who chose the way we should carry it out. So I think I can take the credit for it.'

'All this time, I saw us taking decisions together. I saw us trying hard to win over everyone to our vision of a split that wasn't a trauma . . .' I am speaking slowly, as if I were trying to get used to the idea. 'You, instead, saw me as a passive victim. The woman you divorced, not the woman with whom you worked out a good divorce.'

'Oh, Rosie, what does it matter?' Jonathan tries again to take my hand, but I pull it away. 'The important thing is that we're still –'

'You opted for a kind of life. Now I'm working out mine.'

'You mean . . .' Jonathan looks incredulous, confused, hurt. 'You mean you don't want to give it another try?'

I study my ex-husband's expression of shock, his handsome

if jowlish face. Did he really think I would welcome him back, open-armed, as if he'd gone out for a pint of milk early in the morning for the children's breakfast – rather than left a year ago to find true lust? It's fifteen years ago since I first met him, yet Jonathan still manages to floor me. Who does he think he is? And what does he take me for?

I shake my head. He's not part of the future I see for myself and the children. I won't expose either them or me to the possibility of being left again, should Daddy fall for some new brainy beauty. I don't trust him.

'You are part of my life, Jonathan. Always will be. Despite everything and everyone, we seem to have stayed friends. We can be good parents. But I think the two of us can't do a good marriage. Let's stick to our good divorce.'

It's 6 p.m. and the surgery is uncharacteristically quiet. Someone's in with Ben Shone, but Alicia and Max have already gone for the day. Cora is packing up her rucksack, then spots her cigarettes and lighter, and starts again. Premila applies some chapstick and tidies her side of the reception-ists' desk. For the umpteenth time, I muse over yesterday's lunch with my ex. I replay each scene in slow motion. I see again the bouncy self-confidence with which Jonathan made himself right at home, as if sure of his belonging and my welcome. How humiliating to find out that, while I had thought we were engaged in a joint enterprise, all along my ex-husband had seen himself as the one in charge. He thought HE had handled our divorce in the nicest way possible.

I'm shaken by the realisation. What I thought was a grand,

generous gesture was being misinterpreted by Jonathan as his desperate ex-wife's attempt to win him back. I had seen myself as a self-sacrificing heroine, he had seen me as the loser he'd left behind. It doesn't help, now, that his feelings for me – and Linda – have changed. All I can think of is how deluded I've been, all along, in seeing this as a mutual project, jointly orchestrated by the two of us in order to keep the children from being thrown off course, and our relationship from sinking into irreparable hostility.

I was wrong. Now I feel cross, embarrassed, an idiot. And as for Jonathan: how dare he, how could he? The arrogance of the man. He obviously thought I'd take him back no matter what he'd put us through. Has he no shame?

I fast-forward: Jonathan without Linda? Jonathan on his own? I can't picture my ex-husband surviving more than a few weeks without an admiring audience. Who will he turn to next? And what of the children? I doubt that Linda has come to mean anything to them, but they'll be jolted by yet another change to their familiar arrangements, and they too will nervously wait for Daddy to find himself a new partner. Please, I fervently pray, let her be kind to Kat and Freddy . . .

The in-house phone rings.

'Rosie? Can you come?' It's Jill.

'I've got bad news,' she greets me as I walk through her door.

My best friend sits in a loose turquoise kaftan, a tabletop fan whirring on her desk to help her cope with the August heatwave. On her right sit a pile of brochures: JoJo Maman

Bébé, The White Company, Baby Boden, Baby Gap. On her left a pile of books: *The Little Book of Baby Names*, *Bonding with Baby*, *The First Nine Months*, *Understanding Twins*.

My gaze returns from the desk to Jill behind it. Her expression is so serious, I'm worried.

'What is it? Something I've done?' This job means a lot to me.

'Oh no no, you're doing very well, don't worry. Everyone sings your praises.' But Jill still doesn't smile.

Oh my goodness, something more serious. I gulp: 'The twins?'

Jill shakes her head. 'It's Max. Looks like he's taking up an offer in Kenya.'

'What?!' If I had any doubts about what I feel for Max Lowell, my reaction to this news confirms it. 'Jill, he can't go!' I cry.

'He's decided.' Jill gives me a look of sympathy. 'An NGO, a pittance for a salary and a million miles from his boys. But he says Ellie is making it so difficult for them to see each other that he may just as well be in another continent.'

'Oh, Jill!' My voice breaks.

Jill shakes her head, her hands on her stomach. 'Rosie, if you want that man, you've got to persuade him not to leave.'

'I . . . I don't know that he'll listen.'

'You won't know until you try.'

'Where . . . where is he?' I jump up, as if I could run into his room right now, and throw myself at his feet, begging him not to leave.

'He's gone home.' Jill hands me pen and paper: 'Take this

down.' She reads out the address in her telephone book. 'It's that leafy street off of Camden High Street with the Chinese at the corner. A ten-minute walk.'

Ten-minute walk, five-minute run, I calculate as I pick up my stuff and rush out of the surgery. He can't go, he can't disappear like this! Without Max, nothing would feel quite right. Even now, when he's not talking to me, I feel his presence everywhere in the surgery. At home, I always feel that, if I can just wait a little longer, he'll turn up, boys in tow, ready to give it another go. Even the training somehow has Max in the picture: he was my inspiration, and part of me was looking forward to showing him my progress. I may have told Kat that I was happy, but that was in the hope that soon I would overcome Max's reluctance.

It takes me about six minutes to reach Max's street. I run most of the way, ignoring the curious stares of passers-by and the 'Move!' of a cyclist in fiery red lycra and helmet. It's a quiet tree-lined street. Some of the tall white houses look shabby and as yet un-gentrified; others look like they've been taken over by lawyers, bankers and, yes, doctors, who have spotted a neighbourhood on its way up. I scour the numbers for 24, find the house where Max has a flat, and stand on the doorstep for a second, trying to regain my breath and work up my courage.

'Please, please,' I whisper as I press the buzzer marked M. Lowell.

For what seems like an hour, nothing happens. Then a woman's voice answers:

'Yes?'

I'm petrified: Ellie? A new woman? A girlfriend I never knew about? But I shake off my fears and ask for Max Lowell.

'Doctor not here.' The woman's voice is heavily accented. 'I cleaning.'

'Please. This is urgent. Do you know where he's gone?'

'St Pancras. He leave five, ten minutes ago. He say he go to Eurostar.' The static-filled voice pauses. 'I hope you get better, madam.'

I hope I get HIM. I run down the stairs, feeling only slightly guilty that I've been mistaken for a patient. St Pancras: he's obviously taking the train to Paris. Was that where the NGO was based? Is he off to tell them he's accepting? I'm running again, this time around the corner to Camden High Street where I hope to get a black cab.

Once on the High Street I wave furiously, as if I were drowning and my life depended on being spotted.

Only when the cabbie picks me up and we're rushing towards St Pancras do I realise I'm not sure what kind of reception I will get from Max. He may see my intervention as silly, or arrogant. He may tell me to mind my own business, and that I mean nothing to him and have no claim on him whatever. There's only a tiny, almost insignificant chance that this is what he wants – and even then, I may be too late to change his mind about the job in Africa.

It takes us twenty minutes to reach St Pancras. I pay, run in, and start searching the enormous, bright station for Max Lowell. I'm again out of breath, as I rush past rows of

370

boutiques and signposts and travellers and uniformed railway staff. I bump into a well-dressed woman who gives me a murderous look and trip over a toddler's flimsy buggy. I'm elbowed by a short-necked, red-faced man coming out of the Gents', and warned to 'Watch it!' by a skinny hoodie drinking from a Coke tin.

Beneath the soaring ceiling, I run past Accessorize and Boots and a restaurant, following the signs for the Eurostar. I look for Max in the queue for tickets. It's hopeless: there are dozens of men up and down the station who look vaguely like him from the back – but which one is he?

And then I spot him. He stands by a small café, a cup in his hand, checking his watch.

'Max!' I call.

He turns around and I see an expression of surprise and – yes – pleasure. Then the expression changes to the one I've grown used to: set, impenetrable, unwelcoming.

'Hullo,' he says as I approach. 'What are you doing here?'

'I've come' – I gulp: it sounds so presumptuous – 'to tell you not to go to Africa.'

'What?' Max looks incredulous.

'I . . .' I've drawn up very close to him, and I'm scared that he can see that my whole body is shaking, and my lips trembling. 'I beg you not to go to Africa.' There, I've said it. I shut my eyes, waiting for him to laugh, or push me away, or . . .

'You . . .' Max speaks each word very slowly, as if explaining something complicated to himself, 'don't . . . want . . . me . . . to . . . go . . . to . . . Kenya.'

'That's right. I . . . I don't want to lose you.'

Max frowns down at me. He shakes his head: 'But' – the blue eyes bore into me – 'what about Louis?'

It's my turn now to frown. 'Louis?' I ask, baffled. 'What's he got to do with this?'

'The last time I saw Louis,' Max's voice is dry, emotionless, 'he was wrapped around you in a pretty steamy clinch.'

'What?!' I stare at Max, then splutter, 'When . . .?!'

'I was coming to pick you up, remember?' The voice is dry, noncommittal. 'We were supposed to go out to dinner. I was about to turn into your driveway when I saw the two of you, through the window. Louis and you. Kissing.'

'Oh no! You're wrong! That wasn't us kissing at all!' I cry, almost laughing at the misunderstanding.

'It certainly looked pretty passionate from where I was sitting.'

'Max! Max!' the words tumble out. 'I was waiting for you. The children were too, they wanted to know who my dinner date was. Then Louis came over – to pick up something Kat had borrowed from Molly. And when she went to find it, he and I were on our own, and he . . . he just bent down and forced his mouth on to mine.' I look at Max, trying to impress upon him the truth of what I'm telling him. 'I didn't want to tell you because of Carolyn . . . I thought it would upset you . . .' I almost laugh with relief.

'You mean . . . you mean you're not involved with Louis Vincent?'

'He's horrible. A nasty piece of work. He made some crack

about all divorcées wanting it – it was all I could do not to slap him!'

'God, I would have.' Max's mouth sets in a grim line.

I look up at him, pleading: 'Max, if only you could have told me what it was all about . . . you pulled away, and I had no idea why!'

'I was upset. I'd . . .' A hint of a smile lights his eyes, plays about his lips, 'I'd just decided I was very interested in you.'

My heart leaps and I reach out as if to take his hand – but don't quite dare.

'And there you were, in what looked like a pretty compromising position with your neighbour.' He shakes his head, disbelieving. 'If you had any idea how rotten I felt that night. I thought of all the lies, and the betrayals necessary for that kind of affair to go on. I even began to wonder whether your divorce had been down to you and Louis . . .'

'Oh, Max!' I'm smiling like an idiot. Then, remembering why I'm here: 'But you mustn't leave now that I've found you again!' I take his hand with both of mine. 'Don't get on that train!'

'What train?' Max asks, puzzled, as if we weren't standing in the middle of a train station.

'Aren't you going to Paris?'

'No,' Max laughs. 'I've come to pick up my mum. She's getting in from Paris any second.' He looks into my eyes, smiles fondly. 'Even I don't travel this lightly.' It's true: in my rush I hadn't noticed that Max is not carrying so much as a briefcase.

'What about the job in Kenya?'

Max, his right hand still trapped in mine, looks into my eyes. 'I told Jill I doubted that I would take it. I knew that it would be wrong to go simply because Ellie was being her usual impossible self and you . . . you weren't available.'

'You told Jill you didn't think you'd take it?'

'Yes. This morning.' He bends down to peck my forehead. 'Which is when I said that, if things had been different, I would have loved to get to know you better.'

'She is impossible!' I cry, thinking of my best friend's match-making machinations. But I can't think for long because I'm being crushed in a tight warm hug.

'I'm so glad you're here. I'm so glad you're . . . free.' Max's voice is urgent and low.

'Max!' With my face still on his chest, I hear someone calling him.

'There she is!' Max releases me, waves.

A small, silver-haired woman waves cheerfully back. She approaches quickly, despite pulling a large case on wheels.

'Max!' She beams up at her son as he bends down to kiss her.

'Hullo, Mum. Hope the trip was all right?'

I look from mother to son and see the same blue eyes and open smile.

'Perfect.' Mrs Lowell turns to me. Her expression is friendly, but curious: 'And you are . . .'

'This is Rosie, Mum.' Max slips an arm round my shoulders. 'The woman I've told you about.'

'Ah, Rosie Martin.' I feel Mrs Lowell's eyes appraise me. She takes in my hair, all over the place after our hug, my face, flushed and expectant, my eyes, which keep turning from her to her son beside me. 'Of course. Rosie. Exactly as I pictured her.' Mrs Lowell looks up at her son. She smiles and whispers, but just loudly enough for me to hear: 'Just what the doctor ordered.'

Acknowledgements

Thank you to Anne Applebaum who made me go back to the very beginning. To Jonathan Lloyd and Patsy Baker for giving me confidence. I would also like to acknowledge a huge debt to Julie Lynn-Evans's moving book about divorce, *What About the Children,* and to Ana Diaz for talking me through separation and mediation. Thank you to Clare Smith and Essie Cousins for excellent editing. And as ever thank you, Edward.

About the author

About the book

Read on

Sainsbury's

Book club

Try something new today

sainsburys.co.uk/bookclub

Q & A with Cristina Odone

When did you first realise that you wanted to be a writer?

I was about four when my mum sat with me at our Formica kitchen table – door shut so my little brother wouldn't come barging in – and taught me how to read and write. I still remember the warm scents from the pot on the hob, my mum's undivided attention, the light hanging low over us: I had a real sense of initiation into something wonderful and welcoming. I was hooked – and quickly realised that only making up my own stories could beat reading other people's. The first story I wrote was three or four paragraphs long, about a young inn-keeper's daughter called Bess. I remember vividly how I wrote it at night under the desk in my room, with a torch so no one could see that I wasn't asleep, and how I wept when she couldn't marry her beau. I can't remember HIS name, but he had red hair and freckles, just like Jim, the American boy next door.

When and where do you write? Are your surroundings important?

Every morning I take Isabella, my 5-year-old, to school, then take a walk across Primrose Hill and Regent's Park, thinking about characters, plot, lines. I get home about 11 and sit at the dining room table, which doubles up as my desk (and later as the children's homework desk), then write breathlessly until 3 p.m. when I have to pick Isabella up again. Between tea, homework, and fixing supper, I am forced to take a long break. If I'm lucky, I get a second chance to work between 8 and 11 p.m. The great thing about having worked in a newsroom is that I can work anywhere. Road drilling, neighbours' screeching, dishwasher rumbling, car alarms going off – I can tune it all out. My only requirement is a window to look out of. I wrote *The Good Divorce Guide* looking out on to a crescent in North London, watching neighbours arguing, lovers canoodling on a bench, dog walkers exercising their charges. I sometimes feel guilty about being a peeping Tom – but isn't that what writing is all about?

Who and what are your literary influences?
I can read anything by anyone but I think one of the best disciplines for a comic writer is to read the screenplays for classic comedies like '*When Harry Met Sally*', '*You've got Mail*', '*Groundhog Day*' – all the way back to the fabulous dialogue in Hitchcock's films. Some of the exchanges between Cary Grant and Eva Marie Saint in '*North by Northwest*' and James Stewart and Grace Kelly in '*Rear Window*' are sharper and wittier than anything I've ever read.

You were a columnist for the *Observer* and the *Telegraph* and a former deputy editor of the *New Statesman*. How have you found the transition from writing columns and editing to writing fiction?
Fiction is just like journalism: you want to know who did what to whom, and why. The great difference between the two is ▶

‘ Fiction is just like journalism: you want to know who did what to whom, and why ’

Q & A *(Continued)*

◄ that as a journalist you know you've got to wrap everything up in about 800 words – whereas in fiction, you can take 800 pages. That's liberating but also can present a huge challenge: don't bore your reader.

What triggered you to write *The Good Divorce Guide*?

The thing about writing a book called *The Good Divorce Guide* is that everyone assumes that I've gone through a divorce myself and that I'm sharing my top tips on how to get the best maintenance deal. That's not quite what I had in mind. I've been wanting to write about divorce for years because it has been a big part of my life – my parents divorced when I was 13, my husband was divorcing when I met him, and I live with two step-sons who have survived their parents' (very civilised) divorce.

As a Catholic, I had been taught that divorce was beyond the pale, and to this day I cannot take Communion because I married a divorced man. That hurts, and in a way it has prompted me to analyse the subject more carefully. Every time I read a book about divorce, the author (usually a woman) charts the same journey: wife is left by the cheating husband, is devastated, turns bitter and tries to hit him where it hurts, loses a lot of weight, meets new man, overcomes her grief to emerge triumphant, a new stronger woman. Children might be thrown in, and a job or even a career: but

6 I've been wanting to write about divorce for years because it has been a big part of my life 9

the essential plotline is about horrid man destroying nice unsuspecting wife's life.

And yet many of the divorces I know are not this black and white. Couples' splits are often mutual, two people slipping out of love and out of synch. In these cases, especially when there are children involved, husband and wife seek to keep things amicable and civilised. If it was up to them, they probably would succeed; but once you start the divorce ball rolling, you trigger an avalanche of other interests – from the lawyer (of course) to the dentist and the estate agent.

The book deals with divorce and all the issues entangled with it, but is also a very funny read. How important is humour in your work?
Humour in real life makes everything bearable. In fiction it frees you to say something heart-felt without feeling self-conscious. If you make someone laugh about your slip-up, weight, fear of ageing, fear of staying single forever, no one need know quite how hurtful it is.

Do you identify closely with any of your characters?
I love Rosie, who feels hurt and vulnerable but manages to be generous-spirited. I don't know that I'm like her but I identify with her survival instincts. And there's a lot of Jill in me – I love match-making, telling my friends how to lead their lives, and generally thinking I can fix things if I just try hard enough. Having said that, every attempt I've made to match-make has failed disastrously.

LIFE
at a Glance

BORN

Nairobi, Kenya (11 November 1960)

EDUCATED

Worcester College, University of Oxford

LIVES

London

CAREER

Former editor of the *Catholic Herald*, and former deputy editor of the *New Statesman*. For two years I wrote a column for the *Daily Telegraph*, 'Posh but Poor', which became a novel, *The Dilemmas of Harriet Carew*.

FAMILY

The typical 'blended' family, with husband, two sons from his first marriage, and our daughter.

Q & A *(Continued)*

What do you want people to take away from reading *The Good Divorce Guide*?
Compassion for anyone going through a divorce – especially anyone struggling to keep it friendly.

What do you do when you're not writing?
Children take up a huge amount of time, but I love the feeding, listening, advising involved in parenting and step-parenting. I love walking, and on weekends Edward, my husband, and I usually schedule at least one long walk through the park. I'm very conscious of the need to make time for 'us' moments, as Jonathan Martin would describe them. Otherwise, months pass without your having shared anything more intimate than taking out the recycling together. If you don't make an effort, you can wake up one morning to realise that you're strangers. ■

Top Ten Books

Little Women
Louisa May Alcott

Midnight's Children
Salman Rushdie

Rebecca
Daphne du Maurier

Chéri
Colette

A House for Mr Biswas
V. S. Naipaul

Anna Karenina
Leo Tolstoy

Emma
Jane Austen

Pride and Prejudice
Jane Austen

The Code of the Woosters
P. G. Wodehouse

How to Lose Friends and Alienate People
Toby Young

There is no Enjoyment like Reading

'I declare after all there is no enjoyment like reading! How much sooner one tires of anything than of a book! When I have a house of my own, I shall be miserable if I have not an excellent library.'

JANE AUSTEN

From Socrates to the salons of pre-Revolutionary France, the great minds of every age have debated the merits of literary offerings alongside questions of politics, social order and morality. Whether you love a book or loathe it, one of the pleasures of reading is the discussion books regularly inspire. Below are a few suggestions for topics of discussion about *The Good Divorce Guide* ...

Which character do you most identify with in *The Good Divorce Guide*?

Relationships are central to this book – both those that work, and those that don't. In what ways has *The Good Divorce Guide* informed your understanding of relationships, and what, if anything, has it taught you about how to build a successful one?

How effective a title is *The Good Divorce Guide*? If you could rename the book, what would you call it?

The collapse of Rosie and Jonathan's marriage is a traumatic event, yet *The Good Divorce Guide* is a comedy novel. How successfully do you think the author weaves humour into the plot?

Do you sympathise with Jonathan? Do your feelings towards him change as the story progresses? If so, when and why?

The novel is narrated in the first person, by Rosie. Was there any point in the novel when an omniscient narrator would have worked better?

Have you been through a divorce? Is the range of reactions to divorce explored by *The Good Divorce Guide* similar to those you experienced or are experiencing?

How important is the character of Jill? What, in your opinion, does she bring to the book?

Rosie is determined that her divorce will be a civilised one. By the book's ending, do you think she has achieved this? ∎

If You Loved This, You Might Like . . .

Other titles from HarperPress

The Piano Teacher
Janice Y.K. Lee

It's 1952 when 32-year-old Claire arrives in Hong Kong with her new (and dull) husband Martin. Using her marriage to escape a bitter mother and non-existent home life in England, Claire takes a position in Hong Kong as piano teacher to Locket, the daughter of wealthy socialite Chinese parents. She swiftly becomes intrigued by the family's unconventional English driver, the charismatic and mysterious Will Truesdale. As their love affair blossoms, the tensions and intrigues of 1950s Hong Kong are interwoven with events a decade earlier, during the island's wartime years – another, very passionate, and tragically doomed love affair, Japanese brutality and secrets betrayed.

....

Swap
Daniel Clay

Angela Kenny wants more from her life. Sure, she's got a loving husband and a sweet teenage son, but she can't help feeling that there should be more. She's tired of going to work and filling in spreadsheets, fed up with cooking the same frozen pizzas every evening, and bored of waking up every morning to do it all over again. Lucas – her husband's best friend – seems to share her dissatisfaction, and over slow summer evenings in their small, settled suburb, their friendship slowly develops into a dangerous affair. When John sees his wife in his best friend's arms, his anguish will have devastating consequences for all of them.

Coming soon ∎

CRISTINA ODONE

The Dilemmas of Harriet Carew

Meet Harriet Carew, mother of three and juggler of work, home and family. Harriet only wants to do her best for her husband Guy, her children, and herself. But while their friends flourish, and other parents look on pityingly, the Carews are struggling – and sliding down the ladder of fortune and happiness. Guy is a writer, with a starry past, a humdrum present and unrealistic optimism about the future. Harriet, meanwhile, is torn between wanting to spend more time at home and the need to work longer hours to help pay the school fees. When her ex-boyfriend James turns up, super-successful and single, she has to make some tough decisions.

'Engaging, funny and charming, just like its heroine.'

PENNY VINCENZI